THE WITCH AND HIS DOCTOR

THE KINCAID PACK SERIES BOOK SIX

KIKI CLARK

THE WITCH AND HIS DOCTOR
THE KINCAID PACK BOOK 6

Damien has a secret.

Actually, he has more than one. His entire life within the Kincaid Pack has been a lie. Now that the truth is starting to come out, he's faced with accepting the consequences he set into motion years ago.

And hoping his mate will forgive him.

Except the reckless actions of his past may prove to not only be his own undoing… but that of the pack he's come to love.

Carter gave up on finding his fated mate years ago.

He has a medical practice to keep him busy, a pack he'd do anything for, and a family that's always been a little too nosy for his peace of mind.

Learning the witch he's grown to admire and have feelings for has betrayed them all? Just proves he's getting too old for the whole falling-in-love thing. It doesn't matter that the moment he catches Damien's unaltered scent he realizes another devastating secret the man has been hiding.

The only thing that matters is saving the pack—and its alpha.

With Rick's life hanging in the balance and the pack's enemies moving to strike against them while they're at

their most vulnerable, it will take every scrap of magic and bravery Damien possesses to prove once and for all where his loyalty lies.

This one is for Stew and Molls.

You two have been my support and inspiration for years. Who would have thought the three of us would all end up kicking ass and taking names??

THE KINCAID PACK SERIES

Free Prequel: A New Pack for New Year
(Victor & Cole)

The Alpha and His King
(Rick & Kai)

The Second and His Bonded
(Bennett & Kieran)

The Deputy and His Enforcer
(Marcus & Robson)

The Hunter and His Mates
(Drake & Jamie & Gabriel)

The Enforcer and His Heart
(Nico & Keegan)

The Witch and His Doctor
(Doc & Damien)

AUTHOR'S NOTE

This series has been such a huge part of my life for the last three years, it feels strange to be letting it go. Even though there will be more books and series set within this universe, it's still bittersweet to be saying goodbye.

I hope you've enjoyed the journey so far and that this book meets and exceeds all of your expectations. <3

Below, I've included a brief content warning. It will contain information I'd consider slightly spoiler-y so proceed with caution.

POSSIBLE SPOILERS:

This book contains (off-page) parental death and grief. There is also straight-up matricide, but you won't feel bad about her. LOL

CHAPTER ONE

H is mates were going to kill him.

Gabriel patted Rick's cheek—if anyone asked, he'd deny slapping his alpha—but he didn't rouse at all. His skin was gray and clammy, and his breaths were choppy and erratic, his big chest working way too hard.

"Come on, Rick," he rasped, rubbing his knuckles between Rick's pecs hard, but he still didn't react. "Fuck."

He dug into one of the pockets in his fatigues and pulled out the syringe he'd grabbed at the last second. It was filled with a purple solution he just hoped would work on whatever that asshole Alistair had dosed him with.

"I don't know if you can hear me, big guy, but I'm not sure if this is going to hurt or not. So try not to lash out, alright?" He didn't wait for a response, using his teeth to pull off the cap as he jerked Rick's shirt up to expose his chest.

The wound causing Rick Kincaid to fucking die right before his eyes was only about three inches long, but the edges were black, and dark lines were growing from it like a deathly spiderweb. Jaw tight, he didn't hesitate to jab the

1

needle into Rick as close to the wound as he dared and pressed the plunger down.

He held his breath as he waited to see if something changed. The wolfsbane antidote was for a specific, rare strain, and he had no way of knowing if that was what Rick's dad had hit him with or not. But he and the O'Hares had used that specific strain before.

On Gabriel's mate, Drake, in fact.

For ten of the longest seconds of his life, nothing changed. Rick's labored breathing and ashen complexion stayed the same, his heart racing under the hand Gabriel had resting on his chest, holding his shirt out of the way.

But then...

Rick sucked in a harsh breath, eyes flying open. His irises were glowing hotly, his fangs long and sharp-looking as he opened his mouth and roared.

"Jesus!" Gabriel shouted, jerking back in case he came up swinging.

Instead, as the ringing in Gabriel's ears began to fade, Rick groaned and squeezed his eyes shut. "What happened?"

"Your dad's a real SOB, it turns out," Gabriel said as he leaned in to take a closer look at the wound again. The lines stretching out from it seemed shorter but were definitely still there. The cut itself was smaller, the skin more purplish-red than black.

It should have fully healed though.

If Alistair had coated the blade in just wolfsbane.

"How bad is it?" Rick asked, tipping his head down and squinting before letting it thump back onto the ground.

"It's not that bad." He was thankful he still had the hex bag Tashmica had made him in his pocket, hiding his scent.

Rick lifted his lip in a silent snarl. "Don't lie to me. Not right now."

Sighing, Gabriel scrubbed at his face. "It's bad, Rick. I had a shot of wolfsbane antidote, and that helped but not completely. Something is still preventing you from healing, and I don't like the looks of this wound. How's it feel?"

Rick grunted.

"Descriptive. That mean it hurts?"

"Yeah, little bit."

"So a lot."

"A little," Rick gritted out.

"Can you stand?"

Rick seemed to think about that, his hands opening and closing at his sides and legs shifting. "Doubtful."

"So a lot."

Rick rolled his eyes and tried to sit up, but he sucked in a ragged breath and fell back, clutching at his side. "Fuck."

Dread pooled in Gabriel's stomach as he glanced around. If Rick couldn't stand, it was going to be a real bitch trying to get them out of there. And there was no telling how long Rick had before whatever other poison was coursing through him... killed him. That was if Alistair hadn't had backup waiting not too far away and he came back to finish the job. In that case, they had even less time.

"Did you get him?" Rick asked, panting.

"Your dad? No, fucker got away while I was dealing with his minions," he admitted begrudgingly. He should have taken out Alistair the second he walked into the clearing, then dealt with the others.

"They all dead?"

Gabriel grunted as he checked Rick's pulse, frowning at how fast it still was. "One got away. Stripped and shifted, running the same way your dad went. I might have tried to follow if someone hadn't been so dramatic."

One corner of Rick's mouth tipped up as his eyes closed, chest rising and falling too quickly. "Jackass."

The sun was starting to rise, the sky lightening above

them and making Gabriel more nervous. The darkness—and his ability to hide in it even from shifters—had been the one advantage they'd had. If Alistair's goon or reinforcements decided to come and check to make sure Rick was dead, they'd be way too easy to find.

"We need to get out of here, Rick. Are you sure you can't stand?"

Gabriel grabbed one of his arms and tried to help him up, but they only made it about halfway before Rick was grunting through clenched teeth, sweat beading on his forehead. Even if he got him on his feet, there'd be no way Rick could make it all the way back to the car. And as strong as Gabriel was, there was no way he could carry a guy Rick's size over a mile through the woods.

Lowering him back down, Gabriel swore under his breath and began to pace next to Rick's prone body. He had a burner phone stashed back in the car, but who could he call? They were hundreds of miles from the pack's territory; he wasn't sure Rick had enough time for Dr. Bell to race to Illinois.

But they couldn't just sit there waiting for Rick to get better. Even as Gabriel contemplated his choices, the alpha's coloring leached away, and his breathing became more labored.

"Did you hear what he said to me?" Rick asked suddenly, not bothering to open his eyes.

"No, I was too far away."

"He wants—" A wet cough interrupted him, and Gabriel dropped back down next to him, shrugging off the small pack he had and quickly grabbing his water.

"Here. Take a few sips." When he helped Rick raise his head to more easily drink and the grumpy alpha didn't even try to protest, Gabriel knew they were in fucking trouble. Then he saw the blood on his lips. Freezing for a moment, he felt pure panic swamp him for only the second time in his entire life, but he forced himself to press the bottle to Rick's lips and gently tip some water into his mouth. Once he finished, Gabriel screwed the top back on and looked away, thoughts spinning in a hundred directions. "Maybe I can make something to drag you out—"

"Forget it. Just listen to me," Rick rasped, lifting a hand to grab at Gabriel's wrist. His hold was tighter than expected, and that gave Gabriel a surge of relief. "I need to tell you what to do when you get home."

Gabriel reared back. "I'm not fucking leaving you here to die, so just shut the fuck up."

"He wants the pack," Rick continued like Gabriel hadn't spoken. "That's what the O'Hares are giving him in exchange for his help."

Fury lit up Gabriel's veins. "That motherfucker. Being on the Council isn't good enough? He wants his own pack again?"

"Apparently." Rick stopped to breathe for a few seconds, then peeled his eyes open and pegged Gabriel with a hard look. "You need to make sure Kai is ready. The others will be distracted. I need you to… save my mate and my pack, Gabe. Don't fight fair… Do whatever it takes to win and destroy the Council."

"Rick." Gabriel swallowed and looked away, eyes burning. "We'll beat them together. Tash and Doc will come up with something to save you. We just have to get to them."

Rick chuckled, but it turned into another coughing fit, and they both stared at the blood coating Rick's palm when he finished. "I don't have that kind of time."

"Stop talking like that," Gabriel yelled, grabbing Rick's massive shoulders and shaking him. "I'm going to… I'm going to think of something, just give me a damn minute."

"Okay," Rick said softly, relaxing back onto the ground

and closing his eyes. "Okay. Will you... let me scent you?"

He wanted to scream no. He wanted to scream at him to stop worrying about anything other than getting back to the pack alive. He wanted to just... scream.

He pulled the hex bag Tashmica had given him out of his pocket and tossed it away.

Rick sucked in a deep breath. "Anger is good. Stay angry. The pack will need your fire. They'll need... the hunter. The man who can kill... anyone."

As Rick coughed again, Gabriel scooted back, needing space to *fucking think*. He wasn't that man anymore and didn't want to go back to him. Didn't want to sacrifice the tiny pieces of his soul he'd managed to cling to over the years. But if Rick died...

He was right. The pack would need that man.

The Enforcers would be too consumed with grief to make smart decisions, the same for Rick's mate. Kai was too young, too inexperienced to lead the pack into a damn war on his own.

They needed Rick. Or else... what would be the point of fighting?

Pressing the heels of his palms into his eyes, Gabriel pulled up a map in his head, picturing where the two of them were compared to where the pack's territory was. It was too far to go on their own. Especially in a car. They needed a damn plane or a—

He jerked his head up and stared at Rick's pale, sweaty face.

They needed a helicopter.

"Rick, I'll be right back, okay?" Gabriel pushed to his feet, a plan forming in his head along with a prayer that it would work.

"Don't come back... Just get back to him. Tell him—"

He planted a booted foot on either side of Rick's chest

and bent down so they were face-to-face, then hauled back and smacked the shit out of the biggest, baddest alpha on the continent. His smile wasn't nice when Rick's eyes popped open with a spine-tingling snarl.

"Don't you dare fucking give up. I'm getting us help, and then we're going home so Tash and Doc can work a damn miracle. You hear me?"

Rick stared up at him, looking pissed for the first time since he'd come to. "You should—"

"Remember how Kai smells when he's happy?"

Brows furrowing, Rick didn't answer for a second. "Of course."

"Good. Concentrate on that." He poked Rick right in the chest. "Focus on it with everything you've got left, Rick. If you can't stay alive for yourself, you stay alive for him and those pups of yours." Standing up, he moved a few feet away. "I'll be right back."

Rick swallowed and slowly turned his head to look at Gabriel. "Okay."

Nodding, Gabriel turned and sprinted away. He didn't worry about trying to be stealthy or anything, and he took the most direct path back to where they'd left their car. In less than ten minutes, he was skidding to a stop next to it, chest heaving.

It took him less than sixty seconds to unlock the vehicle, find the phone in the spare tire compartment in the trunk, and turn it on. By the time he found the number for the fake company online—two minutes—Gabriel's breathing was already slowing down, and he didn't hesitate to call.

Someone picked up after two rings. "Yeah?"

"I need to speak with the boss. Tell him it's Gabriel Morde."

There was a click as the other person disconnected, but

Gabriel wasn't surprised. He just hoped Quinten was in a curious enough mood to call back quickly.

He didn't wait around by the car, deciding he'd risk sounding winded and desperate to get back to Rick faster. Another four minutes had passed, and he was maybe halfway back to the spot where he'd left him when the phone started vibrating in his hand.

"Quinten?"

"This is surprising." The familiar, smooth baritone didn't sound surprised at all. More amused than anything else. "What could the great Gabriel Morde need from someone like me?"

Gabriel grimaced at the dig. The last time he'd seen Quinten, he may have said some... choice things about the man's profession. "A favor."

Quinten chuckled. "You're retired. What good does you owing me a favor do for me? Goodbye, Gabriel."

"Wait! Wait, please."

There was a pause, then "I don't think I've ever heard you say please before."

Gritting his teeth, Gabriel stared in the direction Rick was waiting for him. Injured. Defenseless.

Dying.

"Please, Quinten. The favor isn't for me..." He licked his lips and said a silent apology to his alpha. "It's for Rick Kincaid."

Quinten actually made a surprised sound at that. "Really?"

"Yes," he gritted out.

"Now there's a man I wouldn't mind owing me a favor." He didn't say anything else for a long moment, and Gabriel held his breath. Finally, he said, "What does Alpha Kincaid need?"

The relief that coursed through him was so immense

Gabriel nearly fell to his knees. Bracing one hand on a tree, he said, "Your helicopter. And a fucking miracle."

CHAPTER TWO

"No, Mama, that's not what I meant."

Claire Bell huffed out a breath that ended in a soft growl. "Carter, your brothers and I aren't scared of the damn Council or some high-and-mighty witches."

"I know you're not," Carter said as calmly as he could and tried not to break the phone in his hand as he held it to his ear and tried to type with his other hand on his computer. He knew he shouldn't have answered when he saw it was her calling, but then he would have had to deal with Mom Guilt via text messages. "But your alpha—"

She scoffed. "I appreciate your concern, but I can handle your uncle. We're coming to help with this other nonsense, and that's that."

Her tone was one he was achingly familiar with—the discussion was over. Sighing, he rubbed at his forehead. Nearly forty-six years old and still being bossed around by his mother. No wonder he couldn't find his supposed mate. "Okay, Mama. I'll get my guest rooms ready."

Having his mother and all three brothers under his roof at the same time would... be interesting. Though he was the oldest, so he could usually boss the boys around if they got too rowdy. Still, he'd need to make sure his kitchen was stocked with food that had actual nutritional value, or he'd never hear the end of it.

"Okay, dear. Now, I'll also be bringing a cleansing tonic with me that my seer suggested to help you find your mate."

Rolling his eyes, he pushed to his feet. "Goodbye, Mama."

"Oh, fine, be that way. I'll see you in a few days. Bye!"

Who knew what would be happening by the time they arrived.

He glanced at the clock on his wall and grimaced. It had been over thirty-six hours since Rick and Gabriel had disappeared. For the first twelve, no one outside of Rick's mate and Enforcers had known, but when they'd hit the twenty-four-hour mark that morning, Tashmica had called him and a few others to inform them what was going on as per instructions Rick had left with her.

Carter stopped at his office door and squeezed his eyes shut and hands into fists. His bear was ornerier than normal, anxious about his alpha being missing. Maybe hurt.

But he wasn't dead. Tash had reassured him that they'd all feel it if that were the case, the bonds between Rick and his pack so strong that it would hurt if they were severed abruptly.

Which wasn't exactly great to hear, but it was something to hold on to.

If there was no word by nightfall, Tashmica had told him to come to the manor for a meeting so they could discuss next steps.

Though he wasn't sure what other steps there would be other than to go and fucking find Rick and Gabriel. But that wasn't up to him, he reminded himself for the hundredth time and took a deep breath. He wasn't an Enforcer or even a beta.

He was a doctor. A confidant if he was being generous.

But he had no authority to order the others to track the missing two down and bring them back so the pack could figure out what they were going to do about the Council and the O'Hare Coven. Those were supposed to be their concerns at the moment, not a missing-in-action alpha and retired hunter.

As well as their little spy issue.

Just thinking about Damien had Carter's bear getting even more worked up. He planted his palms on his door and gave his whole body a shake, promising himself he'd shift later when he got back home. The full moon run had been two nights ago, but he'd missed out after getting called to the house of one of the pregnant pack members. She was a first-timer, too, and a little on the nervous side, so he'd been out to her place to reassure her and her mate several times.

The monthly pack runs were often the only time he had to run in the woods with his packmates, and his bear was grumpy after having missed it.

But his bear was also a little too attached to the witch currently under house arrest as well.

It was hard for Carter to believe Damien had been sent to spy on them and report back to the O'Hares. The two of them had worked side by side together a number of times and had become—Carter had *thought*—friends. Damien had even opened up to him a few times, telling him several stories about his dad or learning to use his magic as a kid. He'd always clammed up when Carter had tried to ask for more details or attempted to take the conversation deeper, but he'd just thought it was because Damien was shy.

Sweet, shy, brilliant—not someone cold-blooded enough to lie to everyone's faces for two damn years.

The betrayal Carter had felt when he'd found out had been immense—and that was after he'd tried to deny it, not believing it could possibly be true, that some mistake must have been made because there was no way Damien was their *enemy*.

But Drake had finally convinced him, telling him that Damien had admitted in front of the entire war council that he'd been sent by the O'Hares and was Jessica Macey's brother.

He'd wanted to go and see Damien ever since but had talked himself out of it each day. As far as he knew, Tashmica had made it so that Damien couldn't use his magic or leave his apartment, but he wasn't barred visitors. Carter just wasn't sure what he'd even say if he went.

How could you do this?

Why did you do this?

Why did you let me fall in love with you?

He grimaced and slammed his fist against the door, then pushed himself upright and grabbed his white coat from off the hook on the wall. He pulled it on with jerky motions, teeth grinding together.

It was ridiculous, but it was true. In the quiet moments he and Damien had spent together discussing medicine and magic and working on healing injuries, he'd somehow fallen for the beautiful young man.

And he was young. Way younger than Carter.

It had been bad enough before, but now that he knew Damien had been faking everything? All the kind words and soft smiles and quiet laughs that Carter had taken into his heart and held tight hadn't been real. Whatever magic Damien had used to trick them all was incredibly powerful, that was for sure.

In the end though, Carter just felt old and foolish. He'd been so close to just asking Damien to go on a date with him, screw their age difference or his mom's seer having a vision about him having a fated mate somewhere. He'd convinced himself he didn't care about any of that, and neither would Damien. That they could maybe make each other happy. That they could choose each other and fall in love instead of waiting around for some supposedly perfect mate to drop into his lap.

"Such an idiot," he muttered to himself as he straightened his lapels and grabbed his stethoscope.

He should have known better, honestly. Damien had seemed perfectly happy hanging out in Carter's lab, talking science versus magic, and that should have been his first hint that everything was a sham. What kind of young, brilliant witch with the face of a damn angel wanted to spend so much time with an old bear like him?

One looking for inside information, that's who.

Shaking his head, he tried to clear all that noise out. He had patients to see and a pack to worry about—there wasn't any space left for Damien to occupy. It wasn't fair to everyone he had betrayed.

Carter had been happy on his own for nearly fifty years, and he'd continue to be long after Damien was gone. He had his practice and his family and his friends. And after they tracked down Rick and settled things with the O'Hares and the Council once and for all, things would finally calm down and go back to normal.

He didn't need anything else.

Being alone was fine.

Everything would be... fine.

He ended up having his receptionist reschedule most of his afternoon and headed home so he could brood in peace.

His office manager, Kieran, hadn't been there, having spent the last two days at the manor with his mate—the pack's second-in-command—Bennett, so he shot him a text as he walked down the sidewalk to his place next door to his clinic.

Doc: *Any word? I cleared my schedule for the rest of today and tomorrow. Just in case.*

He was just opening his front door when his phone started to ring, and he wasn't surprised to see Kieran's name on the screen. Kicking the door shut behind him, he answered, "Hey."

"I think something's happening," Kieran said so quietly Carter almost didn't hear it.

He froze. "What do you mean?"

"Bennett got a text half an hour ago and raced out of the manor with Tash, and Drake has been prowling in front of the door ever since."

Drake was one of Gabriel's mates. If he or Rick had contacted them, it made sense that the cougar would be anxious to see his mate. "But no one has said anything about… their conditions?"

"No. Maybe… maybe you should get over here."

Carter was rushing into his home office before Kieran even finished speaking. He threw a few extra things into his leather bag that he took with him on house calls and then hustled back through his house. "If Rick is injured… You know what, yeah, it'd be better if I came to him. I'm leaving now."

"Good. Okay, see you soon."

Shoving his phone in his pocket, he opened the door in his kitchen that led to his garage and hit the opener. By the time he was in his truck and ready to go, the door still hadn't finished pulling up, and he forced himself to calm down instead of growling in agitation.

If Rick or Gabriel were injured, they needed him calm and thinking clearly.

As soon as the door finished rising, he hit the gas and drove as fast as he dared through town, not wanting to draw attention to himself. Most pack members knew his truck, and if they saw him speeding toward the manor, people might start panicking.

Nearing the turnoff, he tilted his head as his ears caught a strange noise. It was an engine of some sort, but it didn't belong to any vehicle he knew of. He was almost to the gate when he felt the vibrations and started rolling down his window, sticking his head out to look up.

Coming in fast was a sleek, black helicopter, and it had to be planning on landing at the manor with how low it was. Carter punched in his code for the gate and sped through, parking as far out of the way as he could be from where he assumed they'd touch down.

He climbed out of his truck as his phone started ringing again. Tashmica.

"Yeah?" he shouted over the noise of the chopper as he ran toward it, bag in hand.

"Are you already at the manor?"

"Yes. Kieran gave me the heads-up. Where are you?" He stopped, far enough away that the thing could land without killing him, but his bear was... not happy. His alpha was in there, and he was injured—he could *feel* it.

"Five minutes out. If Bennett doesn't kill us. I had to make a hole for that thing to fly through the warding at the border since it's cloaked in magic, apparently," she explained quickly. "We don't know much. Gabriel called Drake and said they were both alive, but Rick was hurt."

"Badly?" The helicopter was almost on the ground, and he was preparing to duck and run toward it the second it touched down.

"We think so," Bennett said in the background. "Gabe

didn't give details since he wasn't alone, but... Rick wasn't conscious. He would have said something if he had been."

"Okay." He hesitated, not sure they'd listen, but he finally said, "We might need Da—"

"Forget it," Bennett snarled. "He can't be trusted."

"That's not true," Tashmica insisted. "You haven't even spoken to him, but Rick and I have. He messed up, but he had his reasons."

Carter refused to let himself latch onto those words, already heading toward the landed helicopter as the blades began to slow and the side door slid open. His hair was whipping in his face, but he still caught the scent of blood and infection... and magic.

"We need him," he growled, then hung up as Gabriel jumped down. There was another man in the back, leaning over Rick's unmoving body. The scent of unfamiliar shifter so close to his vulnerable alpha had his bear nearly bursting through his skin. "Get away from him."

The guy's head popped up, and he opened his mouth like he was going to argue, but Gabriel calmly raised his arm, and Carter paused, shocked at the sight of the black gun in his hand.

"You heard him, Jimmy."

"This is ridiculous. I can help." The guy moved as far from Rick as he could in the confined space, hands raised up by his head.

"You kept him alive until we got here. That's all I needed you for," Gabriel said, voice oddly flat. "You two can head back as soon as we get him unloaded."

"Mr. Amato said to wait—"

Carter pulled himself into the chopper as he heard Gabriel flick the safety off on the gun.

"And I'm saying to go."

"Fine," Jimmy snarled, then turned to Carter. "Rambo

over there wouldn't let me actually look at the wound, but I injected him with another dose of wolfsbane antidote about twenty minutes ago when he stopped breathing."

When he stopped breathing.

"Thanks," Carter muttered, using his senses to listen to Rick's racing, thready pulse and labored breathing. He didn't bother checking anything else, twisting and throwing his bag onto the ground at Gabriel's feet, and then he slipped his arms under Rick's unconscious body and lifted him.

It was awkward trying to get back out of the helicopter with over six feet of alpha in his arms, but he made it just as he heard Bennett and Tashmica's SUV speed down the driveway toward the gate.

"Shit," he said softly, shaking his head in annoyance. There was no way they had time to stop and grab Damien and already be arriving.

"What?" Gabriel asked, voice still toneless and scent subdued.

"Back me up in there." He didn't want to say more with the unknown shifter and pilot listening.

He caught Gabriel's quick nod as he moved past him toward the manor's front door and heard his softly drawled "Thanks for the lift, fellas" before he was hurrying after Carter.

"Since when do you carry a gun?" Carter asked as he hurried up the steps.

"Don't. Took it off the pilot."

"Ah."

The front door flew open before he even reached it, so he didn't slow down, going past Drake as the cougar rushed straight for his mate, his scent full of relief and anger.

"I'm okay, kitty cat."

"Good. Then I can move directly to the being fucking furious portion of this reunion," Drake snarled.

"Later."

He heard them share a quick kiss, but he was already heading up the first flight of stairs, ignoring the gasps of shock and questions being called at him. When he reached the second floor and started to go up to the third, he caught sight of Kai at the top, hand covering his mouth and tears in his eyes.

"Don't let the pups see," Gabriel said from right behind Carter. When Kai didn't move, eyes locked on Rick's limp body, Carter heard Gabriel sigh softly.

They all reached the top of the steps, and Carter paused when Gabriel put a hand on his shoulder, and then he watched in shock as Gabriel got right in Kai's face and spoke to him in a way no one else would ever dare.

"Kai! Snap out of it. Your kids need you. Rick needs you. Pull yourself together."

Kai's head jerked back, and he finally focused on Gabriel, blinking rapidly. "I... You're right. Sammi?"

"I've got them," Kai's sister answered immediately from one of the bedrooms.

Carter heard Callie, Rick and Kai's little girl, start to cry as they moved past the closed door and Samantha whispering to her that it would be okay. That Doc would make her papa okay.

He prayed she wasn't wrong.

By the time he was lowering Rick to his and Kai's bed, he could hear Bennett, Tashmica, and a few others thundering down the hall toward them. He was glad when Gabriel stood at the entrance, only letting Tash through despite the snarls being thrown at him. Carter needed to focus, not be worried about all the Enforcers watching over his shoulder as he tried to save their alpha.

He ripped open Rick's shirt and frowned at the nasty-looking wound.

"Oh my god," Kai whispered, climbing onto the bed and kneeling next to Rick's head. "What the hell is that?"

"Knife wound," Gabriel supplied as he tossed Carter his bag as soon as he turned toward him to ask for it. "Coated in wolfsbane and something else, I think. I had that antidote that Doc gave us for Jamie before we bonded, and it seemed to help but only some. And within half an hour, he was unconscious again."

He recited everything with that same cool detachment he'd had since the helicopter, but Carter decided to worry about whatever was up with him later. As he opened his bag, trying to decide what he could try and treat Rick with without knowing what else the knife had been coated in, he stared across the bed at Tashmica. "Any ideas?"

She was staring at the wound too, lips pressed together. "It could be any number of things. Or..."

When she hesitated, glancing at Kai, Carter growled and turned to Gabriel. "I need Damien. Right now. Everyone else needs to get out."

"I said no," Bennett said lowly, starting to push past Gabriel until Drake wedged himself between them to block the way as well.

"It isn't your choice; it's mine. I'm his doctor. I need the person in this pack with the most experience helping me deal with magical wounds and who also isn't afraid to say in front of Rick's mate that this might not be a poison at all."

Kai made a soft sound behind him. "What else could it be? Look at it."

"It's magic. A spell created to do something very specific and that isn't just to kill Rick," Tashmica admitted. "Carter's right. We need Damien. He has more experience with spells like this than I do."

"It's out of the—"

Bennett stopped abruptly when Kai said clearly, "Get him."

"Kai—"

Carter glanced at Rick's mate, but he wasn't looking at any of them. He was brushing the hair back from Rick's face and watching him with a desperation Carter could feel coming off him in waves.

"You told me once no one but Rick was above me in the pack," Kai said softly, still looking at Rick. Then he raised his chin and stared at Bennett with glowing green eyes. "As your alpha-mate, I am ordering you to do what Doc says. Get the witch. Quickly."

CHAPTER THREE

M istakes were a funny thing.

In the moment, you can justify your actions all you want, you can tell yourself you're doing the wrong thing for the right reasons, or you can honestly think you are in the right, but in the end, the truth always comes out.

The aftermath... that can often be ugly.

And hurt more people than you can even imagine.

Damien being one of them.

Which was funny, he knew, because he was the one who'd made the mistake in the first place. If he'd known two years ago that one little spell could lead to him locked in his own apartment, magic bound and awaiting judgment after betraying people he'd come to care for and respect, he wondered if he would have still done it.

A lot of bad things had happened, thanks to that spell, but there were good things too.

Or there were before everyone found out who he was and how he'd been sent to spy on the Kincaid Pack. Right before that moment though... he would have said it was a tough call.

And that probably made him an even worse person than everyone thought.

Sighing, he wrapped his arms around himself and curled into an even tighter ball on his bed. His eyes were dry, but that was because he didn't think he had a single tear left inside him. After confessing to Rick and the others about being sent by the O'Hares and being Jess's brother, he'd cried for three days straight in the miserable little jail cell in the basement of the manor. He hadn't felt bad for himself—he was getting what he deserved. No, he'd been so overwhelmed with misery because of the guilt and shame that had been coursing through him.

No one visited for two whole days other than to drop off food, and that was done by a stony-faced beta who didn't make eye contact with him.

He stared listlessly at his closet door and ran his fingers over the leather cuffs on his wrists, intricate sigils carved into them on the inside and outside to prevent him from using his magic. The jail cell had been spelled to hold him— well, spelled to hold a witch. He probably could have gotten free if he'd wanted to, but what would be the point? At the end of the third day, he'd heard the outer door open and hadn't even bothered to look up, assuming it was his dinner being brought and not wanting to see the disgusted look on the beta's face again.

"Make me understand," Rick had said, startling him so much Damien had nearly fallen off his cot. He'd scrambled to stand up and found a frowning alpha and Tashmica, who'd given him a wan smile that didn't reach her eyes. He'd lost even her. "You've been part of this pack for two years and done a lot to help the members here. Explain to me what the point was. Give me a good enough reason why I don't send your head back to the O'Hares."

Tashmica had gasped and turned on Rick like she was going to argue with him, but he'd simply held up a hand and kept his eyes on Damien, waiting.

More than anything, he'd wanted to spill every single detail. Give them all the information they needed to be prepared for when the O'Hares struck again. Tell them the reason why he'd had no choice but to do what he was told. Beg for their forgiveness even if he didn't deserve it.

But he couldn't.

Reaching up, he'd simply tugged the collar of his filthy T-shirt down to reveal the sigil tattooed on his pec, right over his heart, and let the tears continue to fall from his eyes. Rick hadn't gotten it at first, turning to Tash in confusion, but she'd immediately slapped a hand over her mouth and shaken her head like she could deny that he'd been forced to take a Blood Oath to the O'Hares.

They'd left not long after that, voices disappearing as soon as the outer door closed behind them, but the next morning, he'd been cuffed and moved to his apartment. Tashmica and a few other coven members had searched the place and removed any magical objects they'd found and then set warding spells to prevent him from leaving.

A week had passed since then, and he still didn't know what his fate would ultimately be. Rick would have every right to use him to send a message to the O'Hares, but the more time that went by, the less likely that seemed, and he couldn't help but be relieved. Even if he ended up branded and banished, at least he'd be alive and hopefully able to do *something* to make up for what he'd done.

Though he had no idea what that could be.

He knew that Rick and the others would never forgive him or truly trust him again, but that didn't stop him from obsessively thinking about how he could convince them to. If he could just *explain* how he'd ended up being used as a spy and the things he'd done to protect them as best he could, but that would mean breaking the Blood Oath spell, and he wasn't sure he could do that on his own or even if it could be done—

Was Carter thinking about him?

A dry sob broke through his chest, and he pressed his face into his pillow to muffle the sound. No, he wouldn't think about him. He couldn't. It hurt far too much. He hadn't even realized how much his suppressing spell was dampening his own reaction to the man until it had started to wear off the longer he went without his tea. For two years, he'd diligently made sure to drink it every morning, knowing he needed to prevent Carter from scenting that they were... fated.

Damien had still been drawn to the big bear, his quiet, caring personality a balm to the hurricane of fear and regret and shame always bombarding him. When he was alone with Carter, everything would settle inside him, and he felt like he could finally breathe.

He hadn't known the spell had been affecting his own reaction until he'd heard Keegan, a new witch in the coven, talking about how his magic had been drawn to his mate, Nico, the second they'd met. That every time they were near one another before their mating had been consummated, Keegan's magic would reach for Nico, wanting to latch onto the strong wolf inside him and never let go.

Damien had never felt anything like that around Carter. At first, he'd thought maybe he'd been wrong about the doctor being the one he was destined for, but he knew the truth now. The spell was nearly completely out of his system, and it was all he could do at times to stop his magic from trying to break free of the cuffs so they could go and find him.

He wasn't sure how he would have been able to stop it if he'd actually been in the same room as Carter. As much as it felt like a thousand tiny cuts every day that his mate didn't come to see him, he told himself over and over that it was for the best. The last thing he wanted was to make everything worse.

And it wasn't like Carter would even want him. Not now that he knew what Damien had done and who he really was. A traitor.

He squeezed his hands into fists as his magic surged inside him, moaning at the pain of not being able to release any of it outside his body. It was a hundred times worse than the way the cuffs heated against the skin of his wrists, burning him, when his magic got too close to the surface.

He wondered if Tashmica knew how much she was hurting him, the unending torture as his magic surged and ebbed again and again every day, all day. Would she care if she did?

He doubted it. He wouldn't fool himself into thinking that just because she'd gotten him moved into his apartment and out of the cell, it meant she gave two shits about him anymore.

As he started to sit up, needing to *do* something to take his mind off the agony, he heard a noise in the other room. Hurrying, he kept his arms tucked around him as he hustled into his living room just as the door to his apartment opened.

The witch and beta standing in the doorway were grim-faced as they stared at him in silence for a moment. Len, a newer member of the coven and one that Damien had initially hit it off with, looked away first, like he couldn't even stand the sight of him.

Swallowing the bile rising in his throat, he whispered, "What's going on?"

"Put your shoes on," the beta snapped. Damien thought his name was maybe Harry, but he wasn't sure, and it wasn't like any of them bothered to introduce themselves when they came on shift to guard his door. "They want you at the manor."

Shit. This was it. Feeling like he was moving through concrete, he shuffled toward where his shoes were sitting next to the door on a little rubber mat Tash had gotten him when he'd first moved to Michigan. "To protect your floors," she'd said, grinning, "since it's always snowing or raining around here, it seems like."

As he pulled on his tennis shoes, the beta growled behind him, sending a shiver of fear down his spine and making Damien spin around, not wanting the man at his back.

"Hurry the fuck up," Maybe-Harry said, then stomped back out into the hallway.

Damien did his best to go faster, but his hands were shaking so bad he had a hard time tying the laces. Finally, he was ready, and he sucked in a deep breath as he moved toward the door, Len shuffling out of the way so they didn't come anywhere close to touching.

He almost forgot to grab his keys and lock his door since he usually just used his magic, but he remembered at the last second and then hurried down the hallway to the stairs, where the other two were waiting. They led the way down, not bothering to walk with one behind Damien since they knew if he tried to run, the beta would be able to catch him, especially with his magic bound.

There was a black SUV waiting right outside his building, and he climbed into the back seat without a word. Neither of his guards spoke the entire way to the manor, and the tense silence made his skin crawl and set his teeth on edge. He would have preferred they taunt him over the growing sense of doom the quiet caused.

When they reached the manor, the first thing he noticed was Carter's truck parked off to the side haphazardly, and he gasped. Oh no oh no oh no. Carter couldn't be anywhere near him. It wasn't fair to the sweet bear.

For the first time since he'd been escorted to the jail cell, he thought about trying to make a break for it. His mind was frantic—part of him wanting to spare Carter from ever knowing his true mate was a traitorous spy and part of him needing to find him and grab him and never let go.

"Move," the beta barked when Damien hesitated after climbing down from the SUV.

Ducking his head, he hurried after him, stomach twisting so much he thought he might be sick. The second they stepped inside the mansion, his worry over himself began to drain away.

Something was very wrong.

No one paid him any attention, but there were *dozens* of pack members just standing around in the large entrance hall, murmuring to each other and staring up. Damien looked up too, but he didn't see anything on the second-floor balcony that ran above them, connecting the east and west wings.

"What's going on?" he whispered, turning to Len, but he refused to meet his eyes. He and Maybe-Harry just kept going, right past the crowd and up the stairs.

He knew he'd finally been spotted when the gathered pack members got louder, some calling out questions about what he was doing there or just shouting "Traitor!" at him. He flinched and hunched his shoulders, sticking close behind his escorts. When they just kept going up to the third floor, he began to wonder if the crowd downstairs really had been for him. Maybe Rick had put out word that he was being sentenced and people had gathered to watch him be forcibly removed from the pack's territory after being branded.

They didn't go toward the library when they reached the top floor though. Len stopped at the end of the hall that led to the alpha and alpha-mate's private quarters, so Damien did too, not sure where he was supposed to go. There were a few people down at the end, outside Rick and Kai's bedroom, and he realized they were all Enforcers or their mates.

The beta only realized Damien wasn't behind him anymore when he was halfway down the hall and the Enforcer Vanessa pointed behind him, scowling and shaking her head. As Maybe-Harry stormed back toward him, Damien looked between him and Len in confusion.

He wasn't given any more orders, the beta simply grabbing him right above his elbow and dragging him forward. He grimaced at how tight the hold was, but when he saw the Enforcers watching him, he tried to clear his face. Maybe-Harry was going so fast Damien nearly fell twice, which only earned him a harder squeeze and yank. His face was flushed with how hard he was working not to cry out in pain by the time they reached the bedroom door. He was sure that the beta was about to break his arm while everyone just stood there and watched, but then he gave Damien a viciously hard tug past everyone and sent him flying into the bedroom.

That time, he did fall, unable to keep his feet at the momentum he was forced to move at, and he heard a growl and a loud, feminine voice, but he couldn't focus on them.

The entire room was soaked in magic. For a moment, he couldn't breathe it was so thick in his throat, choking him and making him cough and gag. How could the others stand it?

Shaking his head and wiping at his mouth, he pushed to his feet. His eyes went right to Rick's lifeless body on the bed and locked on, not noticing anything or anyone else and forgetting the pain in his arm. His feet were moving before he even realized it, taking him to the side of the bed, and then he was climbing up so he could get closer and see the blackened wound on the alpha's side better. There was a small commotion behind him, but he barely noticed.

"Tell me everything we know," he said, speaking to the room at large as he leaned down and examined the jagged cut, nose nearly touching Rick's skin he was so close. He was raising one hand, about to palpate around the wound, when a firm grip grabbed his forearm, and he jerked his head up to find the pack's alpha-mate staring at him with glowing eyes.

"Tell me you can fix him." The words were an order, but the broken voice Kai said them in made them a desperate plea.

Sitting up, Damien covered Kai's hand on him with his other one. "I'll do everything I possibly can, but I need to know what happened." He paused, licking his lips, then saying carefully, "And I need my cuffs removed."

Angry voices began shouting behind him, but he didn't look away from Kai, not even when he became aware of his magic growing restless as a huge person moved into his periphery. *Carter.* Of course he was there; Rick was injured. Dying maybe.

His wrists grew hotter and more uncomfortable as his magic fought to be free, to reach out to his mate, but he did his best to ignore it all and keep his eyes on Kai. The alpha-mate was nibbling on his bottom lip, staring down at Rick's face.

"He can just tell Tash what to do," Bennett said behind him, and Damien tried really hard not to feel hurt that they didn't trust him not to do everything he could to help Rick. "He can't be trusted, Kai."

He couldn't stop his flinch at the words, finally dropping his gaze so he didn't see Kai agreeing with him. He let his free hand drop to his side and waited, knowing Rick didn't have time for him to argue and that even if he did, they wouldn't believe him.

"Take them off."

At first, Damien couldn't tell who had said it. He tried to glance around without raising his head, but there were too many people crowding into the room. Everyone who had been out in the hallway—and maybe even more—seemed to be right at the foot of the bed. But when his eyes locked with Gabriel's, he realized the hunter had been the one to speak up.

"You don't give the orders around here—" Bennett started to say, face twisted in a snarl Damien had never seen on the usually easygoing tiger.

"Rick gave me my orders," Gabriel said, looking past Damien to Kai, who sucked in a breath and tightened his hold on Damien's forearm. Goddess, he was going to be covered in bruises by the end of the day. "He knew everyone else would be too emotional. My job is to make sure you have a voice of reason helping you right now." A shadow crossed Gabriel's face, then disappeared just as fast, his shoulders straightening a bit more as he said, "And in the future, if he doesn't make it."

No one seemed to like to hear that, voices and growls rising up around them, but Damien was just... really confused. What had happened in the last week that Rick had ended up mortally wounded and asked a human hunter to help his mate in the possible event of his death?

There wasn't time for answers though.

He glanced over at Kai just as he nodded and said, "Tash, remove them. And everyone not needed needs to get out."

Everyone but Tashmica and Carter moved to leave, but Damien called out to Gabriel even as he held out his wrists for Tash to remove the cuffs. "Were you with him?"

Gabriel turned back and nodded. "Yeah."

"Stay and tell me everything you can. I also need something from the shop." He said that to Tashmica, and she nodded as she worked on the cuffs, pressing the tips of her fingers to specific sigils in the unique order required to break the spell.

"The bottle's in the back room, right?" The sigils lit up, glowing a bright orange. She removed her fingers and murmured the incantation to finish breaking the binding.

"Yes. Have someone—" He gasped as the cuffs suddenly split apart, falling into Tashmica's waiting hands, and his magic tried to surge free. Curling over, he grunted as he held it back by sheer force of will, wrapping his arms around his stomach. He was panting by the time the feeling finally began to lessen and his voice hoarse as he pushed himself upright again and wiped at his wet cheeks. "Have someone bring the emerald athame too."

She stared at him in horror, looking at his red and blistered wrists and the cuffs fisted in her hands. They didn't have time for that either though.

"Tash," he said louder, grabbing her shoulders and meeting her wide eyes. "He doesn't have time. Please."

Nodding, she dropped the cuffs to the ground and pulled out her phone. Even as she selected a contact and raised it to her ear, she whispered, "I'm so sorry, Damien."

"Don't be," he said, turning back to Rick. "I deserve it."

He could feel everyone staring at him as he leaned back down and held a hand over the wound, summoning his magic and sending it right into the wound, testing his theory.

"Shit!" he yelled as he was nearly thrown clear off the bed in retaliation, just managing to grab onto the bedding to stop himself from tumbling to the floor.

"Damien!" several people called at once, but he just shook his head and scrambled back over to Rick's side.

"Make it the amethyst athame, Tash," he muttered, gently

laying his hand on Rick's stomach and closing his eyes. More carefully, he used his magic to tell how far the spell had spread, grinding his teeth when he could feel it everywhere he moved his hand on his torso. "Faster. He doesn't have much time left."

CHAPTER FOUR

C arter couldn't stop staring at Damien.

He didn't know how it was possible, but after two years, he could scent Damien fully for the first time. And he was... they were...

Before, he could just detect Damien's emotions and a soft, comforting scent that had appealed to Carter and his bear but not in a way that overwhelmed his senses or drove him to madness. It was why—even though he'd been so attracted to the witch—he'd known since they met that they weren't fated.

But now? His hands were fisted at his sides, so he didn't reach for him, and it was taking everything in him not to shift and attack everyone that was a threat to his mate. Which... seemed to be just about everyone.

He couldn't stop looking at the raw skin on his delicate wrists or hearing his soft voice saying he deserved it. It didn't matter that Carter the man knew what Damien had done and that he couldn't be trusted—his bear wanted him. Needed him.

Had to have him.

When Damien hovered his hand over Rick's wound before getting flung backward, Carter started to lunge forward without thinking, a primal need surging inside him to protect his mate. There was a buzzing in his ears and fire dancing over his skin, and he was pretty sure he was going to lose it in about three seconds.

Then those scared hazel eyes met his for the first time since Damien had gotten shoved into the room, and it was like Carter fell back into his body, aware of the room around him once more.

Their gazes locked and held for only a moment, but it felt like a goddamn eternity, like Carter was falling inside Damien and drowning in his honey-sweet scent.

When his mate bit his lip and looked away, a rosy flush rising in his olive-toned cheeks, Carter had to clench his jaw to hold back a growl. He was suddenly grateful the only other shifters in the room were either unconscious or so distracted they weren't paying attention to how fast his arousal was surging after a moment of eye contact.

Goddess, it was like he was a damn cub again.

"Gabriel," Damien said, turning to the hunter. Carter hated it and wanted to rip the hunter's face off to get his mate's eyes back on him. "Tell me what you saw, heard, felt. Everything."

"I was too far away to hear what was said," Gabriel said, staring at Rick's unmoving body. "I saw the knife in Alistair's hand too late, and he fled while I dealt with his witch and shifter goons. Rick... he went down quick. Like, within seconds."

Kai made a soft, broken sound, and Tashmica hurried over next to him, placing a comforting hand on his shoulder. Gabriel's words were like a bucket of cold water, dousing Carter into reality. He needed to be doing his job, working to save his alpha's life, not panting after a mate he'd be smart to steer clear of. No matter how his bear felt.

He pulled his thermometer out of his med bag and moved up to Rick's head as Damien asked, "What was happening to him? Tell me everything you noticed."

"Same as now. Sweating, hard to breathe. When I checked his pulse, it was way too fast, and…" Gabriel paused, and Carter glanced over at him, unexpectedly glad to see the hunter having some sort of emotional reaction. His hands were planted on his hips, chin tipped up as he stared at the ceiling, but his scent was going crazy. Fury, anguish, fear. Gabriel took two deep breaths, and his scent began to lessen once more as he got himself back under control. "He couldn't see me. He didn't say it, but I could tell. Right before he lost consciousness the first time, he was searching for me with his eyes, and I realized… Well, Drake started losing his sight when the wolfsbane in him built up to blood poisoning, so I pulled out the antidote and hit him with it."

"And that helped." Damien said it like a statement, narrowed eyes moving over Rick's body like it was a puzzle he was trying to solve.

"Yeah, for a little while. He was still too weak to stand, but he could talk." Gabriel's jaw tensed as his anger flared again. "He told me that his dad wants the pack. To be the new alpha."

"What?" Kai's head jerked up. "Why would he want that?"

"We'll figure that out later," Tashmica said softly, checking her phone. "Keegan says he has the bottles and athame and is on his way."

"Good." Carter checked Rick's temp before tucking the thermometer away once more. "He's burning up. I don't know how much longer his body can take whatever that magic is doing to him."

Damien was chewing on his lip once more, arms wrapped around himself and eyes unfocused. He didn't respond, almost seeming to not be aware of what was happening around them.

Carter opened his mouth, about to try and get his attention, but Tashmica stopped him. "Give him a minute."

"What's he doing?" Gabriel asked.

"Thinking," Carter and Tash said at the same time.

A few tense moments later, Damien blinked a few times and refocused on them. "It has to be a Consumption Spell."

"Fuck," Tashmica whispered. "I think you're right, but I really hate those."

Carter looked between the two witches. "What is a Consumption Spell?"

"Nasty bit of blood magic," Tash explained with distaste as Damien climbed off the bed and hurried over to the attached bathroom, the water coming on a second later. "It works like a parasite, burrowing into the recipient and feeding on the magic within them. They're more commonly used on witches, but with how powerful Rick is…" She shook her head, lips pinched together. He really looked at her for the first time since arriving and noticed she looked terrible, like she hadn't slept since before Rick had left, her bronze skin ashen. Black smudges were under her worried brown eyes. "He's chock-full of pack magic. He's brimming with it."

"He was," Damien said, coming back in as he dried his hands. "If we don't stop the spell from consuming his magic, it won't stop until there's nothing left."

"It will kill him?" Kai asked.

"As a byproduct," Damien said, looking at Kai with compassionate eyes. "The point, though, is to sever his connection to his pack, then to his wolf. After that, if he lived, he'd be… weaker than a human."

"Jesus Christ," Gabriel spit out, scrubbing at his face. "Can you stop it?"

Damien didn't answer right away, and everyone in the room turned to stare at him, even Tash, who Carter would have said up until that moment was the most powerful and capable witch in their pack's coven. Apparently, his mate was even stronger.

He really shouldn't feel proud of that fact.

Damien didn't look away from Rick, dry hands starting to twist the towel still in his hands. Finally, he said softly, "Maybe. But then we have to figure out how to replace what it took, to heal the connection, or Rick may wake up wishing he had died."

More than one person cursed at his warning, but before anyone could say anything, there was a commotion outside the closed door right before it crashed open and Keegan ran inside, panting. He shut the door behind him with a flick of his hand, his strange, purple magic coalescing to do his bidding and then disappearing just as quickly as he strode forward, handing over the items he'd brought to Damien.

"Thank you," Damien said, passing the long decorative box to Tashmica and moving back onto the bed with the small glass jar clutched in his hand.

"What is that?" Carter asked, eyeing the bright green liquid inside.

"Harbinger Potion. It's used to decipher blood magic and should tell us for sure if it's a Consumption Spell," Damien answered without looking up, and Carter had to bite back a snarl, not liking not having his eyes on him while he spoke to him.

He and his bear needed to get their shit under control.

"Fucking fuck. Is that what he got hit with?" Keegan asked, moving over to stand next to Carter and studying Rick. He held out one dark-skinned hand and released his purple tendrils of magic, the smoky-like substance dancing over Rick's skin as Damien bent over the wound site again. Carter had never seen magic manifest like that before, and neither had any of the witches in their coven, but after Keegan had mated with Nico, he'd said it was like he'd been supercharged. When he used his active powers now, it was visible to the naked eye. "Holy hell. Yeah, that shit is fucking everywhere inside him."

Damien hummed, not answering as he used the dropper in the lid of his jar to drip three drops of the mixture right into the open wound. Immediately, the skin where the liquid had made contact began to smoke and spark a nasty green-ish-yellow color.

Nodding, Damien put the top back on and moved off the bed. "My best guess at this point, Councilman Kincaid used a knife coated with the spell and dipped in wolfsbane to deliver it. The poison weakened him and helped spread the spell through his system faster, but the doses of antidote slowed things down. If we don't remove the spell, it will keep spreading though."

"Agreed," Tashmica said, opening the box.

"Yup. Tell us where you want us," Keegan said, pushing up the sleeves of his Henley and flexing his hands a few times.

"Tash, you need to cut—"

"You should do it," she said, shoving the open box in his direction. Carter caught the glint of light off the blade inside and widened his eyes, a loud growl coming from the hallway. They all ignored the angry sound. "I've never done some-thing like this, and I don't want to practice on Rick."

Damien turned to Keegan. "Have you?"

"Once..." Keegan glanced around and cleared his throat before saying delicately, "They, uh, didn't make it."

"Damien, just do it," Kai snarled, one hand fisted in Rick's hair and the other brushing tears off his face. "Ignore everyone else and just do what it takes to save my mate."

He nodded slowly as he reached into the box and plucked the thin knife out, glancing once toward the closed door before climbing back onto the bed. There was an almost imperceptible tremble in Damien's hands, and Carter ached to soothe him.

"I got you," Gabriel said, stepping closer to the entrance and raising his voice, even though it wasn't necessary. "Anyone comes busting in here and I'm going to assume it's a threat and start shooting. So unless you want to spend the rest of the day pulling bullets out of your limbs, calm the fuck down and let him work."

Silence was the only answer, and Gabriel nodded before turning and leaning his back against the door, arms crossing over his chest.

"Thanks," Damien whispered, and then he turned to Carter. "You may want to hold him down. Just in case he wakes up."

Jaw tight, Carter didn't hesitate to put one forearm across Rick's pecs and the other over his hips, just beneath where Damien would need to work. He glanced up at Kai. "He probably won't wake up, but keep a hold of his head if he does."

Kai nodded, his knuckles turning white where they gripped the dark brown strands. He gently laid his other palm against the thick stubble on Rick's jaw, leaning down and whispering in his ear, "Don't you give up. I can't do this without you. I need you, Alpha."

Carter turned away, trying to give him what privacy he could, and came face-to-face with Damien as he studied the wound once more. Goddess, how was he still so attractive even while looking like he hadn't slept since the truth about him had come out. His high cheekbones were a little more pronounced and his black hair disheveled.

But still beautiful.

"Tash, Keegan, be ready. I'll cut out the infected part, then lure the spell to the surface. Pull it out as fast as you can." Damien looked up, freezing in place when he found Carter's face right in front of him. They stared at each other for a long second, Damien's honey scent flooding the air around them before he cleared his throat and looked away.

Carter kept staring.

"How will you lure it?" Gabriel asked from across the room.

"Consumption Spells feed on magic. They're attracted to it," Damien said, snapping his fingers and creating a spark, then moving the flame over the blade of the knife until it glowed hotly. The amethyst in the hilt radiated a bright purple. "I'm going to give it something more powerful to go after."

Carter realized what he intended too late, the knife cutting into Rick and the alpha surprising them all by starting to thrash and fight. He didn't open his eyes, but the instinct to protect himself was strong enough that he didn't need to be conscious to try and throw them off.

Grunting, Carter used all of his considerable strength to hold him still, Kai telling Rick over and over that he was safe, but the big alpha kept fighting. Damien didn't stop, didn't hesitate, just kept cutting away at the blackened skin, leaving behind fresh swaths of bloody flesh.

When he finished, he lifted the glowing blade dripping with blood to his mouth and blew on it. The steel cooled in an instant, glinting silver once more. As Carter watched, Damien looked at the other two witches waiting just behind him and nodded. When they returned the gesture, he lifted the blade and sliced through his palm.

Carter roared, nearly releasing his hold on Rick in his need to get to his hurt mate.

Damien flinched at the loud sound so close to him, but he didn't stop, holding his bleeding palm right over Rick's wound and letting his blood fall onto it. Horrified and fascinated, Carter could do nothing but stare as something thick and black began to seep out of the wound and sluggishly flow toward the bloody drops.

"What the..."

"Now!" Damien yelled, jerking his hand back just as the spell began to thin into a black, greasy smoke and rise toward his bleeding hand.

Keegan and Tashmica moved forward, hands outstretched, and began chanting. Keegan's purple magic shot forward, wrapping around the blackness and... consuming it? Carter wasn't exactly sure, except that the two kept chanting as more blackness left Rick, the alpha arching off the bed and howling in pain.

"Come on, Rick, hang in there," Carter grunted, pushing back against him. It concerned him that he was even able to keep Rick semi-still. Normally, the alpha would be strong enough to throw off ten shifters without breaking a sweat.

The bed jostled as Damien edged closer, eyes shut and uninjured hand outstretched. He wasn't chanting like the other two, so Carter assumed he was keeping track of how much of the spell was still inside Rick, but the blood seeping from his cut hand was... starting to get to Carter, the scent flooding his head and consuming his thoughts. He wanted to take care of the cut, to bandage it and scold Damien for using himself as bait for a spell that destroyed magic.

But another part of him wanted... to lick the wound.

That was his mate's blood, and even if it wasn't from a bonding bite on his neck, it still called to Carter like a siren song.

His attention snapped back to Rick when he stopped fighting Carter's hold and sagged back into the mattress, breaths shallow and too far apart.

"Fuck." He dropped his head to Rick's chest and listened, blocking out the noise and distracting scents in the rest of the room, focusing his whole being on Rick. His heart had slowed from its too-fast pace, but it was getting too slow and developing an arrhythmia. Cursing again, he dug his thermometer back out and pressed it into Rick's ear. Sure enough, when it beeped and he checked it, Rick's temp had plummeted. "We have to stop."

"We're almost done," Damien said, eyes still closed.

"So is he," Carter snapped, feeling like shit when Damien's eyes popped open in shock. More gently, he said, "His body can't take much more. You'll kill him."

"How much is left?" Tashmica said, pausing her chanting even as Keegan kept going. "If we leave anything behind, we risk it growing and spreading again."

"Too much," Damien said, turning to Kai. "It's your choice, alpha-mate. Do you want us to stop?"

Carter knew what he was going to say before he even looked up from Rick's pale face and blue-tinged lips.

"Keep going," Kai whispered. "If you leave it… it'll just kill him slower. He's strong."

Not at the moment. At the moment… Rick was barely hanging on.

But Carter could help with that.

"Kai, come over here. You need to warm him up," Carter said, urging him to climb over Rick's body so he was out of the way and then to lie as close as he could, half on top of the alpha. "Keep his core as warm as you can to protect his organs."

Without asking, Gabriel started rifling through the closet and brought over extra blankets, piling them on

44

Rick's chest, arms, and legs but leaving his abdomen clear so the witches could keep working. Carter pulled his bag up from the floor and started pulling things out. Epinephrine to increase his heart rate, another dose of wolfsbane antidote, and a yarrow extract solution. The yarrow solution was his own creation, something he'd developed over the years to help boost a shifter's healing abilities when necessary.

Not waiting, he uncapped a needle, drew out a dose of epinephrine, and hit Rick with it. He pulled out his blood pressure cuff and checked, even though he could hear the muscles of his heart beginning to work faster. His pressure was still a little low but improving.

He could feel Kai's eyes on him as he administered the wolfsbane antidote next, followed by the yarrow solution. As soon as he finished, he met his gaze and gave him a nod, trying to reassure him, even though he still wasn't sure that Rick could handle much more.

Within a couple of seconds, Rick's color improved, and Carter heard his heart even out, his breathing becoming steadier and deeper. He knew it wouldn't last if the parasitic spell and the magic being used to heal him kept bombarding his system.

Sure enough, a few minutes later, Rick's heart started to slow again, and Kai made a sad sound where he was draped over him. Carter glanced at Damien, and he shook his head, grimacing.

Shit.

He got another dose of yarrow extract ready and hit Rick with it again, but the effects weren't as immediate or as strong. Shaking his own head, Carter checked his temp again. "We need to finish this now."

If they were back at his clinic, he could maybe have come up with something more to help stabilize Rick, but he was limited to what he had in his med bag. Which didn't include a defibrillator.

Kai sobbed quietly, holding on to Rick tightly.

"Damien," Carter said, moving over so he was closer to him. "You have to stop. It has to be good enough, at least for now."

Looking torn for a second, he turned and met Carter's eyes. "I have to save him," he whispered. "I can't... I can't fail at this."

Carter had to squeeze his hands into fists to stop himself from gathering Damien into his arms and comforting him. "You haven't. But if you keep going, you'll kill him, and then we'll all have failed."

Chewing on his lip, Damien looked between him and Rick a few times, then nodded. The other two must have been watching because the chanting stopped right away, the room falling quiet except for Rick's labored breathing and Kai's soft sobs.

They all watched Rick, waiting for... something. Some sign the parasite spell was going to come back with a vengeance and sever what was left of Rick's bonds with his pack and his wolf. But nothing happened.

Stepping closer, Carter leaned over, bracing his fists on the mattress, and examined the wound. The black lines around the cut were gone, and the flesh was pink and angry but almost healed closed. He grunted and pushed upright. "It looks a lot better. We'll have to keep an eye on him and maybe pull out any remnants of the spell one more time, but the fact that he's starting to heal seems like a good sign."

"Agreed," Tashmica said, placing a hand on his shoulder. "What was it that you injected him with?"

He waved a hand. "Just a bit of my own magic—science. Something I developed before I moved here that helps boost healing. I've only used it once since joining this pack since our bonds are so strong it isn't usually necessary."

"Drake?" Gabriel asked softly where he was back against the door, even though the crowd in the hall was still quiet.

"Yeah," he said, trying not to remember how frantically he'd had to work on the cougar, almost losing him more than once. Sometimes he still woke up in a cold sweat, the sound of Drake's hoarse shouts and the bone saw in his ears.

"I think it kept him alive," Damien said, staring at Tash's hand still on Carter's shoulder with a peculiar look on his face. Carter scented the air automatically and nearly lunged forward when he realized Damien was *jealous*.

"You all did," Kai said, not opening his eyes or moving an inch away from Rick. "I can't ever thank you enough."

"He's not out of the woods yet," Damien said quickly. "One of you will have to check him frequently over the next day or so to make sure the spell doesn't regrow and his magic heals."

"We will," Keegan assured him. "The pack is strong. Being here will help him get stronger faster." He looked over at Gabriel. "Good job getting him here quickly. Did I hear you stole a helicopter?"

"Borrowed one."

"From who?" Carter asked, moving back to the other side of the bed and straightening his things, anything to keep his hands busy so he didn't try and grab Damien and run back to his house.

Gabriel sighed. "Someone Rick is going to be displeased to owe a favor to."

"And who's that? Another alpha?" Tashmica frowned.

"Worse. A mobster."

CHAPTER FIVE

Damien was in the bathroom, cleaning the athame and washing his hand, when he felt him step into the doorway.

Goddess, Keegan hadn't been exaggerating about the draw a mate had on a witch's magic. Even while he'd been working desperately to save Rick's life, his magic had been brimming at the surface, ready to reach out and touch Carter's. He could feel the big bear just beneath the surface, strong and tempting as sin.

"Let me see," Carter said gruffly, stepping into the bathroom and shutting the door behind him.

Damien sucked in a breath and squeezed his eyes shut. "It's not too bad. I can take care of it."

"Damien…"

He held himself perfectly still, waiting for Carter to say something. To yell at him for hiding who they were to each other. To demand to know why he'd done it. To condemn him and their mating, thanks to Damien's betrayal of the pack.

The cold water running over his hand was turning his

fingers numb, and he embraced the feeling, imagining it spreading throughout his whole body to protect him from the pain of Carter's rejection.

He deserved it.

He definitely didn't deserve a mate like Carter.

"Would you—"

Carter was cut off by a loud banging on the door behind him, the sudden sound making Damien jump. "Wrap it up," Bennett called. "He has to go back to his apartment."

Damien shut off the water and used the towel he'd set on the counter to wrap around his hand. He had bandages back at his place to deal with it. He snagged the athame with his other hand and turned to leave.

Carter had already jerked the door open, enormous arms crossed over his wide chest. "Seriously? What if we need him again? He should just stay in a room here."

"It's fine," Damien said before Bennett could explain how he wasn't trustworthy enough to be allowed to sleep so close to their injured and defenseless alpha. Head tucked down, he moved closer to them. "Keegan and Tashmica will be checking on him. They'll know what to do now. You won't need me."

He slipped past Carter's big body and back into the bedroom, beelining for where Tash was still hovering near the bed. Without waiting for anyone to say anything, he handed the knife to Keegan and then held his arms out to her, waiting for the cuffs.

"No," she started to say, taking a step back. "They're hurting you. I won't—"

"You have to," he said softly.

At the same time, Bennett sighed and said, "Can you guarantee he can't break through the warding on his apartment without them?"

"He wouldn't do that," Tash said loudly, glaring around at

everyone else in the room behind him, and he couldn't help but smile a little. Despite everything, the fact that he still had one person in his corner felt nice. Even if he didn't deserve it.

"Tash, it's okay," he said, raising his arms a little higher, but she just shook her head.

"He could though," Keegan spoke up, sounding regretful as he kept his eyes on the athame in his hands, pressing one finger to the tip until it drew blood. "He's at least as strong as I was before my fucked-up mom broke me."

Damien wasn't sure about that. He knew he was a strong witch, but even he'd heard about Keegan Toussaint and his abilities back before he'd angered his mother and nearly lost all of his magic. Mating with Nico, one of Rick's Enforcers, after joining the pack's coven had replenished his powers and then some.

Regardless, the answer was enough for Bennett, who collected the cuffs from the dresser behind Tashmica and handed them to Keegan instead. "Exactly. And you sliced through our boundary wardings like they were nothing."

Before turning to Keegan, Damien snagged one of Tash's hands and gave it a quick squeeze in gratitude. He might not deserve her trust and loyalty, but he still appreciated it. She tried to hang on to him, but he pulled his hand back from her and extended his arms to Keegan.

"I'm sorry about this," Keegan said, ducking down to meet Damien's downturned eyes.

He believed him, but it didn't matter. He tightened the muscles in his arms to keep himself from jerking back as Keegan wrapped the leather bands back around his burned wrists. As soon as he muttered the incantation to seal them closed, Damien's magic surged inside him, panicked at being trapped again.

The searing pain on his wrists was nothing compared to the fierce cramping in his gut as he fought to pull it back under control. Biting back a whimper, he fell to one knee and pressed his knuckles into the plush carpet, battling himself. If he broke through the cuffs, he was sure Bennett would force new ones to be made, stronger ones. Ones that did more than burn if his magic stirred too close to the surface.

Shoulders hunched and teeth clenched, he held back a scream as his power ricocheted inside him, battering his insides like a caged animal. He was dimly aware of something happening a few feet away from him, but his eyes were squeezed shut as he concentrated.

Finally, it began to slow as he regained control. Bit by bit, he packed his magic away as best he could, trying to contain it without setting it off again. His whole body was shuddering by the time he was done, his panting breaths loud in the tense and quiet bedroom.

He raised his heavy head and found Carter on his knees a few feet away from him, being held in place by Bennett and the tall redheaded Enforcer, Marcus. Carter was straining against them, glowing eyes locked on Damien and fangs bared.

The sight of his mate in distress triggered his magic once more, stronger than before. "Carter…" he moaned, wrapping his arms around his stomach and curling over, "you have to stop fighting them."

He knew it was useless. Carter wasn't in control at that moment, and his bear couldn't listen to reason. All he knew was that his mate was in pain and needed to make it stop. It was sweet in a way, but Damien couldn't fully appreciate it, his whole body heating and vision dimming.

"Oh fuck," he cried just as his magic burst out, frying the sigils on the cuffs and exploding around him, the pain white-hot and never-ending.

Just before he blacked out, he thought he heard someone say, "Holy fucking shit."

🐾

The first thing he felt when he began to regain consciousness was pain. Lots of it.

Moaning, he turned onto his side and tried to make his body as small as it could be. His head felt like someone had stomped on it, pounding with every beat of his heart, and every muscle in his body was sore. But none of that compared to his wrists. It felt like the skin had been flayed off and doused in acid.

Tears streamed down his face steadily as he tried to get his breathing under control, unsure where he was or what had happened. His memory was disjointed, and his thoughts were spinning just out of reach.

Spinning. Spinning.

"Oh goddess," he moaned, dragging himself to the edge of the bed he was lying on as what little was in his stomach hurtled up his throat. Just as he began to heave, someone put a trash can under him and carded gentle fingers through his hair.

The soft touch soothed the pounding ache inside him, and once he was done throwing up, he collapsed back down and croaked, "Carter?"

"He's still at the manor," a feminine voice said, one he recognized.

He forced his eyes open, despite it feeling like he'd even sprained his eyelids, and found Jess kneeling next to his bed. His bed in his apartment. How had he even gotten there? And how was Jess there? Why? He hadn't seen her in over a week, not since she'd raised her hands to him, her magic

53

sparking around her fingers. Not since she'd realized he was a threat. A traitor.

And her brother.

"What happened?" he asked, voice raspy still. His mouth tasted vile, and his throat hurt, but he didn't bother asking for some water. Despite the soft touch while he'd been sick, he didn't think she'd actually come to visit him on her own. The pieces of what had happened back in Rick and Kai's bedroom were slowly beginning to slot in place, so he wasn't surprised when she answered.

"You broke the binding cuffs."

"That's right." He exhaled slowly and let his eyes fall closed again, seeing Carter's fierce face once more. "Is Carter okay?"

When she didn't respond right away, he looked at her again, worry growing in him, but she nodded as she studied him, face closed off in a way he'd never seen it before. She was usually so open, so happy and full of light and humor. He'd been at least partially responsible for the shuttering of her spirit—their mother and her coven also to blame.

"Anyone else hurt? It felt like there was..." He tried to think back, and he remembered feeling like he was on fire, and then—

"There was a small explosion when your magic burst free, but Keegan was able to shield himself and Tash. No one else was close enough."

"That's good," he said softly, relaxing back onto the bed and closing his eyes once more. He felt like he could sleep for a hundred years. "I'm sorry you got stuck watching over me until they could make new ones."

She hummed but didn't say anything, so he didn't push. The longer he was awake, the less pain he seemed to be in, but he was still exhausted. He was just thinking about whether it would be better to force himself up to shower or just go back to sleep when he felt her move. The bed dipped near his feet as she sat on the end.

"Why didn't you tell me who you were?"

He held back a sigh but forced himself to sit up, leaning back against his pillows and headboard. She was holding herself, arms wrapped around her stomach, and the familiar gesture made his eyes burn. He wondered if she was doing it because she needed comfort or because she felt like she needed to protect herself. That's usually how he was feeling when he did it.

"There are things I can't share," he started, trying to navigate the restrictions of the Blood Oath and his desire to get her to understand. It would have been hard normally, but with his brain still fuzzy, it felt like he was wading through sludge.

"Because you took a Blood Oath," she said, distaste evident on her face.

Took implied he'd had a choice in the matter, but he didn't bother correcting her. The intricacies around the spell were one of the things he was unable to share with them because of it.

"Also because I knew it wasn't fair to you. It would have been better if you never knew who I was. If I'd just disappeared one night without anyone knowing who I was or why I was here, it would have been better for everyone." Her. Carter. Himself.

She thought about that for a while, and he let her, giving her as much time as she needed. "We don't look alike."

Of everything he'd been expecting next, that hadn't been anywhere on the list. He laughed softly, then groaned at how much that hurt. "Uh, no. We have different dads. Mine is Latino, his parents from Honduras, and yours is white like our mom, I'd guess."

She nodded as she studied his face, really looking at him. "I guess that makes sense."

He couldn't help but smile at her grudging tone. "He'd like you."

"Who?"

"My dad," Damien said, then immediately regretted it, the sharp stab of missing him surpassing every physical pain he'd been dealt the last week. Clearing his throat, he said, "Anyway, I didn't know who my mom was growing up. Didn't find out until a couple years ago."

She glanced away, voice tight. "She told you to come here because of me. Why didn't you ever try and get me to leave the safety of the pack's territory?"

Damien shook his head. He couldn't tell her about his specific orders; he'd barely been able to confirm for Rick that he'd been sent by the O'Hares. "Can't."

Sighing, she pushed to her feet and tucked her long, brown hair behind her ears as she paced away from his bed. "This is stupid. You can't tell me anything I want to know."

"Sorry." He waited for her to suggest they try and break the spell, prayed she'd say it. He'd thought of little else for two years but had been unable to tell anyone or work on breaking it himself, another failsafe the O'Hares had built in to keep him in line. Frustration mounted inside him as she shook her head and started to leave the room. "Wait."

She paused and looked back at him, eyebrows raised.

He hadn't actually thought through what he'd say if she stopped.

"Um." He cleared his throat, grimacing at the pain. "I can tell you other things. Things about myself. If you want."

They'd known each other—at least in passing since he'd tried to keep his distance in the beginning—for two years, but he doubted she knew very much about him. Like how there was an entire shelf on the bookcase next to her full of science-fiction novels. Or how he couldn't speak more than a few words of Spanish despite his dad's best efforts.

Or how he'd known he had a mate since he cast a spell when he was sixteen because he'd been so fascinated with the idea and jealous of shifters.

He watched a bunch of emotions play out across her face as she nibbled on her lower lip and then tried to hide his devastation when she shook her head again. "I'll just sit outside. Keegan should be here soon with the new cuffs."

"Right," he said softly as she turned and walked away. "Okay."

He felt hollow inside at her rejection, but he told himself it was dumb to feel that way. Why should he have expected any different? No one in this pack wanted him around anymore. None of them trusted him. Well, except Tashmica.

He held on to that thought as he scooted back down on his bed and pulled his blankets over him, curling into a protective ball and trying to breathe through the swell of emotions overwhelming him. He wished more than anything his dad was there to hug him. He'd smell like tobacco and sawdust, the two scents Damien would always associate with being safe. He'd be furious with Damien for putting himself in danger, but he'd also help him get out of it. And tell him he loved him as he kissed his forehead.

A soft sob rocked through him, but he bit it back.

His dad wasn't there, and he didn't have time to wallow in self-pity. No one was coming to save him. He was on his own, and if he didn't focus on figuring out a plan, he'd never see his dad again. There had to be a way to break the Blood Oath spell so he could go rescue him.

As if his thoughts triggered it, the sigil on his chest began to grow hot, and a wet whimper broke free at the feeling. He had no strength left in him, no fight, but he knew better than to ignore the signal.

Pushing to his feet, he shuffled into the outer room and into his tiny kitchen. He knew that if Tashmica had really felt he was a threat to the pack, she would have searched his apartment far more thoroughly and probably found the journal hidden in his freezer. He wasn't sure if he was glad she hadn't or disappointed.

As he pulled the plastic bag it was wrapped in out of the cold depths, he had a feeling he knew what they wanted to know. He unwrapped the leather-bound journal and set it on the counter, opening it to the first page. There, in bright red ink, were the words *Is Kincaid still alive?*

As soon as he read them, they darkened to black and then began to fade. Fingers trembling, he picked up the pen he kept tucked inside the cover and thought about trying to hide the truth. The pages were enchanted to repel lies, and he'd found out the hard way just how the journal retaliated if he tried.

The letters cut into his chest hadn't faded for a month. The scars would have probably been permanent if he hadn't treated them with a powerful healing ointment.

He settled on simply writing, *Yes.* He wasn't surprised when the ink turned black within a few seconds and then disappeared. He fingered the bandage wrapped around his left hand as he waited for a response, dread pooling in his stomach.

Kill him and bring us the abomination. We'll send coordinates as soon as we're in position outside the wards.

He sucked in a breath and squeezed the pen so hard he felt it begin to bend. They were coming here, and he was sure Rick's dad would be with them, ready to swoop in and take over leadership before his son's body was even cold. If the pack resisted, the O'Hares would ensure it wasn't for long. Then they'd take Jess back to their own territory and... make sure she could never fulfill the legend of destroying magic and the parahuman world with it.

Mouth dry, he wrote back quickly, *I can't get close enough to him.*

He hadn't told them about being found out or under house arrest, but it wasn't inconceivable that as far as they knew, he was simply a lowly member of the coven and had no access to Rick or his home. He had never shared even a single word more than he absolutely had to, doing everything in his power to protect Rick, Jess, and everyone else.

His heart was thundering in his chest, his head beginning to ache again, as he waited. When the next message came through, his blood froze in his veins, and tears filled his eyes.

If you ever want to see your father again, figure out a way. You have five days.

CHAPTER SIX

Carter made it back to the manor just before dinner, but the mood around the table was somber, with hardly anyone speaking the entire meal. He understood, but it still grated on his nerves, especially since his bear was still upset about what had happened in Rick and Kai's bedroom just a couple of hours before.

Thankfully, Bennett and Marcus were both absent from the table, or he might not have been able to stop himself from laying into them. He knew everyone who had witnessed him losing his shit had to at least be wondering what was going on with him—but the knowing look Bennett had given him after Damien's unconscious body had been carried out and Carter had tried to follow had said the pack's second suspected the reason behind his behavior.

Which… Carter was still trying to wrap his own head around it. He didn't need anyone else finding out yet. But that hadn't stopped him from trying to help his suffering mate.

Logically, he understood why they'd wanted the cuffs back on Damien, but after working with him all afternoon to save Rick's life, scenting his fear and determination, it had been impossible for his bear to care. All he'd wanted was a few minutes to talk to Damien, and Bennett had acted like that was too much to ask. After everything Carter had done for the fucking pack—done for Bennett's *mate*—he'd thought he'd garnered a little extra trust, but it was like he was just anyone else.

It was infuriating, but then add on top of that watching Damien get recuffed and be in so much pain? He'd been furious, but what had hurt the most was that they hadn't even let him go to Damien to try and offer him some comfort. It wasn't like he could have taken the cuffs back off. He'd simply wanted to give his suffering mate a hug, the need to do *something* impossible to ignore.

And they'd stopped him. Prevented him from touching his own damn mate and sending his bear into a rage. He hadn't been so close to shifting unintentionally in *decades*. He'd heard Damien ask him to stop fighting the hold they'd had on him, but it was like he'd had no control over himself. If he could have in that moment, he was pretty sure he would have attacked all of them to get to Damien.

Which was terrifying.

He'd never been the out-of-control type, letting his bear's instincts control his every whim. He was a doctor, a scientist, and he believed in listening to reason and facts. His animal side was a part of him, but it didn't run the damn show.

Turned out he'd just never had the right motivation.

As soon as he finished eating, he thanked the housekeeper Beth for the delicious food, then headed upstairs with his duffel bag and the defibrillator he'd brought from his office. No one stopped him or tried to talk to him, and that put his nerves even more on edge.

Everyone inside—and those camped outside—the manor were waiting. Most didn't know exactly what was going on, but word had spread through the pack about Rick being injured. The helicopter had been spotted, and too many people had seen Carter carrying his unconscious body inside.

The crowd outside had tried to ask him what had happened when he'd returned earlier, but he'd pasted on his best doctor's smile and told them someone would give them an update when they could. Even if he'd wanted to share what had taken place, he wasn't high enough in the pack to do it. His job was to take care of Rick, and that was it—the others had made that abundantly clear.

As he neared the bedroom he'd been given for the fore-seeable future, he thought about going and checking on Rick, but he didn't want to intrude further. The devastation on Kai's face as he'd stared at his mate had been hard to see, and he wasn't exactly keen on witnessing it again. He'd done what he could, bandaging Rick's wound and helping to dress him so Kai could bring the pups in to see him, and then he'd excused himself.

And now... they just had to wait. Which meant he had nothing to do but think about the way Damien had lost consciousness as his magic had broken through the cuffs and how he'd had to be carried out of the room as Carter fought to free himself from Bennett's and Marcus's holds.

And how Damien had just accepted the cuffs and the pain they caused him as his due.

And how it didn't seem to matter one damn bit to his bear that he'd betrayed the pack and befriended Carter under false pretenses. He wanted him, and he'd been able to scent Damien's honey-sweet desire as well. Even though his witch had barely looked at him as they'd worked, there was no way he could deny the pull between them any more than Carter could.

But what use was it to have the realization? Once Rick

was healed and up and about again, Carter was under no illusions that his alpha would be so grateful for their help saving him that he'd just forgive Damien's transgressions.

So where did that leave Damien? Where did that leave them?

He needed to go and talk to him, to find out why he'd done what he had and figure out a way to convince Rick and the others that he was worth keeping around. Damien was a strong witch with a brilliant mind; it wasn't like it would be a stretch to say he was an asset to the coven and the pack.

But could that make up for his betrayal?

Carter had a feeling it would all come down to what Damien told Rick and how useful the information was. Tashmica had said that she and Rick had talked to Damien and knew more than the Enforcers did, but would it be enough?

Frustrated at his circling thoughts, he grunted and headed into the bathroom attached to his temporary bedroom and started the water in the shower, the stall tiny but useable. It didn't take nearly as long to heat up as his shower at home did, and he was stepping in under the spray a minute later. The hot water hitting the tense, sore muscles in his shoulders and back made him groan, and he took a few minutes to just stand there and try to relax.

Worrying about the future wouldn't solve anything. He needed to gather as much information as he could and come up with a plan. It was what he always did—with his life, with a patient. Making a decision before he had all the facts would be useless.

Nodding to himself, he squeezed some shampoo into his palm and lathered up his hair, trying to simply focus on the next step in front of him. He'd brought his laptop with him so he could dig into any resources he had access to and try and figure out how to keep Rick alive long enough to get the rest of the parasite spell out of him.

When he shut his eyes to rinse out the shampoo, he saw Damien holding his bleeding hand over Rick's open wound, drawing out the spell by using himself as bait. Goddess, he was brave but reckless too. Carter growled, the sound reverberating in the enclosed space, as he thought of how quickly things could have gone wrong.

What would he do if something happened to Damien before he even had a chance to figure out how he felt? Before he had a chance to see if he tasted like honey as well as smelled like it...

His cock began to thicken between his legs just at the thought. He groaned, leaning one forearm against the shower stall and pressing his warm forehead next to it, eyes squeezed shut. After a few deep breaths, he accepted the fact that his body wasn't going to listen to him. Just having the memory of his mate's scent in his nose was enough to overrule his brain and make him forget what a terrible, *terrible* idea it would be to masturbate to the thought of Damien.

Lip lifted in a silent snarl, he reached down with his other hand and wrapped his fist around himself. Fuck it. Maybe it would help him actually sleep instead of lying in bed with circling thoughts for hours.

He tried not to think about anything, to just stroke his hand up and down his shaft and rub at his leaking crown every few tugs.

He lasted less than two minutes.

Smooth, light brown skin filled his head and a soft, shy smile that made him want to see just how innocent Damien really was. He'd done his best not to pay attention to the younger man, feeling like an old pervert whenever his mind had wandered to how good the little witch would taste. How pretty he'd be when he whimpered and begged.

"Fuck." He squeezed his shaft as precome leaked more heavily from his tip.

In the two years he'd known Damien, he'd never seen him out with anyone socially, never heard him talk about seeing someone. Had he known all along who Carter was to him? He had to have—why else would he hide it?

Had he been... saving himself for Carter?

Groaning, he sprayed the wall in front of him with come at the damn thought. He kept stroking, working himself all the way through it and finally letting himself picture all the different ways he'd love to take his witch and show him how good it could be between mates.

When he was spent and sagging, he felt... hollow.

Cleaning up, he realized what a mistake that had been. Would he be able to look at Damien anymore without imagining him naked and aroused?

He finished his shower quickly, his meal turning over in his stomach the more time passed. Mate or not, how could he even be tempted by Damien? He knew who Damien was and what he'd done. It was a betrayal to his pack—to Rick— to think for even a second that the possibility of them mating was worth putting the pack at risk.

He'd never been the selfish type, always putting his family or pack first. How could he suddenly just throw all that away for a man he didn't really know? One who had lied to him for years.

Because he was made for you.

Scoffing at himself, he brushed out his long hair roughly, pulled on a pair of boxers, then grabbed his laptop. He needed to put the whole thing out of his head for now and focus on Rick. He needed Carter's undivided attention. He deserved nothing less.

Climbing into bed, he sighed in annoyance when his phone started to ring. The last thing he wanted was to talk to his mother again—oh *fuck*. He'd forgotten she would be there in a matter of days. After everything that had happened that afternoon and with Rick still hanging by a thread, he needed to convince her not to come.

He scoffed just at the idea. He'd never been able to convince Mama Bell to do anything she wasn't already planning on doing. And if she got even a whiff of how bad things truly were at the moment?

Yeah, there wouldn't be any keeping her away.

Groaning, he picked up his cell, but it wasn't his mom calling. He exhaled slowly as he tossed his laptop onto the bed next to him and answered. "Hey, Tash."

"Hey," she said with a huge sigh, sounding as exhausted as he felt. "I wanted to let you know that Keegan is going to stay at the manor tonight while I do some research here at the shop. If you need me, just call. I'll be up."

"You should get some sleep," he said as he slipped between the sheets of his borrowed bed. "When was the last time you got a good night's sleep?"

"About a year ago," she muttered.

He thought she was joking at first, but then he realized what had happened about a year ago. "Leading the coven has been that stressful for you?"

She sighed again as he heard the familiar *swish* of the beads hanging in the doorway of *Wicca We Can* that separated the public front from the private space in the back. "Leading the coven? No. Figuring out if anyone who was still here had helped Agnes try to kill Kai? Yes. Stepping up the training of every member after realizing how much Agnes had let things slide? Also yes. Convincing Rick to let me rebuild the coven and then dealing with doing that in a safe way—"

"Also yes again?"

"Indeed," she said dryly. "Not to mention the general stress we've all been under not knowing what was happening with the Council and now knowing who's behind things but not knowing what they plan to do next." Tashmica groaned, and something thumped against wood on her end. He hoped it wasn't her forehead on a table. "Oh, and there's the small fact that one of my damn proteges is the reincarnated spirit of a seer who predicted *horrible* things and is now freaking out and afraid to use her magic, and the other one turned out to be a damn spy."

A sharp pain lit up his chest even as guilt swirled in his stomach at what he'd just been doing in the shower while thinking about that very same spy. "Yeah. There's that."

She didn't say anything for a long moment, but he could still hear her breathing and steady heartbeat. The pack had changed so much in the last year, some things for the better, but others...

"How did he fool all of us for so long?"

He jolted when he realized he'd said that out loud, Tash making a soft, questioning noise.

"Do you really want to know what I think?" she finally asked.

Straightening up, he leaned against the headboard. "I do. I've been banging my head against the wall the last week, wondering how I—we—could have missed that he was hiding something so massive."

"I'm not sure he was."

Carter frowned. "He admitted he was sent here by the O'Hares, Tash. There's no getting around that."

"No, that's not what I meant," she said quickly, then huffed a breath. "Listen, a lot of this is just... speculation and my undying hope that I wasn't wrong about him, okay?"

"Okay..."

"Without breaking the Blood Oath, there's no way to really know what his mission was—"

"Wait." Carter sat upright, claws extending from his

fingers and gut tightening. "Did you just say he was under a Blood Oath spell? Like that thing that *killed* Kai's parents?"

"Yes, sorry. I thought you knew. Everything has been so… Sorry." She sounded sorry too, and he began to wonder if Bennett wasn't the only one who suspected why he was so interested in Damien.

"No, I didn't… I didn't know. So he can't tell you anything?" he said slowly, mouth dry as he sagged back against the headboard, and his heart raced. When Tashmica had used magic to try and force Kai's parents to tell them who had been helping them, they'd died horrifically before they could say anything.

Had Damien been living with the fear of that happening to him for two fucking years?

"Very little. He said that he could only confirm about Jessica because we'd figured it out ourselves, so he never had to actually say the words."

Carter grunted, head working fast to try and figure out what that could mean for them. "Can we just play twenty questions with him, then? Get him to confirm or deny certain things to see how worried we should be about the O'Hares?"

Tash sighed again. "Rick suggested something similar, and Damien was, of course, willing to try, but I wouldn't let them. If he pushes the Oath too hard or gets too close to telling us something the spell prohibits without meaning to… I'm not willing to risk his life for half-answers at this point. Are you?"

"No," he said softly. As selfish as it made him, he couldn't find any part of him willing to risk Damien's safety, even if it meant protecting the pack. "So we need to break it then."

"Easier said than done, I'm afraid." He heard some rustling, like she was flipping through the pages of a book. "I haven't had a lot of time to dig into it with everything else going on, but nothing I've found has been... encouraging."

"Meaning?"

"All the examples I found, the person they were trying to remove the Blood Oath from died."

He sucked in a breath. "All of them?"

"Yes. I only found a handful of accounts so far, and most of them are from decades ago, with only vague details given of what they actually tried. Most seemed to use some variation of a purifying spell. But for something as powerful as a Blood Oath given by a coven like the O'Hares, I can't even imagine how powerful the purification would have to be. Even if Keegan and I tried, the process would likely end the same. His body wouldn't be able to handle that level of... cleansing."

Growling, he rubbed at his tired eyes. "We can't just leave it though, right?"

"No, but I think we need to focus on Rick right now. Once we know he's going to be okay, Keegan and Jess and I can come up with something to try."

"Does Damien have any ideas? He's been living with it all this time—surely he's come up with something..."

"He can't tell us even if he has. He could only show Rick and I the mark. When I tried to ask him about it and the parameters set when it was done, he just... shook his head," she finished, but there was something off in her voice.

"Tash. What happened when you asked him about it?"

"It hurt him," she whispered wetly, then sniffled. "I'd guess he was thinking about how to answer, and the mark started to glow orange, and he flinched. I think it burns him as a warning, maybe."

"Fuck."

"Yeah."

They sat quietly for a few more minutes, both lost in

thought before he realized she'd never finished telling him why she thought Damien wasn't the traitor they all thought he was. "What were you going to say?"

"Hmm?" He heard her tapping on something, a nervous habit she rarely let others see, but he had a feeling she didn't even realize she was doing it, so lost in worry.

"You made it sound like you had some theory about Damien that the rest of us were missing."

"Oh right," she said, the thrumming noise stopping. "So you know how I tested the rest of the coven after Agnes and her followers fled?"

"Sure. You gave them all that truth serum stuff and inter-rogated them."

She scoffed. "I didn't *interrogate* them."

Carter grinned. "That's how it was described to me after-ward." It had been, too, by a smiling Damien, who'd been teasing Tashmica where she'd sat three feet from the two of them. Sobering at the remembered memory, he said softly, "How did he trick the serum?"

"He didn't. He couldn't have," she said firmly.

"Tash…"

"Listen to me, Carter. I created that spell myself, and I don't care how strong he is, there is no way he could have figured out how to protect himself from the effects without it being very obvious."

"Okay," he said slowly, eyes squinting as he tried to follow along. As much as he worked with the coven more than most, the intricacies of spellwork were not his specialty. "Then how come you didn't find out he was a spy?"

"Because I didn't ask the right *questions*."

"Meaning?"

"Meaning, I asked things like 'do you harbor any ill will toward anyone within the Kincaid Pack' and 'have you ever tried to harm a member or ally to the Kincaid Pack.'"

When she didn't continue, he sighed. "I don't understand. Did he lie, or did he say yes and you just missed it?"

She made an affronted noise. "Neither, you giant teddy bear. He said no, and it was the truth."

He ignored the teddy bear comment for the moment. "So that means…"

"He doesn't *want* to hurt anyone in the pack. My best guess? They are somehow forcing him to be their little spy, and if I know Damien at all, he's been doing his best to protect us the entire time, maybe even to the detriment of himself."

Carter's gut had been saying the same thing, but his head and heart had been too busy being hurt and insisting the worst. "Forcing him how?"

"I'm not sure," she said, then sighed. "That will have to go onto the list of things to ask once we break the Blood Oath, but we can't focus on that until we get Rick up on his feet. Agreed?"

He echoed her long sigh. "Yeah, you're right. I don't like it any more than he did that we had to leave some of that shit inside him for now, but hopefully, by tomorrow, he'll be strong enough to extract the rest without his heart giving out."

"Hopefully. I'm going to see if I can find something to repair any damage the spell has done. Depending on how much of his magic it managed to consume, he could be in a bad way if we don't replace it somehow."

He nodded absently, wondering if he could cook something up in his lab to boost the alpha's magic enough to repair the bonds to the pack. Even if it wouldn't work on its own, maybe if it was combined with something Tash found, it'd be enough to get Rick over the hump and back in fighting form. Because he had a feeling fighting was what they'd be doing very soon. Once Rick's dad realized his son was still alive and in the spot he coveted, he'd come for him and the pack.

With the O'Hares backing him up, no doubt.

Thoughts turning dark, he asked quietly, "We need to fix him. I don't know how the pack will survive what's coming without him."

She hummed in agreement. "The others should be preparing the pack right now, just in case."

He completely agreed, but it wasn't his place to say anything. "Yeah. Do you think…"

"What?" she asked when he didn't finish.

"Do you think we'll make it through this? Whatever is going to happen?"

She didn't respond for a long moment, and then she let out a quiet breath. "I'm not sure, Carter. But I do know that if we aren't careful, there won't be a pack left to protect."

CHAPTER SEVEN

There was no way Kai could be alpha.

As he held Henry's sleeping body and stared at Rick's unmoving one, he felt sick and empty and terrified all at once. Henry and Callie had been inconsolable after the others had finally left, sobbing and screaming for him and Rick from where Sammi had been keeping them away in their bedroom.

It had been difficult to leave Rick's side, even for the minute it had taken to go and get their pups. Carter had put a bandage over Rick's healing wound and then helped him dress his mate before leaving him to deal with his broken family.

How could Rick have done this?

Tashmica had brought him a letter Rick had written for him the morning before, her orders having been to deliver it once Rick and Gabriel were far enough away that it'd be difficult to follow. She'd brought one for Bennett as well and then told him that Rick had left her with letters for Samantha, Callie, and Henry for later. She hadn't said it, but it had been crystal clear what she'd meant.

If Rick never came back.

A sob ripped from Kai's soul at how close they'd come, at how they still weren't out of the woods, as he fell to his knees and held Henry even tighter, the pup whimpering but not waking.

Damien hadn't wanted to stop, but Carter had convinced him, and that meant there was still some of that parasite stuff left inside him, waiting for them to turn their backs and then rip away the one person Kai needed above all others.

How could Rick have done this?!

Never in his entire life had Kai ever wanted to hit someone as much as he did Rick in that moment. As he knelt next to their bed, holding their pup in his arms and listening to his mate's unsteady breathing, he realized a part of him hated Rick for doing this to him. For putting their family in danger of losing him. Of risking the future of their pack.

He wanted to throw things. He wanted to burn the manor down around them. He wanted to scream at Rick, slapping and hitting him until he hurt as much as Kai did.

He wanted to *rage*.

Then he wanted his damn mate to put his big, strong arms around him and hold him until he didn't feel like he was falling apart anymore. Until it didn't feel like he was shattering into a million pieces. Until his insides stopped shaking with terror.

He couldn't be the alpha.

He needed Rick. They all did.

Rocking back and forth, he continued to cry as he gentled his hold on Henry, not wanting to wake him now that he was finally asleep. Callie had passed out over an hour ago and been carried away by the silent ghost Sammi had become, her tiny body exhausted after the tears and scary feelings she'd been experiencing since they'd woken up yesterday and found Rick gone. Kai had tried to reassure her, but even at five, she was learning so fast how to scent and understand other people's emotions, and she'd known he was scared.

How could he take care of a whole pack when he couldn't even hold it together for his family?

A soft knock behind him startled him out of his downward spiral. He turned and scented the air and then bit back a groan. "I'm fine, José."

"I don't mean to disagree with you, sir, but we both know that's not true. May I come in?"

Sighing, he pushed to his feet. If he didn't like the young beta so much, he'd be pissed at his presumption. He padded over to the door and opened it carefully without jostling Henry too much. His sweet boy was getting so big it was getting awkward for Kai to cart him around, but after everything that had happened the last couple of weeks... He needed him close.

José was standing just on the other side of the door, a covered plate in his hands and a worried frown on his handsome face. When he took in Kai's appearance—which had to be terrible, but he hadn't looked in a mirror in days—his mouth tightened. "Kai, you need to eat something and then get some rest."

He wasn't hungry. His appetite had disappeared when his mate had and hadn't come back yet. Without answering, he tipped his head down to stare at Henry's round face, his mouth slack and parted, dried tears and snot streaking his cheeks. He didn't like being away from him, not after Keegan and his dead grandma had translated some stupid prophesy about... about him...

It wasn't rational, but Kai felt like if he kept Henry close, held him tight and never let him go, then he could stop anything bad from happening to him. Screw what some long-dead seer had said.

But his sweet boy needed a good night's sleep, and he

wouldn't get that if Kai held him the whole time. Leaning down, he gently rubbed his cheek against the side of Henry's face, scenting him, then nodded down at him. "Will you take him to his room, please?"

"Of course," José said quickly, spine straightening just a little at being given the task.

He stepped just inside the bedroom, only far enough to set the plate on a dresser and accept Henry's small form, and then he backed up again, but he didn't walk away. His gaze slid past Kai to the bed behind him, and even though Kai trusted José with his life and the life of his children, his wolf surged to the surface. He stepped over, blocking the beta's view. Letting a young, strong member of the pack see their alpha while he was weak and injured set off Kai's instincts in a way he rarely experienced.

At his defensive posture, José dropped his eyes and took several steps back.

"Then the rest of the evening is yours," Kai said lowly.

José glanced up at him, jaw tight, but he finally just nodded. "Try to eat something. You need to keep up your strength, alpha-mate."

Alpha-mate.

The title rang in his ears as José turned and left, carrying Henry down the hall to his bedroom and slipping inside. As soon as he was out of sight, Kai closed the door, fingers lingering on the lock but falling away before twisting it. If he needed help quickly, he didn't want Carter or one of the Enforcers to have to break down the door. He took a few deep breaths and reminded himself that he trusted all of the Enforcers and all of the betas with access to the third floor.

No one was going to slip into their bedroom and try to kill his injured mate so they could become alpha.

His wolf was still on edge though, prowling in his chest and urging him to barricade the door and keep watch until

Rick was able to protect himself again. As he paced for the next half hour, he fought to keep himself under control, his claws extending and retracting over and over.

When he heard someone approaching, he was still on edge, not relaxing until he caught Keegan's scent of magic and Nico. He was opening the door before he could even knock, Keegan's brows rising in surprise.

"Everything okay?" he asked, glancing past Kai to check on Rick.

"Yeah, sorry." Kai rubbed at his face and scooted back enough to let him inside, shutting the door firmly behind him. "My wolf is just on edge. I thought it was bad before, while he was gone, but now... The later it gets, the more agitated I'm getting."

Keegan nodded as he moved to the foot of the bed, studying Rick. "I suppose that makes sense. To your wolf, nighttime is the most dangerous. Everyone is sleeping, it's dark. It'd be easier for a threat to get to him while he's vulnerable."

If anything, hearing the words made Kai feel worse. "Yeah, exactly."

"I can stay if you want, and we can take turns keeping watch. Or you can have some of the Enforcers come help," Keegan offered easily, raising a hand in front of him. His purple magic appeared, dancing in the air over Rick, and Kai waited for him to finish to answer.

"That's okay. I don't think I can let another shifter in here right now," Kai said, voice slow and embarrassed. "Is he... better?"

Keegan shoved his hands in his pockets and gave a one-shoulder shrug. "About the same, but I'd say that's good news."

"Really?"

"Yeah. Right now, we're mostly just hoping the spell

doesn't grow again inside him. Then when he's a bit stronger, we can pull the rest of that shit out, and that should help with his healing and regaining his strength. So the same is definitely good."

Kai let out a relieved breath. "Okay, yeah. That's... yeah, that's good."

Smiling, Keegan stepped closer, then slowly raised one hand, giving Kai a chance to step back if he wanted. When he didn't, Keegan lightly touched the side of his neck before pulling away. It wasn't as comforting as when another shifter scented him, or someone he was especially close to, but it did seem to settle his wolf a little.

"Thanks," he said softly, and Keegan just nodded, heading for the door.

"I'll be back in a few hours. Try to get some sleep. The pack needs you strong right now," Keegan added, pausing at the door and looking back at Kai with knowing eyes. "You have a good support system around you, so use them. It's not all on you."

Kai pressed his lips together and glanced back at Rick, not sure he believed that. Keegan didn't wait for a response though, slipping back out of the room and heading down the hall to the room he was crashing in for the night. If Rick... If he didn't make it, everything would fall to Kai.

He didn't know how to be alpha.

He clenched his hands into fists and slowly moved over to the bedside table he used, pulling open the small drawer and staring at the folded piece of paper inside. Fingers trembling, he reached in and pulled it out, even though he had the letter memorized after having read it so many times the day before.

Kai,

I know you probably won't understand why I'm doing this, but just know that it's for us. Everything I do, I do to make sure you and our family is safe, so I have to do this. You need it and that means I have to give it to you.

I'm sorry, pup. I know you're going to be furious, but I'll make you feel better when I get back, I promise.

You can ask Tashmica for more details, but after I spoke to her, I felt like this was the only option to make sure Henry stays safe. I know you're scared about his future and so am I, but I can't just sit around and watch you kill yourself trying to find answers in old dusty books.

Tash and I agree—the only way to stop the Fourth King Prophesy is to stop another of Angeline's visions, and that's what I'm going to do. The Council doesn't deserve our help, but if that's what it takes to keep him safe, I'll do it. I'd do anything for you and him.

I love you so much, pup. I need you to be strong right now, for our family and for the pack. While I'm gone, you're the acting alpha. Listen to B, but trust _your_ instincts. You are smart and strong and capable. The pack is in good hands.

I'll be back as soon as I can. Scent the pups for me.

Your mate,

Rick

Shuddering, he let the paper drop from his numb fingers and began to pull off his clothes, shifting as soon as he was naked. He shook out his white fur, then whined and jumped onto their bed, sniffing at Rick's unmoving body. He wanted his mate, needed him in that moment so much he cried out for him, his wolf releasing sad, longing howls as he nosed at Rick.

In this form, he could smell the lingering magic on him and the pain. God, there was still so much pain coming off him. Anxious, he licked at his mate's face and throat, trying to soothe and scent him, before using his snout to shove

Rick's shirt up so he could sniff at the wound there. The strong smell of the magic caused him to sneeze, his nose tickling.

After checking his whole body, Kai finally huffed and settled next to him, resting his head on Rick's stomach to protect him. He didn't think he'd sleep, too scared and worried, but even with the smell of magic and pain on him, Kai couldn't resist the scent of his mate thick in his nose. It eased some of the tension inside him, and his muscles began to relax, one after the other, until he finally drifted off, knowing he'd wake if someone tried to come in or if Rick stirred.

He wasn't sure how long he slept for, but he was groggy and disoriented when he roused, and the room was completely dark because he'd forgotten to turn a lamp on. He listened for a moment, assuming Keegan's approach had woken him, but the hallway was silent, and he couldn't detect any lingering scents like someone had been there recently and left.

He couldn't figure out what had woken him up, even as a terrible feeling began to grow in his stomach, twisting and tugging until he thought he was going to be sick.

Even in the dark, he could see well enough in the room, and he checked all the shadows once more, but they were still alone. As he started to lower his head back onto Rick's stomach, the feeling in his gut didn't go away. If anything, it was growing even more insistent.

Something was wrong. Something was very wrong.

The silence of the room began to prickle at his skin, and then it hit him like a sledgehammer to the head, and he jumped to his feet.

The room was *silent*.

He shifted back into his human form and knelt next to Rick's head, placing a hand on his chest even though his ears were already telling him what his brain didn't want to accept. No heartbeat. No breaths.

"Rick!" he screamed, gripping his mate's face and giving him a rough shake. "Wake up! Oh my god, Rick! Someone help! *Someone please help me!*"

CHAPTER EIGHT

Damien jolted awake, heart racing and pain throbbing behind his right eye.

He pushed up from where he'd fallen asleep on the open books spread across his small kitchen table, running a hand through his hair as he tried to clear his head enough to figure out what had woken him up. It was dark outside, the floor lamp behind him providing the only illumination in the apartment.

As he fumbled to his feet, intent on checking the time on his stove and flicking on another light, someone pounded on his door, startling him so badly he windmilled for a second before catching himself on the counter.

"Damien! I'm going to come in, okay?" Tashmica called as he heard his lock flick open.

The strain in her voice had him hurrying across his apartment and worry beginning to build inside him. As she stepped inside, frantic eyes searching for him in the dim lighting, he asked, "Is it Rick? What happened?"

"He…" She stopped a few feet away, one hand going to her chest and eyes squeezing shut.

"Tash," he croaked, horrified by the pain clear on her face. Knees weakening, he braced a hand on the back of his couch. "Don't say it. Please."

"He's still alive," she whispered, stepping forward and wrapping him in a tight hug.

It was so unexpected he stiffened at first, but when she murmured an apology and started to pull away, he made a soft, broken sound and hugged back, squeezing harder than was probably comfortable. He wanted to know what had happened, why she had come to his apartment in the middle of the night looking heartbroken, but first, he needed to take a moment to accept the comfort she so freely offered him. No one else was coming around to give it to him, and his soul *craved* it. The warmth and soft curves of her body, combined with her light floral scent and the barely there staticky feeling of her magic to ease some of the tension he'd been carrying for years.

He knew it wouldn't last, but he still sucked it up like a parched plant.

He could have stayed with his face buried in her soft curls for hours, but he forced himself to pull back after a minute. Turning his face away, he wiped at his damp eyes and cleared his throat. "You scared me. What happened?"

She waited for him to face her once more, her soft, understanding smile bringing a lump to his throat. "I'm sorry. About fifteen minutes ago, his heart stopped."

Damien sucked in a breath, feeling lightheaded. "But he's..."

"Carter was able to shock him a few times and get it going again, but he's concerned that even with how much of the Consumption Spell we removed, he's just too weak to get better on his own."

He ignored the way his belly fluttered at Carter's name, turning toward his kitchen and striding over to the books he'd left out. "I was worried about the same thing. The few volumes I had here were useless though. I couldn't find anything about combating the effects of a parasite or any accounts of those who've survived."

"I don't know that there are any people who've survived them," she said behind him, sounding like she was almost speaking to herself.

"Well, Rick will," he said firmly, snapping closed the book he'd fallen asleep on. Meeting her dark eyes, he took a few deep breaths to calm himself. "We have some of the most powerful witches in the world in this pack. Nothing is impossible. We just have to figure out *what* we want to do and then do it."

She stared at him, unmoving and looking like she was barely breathing, and then she let out a breath in a big rush and nodded. "You're right. I came to get you. We need to go back to the shop and put a plan together. Keegan and Carter are going to keep eyes on Rick all night and let us know what's going on, but you and I need to hit the books hard and find something that will fix his broken bonds so he can get his strength back."

Swallowing, he ran his hands through his hair and nodded, looking around the apartment but realizing quickly he didn't need anything there. The few books he'd been left with were informative only, and none of them had contained anything useful. As soon as they exited his apartment, the beta on duty was in his face, jaw tight.

"He can't leave his apartment without Enforcer approval," he said to Tashmica without taking his eyes off Damien or stepping back. There was another coven member standing back behind him, a frown on her face, but she didn't speak up.

"I need him, Charles. If you have a problem with that, you can take it up with Kai since it's his mate we're trying to save." Tash's voice was colder than Damien had ever remembered hearing it, his head jerking over to look at her and eyes widening at how pissed she appeared to be.

At the mention of Rick, the beta deflated and stepped back, rubbing at his temples. "Right, of course. We'll come with you and keep an eye on him."

Tashmica reached over and grabbed Damien's forearm, lifting and waving his newly cuffed wrist in the beta's face. "I think we're good. Head back to the manor and see if they need you there." She glanced at the coven member, her whole demeanor softening. "Go home and get some sleep, Bev. We'll call in the morning if we need you again."

The witch nodded and left without a word.

The beta gaped at Tash. "I can't just let you take him. He's my responsibility."

Tash sighed and started heading for the stairs. "Fine, but I'll probably put you to work."

Damien exchanged a glance with the beta, then slowly stepped forward to follow her. He half expected the beta to grab him roughly like the one yesterday, but Charles seemed fine with following the two of them down two flights and out to Tash's VW. He did balk when Tash tried to make him squeeze in the back seat though.

"I'll follow you in the SUV," he said, sounding grumpy but resigned.

Damien sank into the passenger seat, eyes on the beta's retreating form in the review mirror. "I can't believe he just walked away like that."

Shrugging, Tash started the car and threw it into gear. The car jolted forward, leaving Damien's stomach behind and him scrambling to put on his seat belt. "My guess is he heard about you busting through the last pair of cuffs and knows that if you wanted to get away, there isn't a single thing he could do to stop you."

Damien's heart sank as he rubbed at his wrists under the cuffs, remembering the pain. "I passed out last time. I don't think I could exactly make a run for it after breaking them."

"Exactly," she said, like he'd proved her point, "so there's no point in him hovering over you every second."

As they passed *Magic Beans* on their way down Main Street, she groaned and looked at the dark windows longingly. He couldn't help but smile, face turned away so she wouldn't see. "It'll open in a few hours. We can probably send Charles to grab some coffee for us then."

"And pastries," she grumped, turning sharply into a spot right out front of *Wicca We Can* and sending him into the door so hard he whacked his elbow. "If I have to be up all night straining my eyes on dusty old tomes, then I want a damn donut."

Rubbing at his arm, he climbed out of the car. "I'm sure we can get those too."

As they climbed the couple steps to the front door, he glanced over at her, noting her strained face. As much as she was joking, he knew it was killing her that they didn't know how to help Rick. But they'd figure it out. They had to.

The beta followed them in, silent and looking bored since Damien didn't actually try to make a run for it. He pulled out his phone and started thumbing through it, so Damien decided it was safe to ignore him and focus on the task at hand.

He and Tash headed straight for the back room, not pausing to grab any of the books in the front of the shop. Most of them were useless or only had history of magic or packs—things for locals or tourists to pick through but nothing truly dangerous.

All the valuable books were kept in the back. Dozens and dozens and dozens of old grimoires and recorded histories and guidebooks. The collection was impressive. The only one he'd seen that was bigger was his dad's. A soft ache bloomed inside him as he wondered, not for the first time, what had become of his and his dad's home. When the O'Hares had come for him—and later his father—they hadn't exactly had a chance to pack up the house or call someone to come and check on things.

He hoped what was left of the warding spells had at least kept nosy humans away, even if they hadn't proved to be strong enough to keep out his mother.

Sucking in a deep breath, he pushed the thought away and headed for the bookcase in the back corner of the small room. "Do you have an idea of where you'd like us to begin?"

"Not really," she admitted, perching on the edge of the round table where they'd often worked together, a small stack of books by her hip. She gestured at them. "The books I've checked so far have covered how to perform a Consumption Spell, but I haven't found anything on successfully breaking it or how to repair the damage done."

"Hmm." He planted his hands on his hips and studied the spines in front of him. He'd spent a lot of time in this room, familiarizing himself with the information as best he could in case it would come in handy. And because he enjoyed learning, always had. His dad used to tease him about it. How he was his little sponge, soaking up information like water. Clearing the emotions out of his throat, he said slowly, "Maybe we're thinking about this wrong."

"What do you mean?"

"Well… Let's remove the Consumption Spell from the equation for a minute."

"Okay?"

He spun around and faced her. "What does that leave?"

"Rick's diminished magic." She nodded along as she said, "And his severed bonds."

"Right. Okay." Damien twirled back to the bookcase. "We

should have C-Carter get us some of his blood. See if we're right about the bonds being severed. Because that... I think that is where we should focus." He pulled several books off various shelves, ignoring how he'd stumbled over Carter's name. "Because we can boost his magic easily enough, right? Give him a temporary infusion from one of us if need be or tap into the pack's magic somehow. But the severed bonds are going to be the trickiest part. Without those... he's just a regular shifter. Not even a member of the Kincaid Pack, technically. He'd be as weak as any other nomad, weaker if we don't give him a big enough boost."

He realized he was rambling and turned around with a grimace, the books overflowing in his arms. Tashmica was staring at him with a familiar fond expression that made his eyes prick with tears. "Okay," she said gently. "What are you thinking?"

He dumped his load onto the table and started spreading the books out. "I think... I think we need to focus on mating magic."

Her eyebrows shot up as she hopped down from the table and turned to face it, examining the books he'd chosen. "Why's that?"

"It's the strongest bond a shifter can have. And it's... the beginning of Rick's connection to his pack. Everything else flows through his tie to Kai." He scrunched up his face. "Sorry, I'm explaining this terribly."

"We're all tied to Rick," the beta said from the doorway, startling him and Tash. His arms were crossed over his wide chest, a deep furrow between his brows. "You can feel it when you're near him or if he gets mad enough."

Tash turned to Damien with raised brows. "He's right. I can't feel it like a shifter, but the pack bonds are what make us so formidable and Rick so strong."

Nodding, Damien huffed out a breath and glanced

around, finally focusing on the old, decrepit printer tucked in a corner under six inches of loose papers stacked haphazardly. He strode over and jerked the tray open, grabbing a sheet of white paper and a marker from out of a cup on a shelf on his way back to the table.

"Okay," he said, slapping the page down on the table by Tash and gesturing the beta over. "So, this is Rick."

He drew a circle in the middle, then a half dozen circles around Rick, then a dozen more surrounding that ring, and then two more.

"Looks like a shitty solar system," Charles mumbled, but Damien ignored him.

"This is Rick," he said again, pointing at the circle in the middle. "These are his Enforcers." He drew lines from Rick to the circles in the first ring around him. "These are the betas." He connected the Enforcers' ring to the betas'. "And then the coven, committees, and others who have semi-regular contact with him." He sloppily connected the two rings. "The last group, the farthest from him, are the rest of the pack. The majority of members who rarely, if ever, see him and just go about their lives."

"Okay," Tash said slowly. "I don't understand—"

Damien kept going. "But this"—he forcefully tapped the now-capped marker on the drawing twice—"this represents the pack from *before* he mated with Kai."

He flipped the page over and swiveled it so it was vertical, drawing a circle at the top, one just beneath it, and then connected the two, running the marker back and forth several times to make it extra thick. Underneath, he drew three circles in a line, then did a row of six, and then twelve, connecting each one as he went to the row above it.

"This is the pack now," he said slowly as he finished, then recapped his marker and pointed at the very top. "This is Rick now, and that's Kai. Their bond supersedes *everything*.

Even his bonds to his pack. The rest of his bonds are now *dependent* on that bond. Does that make sense?"

He turned to Tashmica and the beta, using his thumb to push the top off the marker and then push it back on with a soft *click* over and over again. They were both studying the picture curiously.

"How do you know this?" Charles asked finally. "And how can we trust that you're telling the truth? Maybe you just want to distract Tash and the others to buy time for Rick to... get worse."

The accusation felt like a punch to the face, rocking Damien back so hard he had to take a step back to stop himself from losing his balance. "I wouldn't..."

He made himself stop, slowly lowering the marker to the table and tucking his chin down. He'd gotten so caught up he'd forgotten he'd destroyed any trust the pack had had in him. Tashmica might still believe in him, but even she looked reluctant to abandon the direction she'd been spending hours researching and just blindly trust he knew what he was talking about.

Clearing his throat, he took a step back from the table.

"Damien—" she started to say, looking apologetic.

"It's fine." He kept his voice soft, trying to hide the emotions from them, though he wasn't sure why he bothered. Tash knew him well enough to read him easily, and the beta could scent how he was feeling without even trying. "Um. You can use an effigy diagram." He pointed at the book all the way on the left. He'd seen the spell she'd need in there a few months ago while he'd been looking for something else. "If you use a representative for each layer—family, Enforcer, betas, etcetera—then you just need a handful of people's blood. Then take a few drops of Rick's and cast the Seeing the Unseen spell. Since the parasite would start with the weakest connections first, that should let you see how far up the bonds have been destroyed."

Tashmica was reaching for the book he'd gestured at, flipping through it before he'd even finished explaining his idea. She probably could have figured out another way to check the bonds—she was a *brilliant* witch, after all—but she had asked for his help. And while his focus of study had usually been mated bonds and the intricacies of them, he'd found there was often a lot of overlap with pack bonds.

He turned toward the silent beta. "You can take me back to—"

"Not happening," Tash said without looking up from the book. "I hadn't even considered the impact of his mating with Kai on his bonds with the pack. You're staying and helping me." She glanced up at Charles. "And you're going to need to donate a little blood."

Sighing, the beta rolled his eyes and extended his hand. "Whatever it takes to save Rick."

It took nearly three hours for them to collect samples from representatives of each pack level and set up the diagram on the floor of the shop. Damien was lighting the candles and double-checking the ingredients when Charles barreled through the front door, looking disheveled and holding up a small vial.

"Got it."

"Thank you," he said, hurrying over and taking the sample of Keegan's blood.

He'd realized right before they'd been about to cut Tashmica's finger that he wasn't sure where she fell in the pack hierarchy anymore. Yes, she was the leader of the coven, but she was also a close confidant of Rick's.

For the spell to work correctly, they needed someone from *each* layer of the bonds within the pack, and he couldn't say confidently that she wasn't closer to the Enforcer level than the coven's. She hadn't been able to disagree either. And he couldn't be the representative because it was entirely possible Rick didn't consider him a member of his pack anymore.

While that thought had hurt, he'd pushed the feeling aside and focused on finding another source. They'd needed someone who was a member of the coven or one of the pack's committees.

Considering it was the middle of the night, only one person had come to mind that wouldn't require trying to wake someone up.

So Charles had gone back to the manor and gotten Keegan's blood.

"This should work," Damien said, stepping carefully through the diagram and pouring the little bit of blood from the vial onto the small cloth model he'd constructed to use for each layer as an icon.

"Should?" Charles asked from behind him.

"He's mated to an Enforcer," Damien said absently, running his eyes over each row to make sure everything lined up correctly. "That could have moved him up in the hierarchy."

"Oh, for fuck's sake—"

"But he's also brand-new," Tashmica finished for him, sweeping in from the back room with the bowl she'd been preparing Rick's blood in. "The bond between him and Rick will be weaker since it's so new. I'm sure it will be fine."

Damien joined her at the top of their makeshift pyramid. "Exactly. Ready?"

"Yes. Everything ready out here?"

He nodded.

"What's going to happen?" Charles asked as he shuffled closer to them, eyes on the large diagram taking up most of the space of the shop's front-room floor.

"The spell will show us how far Rick's connection to the pack still reaches," Tashmica said as she knelt by the Rick effigy. "The lines representing the bonds between each layer will light up the farther his connection reaches. Hopefully, it'll reach the bottom."

Damien glanced at her, eyebrows raised.

"I said hopefully."

Charles looked between them. "What's more likely going to happen?"

Damien gestured toward the middle. "More likely, it'll show his connection to the lowest levels has been severed and will need to be… rebuilt."

"How do we do that?" Charles asked, eyeing the diagram with more wariness.

"One problem at a time," Tashmica mumbled as she poured the blood mixture onto the icon and said the incantation.

Damien felt the swell of magic in the air, but for several seconds, nothing happened. His stomach dropped. Had they messed up the spell?

Was Rick's bond… irreparable?

Charles dropped to his knees and bent forward over the line connecting Rick to the Kai effigy. "You call that lighting up?"

Damien knelt as well, shuffling forward to see as all three of them peered more closely. There was a faint glow, barely perceptible. Swallowing, he turned his head and met Tashmica's terrified eyes as Charles knee-walked to the next level— the one connecting Rick and Kai to Kai's siblings, two of which were like Rick's own pups—and huffed.

"I don't see anything on these lines. Are you sure this worked?"

Damien sat upright, resting on his feet and covering his face with his hands, trying to take a few deep breaths to steady his panicking heart and thoughts. Eyes stinging with unshed tears, he shook his head as the beta called his name several times.

He needed... he needed to think.

They could... They just needed to...

He didn't realize he was panting or rocking back and forth until Tashmica's strong arms wrapped around him, engulfing him in her comforting scent for the second time that night.

"Damien," she whispered hoarsely, "what do we do?"

"I don't know."

CHAPTER NINE

Carter's tired eyes popped open when a mug of coffee got shoved under his nose. "I wasn't sleeping."

"I know," Keegan said softly, trying not to disturb the couple a few feet away.

Pushing up from where he'd slumped down in his chair, he ignored how his lower back screamed in protest and accepted the dark liquid, drinking half the mug down in a single scalding swallow. Even as he rubbed at his scratchy eyes and throbbing temples, he had both ears trained on the bed five feet from him, making note of every single thump of Rick's heart and *whoosh* of his lungs.

"Any news?" he mumbled, watching how Kai clung to Rick even in his sleep, his face still lined with worry while he rested. He looked... terrified. And older. Like the last few days had aged the young alpha-mate a good ten years.

Keegan licked his bottom lip, glancing at the pair on the bed, then nodded. The fact that he was hesitant to say out loud what Tashmica and Damien had found with their spell had the coffee he'd just ingested souring in his gut.

"Fuck." He pushed to his feet and gestured with his head

toward the small sitting room just off Rick and Kai's bedroom. As soon as Keegan stepped inside, Carter quietly pushed the door shut. He could still hear both of the occupants of the other room, but hopefully, they wouldn't disturb Kai. He'd only just fallen asleep maybe an hour before. "What is it?"

Keegan rubbed at his jaw. "It's bad, Doc. The spell showed Rick's bonds with the pack have almost been completely severed."

Feeling like a boulder had taken the place of his stomach, Carter sucked in a breath. "Okay. That's… That's bad, but we assumed there'd be some loss. That's the nature of the parasite inside him, right?"

"You aren't hearing me," Keegan said. "Tash said there's barely even a connection between him and Kai at this point. If we don't do something *today*, there won't be anything left to repair. He'd be… shit, he'd be basically human."

Carter heard the words Keegan didn't say. *Weak. Vulnerable.*

Easy for his father to come and finish the job.

Setting aside his coffee mug, Carter used both hands to scrub at his face, then quickly tied his hair up into a messy bun with the elastic band he kept around his wrist. "Okay. What's the plan? How do we strengthen their bond while he's still unconscious?"

"I got no fucking idea," Keegan said, pulling out his phone. He quickly called Tash and put it on speaker. "You've got me and Doc. We need a plan. Something we can tell Kai when he wakes up in a couple of hours."

She sighed over the line. "We… we don't really have one."

"That's not really going to fly," Carter growled. He jutted a finger at the closed door. "I'm working my ass off keeping him alive, but we might as well let him go if he's going to wake up and not *be* Rick Kincaid anymore. So we need to come up with something right fucking now."

No one said anything for a moment. If Keegan's shocked face was anything to go by, he assumed he'd surprised Tash as well with his harsh words, but he didn't care. He was exhausted and hungry and missing his mate and feeling guilty for that and terrified out of his mind for his alpha.

"What does Damien say?" he finally said when the silence started grating on his nerves.

There was a muffled sound, and then Damien's soft voice hit him, cooling the anger in his blood. He let out a quiet breath as the tension slowly seeped out of his muscles, even as Damien delivered less-than-great news. "Most of what we'd come up with to do was dependent on using the strength of the bond between Rick and Kai."

Keegan grimaced. "That makes sense. Nothing's stronger than the bond between fated mates."

Damien cleared his throat, and Carter wished more than anything that the two of them were in the same room at that moment. His witch had to be thinking about their potential bond and what it could mean, which meant he probably smelled flustered and a little embarrassed... and aroused. Fuck, Carter could just imagine his honey scent surrounding him, so thick it coated the back of his throat.

Keegan was looking at him strangely, but Carter was positive he hadn't actually groaned out loud. Luckily, Tash-mica broke in and distracted him before he noticed the slight tenting of Carter's sweatpants. "Right. So without being able to tap into the magic of their mating bond, we're trying to come up with another way to repair his connection to the pack. We can give him a boost of magic, but it would be temporary."

"Without the strength of the pack helping him," Keegan

said, finishing the thought, "he and his wolf won't heal on their own."

A heavy silence filled the room, making the out-of-sync beating of Rick's and Kai's hearts oppressive. Like a clock ticking down the minutes until they lost him for good.

Fuck that.

"What are our options," Carter growled, looking between Keegan and the phone. "Come on. You three are fucking brilliant. You have to have some sort of Hail Mary we can try. Some out-of-the-box plan that's just risky enough that it'll work."

Keegan ran a hand over his short curls. "We could…" His eyes widened as he jerked his head up to meet Carter's gaze. "We can swap their bond with another pair's."

"Keegan—" Tashmica said, a warning clear in her voice, but he just kept talking.

"No, hear me out. If we use another pair of fated mates, we could theoretically replace Rick and Kai's weakened bond with a healthy one. Then we'd be able to—"

"That would kill him," Damien cut in harshly. "And possibly Kai. And maybe the pair we ripped the bond out of."

Keegan's dark cheeks flushed as he rubbed at his forehead, shoulders sagging. "Shit. You're probably right."

Reaching over, Carter clasped the side of Keegan's neck, offering him support and his scent. Even without a shifter's senses, it would help soothe his agitation. "Okay, maybe not that far outside the box then. What else have we got to work with?"

"Rick and Kai are the only ones who can strengthen their bond," Damien said slowly. "I think… I think it was fractured before Rick was injured by his leaving. He needs to repair the hurt he caused his mate and then reaffirm their bond through—" He cleared his throat again. "—uh, mating."

"Even if we could wake him up long enough to grovel to

Kai," Carter said, shaking his head and ignoring the fact that Damien just muttered the word *mating*, "there's no way he'd be strong enough for something that... physical."

"Dear goddess," he heard Tashmica murmur softly somewhere in the background. "These two."

Louder, Damien said, "We can help with that. The strength of the pack is still there; Rick just can't access it right now. If we can tap into it and funnel it into him, it should give him enough of a boost in his magic and strength for him to be able to wake up and... do what needs to be done."

"Repair his bond with Kai," Carter clarified, turning to face the closed door like he could see the bed through it. "If we give him an infusion of magic, his body may be able to handle getting the rest of that shit out of him too."

"Yes," Damien agreed quickly. "Though we'll need to be careful about—"

"Something's wrong," Keegan said, drawing Carter's attention back around. He was frowning and rubbing at his chest with his free hand.

"With the plan?" Damien asked carefully.

"No. It's Nico. He's—" His phone vibrated in his hand at the same time Carter's went off in his pocket, and he could hear the soft ping of Tash's notification as well as Kai's phone in the bedroom.

"What the hell?" Carter pulled out his own cell and found a text in a group thread that seemed to just be him, the Enforcers and their mates, Kai, and the witches. Carter knew Rick had been meeting with a wider group of individuals— which Gabriel had started referring to as the War Council— but this was a much smaller number of people.

When he read the text from the hunter, he understood why, even as his blood turned to ice in his veins.

Gabriel: *Councilman Garcia and Councilwoman Voight are* *dead. Kincaid is claiming Rick is responsible and it's already picking up steam. Library in one hour. We need to prepare for an imminent attack.*

🐾

"This can't be happening," Kai said brokenly, arms wrapped around himself and looking too thin and pale. He was pacing back and forth, refusing to sit, and his gaze kept creeping toward the door, letting them all know his main focus was still on his incapacitated mate.

"Where's Gabriel?" Bennett snarled, eyes glowing as he glared at the library's open door. "He called this damn meeting at the crack of dawn and then can't be bothered to show up."

Carter's hackles rose at the tiger's aggressive tone, still pissed about what he'd done to Carter and Damien the day before. His hands curled into fists, but he stayed where he was, leaning against the wall next to the large picture window overlooking the manor's backyard.

"Easy," Kieran said lowly, setting a gentling hand on one of his mate's massive shoulders and guiding him down to a chair. "He's not the only one still on the way, so let's just take a few breaths, okay?"

B sucked in a deep inhale through his nose as he wrapped an arm around Kieran's waist and tugged him onto his lap, burying his face in Kieran's neck. "Sorry, sweetheart," he murmured, though all the shifters in the room could still hear him. "I just can't seem to calm down. It's like my skin is on fire and my tiger wants to make someone pay for what happened to him."

Carter forced himself to relax and looked away from the couple. He still wasn't okay with how Bennett had handled things with Damien, but the reminder that he was feeling as lost and scared as the rest of them helped cool his ire. Bennett and Rick had known each other their whole lives— were as close as brothers.

His best friend was hanging by a thread, and he'd had to stand by and let a man he considered an enemy help him.

Carter felt for him, truly, but his bear didn't care. He just hoped their plan to help Rick would work and fast so he didn't have to try and control himself if B pissed him off again.

"Who are we missing?" Nico asked from where he was perched on one end of a couch, laptop balanced on his knees as he typed.

"Morde and his mates," Bennett muttered.

"And Tashmica," Keegan added, perched on the arm of Nico's couch.

"We're here," Tash said as she hurried through the door, Jamie and Drake right behind her.

He was about to say something to her as she approached him, but even without looking, he knew the moment Damien stepped into the room. Head jerking around, he locked eyes on him as he sidestepped out of the doorway, keeping Gabriel between him and the rest of the room.

Gabriel swung the door shut hard enough for it to slam, stopping Bennett and Vanessa where they half stood, looking pissed. "I don't want to hear a word about him being here. They have a plan to help Rick, and he's needed. There was no point in bringing him back to his apartment, coming for the damn meeting, then going back and getting him."

The hunter stood braced and ready, like he was prepared to take on the two Enforcers if need be. Carter started to move forward without thinking, but a warm hand on his wrist stopped him, Tash shaking her head slightly when he glanced at her.

"We've got bigger problems at the moment," Kai said into

the tense silence, effectively puncturing the oppressive outrage and causing Vanessa and Bennett to sag back into their seats. "What happened to Voight and Garcia? Are you sure they're... dead?"

Gabriel nodded, placing a hand on Damien's back and ushering him farther into the room and toward where Tash and Carter stood off to the side. "That's what took me so long. I reached out to a few sources to independently verify whether they were even really dead. Two of the three got back to me and said it was true. I think we need to accept that Alistair killed our only two true allies and is making his move. Right now."

Several people started speaking at once, offering suggestions and asking who Gabriel's sources were and just generally talking over each other. Rolling his eyes, Carter turned to where Damien stood on the other side of Tashmica, head tucked down, and looked him over carefully before settling on the new cuffs on his slender wrists.

His lip curled at the sight of them. "Are you okay?"

Damien's head shot up at his gruff question. As soon as their gazes met, Carter's stomach somersaulted, and his heart picked up speed, his bear crowding beneath his skin and yearning to get out and scent their mate. He wasn't sure how long they stared at each other before Tashmica cleared her throat delicately, causing Damien to jolt and his cheeks to flush red.

"We're pretty confident, yes," Tashmica said, throwing a look at Carter. "Doc will be on hand to make sure he remains stable during the process, and then it will be up to Rick and Kai."

Carter forced himself to turn back to the room at large and caught Kai nibbling on his bottom lip, eyes downcast and arms still wrapped around himself. Keegan glanced over at Tash and Damien, eyebrows raised, then offered, "It might sound complicated, but this is his best chance. Do you have any questions, Kai?"

They all watched him as his shoulders rounded farther, and he pulled in on himself even more. "What if I can't forgive him?"

Carter's eyes shot around the room, sure he'd misheard, but everyone looked just as shocked as he felt at Kai's soft words. Tashmica started to move forward, probably intending on offering the young man a much-needed hug of support, but Gabriel was quicker, having settled not too far from where Kai was pacing.

He gripped Kai's biceps. "You will."

Angry green eyes started to glow as he glared up at the hunter. "You can't know that. He broke his word to me. He *left* me."

One side of Gabriel's mouth lifted in an arrogant grin. "I do know that. He knew you were strong enough to do this. To even carry on without him if need be. You were *fated* for one of the strongest alphas in shifter history, Kai. You're his equal. His perfect match. There isn't anything you can't do."

Kai's chest heaved as he breathed heavily, tears filling his eyes as they dimmed and all the anger drained out of him. He collapsed against Gabriel's chest and moaned brokenly, "I just want him back. I don't want to do anything without him."

Relief was palpable in the room at his admission.

"Okay," Bennett said, rubbing one big palm over Kieran's legs absently, "while the witches work on that, the rest of us need to come up with a plan to defend the pack if Alistair arrives at the border before Rick is at a hundred percent."

There were some general murmurs of agreement from the Enforcers as Keegan and Tashmica started for the door. Carter followed, figuring he wasn't needed for tactical discussions, but paused when he realized Damien hadn't moved.

He glanced back and saw he was staring anxiously at the brainstorming Enforcers, hands twisting in front of him. As Carter watched, he opened his mouth, then winced and whimpered, slapping a hand over his heart.

"Wait." Carter studied Damien a moment longer, but when his panicked eyes met Carter's, he nodded and turned to the others. Even Tash and Keegan had paused near the library's door. "We need to make breaking Damien's Blood Oath a priority."

Bennett scoffed. "Rick is the priority. We're not going to risk his life because some spy was dumb enough to—"

The snarl Carter released was so loud it seemed to reverberate around the room. Several Enforcers slowly stood, eyes glued to him, but Bennett didn't move, just stared at Carter through narrowed eyes.

"You need to watch how you fucking talk about him."

Damien sucked in a shocked breath, but Carter kept his attention on the biggest threat in the room. B ignored his mate's soft plea to drop it, carefully moving Kieran off his lap and then pushing to his feet. The second-in-command was big—but so was Carter. He wasn't intimidated, straightening up to his full height and widening his stance just a little.

"Alright, that's enough," Gabriel said, getting between them.

"You're not in charge here, hunter," Bennett said, not taking his eyes off Carter.

"Neither are you. And if you think getting between a shifter and his fucking mate is a smart play, you're not nearly as smart as I thought you were, *tiger*."

"Oh fuck," Keegan said. "That seriously explains a *lot*."

"It doesn't matter," Bennett argued. "Damien betrayed this

pack. He and whatever oath he took are not going to get the focus right now."

"He knows what the O'Hares are planning," Carter said like it was obvious. He was pretty sure it was true and was grateful as hell when Tashmica backed him up.

"It's true. The Oath prevents him from telling us anything, but he no doubt has vital information we need. Breaking it needs to be the next thing we do after waking up Rick."

"If he can help us kill Alistair and those fucking O'Hares, then just do it, Tash," Kai said, face set in determination. He looked across the long room at where Damien was still standing frozen in front of the window, the orange sky framing him beautifully. "Do you know how to break it?"

Damien's jaw flexed as he nodded. "But I can't do it myself, and I can't talk about... it. At all."

Tashmica took a few steps toward Damien. "Wait. You figured out how to break it without killing you?"

"Killing him?" Carter snapped, looking back and forth between the two.

Damien shot him a sad smile before telling her, "Seventy-thirty."

Knees damn near giving out, Carter grabbed the back of the couch in front of him. "Seventy-thirty?" he repeated weakly. "As in, there's a thirty percent chance the method you figured out could *kill* you?"

"Better than what I've been able to find," Tash said softly. "Everything I've been able to dig up in the last week had a hundred percent fail rate. I'll take seventy-thirty."

"If he can't tell you..." Bennett started, and then realization dawned on his face. "You left a clue or something somewhere, didn't you?"

Damien gave them all the smallest smile imaginable. As his lips parted—to confirm or deny, Carter wasn't completely sure—he hissed and dropped to one knee, hand going to his chest again.

Carter was kneeling next to him a split second later, gently laying a hand on his trembling back. "It's okay. You're okay. I've got you."

Taking a couple of shaky breaths, Damien whispered, "Hurts."

That one word was like a knife to his heart. He never wanted Damien to ever be in pain, no matter how much him keeping their mating from Carter had hurt him. Slowly, so he could pull away if he wanted, Carter gathered his slender body into his arms and against his chest. His warmth and scent nearly overwhelmed Carter, his bear humming in happiness at having their mate so close.

Damien gripped the front of Carter's shirt, shivering against him and sniffling, and Carter couldn't take it any longer. Pushing to his feet, he raised Damien up with him, keeping him as close as possible, wanting him to feel safe and send a clear message to everyone in the room that they needed to back off.

He wasn't sure what had caused Damien to become a spy, but he was becoming more and more sure he was no traitor.

Which meant he needed saving just as much as Rick did.

CHAPTER TEN

The burning pain from his Blood Oath tattoo was finally beginning to subside as Carter carried him from the library, a few people murmuring behind them but no one stopping his big, grumpy bear. As it lessened though, Damien's brain came more and more online—including his worries and fears.

At the top of those was that Carter was only reacting because of his bear's instincts to protect his mate, not because he actually *wanted* Damien.

Just the thought hurt nearly as much as the tattoo had when he'd tried to warn the Enforcers about the O'Hares' impending arrival. He tried not to lean into Carter's warmth or inhale his comforting scent too deeply, knowing it was going to be so much worse when he didn't get to have those anymore. He just hoped he didn't have to witness Carter realizing what his bear had made him do; he doubted his heart could handle it.

"Relax," Carter rumbled, his deep voice vibrating out of his massive chest and into Damien's body where they were pressed together. "We'll figure things out. We always do, don't we?"

Damien couldn't stop himself from tipping his head back to get a better look at Carter. He didn't sound annoyed or like he regretted all those late nights the two of them had spent together in the lab or at the shop, trying to find ways to help Drake after he was injured, then to figure out why Marcus's human mate had developed advanced healing after they mated. The two of them would spend hours discussing the magic versus the science.

They had been the best moments of Damien's life and what he'd held on to every time his chest had burned and he'd received another message from his mother. He'd known those times would probably be all he'd have to remember his mate by if he managed to survive whatever the O'Hares had planned for him and the Kincaid Pack.

He couldn't see all of Carter's face, but what he did see made him frown with worry. His big, strong jaw was rough-looking with salt-and-pepper stubble, and the side Damien could see had a haggard tiredness that concerned him. Without thought, he reached up and brushed the tips of his fingers over Carter's cheek, just beneath the dark circle under his eye.

He realized what he'd done when Carter stuttered to a stop in the middle of the hallway, dropping his full attention to Damien. Jerking his hand back, he tucked it against his stomach. "I'm sorry. You just... You look so tired."

He couldn't meet Carter's serious blue eyes for more than a few moments, ducking his head back down and holding his breath. Waiting for Carter to come to his senses and set Damien down before striding away without looking back. His bear may be confused about how he felt, but Damien knew that Carter the man didn't have such a compunction.

It didn't matter what his instincts said—Damien was a traitor to the pack.

Carter didn't say anything, simply bending forward and pressing his face into Damien's hair for a moment, inhaling deeply, before continuing on his way once more. They turned down one more hallway, and then Carter was pushing open a partially closed door and stepping inside, kicking it closed behind them.

Damien glanced around and swallowed, his eyes widening at the sight of the bed, covers thrown back where a big body had been lying. "What are we doing?"

In response, Carter just strode over to the end of the bed and sat, still not releasing his hold on Damien. He easily maneuvered Damien's legs and body, situating him just how he wanted him and sending Damien's internal temperature and heart rate through the roof.

"We're taking a minute to talk while Tash and Keegan get the spell ready," Carter finally said, sounding nonchalant. Like the two of them... cuddled every day. "Are you still in pain?"

Damien squeezed his eyes shut, everything inside him melting at the fact that was the first thing Carter asked. His nose prickled, tears wanting to come at his gentle kindness, but he clenched his jaw, fighting to keep them back.

A big, warm hand cupped his chin and tilted his face up. "Damien, tell me. Is it still hurting?"

"No," he whispered, keeping his eyes closed. He couldn't handle seeing Carter's concerned face turned on him. He'd fall completely apart, and they didn't have time for that—nor did he feel like he had the right. Everything he was dealing with was his own fault. He didn't deserve Carter's kind words and touches. "I'm fine. We can go back."

Carter scoffed, his warm breath cascading over Damien's

still-tipped-back face and shooting shivers down his spine. "I finally have you alone for a minute. We're going to have a real conversation. Can you look at me? Please?"

Sinking his teeth into his lip to hold back a whimper, he forced himself to look at the man he'd been in love with for years. Who finally knew they were preordained. Destined. Fated.

Cursed.

His eyes ran over Damien's face, studying him with a divot between his thick brows. "You smell so sad, beautiful," Carter said softly, leaning in and nuzzling against Damien. His stubble scratched at his cheek and jaw, making him gasp as goose bumps erupted all down his arms and heat pooled low in his belly. "That's better. I can't handle you being upset on top of everything else right now."

The words were like a bucket of water getting dumped in his lap, jerking him upright from where he'd unconsciously started to sag into Carter's unwavering strength. Clearing his throat, he pulled free of Carter's hold, grateful when he let him go without question.

Of course he didn't want to be distracted by Damien's scent. They were about to do incredibly complicated and potentially dangerous magic on the pack alpha. Everyone needed to be focused.

Swiping under his eyes with his back to Carter, he said carefully, "Sorry. Um. They took my scent-suppressing tea when they searched my apartment. I'll try not to be so distracting though."

"Damien."

"We should just... stay focused on Rick. He's what's important." He didn't turn around, knowing his face would confirm what his scent was probably telling Carter. That he was devastated and scared and just wanted Carter to hug him.

But he didn't get to have that, and he needed to remember it.

Taking advantage of Carter's instincts while he was already worried for his injured alpha would only lead to further heartache for both of them. And maybe worse. He didn't want Carter to ever think for one second that Damien had used his shifter instincts against him, trying to garner favor or an ally through their connection.

If Carter ever felt that way, Damien wouldn't be able to handle it.

"Damien," Carter growled, gripping Damien's arm and turning him around. Unfortunately, he grabbed the same spot the beta had the day before, pressing into the fresh bruises and causing Damien to wince. He jerked his hand back like he'd been burned. "I'm sorry. I didn't think I was using too much—"

"You weren't," he rushed to reassure him. He pushed the sleeve of his rumpled polo up to show him the dark purple spots left by the beta's fingers. "It's not your fault. Please don't worry about it."

If he'd thought showing the bruises to Carter would calm him down, he'd been dead wrong. His sweet bear's eyes lit up with fury, glowing in the dim room, and his canines extended.

"Who the *fuck* did that to you?"

"It doesn't matter," he said quickly, holding both hands up in front of Carter but being careful not to touch him. He didn't feel like he had the right to lay his hands on him. "Everyone is incredibly stressed right now. I'm sure it was an accident."

It absolutely hadn't been, and he should have known better than to try and lie to a damn shifter. Carter's eyes narrowed a little. "Why are you protecting whoever did that?"

He opened his mouth, not sure what was going to come out and surprised as hell when he said, "Because this isn't you. This is your bear reacting to everything. We should... keep as far from each other as possible moving forward."

Carter's jaw bunched. "As far as possible."

Damien couldn't read his face, but his hands were fisted at his sides. Running his teeth over his bottom lip, Damien nodded and glanced away. "I don't want you to do something you'll... regret."

"Like what? Kill the asshole who—" Carter sucked in a breath, drawing Damien's eyes back to him like a magnet. "That fucking beta yesterday. He shoved you into Rick and Kai's bedroom. He did that, didn't he?"

Hands wringing in front of him, Damien shook his head. "Carter, please. Just let it go—"

"He put fucking bruises on my mate!" Carter roared.

Damien stared at him in shock. He'd never seen or heard Carter get so upset before, but that wasn't what had him frozen in place. Carter had never called him his mate before. Even having known it for years and knowing that Carter had realized it the day before, hearing the words was like the sweetest of torture.

A taste of something he could never actually have.

When tears filled his eyes, Carter's entire demeanor changed, all the anger leaving him as quickly as it had come, replaced by worry as he hurried forward. "I'm sorry. I didn't mean to frighten you or make you sad again."

"You didn't," he whispered brokenly, sagging against Carter and completely giving up on trying to keep any distance between them. At least for the moment. He was too tired. Too sad. He needed comfort and a chance to catch his breath. "I just... You called me your mate."

Carter's arms tensed around him. "Didn't you already know that?"

He nodded, pressing his face closer into Carter's warm chest. "I've always known, but I never thought I'd hear you say it. I tried so hard to keep it from you, knowing it would hurt you so much more to find your mate and lose him than to never find him at all."

"I'm not losing you." Carter's arms tightened almost painfully, but Damien welcomed it and the certainty in his voice, even though he knew it wasn't true. "We'll figure out how to break the Oath and beat the O'Hares, and then you and I... We'll get a chance to start over. To do things right."

It was a nice thought, a dream to hang on to, but Damien couldn't fully convince himself. There were too many things stacked against them. Rick's injury and broken bonds, the strength of the O'Hare coven, the murders of the two council members they'd counted on as allies...

It would take a damn miracle for the Kincaid Pack to make it out of the upcoming battle unscathed, and Damien knew that if sacrifices had to be made, he'd be the first thrown to the fire.

He didn't say that though. Didn't agree or disagree with Carter's claim. Just let his big bear hold him and soothe his agitation, knowing what was coming next would be a test of his, Tash's, and Keegan's abilities.

"What did you mean?"

Damien stirred from where he'd zoned out in the comfortable little valley between Carter's pecs. "Hmm?"

"You said you'd always known we were mates," Carter repeated slowly, big hands rubbing up and down Damien's back. "What did you mean by that?"

"Um." He definitely hadn't meant to spill the beans on his obsession. "Well... I sort of cast a spell when I was sixteen to see if I had a fated mate because I was jealous of shifters."

One of Carter's hands slid up to the back of his head to thread through his hair and gently force him to tilt back. He met Carter's curious eyes. "You've known I was your mate since you were sixteen? That was like…"

"Nine years ago," he supplied helpfully. "But I didn't know it was *you*. I just knew you were out there. Somewhere in the backwoods of North Dakota of all places."

Carter snorted, a small smile teasing at his lips. "My family's pack is from there. I only came here about—"

"Four years ago," Damien said sheepishly, biting at his lip. "Um. I kept recasting the spell over the years to keep an eye on them. You. When you moved to Michigan, I got really excited. It seemed like you were finally close enough for us to meet since my dad and I lived in South Carolina."

"Why didn't you come find me?" Carter didn't sound upset, just curious. He also didn't seem to have noticed he was running his fingers through the short hair on the back of Damien's head over and over in a way that could probably put him to sleep if he wasn't careful.

"I wanted to," he told him quickly, meaning every word. "I was twenty-one, and I felt like I was old enough to come and find you on my own, but my dad was concerned about me traveling so far by myself."

"Understandable," Carter said with feeling, his grip on Damien's hair tightening. "Fuck, you're so young."

Blushing for some reason, Damien glanced down and cleared his throat before continuing. "We fought about it, but I finally agreed to wait until he could travel with me. But then a couple of years passed, and we just kept working another job and another job. I think that's why I got impatient and—"

Searing pain ripped through his chest, and he grunted as he squeezed his eyes shut. The world spun around him as Carter lifted him back into his arms and carried him to the bed, laying him on the soft sheets. Damien focused on his breathing and the feel of Carter's huge hand resting on his chest.

Once he felt like he could open his eyes without throwing up, he met concerned blue eyes, Carter having sat right next to him on the edge of the bed. "Sorry. Goddess, I didn't even say—" He cut himself off, afraid of setting the Blood Oath off again. "Anyway. I… I knew who you were the first time I laid eyes on you."

Carter didn't say anything for a long moment, staring down at Damien with a slew of emotions running over his face. Finally, he slid his hand over so it was right over the tattoo. "We're going to get this off you."

Goddess, he hoped so. He wanted to be able to tell the pack everything he knew and to tell Carter anything he wanted to know. And—if he was really lucky—come up with a way to save his dad.

Just at the thought of him, his heart twisted. Like he felt it, Carter made a soft noise and leaned down to press his face into Damien's throat, inhaling and then exhaling his hot breath right onto his sensitive skin. Scent marking him.

Damien's hands fluttered in the air above Carter's shoulders for a second, wanting to touch but not wanting to press his luck, but when he felt Carter's warm, wet tongue lick up the column of his neck, he grabbed at his upper back and arched off the bed. "*Carter.*"

"Goddess," he grunted, then licked him *again.* "You do taste like honey. So. Damn. Sweet."

"Oh gracious." Damien tried to think of literally anything other than how sexy Carter was to try and prevent his dick from reacting, but it was no use. His entire being was focused solely on his mate and wouldn't be diverted.

Tipping his head back, Damien whimpered at the low growl he felt pressed against his throat. Not from fear. Goddess no. He'd never been so aroused in his entire life.

Sharp teeth nipped at the delicate skin, causing him to gasp and dig his heels into the bed, trying to get his bearings. "Carter, you… you're just… we…"

Chuckling, Carter lifted his head, beautiful eyes glowing once more. "Are you trying to tell me this is just my bear's instincts again?"

He sucked in a ragged breath and nodded. "It's natural, but we can fight it if we just—"

"I don't want to fight it, mate. Why fight the inevitable?"

"Because—*oh*!" Damien's whole body jolted at the unexpected pleasure of Carter's teeth sinking into his earlobe. When he sucked it into his mouth, running his tongue over the abused flesh, Damien moaned.

Loudly.

"Shh. No one gets to hear your sexy noises but me."

Damien slapped a hand over his mouth automatically before lifting it briefly to hiss, "This is a mansion full of shifters."

"We'd better do our best to be quiet then," Carter whispered against the shell of his ear, and Damien gritted his teeth together to hold back a whimper.

His seductive bear was *killing* him.

Sharp teeth nibbled along his jaw, and Damien's dick throbbed in his underwear. Dear goddess, he wanted Carter to stop before he embarrassed himself, but he also wanted Carter to never, ever stop touching him like this. It was *everything* and was soothing a part of him that had been broken and aching for years.

When Carter slid down to lay soft, wet kisses on his throat, Damien couldn't stop himself from grabbing onto him with both hands. He felt like he was lost in a sea of sensations, his entire body tingling with pleasure and his mind unable to wrap around the fact that he was finally getting to touch his mate.

That he was being touched by *Carter*.

Biting back a groan—mostly successfully—he peeled his eyes open just enough to see what he was doing as he carefully removed the hair tie from Carter's long hair. As the dark brown strands fell around them, surrounding Damien in his herbal scent, Carter lifted his head. Their gazes connected and held as Damien delicately ran his fingers through the thick tresses.

Eyes glowing just a little and the tips of his fangs peeking out behind his parted lips combined with his loose hair made Carter look more wild than Damien had ever seen him. His shining blue eyes dipped down to Damien's mouth, and he couldn't stop himself from darting his tongue out to wet his lips.

A deep growl began to grow in the large chest pressed to him, vibrating his skin and his damn soul. He held his breath as Carter's head lowered toward his own so, so slowly.

Was it really happening? Was Carter actually going to kiss him? Should he stop him?

As fast as the last question popped into his head, Damien shoved it back down. In that moment, he didn't care if it made him a terrible person—he wouldn't do anything to stop what was about to happen. It was something he'd dreamed about for years—long before he'd even met Carter, but on a near constant loop since he had. His fantasies of strong arms around him and uncontrollable passion being leveled at him had been the only things to keep him sane the last two years. Even if he'd always assumed they'd have to stay fantasies.

But now he was actually going to get to—

A sharp knock at the door froze Carter half an inch from Damien's lips.

"We're ready," Tashmica said, just loud enough for Damien to hear, then something too soft for him to catch.

Carter groaned in frustration as he pushed himself

upright, leaving Damien cold and aching. Feeling embarrassed and disappointed, he scrambled upright, pushing himself back against the headboard to put as much space between them as he could.

He pulled his knees up to his chest and wrapped his arms around them, taking a few deep breaths to slow his libido. "What did she say?"

Carter was watching him, a deep furrow between his brows, but all he said was, "That the others are impatient to start. And that she was sorry for interrupting."

Damien's entire body flushed with humiliation. If Tashmica had known what they were doing, that meant one of the shifters must have told her why they were taking so long to join them. "Oh goddess."

A big hand gripped one of his ankles and gave him a slight shake so he'd raise his head from his knees. "Don't be embarrassed, beautiful."

His mouth moved without anything coming out. How could he explain that he wasn't just embarrassed about being caught doing... whatever they'd been about to do. But also that he still felt guilty, like he should have done more to convince Carter that he was only reacting because of his instincts.

Head cocked to the side, Carter studied him a few moments longer, then turned his head toward the hallway and sighed. "We need to go."

Swallowing, Damien nodded and uncurled his body as soon as Carter stood. Once he was on his feet, he closed his eyes for a second and shook out his arms and rolled his neck. He needed to focus. Rick was all that mattered, and the spell they were about to try and perform was complex. He couldn't let himself get distracted.

When he opened his eyes, he found Carter watching him, a small smile on his face. "Ready?"

Straightening his shoulders, he nodded. "Let's go wake him up."

CHAPTER ELEVEN

The first thing Rick Kincaid noticed was his entire body hurt, aching in a way he was unfamiliar with. Like an elephant had stomped on him repeatedly, leaving his insides and outsides bruised and broken and he was just beginning to heal.

As his brain started to come more online, he noticed something else.

The scent of his mate's tears was burning his nose.

"'S'okay, pup," he tried to say, but his throat was so dry his voice came out as a scratchy whisper.

"Rick." He felt his mate shift closer, but he couldn't convince his eyes to open quite yet. They felt weighted down, even as he could tell his body was improving but at a fraction of the pace he was used to. "Here. Take a sip."

Fingers slid into his hair, scratching lightly at his scalp before a straw was pressing to his chapped lips. He sucked down as much cool water as he could handle before his stomach started to revolt, but it was enough to start to clear out the rest of the cobwebs in his head.

There were people in his den.

He reacted without thought. He shoved the water bottle out of the way, spraying himself and Kai as it arced through the air, and leapt up to crouch in front of his mate, fangs and claws extended and eyes glowing so brightly they could probably illuminate the entire room.

"Holy fuck," someone said.

Rick jerked his head in that direction, blinking the last of the fuzziness from his eyes, and zeroed in on Keegan where he was standing between Tashmica and Damien right next to his and Kai's bed.

"Rick," Kai said, placing a hand on his back, but he shook it off.

"Step back," he snarled, unable to control his wolf's instincts for some reason. His gaze narrowed on Damien, and his heart rate kicked up another notch. Traitor.

A large body stepped between him and the witch, hands out to the sides. He ran his eyes up the tall frame, and his wolf relaxed a little at the sight of Doc's calm face. Pack.

"You're safe," Doc said evenly. "Try taking a few deep breaths to calm your wolf."

Rick shook his head, even as he sucked air into his lungs. His skin was prickling with awareness, and he felt like he was thirty seconds from shifting and attacking everyone standing in his den, too close to his mate.

Slender arms wrapped around him from behind, and a familiar face pressed into his neck, right over his bonding bite. "Shhh. Our pack won't hurt us. I'm safe. Our pups are safe. You protected us, Alpha."

Even as his wolf finally loosened his grip on him, Rick knew that wasn't true. Memories began to come back to him. A sharp pain. His father's sneering face. Lying in the dirt.

Dying.

His darting eyes finally landed on the tall blond standing at the door, face grim. Gabriel lifted his chin in acknowledgment. "About time you quit lazing around. We've got work to do."

He ignored the words as he laid his hands over Kai's where they rested on his abdomen. "You actually got us home."

Gabriel lifted a shoulder. "Had to call in some help. You're probably not going to like who you owe a favor to now."

Looking down, he held on to Kai's trembling fingers and swallowed roughly. "Thank you, Gabriel."

He didn't look up until Gabriel stepped right up next to the bed, then met his tired dark green eyes. Not hesitating at all, the hunter reached out and laid a hand at the juncture where his neck met his shoulder, scenting him. Leaning in, he said quietly, "You wouldn't have left me, but don't you ever fucking do that to me again."

He released one of Kai's hands so he could grab the back of Gabriel's neck, giving him a reassuring squeeze and holding their foreheads together. There were no words for how grateful he was to Gabriel for returning him to his mate and family. He didn't care who he owed a favor to—he'd pay it without hesitation and with a fucking fruit basket.

Gabriel took a couple of shuddery breaths, scent spiking with the agitation and fear he hadn't let himself feel while taking care of Rick, and then it began to ease, his breaths and heart slowing and scent settling into his base notes—a mixture of his mates, Drake and Jamie.

With one more squeeze, he released his hold, and Gabriel straightened up, clearing his throat and looking away with suspiciously damp eyes. "You need anything before I go catch a little sleep? I know we'll need to assemble the War Council soon, but I'm about to crash."

Rick shook his head as he rubbed Kai's hands and arms, soothing himself and his mate as best he could. The dampness on his neck where Kai's face was still buried was beginning to set his wolf on edge again. He needed to clear out their bedroom and take care of his mate as quickly as possible. "No, but just so you know, you'll be attending that meeting as a pack Enforcer."

Gabriel's eyes widened. "Rick—"

"No arguments." He threw a look around the room, focusing the longest on where Bennett was frowning fiercely. "You saved my life. You've been an invaluable member of the War Council, and your experience as a hunter has brought in a perspective we were sorely lacking in this pack."

"But he's a human," Bennett said slowly, like Rick may have forgotten while he'd been unconscious.

"My pack. My choice," Rick said clearly, holding his second's eyes until he looked down, tipping his head to the side a fraction in submission. He glanced around to see if anyone else was going to argue, but Keegan, Damien, and Doc just looked surprised. Tashmica was grinning at him with pride. "Don't tell me you knew this was going to happen…"

She quickly shook her head. "Goddess no, but I'm pleased you recognize how valuable he is."

He narrowed his eyes, still not sure he believed her. "But you insisted I take him with me. You're telling me you didn't have any kind of premonition?"

Face sobering, she crossed her arms and pegged him with a glare. "Yes, that's what I'm saying. I insisted you take Gabriel because I knew you shouldn't go alone, and he owed me a favor, so he wouldn't argue with you about the plan."

"Yeah, and we're more than fucking square," Gabriel muttered, striding for the door.

"We are," she said clearly. "Thank you."

He threw up a hand in acknowledgment but didn't pause, cracking open the door and slipping out. Rick frowned at the door once it was closed again. He'd been so focused on the people in his den he hadn't given much thought to the small crowd hovering outside.

Turning to the people who remained, all watching him with varying levels of apprehension, he sighed. "Can you all give my mate and I some privacy?"

Tashmica and Doc exchanged a look.

"What?" The burst of energy he'd felt when his wolf had thought they needed to protect Kai was beginning to fade, exhaustion scratching at the edges of his consciousness. He wasn't sure what had happened since he'd been stabbed, but he was guessing he'd have to give his body time to completely heal.

Tashmica glanced at Keegan and Damien. "Will you two go wait in the library?"

Both nodding, they started for the door, but Bennett stepped in their path. "Cuffs first."

A low snarl had Rick's wolf surging to the surface once more, and he was shocked to realize the threatening sound had come from Doc, his gaze locked on Bennett. The bear shifter's shoulders were hunched over a little, the tips of his fangs peeking out and hands fisted at his sides.

He looked ten seconds away from throwing a punch at Bennett.

"Hold," Rick called, throwing a little of his alpha voice into the mix to make sure Carter actually heard him over his bear's instincts. When he froze but didn't take his eyes off Bennett, Rick raised a brow at his second, who looked... constipated. "What the fuck is going on?"

Cheeks flushed, Damien darted back over to Doc and placed a hand on his chest with a glance at Rick. "Carter. It's okay."

"They hurt you," Doc said through his teeth, not taking his eyes off Bennett.

"I can handle it."

That got Doc to finally look away from his target, his face dropping to look into Damien's upturned one. "This is bullshit. You just helped save Rick's life too. Morde got to become an Enforcer, and you're getting shoved back into shackles."

Damien grimaced, but Rick spoke up before he could say anything. "Gabriel never lied about who he was or what had brought him to this pack, and he damn sure never spied on us for our enemies."

Flinching, Damien removed his hand from Doc and wrapped his arms around himself, face tucked down. When Doc turned on him, outrage and hurt in every line of his face and body, Rick sighed.

"Until we can ascertain what he told the O'Hares and how big of a threat he is, he can't run around without the cuffs." Doc opened his mouth to argue but snapped it shut when Rick narrowed his eyes. "My decision is final."

Damien didn't look at him or Doc, just turned and walked over to where Tashmica was holding the wrist cuffs, looking mutinous. She didn't say anything though, and a moment later, they were wrapped around Damien's wrists, and he was curled over, scent spiking with pain.

Doc was next to him, wrapping his arms around him, before Rick could blink. "Breathe through it, beautiful. You're okay. It'll pass."

Rick's eyebrows shot up as things began to click into place. He glanced around, wondering if the others had realized before that moment who Damien was to Carter, but they were all staring at the young witch with apprehension, almost like they were waiting for something to happen.

It took nearly a full minute, but the tension in Damien

did begin to ease, and he sagged against Doc, sucking in a couple of deep breaths as everyone else in the room relaxed too.

"I'll come find you in a few minutes." Doc pressed a kiss into Damien's hair before releasing him. He kept his eyes on him until he and Keegan left the room, and then he turned to Rick, face stony. "I need to give you a quick exam."

He didn't love the sharp edge to his voice, but considering it seemed like it was his *mate* who was persona non grata with the pack at the moment, he decided not to remind him of his place in the pack. He eased out of Kai's hold—lifting each of his hands up to press a kiss to his palms first—before moving to get out of the bed.

"You don't need to get up," Doc said, a little frostiness having melted away. "Lie back so I can see the wound site."

It set his wolf on edge, reclining into such a vulnerable position in front of two strong pack members, but he breathed through it and relaxed back against the mound of pillows Kai insisted on. "My body kind of aches still, but it doesn't hurt where he stabbed me anymore."

Kai made a broken sound at his words, so he reached for him, grateful when his mate took his offered hand without hesitation. "He infected you with a parasite."

Rick stared at Kai for a moment, then turned to Tashmica and Doc. He flinched when Doc raised his shirt, exposing his belly, but pushed past it. "So it wasn't wolfsbane?"

"It was that too," Doc said as he palpated the area where the wound had been. "But he had someone—the O'Hares, no doubt—coat the blade with a spell as well."

"A Consumption Spell, also known as a parasite," she said, planting her hands on her hips. "If Gabriel hadn't gotten you back here as fast as he did and Damien hadn't been familiar with those kinds of spells…"

She glanced away and ran her teeth over her bottom lip,

drawing his attention to the fact she wasn't wearing lipstick. He wasn't sure he'd *ever* seen her without it, and she was dressed in jeans and a T-shirt that looked to be a few sizes too big. He glanced at Doc and his hastily tied-back hair, dark circles under his eyes, and gray sweatpants.

"It would have killed me," he finished for her, voice hollow.

"Nearly did," Doc said, pulling out a pen light and flashing it in his eyes. "Your heart stopped three times. Twice before you even made it back here. You were lucky."

"How's that?" he asked hoarsely, staring at his mate's tear-streaked face.

"Anyone else definitely would have died. Even another alpha. But the strength of your wolf and pack helped keep you alive and then the fact that you had three very powerful witches able to work to bring you back from the brink." Doc clicked off the light and frowned at him as he stepped back.

Tash cleared her throat, drawing his attention back to her. "We had to… use a spell to give you what basically translates to a magical transfusion. We were able to remove the remainder of the wolfsbane and Consumption Spell from your system once you were strong enough to withstand the process."

Rick shook his head. "I don't understand. Magical transfusion?"

"You got a boost directly from the pack," she said carefully. "We tapped into it and funneled some directly into you since you weren't… connected anymore. You feel good now, but the transfusion will wear off without the bonds holding you and the pack together. It's temporary."

He shoved upright, eyes narrowed. "Meaning what? Get my fucking affairs in order?"

"We have to fix our mating bond," Kai said so softly Rick thought he'd imagined it for a second.

Jerking his head around, he stared at the love of his life. "What do you mean?" When Kai just looked at him with wet, sad eyes, he twisted back around, finding Doc and Tash watching him with worried faces. "What the fuck does that mean?"

🐾

As the door closed behind Doc, Tashmica, and Bennett, Rick felt almost numb.

How could he have been so fucking reckless?

He looked at his mate and thanked anyone who was listening that he at least had the chance to try and make up for his mistakes. Kai was still kneeling next to him on the bed, clinging to his hand, and it was giving him strength and hope. It wasn't too late to fix what he'd fucked up.

Tashmica's careful explanation of how the parasite had eaten away at his bonds to the pack and his mate was ringing in his ears—especially when she'd reluctantly explained that they were pretty sure his bond with Kai had already been frayed.

Because he'd broken his pup's heart.

And his trust.

Fucking hell.

"Kai…" He paused, unsure what to even say or where to begin. When large green eyes swimming in tears met his, he hated the apprehension he could see on his mate's face. Jaw tightening, he gestured Kai forward. "Come here, pup. Let me hold you."

His heart cracked apart in the half second his mate hesitated before crawling into his lap and wrapping his arms around Rick's waist. "You broke your promise."

His stomach twisted so hard he thought he'd throw up. Gently, he gathered Kai in his arms and pressed his face into his messy hair, breathing in his scent. "I did. I'm so sorry."

He'd promised his mate that he'd always tell him the truth, that he wouldn't hide things from him or try and protect him from any threats to the pack. It was a promise he'd kept with ease for a year.

"I thought…" His guilt and sorrow were so thick in his throat he had to cough to clear it out. Kai raised his head to stare up at him with solemn eyes. "I thought I could save him, but I knew you wouldn't like it."

Kai's face hardened, but he didn't pull out of Rick's embrace. "No, you knew I'd never agree, and for good reason. Look what your father did to you! You walked into that meeting with barely any backup and almost *died* for it. What use to Henry would you have been then?"

Rick flinched, but Kai wasn't done.

"What would the pack have done if you'd died, Rick? Did you even think about that?"

"They would have had you," he said carefully, reaching up to cup Kai's face, but he swatted Rick's hand away, stunning him.

"Don't."

"Kai—"

"No," Kai said, real anger souring his scent as he pushed out of Rick's hold and climbed off the bed. As soon as his feet hit the ground, he began to pace. "I can't be alpha! I don't know how. I wouldn't have the first clue what to do."

Rick studied his mate as he prowled back and forth next to their bed, his agitation and fear coating the back of Rick's throat. He knew he'd fucked up, but a part of him knew he'd choose the same thing again if it meant there would be a chance to save his son.

He'd sacrifice anything for his family. Even his own life.

Even his pack.

"Do you remember that day I found you in that shed?" Rick asked, his voice low.

Kai paused his pacing and glanced over his shoulder to peg him with a dubious look. "Of course I do. You saved my life. Our lives."

Rick shook his head and slowly slid over to the edge of the bed. Rising to his feet, he closed the distance between him and his mate. "Pup, if anyone did the saving, it was you."

Kai rolled his eyes and turned to face him fully, arms crossed over his lean chest. "I meant physically or whatever. I know I... helped you too. Made your life better and showed you that there could be balance between work and life. That you deserved that even if you were the big, bad alpha."

Grinning, Rick cupped Kai's sweet face. "I don't mean me —though you did all that and more." He moved slowly, leaning in to brush a soft kiss against Kai's forehead and then murmuring against his warm skin, "Kai, you saved your family long before I came along. And that day, you came out of that shed swinging the only weapon you could get your hands on, attacking even if it meant putting yourself at risk."

"Anyone would have done the same," Kai said, eyes shifting away.

Rick tightened his hold on him a little, making sure he had his attention before saying, "No, they wouldn't. You are stronger and braver than anyone I've ever met. You not only survived something horrible—you protected your siblings from it too. You let them lean on you. You took the worst of the abuse to keep them safe. You are... more precious to me than words could ever express, but you don't need me."

Kai's mouth opened in protest, and Rick dipped down and pressed a kiss to his lips, silencing him.

"You don't," he said against his mouth, sliding over to pepper kisses along Kai's jaw and then down his neck. "But I need you. You and our family. I need you to be happy and healthy and safe, or else I can't do my job. Or else there is no point in me doing my job because I could not survive a life without you and them again."

Kai sucked in a breath, both hands coming up to grip Rick's hips in a tight hold as he swayed unsteadily. "Rick..."

"It's true, pup. You breathed life into me that day, and I'd suffocate without you. You're stronger than me. You always have been." He pinched the skin of Kai's neck between his teeth, right over where the scar of his bonding bite was. The soft shudder that shook Kai's body made his limbs weak with relief.

"You're ridiculous," Kai said wetly, shaking his head.

"I'm pragmatic." Rick licked up the smooth column of his throat, then whispered into his ear, "And dead serious. I love you more than life itself, mate. I'd kill or die for you without thought or question. I may be the alpha, but you are my home. My everything. My reason for being. I couldn't handle seeing you so afraid and worried for Henry."

A soft sob broke from Kai, nearly sending Rick to his knees. His slender arms flew around Rick's neck, and he held on for dear life. "I'm so scared for him, but I'd rather face his unknown future with you than by myself."

Rick enveloped his mate with his body, wrapping around him as tightly as he could. "Considering I failed at stopping Angelique's vision for the Council, that's pretty much guaranteed. But we'll keep him safe."

"Together."

Rick nodded against his soft hair, sucking his comforting scent into his lungs. "Together."

"And no more half-baked plans," Kai scolded, even as his hands gently ran over Rick's back and shoulders. "If I'm so damn important to you, then you better not leave me again."

"Never," Rick said softly, cupping the back of Kai's head.

For a long moment, he just held his mate, soaking in the feeling of having him in his arms again after thinking he was going to die in the woods. "I'm so sorry I left without telling you, Kai. I love you and our family so much, and it... I've never felt so helpless. I needed to do something to make it better, and I nearly ruined the best thing to ever happen to me."

Kai took a deep, shuddery breath, then let it out slowly. "I love you too. I..." He swallowed thickly before pulling back just enough to prop his chin on Rick's chest to peer up at him. "I know I went a little crazy after we found out about Henry's role in some doomsday prophesy—"

"We don't know for sure—"

Kai narrowed his eyes at him. "Don't. Don't try and placate me."

Nodding, Rick sighed. "You're right. We'll figure out what to do about that after we deal with my father and the O'Hares." When Kai's eyes flicked away and his heart tripped, Rick realized there were more things that he'd missed while he was unconscious. "What happened?"

Shaking his head, Kai slid his arms up to wrap them around Rick's neck and then tug him down. "Later."

"Kai—"

"Shh." Kai laid a slow, thorough kiss on him that had Rick's head spinning by the time he pulled away. "Later. First, you need to do something for me."

"Anything." He meant it with every cell of his being. He'd give his mate whatever he needed to solidify the bond between them once more. He'd fall to his knees and grovel for hours if that's what it took to earn his forgiveness.

Eyes beginning to glow and scent deepening, Kai pushed up to his toes and whispered in Rick's ear, "Remind me I'm yours, Alpha."

A low growl built in the back of Rick's throat as his

canines began to lengthen. "Are you sure, pup? We can talk mor—"

Kai shook his head and stepped back, pulling his shirt off in a quick move, then pushing his sweats down over his plump little ass and letting them fall to the floor. Stepping free, Kai climbed back onto the bed. Rick's breaths sawed in and out of his chest at the sight and then froze in his lungs when Kai stopped right in the middle and lowered to his forearms, pushing his ass up into the air.

He looked back at Rick, eyes half-lidded. "I'm sure. I need you, Rick. Need to feel connected to you and remember I don't have to be strong when I'm in your arms."

He was moving before Kai finished, ripping his clothes off and leaving the shredded pieces on the floor at his feet. Rick prowled toward the bed, his wolf howling with excitement as he caught the familiar scent of his mate's precome.

As he plastered himself to Kai's back, notching his hardening cock between his cheeks and giving a rough thrust, he laid his hands over Kai's and threaded their fingers together. "You don't ever have to be strong again, pup. Not if you don't want to. I will gladly spend the rest of my life taking care of you and our family."

Kai chuckled huskily, arching back against Rick and rubbing himself against his dick. "What am I supposed to do? Lay in bed waiting for your cock?"

Rick snarled at the enticing idea. "Sounds like a plan to me."

"You're ridiculous," Kai said again, but his voice was soft and full of love and affection.

Rick grunted in fake annoyance, even as he freed one of his hands to reach over and pull open their bedside table, retrieving the lube from inside. "Fine. You may leave our bed. But you'll only have one true responsibility."

"Oh yeah?" Kai turned his head, and Rick couldn't resist

swooping in and latching onto his smiling mouth. As soon as Kai moaned, Rick plunged his tongue inside him, reveling in his intoxicating taste and easy submission. The way his whole body relaxed beneath Rick's bigger one, his mouth softening and giving up control of the kiss.

He was telling the truth when he told Kai that his sweet mate didn't need Rick the same way Rick needed him—but he'd still gladly spend the rest of his life loving him and giving him everything he desired. Whether that was Rick's support or dominance or protection, it didn't matter.

Kai was his. To care for and sacrifice for and love.

End of story.

Ripping his mouth away, he palmed Kai's hips and flipped him onto his back, dodging one of his feet that nearly smacked him upside the head, then leaning in and sealing their mouths together once more. Kai clutched at him, scratching at his shoulders in delicious agony and locking his legs around his waist to hold them as close together as possible.

Rick could be the alpha of a pack ten times the size of his current one and he'd still never feel as powerful as he did when his mate tipped his head back and whimpered, begging for him to touch him.

With a snarl that shook the lamp on their bedside table, he latched onto Kai's throat, licking and sucking and nibbling, as he slicked his fingers and pressed two against Kai's entrance. Despite his desire to get inside his mate as quickly as possible, he forced himself to slow down, circling the puckered opening over and over until it was soft and giving.

"Stop teasing me. I need you," Kai gasped out, slapping at one of Rick's shoulders.

The ache in his voice nearly did Rick in as he pushed inside and bit back a damn howl at how perfect and tight his mate was every fucking time. He tried to go slow, to work Kai open with gentle touches and easy stretching, but his pup wasn't having it. He rocked back against Rick's hand hard, growling and sinking his claws into Rick's back.

Hissing, Rick lifted his head and peered down at Kai with lust-clouded eyes, pushing another finger inside him and rubbing at his sweet spot that always drove him to the edge. Kai's reddened and swollen lips parted as he gasped, eyes rolling back.

"*Rick.*"

Fucking hell. He could listen to Kai moan his name like that on repeat for the next fifty years and never get enough. The sound was still ringing in his ears when he yanked his fingers free, lined up his weeping cock, and shoved inside.

Kai's back bowed off the bed as he yelled, and Rick wrapped a hand around the base of his dark red cock and squeezed, stopping the orgasm that was about to burst out of his mate.

Kai's lashes fluttered as he whimpered and struggled to focus on Rick's face. "Please…"

"Not yet, pup," Rick grunted, working the rest of his shaft inside his pulsating ass. "Not 'til my knot is wrecking this hole and my teeth are buried in your neck again."

Kai sucked in a breath, then moaned long and loud as he did his best to try and fuck himself back on Rick faster. "God yes. That's exactly what I need."

"I know."

Rick kept one hand on Kai's throbbing cock as he shuttled in and out of him, slowly building up speed and staring down into his glowing, wet eyes. His face was flushed, and his dark hair was a complete mess all around his head—he'd never been more beautiful.

He couldn't resist dipping down for another long kiss, licking inside over and over, fucking his sweet mouth just as well as he was his ass. When he had to break away to catch his breath, he picked up the speed of his hips, driving into Kai so hard their massive headboard slammed against the wall repeatedly.

Panting, Kai held on to him as tiny grunts fell from his lax mouth each time Rick's groin smacked against his ass, the slap so loud and perfect it was driving Rick out of his mind.

Just as he felt his knot beginning to grow, Rick slowed his thrusts and slid his free hand up Kai's chest until he could press his palm to the front of his throat and wrap his fingers around the back of his neck.

Kai moaned, pushing up into his hold. "*Alpha...*"

Rick snarled. "That's it, mate. Give everything to me. That's your only responsibility. You hear me? Give. Me. Everything."

He emphasized his words with hard, almost punishing thrusts, reminding his mate where he belonged and that their bond was stronger than any fucking spell. He ground his cock as deep as he could go and growled as his knot began to grow, locking him in place. Inside his perfect mate.

His claws pricked at the vulnerable flesh of Kai's throat, but he didn't flinch, staring up at Rick with absolute love and trust.

Releasing both hands at the same time, he fell upon Kai and sank his teeth into the side of his neck as he felt him erupt between them, screaming and clamping down so hard on Rick's cock that he grunted around the flesh in his mouth.

Then Kai's sharp teeth were biting into him, right over his bonding bite scar.

A hot wave of possession and rightness flooded through Rick, even as he felt his body refilling with power. It was like getting hit with a tsunami, the magic growing so fast inside him he thought his skin would break apart.

He threw his head back and roared.

He was the motherfucking alpha. Let his father try and come for his pack—him and the damn O'Hares. He'd soak the earth with their blood for daring to try and take what was his. For trying to break his bonds.

None of them would make it out alive.

CHAPTER TWELVE

Damien shifted in his chair for the third time in ten minutes, doing his best not to think about what was happening a few halls away from where he and the others waited. It was just so... weird. They all knew Rick and Kai were making up, and then they'd be... *making up*.

Heat flooded his cheeks as he did his best not to look at where Carter was pacing behind the couch across from where Damien was sitting, eyes glued to his phone as he typed. He thought he was doing a good job keeping his discomfort to himself until Keegan's mate, Nico, threw himself down onto the couch and studied him.

"What's up?" Nico asked, brows furrowed. "Your scent is going nuts."

"Nico," Carter growled without looking up from his phone. "Leave him be."

Nico rolled his eyes and leaned forward, planting his forearms on his knees and grinning. "No, seriously. Didn't you grow up in a pack? How are you still embarrassed about—"

"Nico." Keegan's stern voice from right behind him

caused Damien to jolt, but Nico just smiled even wider, settling back on the couch once more. Huffing, Keegan stepped around the chair Damien was in and threw him an apologetic grimace. "Sorry about him. He doesn't mean anything by it."

Damien swallowed and glanced around the room. Bennett had excused himself not too long after he, Tashmica, and Carter had walked in, muttering about checking on something. But Nico had joined their weird waiting room along with Gabriel's mates, Jamie and Drake, though the hunter himself was missing. Damien didn't know either of the Enforcers or Jamie that well, but none of them had been hostile toward him. The pack's second and some of the betas were the only ones who'd made him uncomfortable.

"Um. I didn't grow up in a pack."

Tashmica glanced over at him from where she was leafing through a book, face curious. "Really? Considering your knowledge of mates and pack bonds, that's very surprising."

"Very," Nico agreed, slipping one of his hands into Keegan's as soon as he sat next to him. He did it without looking and seemingly without thought, the sweet, simple gesture tugging at Damien's heart and stirring jealousy in his gut. "Though I guess that explains why you're sitting over there squirming."

Damien sent him a flat look. "It's simply strange to me that we're all sitting here waiting for Rick and Kai to…"

"Mate," Nico finished with a grin. "It's okay. It's not a bad word. It's the most natural thing in the world for shifters."

Shrugging, Damien glanced away. "I've visited a lot of packs before coming here, but none long enough to get that familiar with the members."

"With your dad, right?" Carter asked, having slipped his phone away and turned his full attention to Damien.

His heart tripped as he met his serious eyes, mouth

drying up and palms beginning to sweat. Goddess, the effect the man had on him. "Correct. He was unaffiliated."

Keegan made a soft questioning noise. "I didn't know that. So he visited packs that didn't have their own covens?"

Damien nodded and blinked the burn out of his eyes. It was hard to even think too long about his dad without getting consumed with worry and guilt. "Yeah. They'd hire him to do warding spells or provide certain tonics, elixirs, or hex bags so they could have them on hand when needed. We actually made most of those at home and shipped them directly to the packs who ordered them." He shrugged wistfully. "Packs from all over would call on him for help, knowing he was powerful but fair."

Keegan's dark eyes narrowed as he looked at Damien closely. "What was his name?"

"His name is Pedro Alvarez."

Keegan and Tashmica exchanged stunned looks before turning back to stare at him. "Wait, you're Pedro's son?"

Damien nodded, a soft smile curling his lips despite himself. He'd always been so proud to call him his dad, even when they fought about Damien leaving to find his mate. He'd always respected his dad. "Yes."

Tashmica faux glared at him. "You're Damien *Alvarez*."

He nodded again, heat hitting his cheeks.

"Wait," Nico said, looking between the three witches, his face scrunched in confusion. "I thought your last name was—"

"I lied about my last name." Damien ducked his head as shame hit him.

"Why?" Nico asked, not sounding accusatory.

"Wait wait wait." Keegan waved his hands, nearly smacking his mate in the face in the process. "You said *is*."

Frowning, Damien shook his head. "I don't know what you mean…"

"Your dad," Keegan said impatiently. "You referred to the work he did in the past tense, but when I asked what his name *was*, you said 'his name *is*.' I've heard of Pedro Alvarez, but a couple of years back, rumor had it he'd disappeared. Him and his son. Everyone assumed they'd either fled an angry customer or been killed."

Damien froze, staring at Keegan with wide eyes. "I... We..." Goddess, what could he even say without setting off the Blood Oath? "It's... complicated."

He didn't realize he was rubbing the tattoo on his chest, his breathing getting more and more unsteady, until Carter was kneeling next to him, one of his big hands covering his own and stopping the worried motion. "Take a deep breath, Damien. Good. Another."

He stared into his mate's eyes as he did as he was told, focusing on nothing except their joined hands on his chest and slowing his breathing to match Carter's. The entire room faded away, leaving only the two of them and the safe little cocoon Carter created with his immense presence and warm touch.

"Good boy," Carter murmured, rubbing his thumb over the back of Damien's hand. "That's much better."

The soft praise and tiny touch flooded Damien's body with heat and a wanting so deep it nearly stole his breath once more. As his heart rate ticked up, Carter's eyes dropped to his chest before returning to his face, his beautiful blue irises glowing faintly.

"Whoa," someone said, jarring Damien out of the moment.

Swallowing, Damien tucked his chin down and turned his face away, even more embarrassed that the shifters in the room could scent and hear his desire for Carter than he had been about all of them waiting on Rick and Kai to make up. Good goddess, he needed to stay focused on what was important and not let his fanciful daydreams about his mate distract him.

"We need to get that Blood Oath broken," Tashmica said into the strained silence, and Damien could have kissed her. He glanced over at her and found her dark brown eyes studying him. "Once we know Rick's bonds are on the mend, I'll head back to the shop and start looking for the research you did. Don't suppose you can give me a hint?"

Even thinking about telling her where he'd left his notebook—half-baked ideas filling most of it until he finally found something he was almost sure would work but the Oath preventing him from doing anything more—the tattoo on his chest warmed. He shook his head regretfully.

"Don't worry," she said, drawing his eyes back up to her face. Despite how tired and out of sorts she'd seemed not too long ago, she held his gaze with so much conviction that it had hope blossoming in his chest for the first time in two years. "I know that shop inside and out. I'll find it, and we'll get you free of that damn Oath."

"I'll come with you," Keegan piped up, surprising Damien a little. He hadn't known the other witch for very long— though he'd heard of him long before he came to Michigan with his daughter to try and win Nico back—and hadn't even been sure Keegan liked him. Smirking, Keegan said, "I may know a spell that could help us narrow down where to search."

"Thank you," Damien said softly, looking at both of them and doing his best to express how much he meant it.

Keegan shrugged and leaned back, half on his mate's wide chest. "We don't know each other well, but everything I've ever heard about your dad—and you, by extension—boiled down to him being a good man."

Tears pricked at his eyes once more, but he did his best to blink them away. "He is."

"And I'm guessing it's no coincidence that right around when he went missing, you arrived here," Keegan said, face neutral but eyes burning with a fury Damien barely understood. "And the fact that you can't even tell us where he is right now is all the confirmation I need. They have him, right? That's why Pedro Alvarez's kid is spying for the O'Hares."

Damien sucked in a breath, barely able to believe Keegan had actually figured out something he'd kept hidden for years. Then again, it wasn't until recently that anyone really noticed him or asked questions. He'd been nearly invisible unless he was doing work for Tash or someone came to him for help with their bonding.

Carter made a growly grumbling noise where he still knelt next to him. His handsome face was fixed in a scowl, and Damien reached out without thinking, wanting to soothe him. He gently caressed his bristly cheek and ran his thumb along his cheekbone.

"What do you think the chances are he's even still alive?" Nico asked carefully.

Damien's head jerked around so quickly he nearly gave himself whiplash. The big Enforcer wasn't looking at him though. He was looking at Keegan, who seemed to be considering his question.

"Without knowing if Damien has spoken to him, it's hard to tell. If I were them…" He shot an apologetic look at Damien. "Depending on how they communicate with him, they may be able to trick him into thinking he's still alive. Two years is a long time to hold someone prisoner. Especially someone as powerful as Pedro Alvarez."

Damien let out a wet breath, dashing the tears from his cheeks. As much as he wanted to scream that his dad was alive—that he knew it in his heart and soul—Keegan wasn't wrong. He asked to speak to his dad as often as he dared, but it had been months since he'd actually heard his voice.

But without knowing for sure, he had to hold on to his tiny kernel of faith. He couldn't just give up on trying to save his dad.

Not when it was his fault his dad was taken captive to begin with.

Their small, strange group eventually wandered downstairs to get something to eat, unable to just sit and do nothing. Several other people were already in the dining room for lunch, munching on what looked like steak sandwiches. Even though his stomach felt like it was trying to eat itself, he resigned himself to nibbling on the chips set out in large bowls and sipping on a glass of water.

When he refused a sandwich from Carter—who'd grabbed two for himself off the platter the housekeeper brought in a minute after they arrived—his mate narrowed his eyes at him. "I know you're hungry. You can have one—there's plenty to go around."

Damien avoided the curious eyes watching them and shook his head. "Um. No, thank you. I don't..." He swallowed before whispering, "I don't eat meat."

Carter's eyes widened comically, and several people around the table noticeably paused what they were doing—making a plate or already digging into their food—and Damien could feel their eyes on him.

"You..." Carter seemed shocked to his core.

Damien pressed his lips together, doing his best to suppress the inappropriate laughter trying to bubble up. When he glanced over and saw Nico's horrified face, he couldn't stop himself, humor spilling out of him in a snorting laugh that had him slapping a hand over his mouth.

"Wait, are you fucking with us?" Keegan asked from the other side of Carter, peering around his big bear's body to look at Damien. "I've never met anyone in a pack who was a vegetarian."

Damien shook his head. He slowly lowered his hand, worried he'd start laughing again and need to suppress it once more. Taking a deep breath, he managed to say, "I'm not messing with you. And I'm technically pescatarian. I eat seafood. Just nothing… cute."

Carter lowered himself unsteadily to his chair, still looking shaken. "How did I not know this about you?"

Shrugging, Damien sat next to him and pulled the closest bowl of chips over to pour some onto his empty plate. "We've never eaten a meal together, I don't think. We're usually at your office or in your lab. Or at the shop."

Huffing, Carter rolled his eyes and pushed back to his feet. Worried he'd actually upset him, Damien started to stand too, but Carter put a hand on his shoulder and eased him back down. "Stay here."

"Um, okay." He watched Carter walk around the long dining room table and then out the swinging door. As soon as he was out of sight, Damien's stomach tightened, and he dropped his eyes to his plate. He knew it was silly, but he felt abandoned—especially since Tashmica had slipped away when they'd all come down from the library.

Even though his appetite had disappeared, he picked up a triangular chip and nibbled on one corner, hoping that if he stayed quiet and didn't engage, the others around the table wouldn't bother him.

"That's bullshit," someone exclaimed as they came into the room, startling Damien and drawing his eyes up.

Bennett's intimidating scowl was pointed at someone else

—thank the goddess—but it didn't make Damien feel much better. Rick's tiny assistant, Jamie, threw up his hands in frustration, not bothered by Bennett's larger stature or obvious displeasure.

"Why would they make this up?" Jamie asked, then turned and looked around the table. When he spotted Vanessa and a couple of betas at the end opposite Damien, he beelined toward them. "José, Ericka—tell B what you told me earlier."

Ericka's normally wide smile and badass attitude disappeared at Jamie's demand, the young blonde looking incredibly uncomfortable. "Maybe we should talk in private..."

Waving his hand, Jamie shook his head. "Everyone here is fine to hear."

She looked right at Damien for a moment—just long enough for his face to heat as he dropped his gaze back to the table—before saying carefully, "At least a dozen people have left the territory in the last day. Probably more."

José added evenly, "Without a thorough head count, it'd be hard to tell, but what's worse is that some people are staying... but are getting *vocal* about their diminished faith in Rick as leader of the pack."

Damien sucked in a breath as several people around the table cursed. He glanced up to check how Bennett was taking the news, and he was rubbing his smooth scalp, shaking his head. The fact that he was unsurprised was even more shocking, considering he'd tried to tell Jamie it was bullshit.

"Dammit," the big second muttered as he pinched the bridge of his nose. "Fucking cowards, slipping away without a damn word. Who's stirring up the ones expressing their discontent? There's always a ringleader."

The two betas exchanged a look, and then José said, "You remember Todd?"

Jamie made a sharp screeching noise. "The beta I had demoted because he refused to follow orders?"

"He didn't take that well," Ericka said, grimacing. "We all kind of thought he'd leave. I mean, how do you come back from something that humiliating? But he didn't. I think he was waiting for something like this to stir up trouble."

"He has to know it won't go anywhere," Nico interjected, frowning. "Once Rick is back up on his feet and we make a plan for these assholes coming for us, people will settle back down. They're just restless right now because they don't know what's going on, but they know he was hurt. Too many people saw him getting carried in here unconscious."

José and Ericka exchanged another look, and then she shrugged and said, "Maybe. But other alphas have been taken down with less…"

She was right, and the silence around the room spoke volumes. Once an alpha lost the faith of their pack, it was nearly impossible to come back from that.

Before anyone could figure out what to say, the door swung open and Rick and Kai walked in, surprising even the shifters in the room. People jumped to their feet—Damien included—but Rick waved a hand, then wrapped an arm over Kai's shoulders as Carter slipped in behind them with a plate in his hands.

Damien tried not to notice how flushed Kai's cheeks were or that both he and Rick had scabbing bite marks on their necks. He focused on Carter instead and ignored the wave of heat licking down his limbs.

Carter's face was lined with worry, just like the others, so he must have heard at least part of what had been said while he was gone. As he reached Damien, he slid the plate he was carrying onto the table in front of him, pushing the one with chips out of the way.

Damien stared down at the mountain of shrimp and a small bowl full of cocktail sauce, adoration spilling out of him in the form of tears and a wide smile, even though it was completely inappropriate at the moment. He couldn't stop it though. Despite his horror that Damien didn't eat meat, Carter had gone out of his way to provide a meal for him.

It had been years since someone had taken care of him, but nothing had ever felt like it did when Carter slid the plate in front of him without a word, then gave his knee a gentle squeeze beneath the table without taking his eyes off Rick and Kai.

Damien quietly cleared his throat and refocused on what Rick was saying.

"Let them leave." There was a hard edge to the alpha's voice, but his hand on Kai's hip was gently caressing the sliver of bare skin there, and his mate was staring up at him like he'd hung the moon. "For years, I have welcomed anyone who was willing to pledge their loyalty, sharing our resources and helping any who needed it. If they are so willing to abandon me and our pack in our hour of need, then I don't fucking want them here."

Some low grumbles of agreement echoed around the room. Damien didn't join in, but he couldn't help but agree as well. He'd witnessed it firsthand for years, Rick's willingness to accept members into his pack who had been ejected or abandoned by their own. Sometimes because they fell in love with a human. Sometimes because they disagreed with the way their old alpha did things.

Sometimes because they'd been hurt or threatened.

The last year, Rick had been a touch more discerning about who he let in after being betrayed by Agnes and some of the other coven members, but he'd never closed the borders completely. And now that he needed his pack's support to face an enemy that was more powerful than anything he'd faced before and some of them were fleeing instead?

They were cowards and didn't deserve to call themselves

members of the Kincaid Pack, as far as Damien was concerned. He'd give just about anything to truly be considered a member, and yet there were people willing to throw away Rick's trust and protection.

"After I eat, I need to get brought up to speed on what happened while I was unconscious," Rick was saying, looking at his Enforcers. "Put out the word about a War Council meeting in an hour. Nico, I want you to draft a message to go out to pack members."

"How transparent do you want me to be?" Nico asked as he picked up his phone and started typing.

"Completely." When Nico glanced up in surprise, Rick nodded. "Tell them I met with a Council member to broker peace and was attacked. Tell them he's working with a strong coven who has used illicit magic against me and my pack. And then tell them that if they want to leave, they better not ever come back. Not everyone will be expected to fight, but abandoning the pack right now is not something I will forgive. Got it?"

"Got it." Nico pushed up from his seat and walked out of the room, all without looking up from his phone.

Keegan watched his mate with a soft smile, but when Damien caught his eyes and subtly gestured at Rick, he sobered and nodded as he stood. "Sir, we need to recheck your bonds before you start going all war general."

Rick looked between him and Damien, eyebrows raised, then sighed. "Fine, but make it quick. Where's Tash?"

"She's at the shop, looking for Damien's solution to breaking the Blood Oath spell the O'Hares forced on him," Keegan said as he moved around the table. He swiped up an empty glass as he passed and pulled a small knife from out of somewhere Damien didn't catch. "I just need a little blood, and then I'll take this back there and perform the spell to check—though, based on the look of you two, I'd say it was successful."

Kai turned a little into Rick's side, but his satisfied smile was still evident.

Rick grunted as he held out his free hand, not even seeming to notice when Keegan sliced into him. "Definitely. I felt the power come back."

Nodding, Keegan smiled. "Good. I'll let you know for sure as soon as I get to the shop. Tash and Damien left everything set up to recast the spell, so it'll just take a minute."

Damien nodded in agreement, even though no one was paying attention to him as he dipped shrimp into his sauce and savored them. It wasn't a gourmet meal or anything, but the fact that his mate had gotten it for him made it the best thing he'd ever eaten.

When a minute or so of silence passed, he glanced up and found that everyone was staring at him. He frowned and glanced at Carter, who was smiling at him softly. "Why's everyone looking at me?"

Rick answered him as he settled into the large chair at the head of the table, pulling Kai down onto his lap immediately. "I asked why Tash was looking for your notes."

Flushing, Damien set the shrimp he was holding back down on his plate, then wiped his fingers on his napkin over and over. "Oh, I'm sorry. I didn't hear that."

"Clearly." There was still a harshness to Rick's voice that Damien was growing used to, but he tried not to take it personally.

"Um." He squinted at the table, trying to figure out how much he could say.

"We need to break the Blood Oath so we can figure out what he knows about the O'Hares," Kai said as he pulled a half-empty platter of sandwiches over to him and Rick. "He must have figured out how to do it."

Carter nodded, still watching Damien in a way that made him blush for a completely different reason. "He did. But he can't tell us. Tashmica and Keegan realized he left the spell at *Wicca We Can* so they could find it. Oh, and the O'Hares have his dad."

"I see." Rick was studying him, but unless he was mistaken, some of the frostiness from before had thawed. He glanced at his mate, who was chowing down on a sandwich, and smiled softly. "I understand doing things you never thought yourself capable of to protect those you love."

Damien's stomach twisted. Hopefully, understanding would turn to forgiveness when Rick and the others found out everything.

Like the secret he was still keeping and how he was the one who'd started the whole mess.

CHAPTER THIRTEEN

E ven though he understood the logic behind the decision, Carter and his bear were unhappy when Damien was taken back to his apartment instead of being allowed to sit in on the War Council meeting.

Though he wasn't quite sure why *he* was asked to be there.

He agreed even though he had a ton of work to get caught up on and patients to reschedule and his family to prepare for. Despite all of that, there was no way he'd say no when Rick looked him in the eye and asked him to be there. It didn't matter that he was still peeved at some of his Enforcers—Rick was his alpha, a man he respected, and a dear friend.

He found a seat in the Great Hall, lowering himself to one of the chairs set up in a large circle and eyeing the other occupants of the room. Gabriel and his mates were already there, the hunter looking like he'd showered and gotten some sleep. His mates sat on either side of him, seemingly unable to take their hands off him. Drake especially—the cougar kept leaning over and rubbing his face against Gabriel's neck like he couldn't help but scent him. Gabriel simply accepted the touches and scent marking, rubbing the back of both of their necks periodically and pressing kisses to their mouths or hair.

A handful of betas were lingering against one wall, looking about as comfortable as Carter felt.

When Colt and Fiona walked in—the tiny hawk talking about something that had her hands flying around and Colt nodding—he was surprised when the two Enforcers walked right over to where he was sitting and settled next to him. Colt even gave him a small smile as he knocked his fist against Carter's knee in solidarity.

"But see, if you kill the guy inside the back room, you end up getting pinned down in there," Fi was saying. "You have to go around to the back of the building and—"

"Are you seriously still talking about that dumb video game?" Vanessa asked as she entered the circle of chairs and rolled her eyes.

"It's not dumb. Research shows that—"

"Yes, yes. Improves spatial awareness and hand-eye coordination." Vanessa sighed as she flopped next to Fi. "That doesn't mean you have to yammer on about it. Poor Colt must be bored out of his mind."

Carter raised his eyebrows as Fi turned an expectant look on Colt. "You don't mind, do you?"

He knew Fiona and Colt had been best friends for years, but he'd never witnessed *this* side of their friendship. For a long time, a lot of people in the pack had thought the two were in a relationship since they spent so much time together and then moved in together after Colt's brother passed. Fi had gone on a furious campaign after that—explaining to anyone who would listen that she was ace and what asexuality was and wasn't and that they had only ever been friends. Colt had never said much about the rumors—not that the big wolf said much of anything—but Carter had seen the results firsthand of what he would dole out to anyone who didn't treat Fi and her sexuality with respect.

"It's fine," Colt said, voice a deep rumble and scent full of fondness.

Fiona turned to V with a wide grin. "See?"

Vanessa opened her mouth, but before she could say anything, she tilted her head toward the doors. A second later, Carter caught the sound too. The heavy footsteps of a man in charge.

Both doors to the Great Hall burst open and Rick prowled in, Kai, Bennett, and Nico right behind him. Before the door closed behind them, another small group of betas and several coven members entered.

Then Marcus and his mate, Robson. Then some more betas.

Within a few minutes, every Enforcer, beta, and coven member—minus Damien, Tash, and Keegan—was packed into the large room, as well as a few people Carter recognized from around town or pack events but he knew for a fact were outliers like him—not a beta or Enforcer, yet they'd obviously been invited to attend.

Rick was sitting with his nose buried in Kai's hair, waiting. There weren't enough chairs for everyone, but folks just stood behind the circle, giving Rick their attention. There was one empty spot next to Marcus, who kept glancing at the door.

Just as Carter was beginning to shift in his seat, growing impatient, one of the doors pushed open just enough for a short, sickly thin woman to slip inside. Carter sat forward, shocked at the sight of Wendy. He rarely saw her outside of checkups at his office, even though he knew for a fact that he wasn't the only one who regularly visited her and tried to coax her into leaving her apartment more often.

The scars on her face and neck were the only ones visible, but Carter knew there were others hidden beneath her long-sleeved shirt and jeans. She'd nearly died to bring Marcus a letter from the late Councilman Gregson, slashed to pieces by some unholy beast the O'Hares must have cooked up. The letter had proved to be vitally important, leading them to the original Council charter and a journal of prophesies from the long-dead seer Angeline Pierre-Louis, who foretold of the Council's fall. And her own reincarnation.

Carter's eyes darted over to where Jessica Macey stood as far as possible from the others while still being part of the outer circle of people standing, her arms wrapped tightly around herself and face downcast. She looked like she'd barely slept in weeks. It was obvious that Tash was right—the young witch was spiraling, afraid of what she might become based on some vague myth. She didn't trust herself or her magic anymore and was isolating herself from her friends. Even as Rick stood to start the meeting, Kai was watching his friend with sad, hurt eyes. It had been painfully obvious the last few days that she hadn't been there for him while Rick had lain dying.

Wendy stopped behind José, but the beta stepped out of the way as Rick gestured her forward. Pointing at the empty chair next to Marcus, Rick said, "Take a seat, Wendy. Thank you for coming."

She nodded, offering a wan smile to Marcus when he put a hand on her shoulder. While Carter and Damien may have saved her life when she'd arrived at the border, barely clinging to life, it had been apparent very quickly that not only would she have to live with the scars of the attack forever despite their best efforts and her shifter healing... but she wasn't the same woman after the attack. The trauma had been too profound *not* to change her.

Rick looked around the room, nodding slowly. "Thank you all for being here on such short notice."

There were some general murmurs, but no one spoke up or asked the questions everyone had to be dying to know. What had happened to Rick? Was he okay now? Were they at war?

Sighing, Rick planted his hands on his hips. "Most of you are aware of the prophesies Keegan and his grandma translated for us, but for those who aren't, there was one that interests us as a pack. And one that was very personal for me and my mate." He glanced back at Kai. "To stop the one about our boy, I decided to try and stop the other. The one that said the Council would dissolve when Angeline was reincarnated."

Surprised noises rippled around the room.

Rick turned to Jess. "Angeline was an extremely powerful half-witch, half-seer. We happen to have one of those." Jess flinched like he'd struck her, but Rick kept going, turning to the others as he said, "Tashmica determined Jess was indeed the late seer's reincarnated spirit, but it wasn't until we found out that certain witches and covens believe some bullshit about her losing control and destroying magic that we realized where the threats against the pack have been coming from."

"How do we know it's bullshit?" one of the betas Carter wasn't familiar with asked. He glanced at Jess and grimaced apologetically. "No offense. It's just... we're putting a lot of credence to the rest of the prophesies; why not the one about some witch destroying magic?"

"Because that one didn't come from Angeline," Tashmica said as she strode into the room.

Carter wouldn't have put it past her to wait outside for

the exact moment to have the most dramatic effect. His lips twitched as her long skirt swirled around her legs, the energy in the room crackling for a moment before dimming once more. She must have stopped at her house to change and do her hair and makeup, the tired, run-down woman from the last few days replaced by the fierce, red-lipsticked witch they all knew and trusted.

Keegan was behind her, moving slower and biting casually into an apple as he shot Carter a thumbs-up. His heart thudded behind his ribs. They'd found the notebook.

Thank the goddess.

"It's an old legend that predates Angeline," Keegan said around his mouthful, strolling over to Nico and leaning his forearms on his mate's wide shoulders and propping his chin on top of his head. Nico didn't pause his typing, even as he turned just enough to snap up a bite of apple. "There's no evidence it's based on anything other than folklore. A story to scare baby witches into being afraid of growing too powerful."

Not everyone looked convinced, Jess included, but Rick picked up where he'd left off. "Regardless, we now know my father—and probably several other Council members—are working with the O'Hare Coven to come after us. I'd hoped" —Rick glanced back at Kai, who stared back steadily—"that by offering Alistair help to prevent the collapse of the Council, we could circumvent the other prophesy."

"A seer as powerful as Angeline would have had visions built on top of each other. They all came true because she could see the threads that connected each event," Tashmica explained to the non-magic users in the room. "In theory, if we could stop one and sever its connection to the next, the proceeding visions would fail to come to pass."

"Like taking a single card out of the middle of a house of cards," Keegan said, standing up straight again and waving his half-eaten fruit at the group. "Everything beneath it is fine, but everything above? Collapses. The integrity has been compromised, and now you're left with a pile of loose cards on the ground."

There was some nodding and murmurs, even as folks glanced at each other uneasily.

"Your old man wasn't interested in your help though, huh?" José asked. "My dad can be a stubborn d-bag too."

Carter snorted at the young beta's words but tried to cover it with a cough. Rick rolled his eyes but nodded. "Essentially. It turned out he was more interested in regaining the power of being the alpha of a large and prosperous pack than staving off the collapse of the Council."

"Fucker," Keegan grunted none too quietly. Several people nodded in agreement.

"Let me guess," Robson Medina—former deputy and human mate to Marcus—spoke up for the first time. "He's got a nice pack picked out that he'd like to take charge of."

Rick's lip lifted in a low snarl. "You could say that. When I offered him and the rest of the Council help, his response was to stab me with a knife infected with a spell intended to completely sever my connection to the pack even if I lived."

"Holy shit," one of the people Carter didn't know said, shaking his head in astonishment. "That explains the helicopter, I guess."

"Needed quick transport back here," Gabriel said without raising his voice or looking up from where he was smoothing a hand down Jamie's back, the hawk having crawled into his lap at some point and plastered himself to Gabriel's chest. Drake didn't look much better; his entire body vibrated with tension at the reminder of how dangerous things had been while one of his mates had been too far away for him to help.

"I saw the company name on the helicopter," Tashmica

said, looking at Gabriel curiously. "How on earth did you get Q to agree to help you?"

"Q?" Bennett asked, frowning.

Gabriel sighed, his breath ruffling Jamie's neat hair. He looked at Rick, who shrugged and gave a *go ahead* gesture. "Quinten Amato. CEO of Amato Imports. Oh, and basically a mafia don."

"What?" Vanessa leaned forward, curiosity leaching from her. "A human mobster helped you save Rick?"

Gabriel nodded. "He is human, but the less-than-legal shit he does revolves around the parahuman world. And the only reason he agreed to help was *because* of who Rick was. As a retired hunter, I didn't have anything of value to offer."

"What will he ask for in return?" Kai asked quietly, looking worried.

"It doesn't matter," Rick said, moving closer to his mate so he could run his fingers through his hair soothingly. "I'll give him whatever he wants. He saved my life."

"How did I not know there were parahuman mobsters?" Fiona hissed at Colt. When he just shrugged, she poked his leg. "Did you know?"

"I've heard… things."

"Wait." Nico finally stopped typing on his phone and looked up. "Amato? Any relation to Liam Amato, alpha of the Silver Oak Pack?"

Gabriel nodded. "Brothers. Well, stepbrothers. Rumor has it that Q's dad mated Liam's mom when Liam was really young, and Q basically raised him." He shrugged. "If you believe the rumors. Either way, Liam isn't involved in the shady shit his brother is. You and Keegan were safe with him."

"Except now we have to worry about some shady mobster coming to collect the debt owed to him," Bennett said. Kieran slipped his hand into his mate's and gave him a reassuring smile that seemed to ease a little of the tension in the big tiger's shoulders.

"We won't hear from him anytime soon," Gabriel said confidently. "He'll wait until things settle with the Council and O'Hares before popping up. He'll want to see how things resolve first."

Bennett grunted, less than reassured.

Stepping back into the middle of the circle, Rick crossed his arms over his chest and sighed. "We'll deal with Amato when the time comes. For now, we have much bigger issues to attend to. Not only did my father turn down my offer for help—with prejudice—our only true allies on the Council are now dead. I'm confident that he orchestrated it though he's pointing the finger at me." When several people started talking at once, he held up a hand, and silence fell immediately. "Gabriel confirmed their deaths with multiple sources. Garcia and Voight were both found dead in their chambers in Mehko in the middle of the night."

Wendy gasped and covered her mouth, tears in her eyes. She'd worked in Mehko for the Council for years—it wasn't surprising she'd be upset at the news. Carter didn't know if she'd kept in contact with anyone, but it was obvious she hadn't heard about their deaths.

Gabriel nodded. "One of my contacts works in Mehko, and they told me that no one seems to know *how* they died, but they saw the bodies with their own eyes. Alistair doesn't even seem to care that people are already asking how Rick supposedly snuck into the most secure place on the continent, killed two Council members, and snuck away without being seen by a single person."

"So people don't really believe that Rick did it," Vanessa chimed in, sounding relieved.

"Well," Gabriel said, tilting his head back and forth. "Many people seem to be quietly questioning it, but most aren't publicly sticking up for Rick. And those who are making public statements are Team Council and are spreading the word loudly and with relish. I've already heard three versions of what allegedly happened. We can't assume just because it's ridiculous that people won't side with the Council."

"This is fucked up," Drake said, gently carding his fingers through Gabriel's long, loose hair even as he scowled at the room at large. "I never would have guessed so many shifters could be such fucking cowards."

"People are scared," Kieran spoke up for the first time. Carter watched his soft-spoken office manager meet the eyes of all the pissed-off parahumans around him. "Scared of what the Council will do to them if they speak up. Scared of what could happen if they did stand up in opposition."

"The devil you know..." Keegan said, tossing his apple core toward a trash can in the back corner of the large room, using a soft burst of magic to get it all the way there, the purple swirls carrying it gently into the tall metal container.

"Exactly." Gabriel shook his head, looking disgusted. "The excuses I'd see packs make for the Council's behavior never failed to surprise me. People are somehow more scared of what the world could look like without the Council being this all-powerful entity controlling their lives than of the atrocities they are committing against anyone who defies them."

Rick grunted and rubbed at his chin. "Too bad for them because I intend on making sure that by the end of this, the Council will be nothing but a bad memory. All of Mehko will be burnt to ash, and a new system of governing and protection will be put in place. One where packs actually have a voice and are heard and respected like they should be."

Carter stared at him in disbelief, the words popping out

before he could stop them. "You want to stage a coup against the *Council*?"

A smile spread across Rick's face that sent a shiver down Carter's spine. He was damn grateful he wasn't the man's enemy. "Yeah, that's exactly what I want to fucking do. Who's with me?"

CHAPTER FOURTEEN

Damien was just finishing putting the last letter in its envelope when a soft knock on his door startled him. He frowned, staring at it for a second as he shuffled the pile of sealed envelopes together and shoved them half under a pile of books.

The beta who'd shown up after Rick's meeting ended had already let him know he was out there, even going so far as to thank Damien for not trying to leave while they'd left him unattended for the all-hands-on-deck gathering at the manor. Damien had been tempted to ask how things had gone and if anything had been decided but didn't want to push his luck.

The sun was still out, but it'd be heading down for the evening soon and taking day two of the five-day deadline his mother had given him with it. When he showed up without Jessica or confirmation that Rick was dead, would she kill him right away?

Or keep him alive long enough to watch them destroy the pack he'd come to love?

Agitated and distracted by his thoughts, he could only

stand there and stare at the wide chest in front of his face when he opened the door. Slowly, he tipped his head back, letting his eyes take in the massive breadth of shoulders, strong jaw, and loose, wild hair falling into Carter's achingly beautiful face.

"Carter." The word came out breathy, barely more than a sigh, as the tension from a moment ago began to melt away.

One side of Carter's mouth tipped up as he raised a hand and caressed Damien's cheek with one crooked finger. "Hey, beautiful. Can we come in?"

We? Blinking, Damien finally noticed Tashmica peering around Carter's large frame. She smiled and waved, but it didn't quite meet her eyes. Had something else happened already?

Quickly, he moved out of the way. "Yes, of course. Sorry."

Carter tapped the bottom of his chin as he passed, stopping him from tucking his face down. "You don't have to be sorry."

There was something in his voice that made Damien's blood begin to heat, even as he flushed. A sort of smugness, like Carter enjoyed the fact that Damien had been distracted by his presence. Damien couldn't even deny it—it had always been a problem for him. With his scent and mating drive suppressed by his tea, he doubted anyone had ever noticed.

Now though… it was painfully obvious.

Ignoring the knowing smile on the beta's face, he shut the door behind Tash and led them over to his dining room table, pushing some of the books out of the way. He bit his tongue to stop from apologizing again. "Can I get either of you anything?"

They both shook their heads as they sat, Carter looking even larger than normal in the regular-sized chair.

"Unfortunately, this isn't a social visit," she said, pulling a familiar notebook from her bag, then folding her hands over it. "Some things were decided today that necessitate we speed up the timeline with breaking your Blood Oath."

Damien swallowed and glanced at Carter, who looked unhappy but didn't interrupt. "Okay…"

"But I have some concerns about the spell you came up with." She pegged him with a glare that raised the hair on the back of his neck. "You modified a Cleansing Ritual to such a degree that it's very possible it could strip away your magic or kill you."

He raised his chin, despite her sharp words making him want to flinch. That time, he didn't look at Carter, positive he didn't want to know how he was feeling at her declaration. He couldn't argue with her without setting off the oath, but he was pretty confident it would work without doing either.

After glaring at him for a minute, she sighed and moved her hands, opening the notebook to a marked page. "The fact that your affinity is water is probably why you used a spell like this," she muttered as she ran her finger down the page over his messy scrawl. "But it's still a risk."

He squeezed his hands into fists in his lap, frustrated that not only could he not say anything but that she didn't seem to trust him to know how much he and his magic could handle. "Seventy-thirty," he said neutrally.

There was a loud creak that had his eyes snapping over to Carter to find him gripping the edge of the table so hard he looked about two seconds away from snapping it like a twig. "I don't like those odds," he grumbled lowly, glowing eyes pinning Damien in place.

Goddess, what those eyes did to his insides…

"I know," he said softly, sliding an arm across the table and laying a hand over his white-knuckled one. "Trust me."

Carter stared at where they touched for a long, heavy

moment, then raised his eyes to meet Damien's, letting out a long breath. "I do."

The words were simple, like it was a given, and yet they hit Damien in the chest like a truck, stealing his breath and bringing tears to his eyes. Vision blurry, he tried to blink them away as Carter covered his hand with his other one, sandwiching it between both of his.

"I do too," Tash added, drawing his attention back to her as he swiped at his damp cheeks and sniffled. "But I think the other idea you had will be safer—"

He was shaking his head and pushing to his feet. "No," he croaked out. "No, not that one."

His chest was starting to burn, but he pushed it down, needing Tashmica to hear him and understand. The first idea he'd come up with may have been a little safer, but it would be colossally unfair.

"Please," he gasped, pushing at the heating mark and sinking back into his chair. "Don't."

Carter's head whipped back and forth between them. "What other idea? If it's safer, then that's what we should do."

Damien kept shaking his head, but Tashmica flipped the notebook back to near the midpoint and pointed at the half-worked-out spell. "Keegan and I would have to finish it, but it's nearly there. Damien realized that removing the Blood Oath completely might be too dangerous, but we could probably alter the spell enough that it would transfer the compulsive loyalty to another person."

Thick, tension-filled silence weighed on him as Carter stared at her for a moment before turning to him to study his trembling frame. The last thing Damien wanted was to be tied magically to anyone other than his mate—but he would never forgive himself if Carter's instincts convinced him it would be a good idea to take on the role of holder of the Blood Oath.

Damien could see it in his eyes the moment he decided to sacrifice himself.

Oblivious—or at least pretending to be—Tash continued. "I spoke with Rick, and he's willing as your alpha—"

It was Carter's turn to shove to his feet, his big body sending his chair crashing to the floor and nearly tipping the table. He didn't seem to notice. Turning on Tashmica, he snarled, "Not. Happening."

Eyebrows raised to show how unimpressed she was with his display, she turned back to Damien. "He said that he'd take on the role as your alpha. Though Carter is also another choice, of course."

Damien shook his head, burying his face in his hands. He didn't want that. Well, he did, but not *like* that. He wanted Carter to choose him freely. To love him and trust him and want to spend the rest of his life with him.

Not feel obligated to throw himself onto the grenade that was Damien's life.

His shoulders shook as he did his best to hold back his tears without much success. When a big, warm hand landed on his upper back, rubbing soothingly, it was all he could do to not throw himself into Carter's arms and let him make everything better.

"Damien—"

"You'll hate me," he whispered hoarsely, scrubbing at his face to try and get himself back under control. Goddess, everything felt so out of control the last few days, the last few years. He just wanted to be able to take a deep breath again. Using his forearm, he swiped at his wet cheeks and forced himself to meet Carter's eyes. "When you know everything, you might hate me. Don't ruin your life for me."

Carter's eyes widened, looking devastated and worried. He started to shake his head, but Damien decided to go around him.

Sucking in a deep breath, he braced himself before forcing out, "Use the Cleansing Ritual."

Pain flared in his chest, white-hot and all-consuming. For a second, he thought it would kill him. That he'd pushed too hard and would pay the price. But even as he cried out, skin feeling like it was being dipped in acid, he felt the cuffs snap open. He didn't understand at first, too distracted by the agony to realize his magic was fighting back, surging to the surface to protect him. Once free of the bindings, it burst out of him.

And latched onto Carter and Tashmica.

He hit the floor, trying to pull it back, but for the first time in his life, his magic didn't listen to him. It drew on the power in the other two people in the room, using it to grow and strengthen before diving back into Damien, crashing over him like a tidal wave and cooling the burning agony.

He lay there gasping, eyes squeezed shut, for a long time. His magic was still pulsing just under his skin, making him hyperaware of his clothes and the hardwood floor beneath him and how close Carter was kneeling to him.

Goddess, his magic wanted to consume his sweet bear.

Whimpering at the dangerous thought, he curled onto his side, away from where he could feel Carter hovering. "'M sorry. Didn't mean to."

Tash was in front of him a second later, laying her soft hands on his hip and shoulder. "Shh. You're okay. Carter, put your hands on him. Good. Damien, breathe with us, okay? Focus only on that, and let your magic settle back down. You're safe. We have you."

When Carter's hands had landed on him, his whole body jolted with the need to get *closerclosercloser*, but he kept his focus on Tash's words, doing as she instructed and taking deep, even breaths.

"Good boy," Carter said softly, smoothing one hand up his spine to cup the back of his neck.

Damien moaned—at the touch or the words, he wasn't sure. He was so oversensitive at the moment that the light hold made his entire body tingle. He kept breathing though, and soon, he started to feel almost back to normal.

Then the embarrassment and horror hit.

Scrambling on all fours, he hurried away from them, not stopping until he hit the wall, then curling himself into a ball in the corner. "I'm sorry. I didn't know that would happen."

Heavy steps vibrated the floor beneath him, and Damien buried his face farther into his knees. Goddess, how could he have done something as dangerous as lose control of his magic and then try and siphon off the two people he cared about the most in the pack? The only two that seemed determined to help him, despite him lying to them for years.

He was the lowest of the low.

He was despicable.

He was—

—being lifted into the air.

Flailing, he twisted to grab onto Carter's shoulders. "What are you—"

His mate didn't respond, just walked the few steps back over to the table and sat in Damien's abandoned chair, settling Damien in his lap. Tashmica righted Carter's chair once more before sitting on it, reaching over and grasping his hand firmly.

"We're not mad," she said clearly. "You didn't hurt us."

Damien stared at her, then peered up at Carter for the first time. The lines around his eyes seemed a little deeper as he studied Damien right back, but otherwise, he looked the same. They both did. "But I thought... I felt myself lose control of my magic, and then it attacked you two."

"It didn't attack us." She rubbed her thumb over the back

of his hand, smiling at him like he was a few crayons short of a box. "It did latch on for a second, but I'm guessing once it had what it needed to bolster itself, it let go. No harm done."

"Just sort of tickled and stirred up my bear," Carter added quietly, his deep rumble soothing to Damien's fried nerves. He leaned harder against his chest, wanting to feel the vibrations even more fully.

"I thought I was going to die," he admitted. "But when it came back to me, it cooled the spell immediately."

She nodded, looking thoughtful. "Show me the tattoo."

He furrowed his brows, even as he gripped his neckline and tugged it down. At her soft hum, he glanced down at it too and jolted in surprise. The black lines of the ruin looked... lighter. "It's—"

"Definitely," she agreed, leaning forward to examine it more closely.

"What?" Carter asked, arms tightening around Damien.

"It seems the spell has been weakened. The ruin has faded a hair," she explained, reaching forward and running the tip of one finger over the bottom corner, where a line seemed shorter.

"What does that mean?" Carter asked tightly.

"It means that I'm much more willing to try the Cleansing Ritual," she said, sitting back and smiling. "After I make a couple tweaks." She shot Damien a look. "Your version is a little too all or nothing for my tastes, but this proves we may be able to weaken it enough for you to share what we need to know."

"You think so?" Damien asked, releasing his neckline, then laying a hand over the spot where he knew the tattoo was on his skin.

She nodded, pushing to her feet and collecting the notebook. "I do. Even if it doesn't work as well as I'd like, we may be able to make a few adjustments and try again or revisit the transfer idea. Either way, I'll need you at the pond behind the manor at sunrise in two days."

He tensed. That wouldn't give them much time to prepare, assuming even that it worked and he'd be able to share the O'Hares' plan right away.

"Why not tomorrow?" Carter asked.

She made an apologetic face. "There's too much prep work to get it finished before tomorrow's sunrise. The spell would be most effective during a new moon, but since we don't want to wait two weeks, sunrise will be the next best time for a cleanse like this."

Damien sighed, sagging against Carter. She was right, of course, but he didn't like it. If he could help with the prep, then they might have been able to pull it off faster, but without him, she and Keegan would be on their own. He knew she wouldn't trust anyone else in the coven with a spell this complex except maybe Jess, and she wasn't exactly helping out at the moment.

"Okay," he said, nodding. Maybe in the time before they performed the Cleansing Spell, he could come up with a plan to present to Rick and the others. Something to stop the O'Hares and save his dad…

"Oh, and congratulate me and Carter," she said as she walked over to the door, throwing a smile at him over her shoulder. It was a real smile, unlike the one she'd been sporting when they'd arrived, and it made him feel better despite everything still being on edge.

"Um." He glanced between the two, noting Carter's eye roll. "Congratulations?"

She cackled as she walked out, closing the door firmly behind her.

He shifted on Carter's lap, suddenly much more conscious of where he was sitting now that it was just the two of them. "What did she mean?"

Carter sighed, looking annoyed, even as his big hands gently adjusted him, cradling him even closer. "Rick... He asked Tashmica and me—and the betas José and Ericka—to become Enforcers along with Gabriel."

Damien stared at him in shock, pushing upright. "Are you serious?"

Nodding, Carter ran a hand through his loose waves, cheeks coloring a little. "Yeah. I don't know why he asked me, but the others I get."

Damien frowned, then clambered around so he was facing Carter, legs splayed over his thick thighs. "I do. You are selfless and kind. You always put the pack first. You have gone above and beyond for him and his family and the other Enfor—mrph!"

His tirade was cut short as Carter slammed his mouth down on Damien's and *devoured* him.

Every thought in his head scattered like dandelion fluff in the wind, his hands fluttering in the air before settling on those massive shoulders he'd admired for so long and clutching at the soft flannel Carter was wearing. His lips started out almost harsh but quickly softened, moving over Damien's slowly and allowing him to catch up. He tried to mimic what Carter was doing, but he kept getting distracted by how good it felt.

He whimpered when Carter pulled away, even though he only put about a millimeter between their mouths to say, "Baby boy? Is this... is this your first kiss?"

Damien sucked in a breath, then sank his teeth into his bottom lip. *Was it that obvious? Oh goddess...* "Is that okay? I'm sorry if it isn't good."

Firm fingers gripped his hair and eased him back, the tiny licks of pain doing nothing to calm the heat building in his pants. Carter's softly glowing eyes ran over his face before landing on his lips for a long moment, then darting up to hold his gaze. "Everything we do together will be good. Because it's us, beautiful. I just... Fuck. I wasn't expecting that, and now it's all I can do to keep my bear under control right now."

Damien shivered. A part of him wanted to encourage Carter to just let go of his control and allow his bear to do whatever he wanted. But the part of him still afraid of Carter not wanting him after he knew the truth was louder. He didn't want Carter to ever regret anything they'd done together... but what if he never got another chance?

"Can I ask why?" Carter asked softly, smoothing a hand up and down Damien's back a few times before letting it settle just above his ass.

Nibbling on the inside of his lip, Damien could barely focus on anything but the heat of those hands—one still holding his head where Carter wanted it and one temptingly close to a part of him that had never been touched by another person. "Why what?"

"Why you've never kissed anyone before. You're a very attractive man, Damien. I can't imagine you've never been propositioned..." There was an edge of jealousy to the words, the fingers in his hair tightening a fraction.

Damien's eyes fluttered closed as he whimpered. "Why would I want to kiss someone else when I knew you were out there somewhere?"

Swearing crudely, Carter pushed to his feet so fast Damien yelped and wrapped his legs around his waist, eyes flying back open. "Is that your bedroom over there?"

He was already taking a step before Damien answered, but he laid a gentling hand on the side of Carter's neck. "Wait."

His mate froze in his tracks. "What's wrong?"

Damien shook his head, allowing himself to brush his fingers through Carter's glorious hair while his other hand pressed a little more firmly right where Damien would leave a bonding bite. If they bonded. "Nothing's wrong. I just... We can't..."

Carter settled back down onto the dining room chair. "Shh. It's okay. We can go as slow as you want, beautiful."

Tears pricked at his eyes as he looked away. "Until you know everything, we shouldn't... *be* together. Just in case."

When Carter didn't respond right away, Damien finally peeked back up at him, surprised to find him frowning in confusion. "Just in case of what?"

Damien let out a shuddering breath. "Um, you know... In case you change your mind. About me. And our... mating."

"Do you really think that will happen?" Carter's voice was neutral, but his eyes were angry, losing their lovely glow.

Damien shrugged, twirling a section of Carter's dark hair around one of his fingers gently. "Maybe. There are things about me you don't know, Carter. Things I've done. Things I'm... capable of."

The silence that swallowed them did nothing for his nerves, and then Carter was sighing heavily, the hand on the back of Damien's head guiding him forward to rest under his chin, against his vulnerable throat.

Damien tried to swallow down his emotions and ignore the significance of that.

"I can wait."

Disappointment soured his gut. Goddess, he was a wreck. He'd wanted them to wait. Or at least that was what he'd told himself...

Carter chuckled, running his fingers through the short hairs on the back of Damien's head. "How did I never notice how muted your scent was before? Now your emotions are so clear to me it's almost like I can read your mind."

Damien squirmed closer, a little embarrassed but willing himself to ignore it. "The tea I made suppressed our connection more than anything. Though my general scent was affected too. Unless I was experiencing strong emotions, most probably didn't notice."

Carter hummed and rubbed at his low back. "I like it better this way."

"I'm sure," Damien said with a snort. "You get an all-access pass to my every thought and emotion, whereas my weak human nose only knows you smell really good."

The arrogant noise Carter made at the admission should not have been sexy.

"You think I smell good?"

"Shut up," Damien muttered, swatting at his chest, then curling even closer. The peace he felt pressed against Carter was better than he could have ever imagined, and the more time they spent together, the less his guilt plagued him. It was so hard to resist his instinct to lean into his mate and just let himself be soothed.

Whether the Cleansing Spell worked or not, everything was about to change, so he'd take what he could get, even if it did make him selfish.

"It's going to be okay," Carter said softly, wrapping his arms around Damien and holding him tightly. "You'll see. Soon, all this will be behind us, and we'll be able to start over."

Goddess, he really hoped so.

CHAPTER FIFTEEN

"Mama, why did you bring a U-Haul for your visit?" Carter stared at the large truck his brother Asher had driven up to his house behind his mom's SUV. She and his brothers Onyx and Wren were already climbing out of the vehicle, Wren slapping a dollar into O's outstretched hand.

"Told you it'd be the first thing he said," Onyx crowed, pocketing the bill.

"You could have at least said hello first," Wren grumbled, going around to the back of the SUV and opening the hatch to start removing luggage.

Carter ignored both of them, crossing his arms and facing the woman who had birthed him, who had the audacity to smile sweetly as she hurried over and wrapped her arms around him. She barely reached his chin, but her grip was strong as she held him in the hug longer than was probably necessary.

"My sweet boy!" She finally released him, but only so she could grasp his face in both hands and peer up at him. "You look tired, baby. Are you tired? Have you been getting enough sleep? You need to make sure—"

"Mama," he growled, then cleared his throat and grimaced apologetically when she leveled him with her Mama Bear Glare—patent pending. "Mama," he said more evenly, "why is Asher driving a U-Haul?"

"I told you we were coming," she said, stepping back and waving at him like he was being ridiculous.

"For a visit! Not to move here. Mama, you can't just move into a pack's territory—"

She rolled her eyes. "Yes, thank you, dear. Luckily, I do know a thing or two about pack politics."

He took a deep breath, feeling a headache beginning to throb behind his eyes. "I know you do, so what makes you think you can just come here with all of your things and—"

"Dear heart, your brothers and I became official members of the Kincaid Pack a month ago. I asked Alpha Kincaid not to tell you because I wanted it to be a surprise, but I can see that wasn't a great idea." She planted her hands on her round hips. "Are you really upset we're here to stay? It's been so hard being separated…"

"Of course not," he said quickly, scrubbing at his face. It had been hard for him too, but he'd butted heads with his uncle too much to stay in his old pack. He'd never wanted to challenge him to be alpha, but staying where he hadn't respected the person leading the pack had gotten to the point where if he didn't leave, he would have become alpha.

But his family was moving to Meyerville at the worst possible time.

"It's just… there's so much going on right now," he said carefully, eyeing his brothers where they looked to be squabbling over something at the back of the SUV. "And housing is limited at the moment—"

"Well, I sold my business," she said, moving around him

and toward his front door. "I couldn't very well continue it from here. I've already picked out a plot of land, thanks to that lovely Enforcer Nico, and am working on having a house built. We can just stay with you until it's done."

Stay with him?

Goddess save him.

Groaning, he hastily pulled his hair back up into a loose bun and strode across his front yard. "Asher, you can't leave that damn thing there. Park it around back behind the clinic in the parking lot for now. Onyx, Wren, start grabbing bags and carrying them inside."

"I haven't missed you barking orders at us, asshole," Asher said, even as he came over and gave Carter a quick hug.

"He can't help it," Onyx said, picking up a suitcase that looked like its zipper was about to burst.

"He's the oldest," all three said at once.

He flipped them the bird as he grabbed some luggage and started hauling it inside. Having the four of them all staying in his house was going to be... a lot. It wasn't that he didn't have the space. He'd picked out the house and built the clinic next to it specifically so there would be enough space for all of them to visit him at once, but it was rare for that to happen.

As he set his mom's suitcase in the room next to his own since it was the second largest, he made a mental note to get her noise-canceling headphones. He wasn't necessarily embarrassed about what she may or may not hear—he'd grown up with shifters and lived among them his entire life —but things with Damien were so new, and his sweet mate *wasn't* used to it. That had been adorably apparent when he'd been embarrassed for Rick and Kai, even when he hadn't actually been able to hear the two of them making up himself.

Heading back down to the first floor, he found Asher

185

hissing at Onyx as they fought for the remote to the TV. Rolling his eyes, he walked over and gently cuffed both of them on the back of the head.

"Anything you three destroy in my house, you will be paying to replace."

Wren's head popped out from the kitchen, cheeks already full of something. "What the hell did I do?"

"Language, my love," he heard his mom say from behind Wren.

Carter gave O and Ash each a quick scenting, rubbing his palms from the top of their heads, down the back, to the side of their necks, before moving toward the rustling in his kitchen. Bears weren't necessarily as scent-oriented as some other shifters, but he'd learned when his brothers were cubs to be more free with his touches to help settle them. They pretended they didn't need it anymore, but they both settled on the large L-shaped couch afterward, tussle forgotten.

His mom and dad were both bear shifters, but they hadn't been fated mates. Most shifters never found their other half and settled for choosing a mate that they grew to love and respect. Except Carter's dad *had* ended up meeting his fated mate when Carter was twelve and he was off on a business trip on the other side of the country.

He'd never come back.

At first, Carter had been angry all the time, but he'd realized quickly he didn't actually miss the man, and his mom more than made up for his absence. She'd been lonely, he'd known that, but had never mated again.

She had, however, taken in a few other cubs.

He remembered the day she came home carrying baby Asher like it was yesterday. He'd been struggling with a paper, erasing and rewriting over and over until he put a hole through the page. Just as he'd been about to give up to go and play outside, she came home and smiled at him, smelling so happy and full of joy he could only stare at her.

"This is Asher," she'd said, coming to sit near him so he could more clearly see the tiny bundle in her arms.

He'd leaned in and inhaled deeply, then promptly sneezed. "Why's he smell funny?"

"He doesn't smell funny, dear heart. He's a panther, not a bear. But his mama couldn't take care of him, so we're going to. How does that sound? Do you want a baby brother?"

He had.

And then he'd said yes again to the tiny wolf pup, Onyx.

And then to the falcon hatchling, Wren.

The five of them had become a family, loving and caring for one another just as deeply as one tied together with blood.

Though if they ate him out of house and home, he'd kick them to the curb, brothers or not.

Entering the kitchen, he saw his mom already had something simmering on the stove somehow, and Wren was half-buried in the fridge. He was almost as tall as Carter but lean, unlike his massive bulk. The artfully torn jeans and retro band T-shirts he was fond of sporting gave him an artistic appearance—but Carter knew the man was tone-deaf and all thumbs when it came to trying to learn an instrument.

"Didn't you all stop for food on the way?" he asked as he flicked at the bare patch of skin showing above Wren's tight pants. He snickered when his brother nearly smacked his head when he startled. "It's hours until dinner."

"Wrenny got carsick," his mom said, shaking more dried oregano into the sauce she was fussing over. "Poor thing. Long car rides just don't agree with him."

Frowning, Carter urged his brother upright, then started looking him over, pushing his dark red hair out of the way so he could put a hand to his forehead and then checked his pulse. Wren rolled his eyes but put up with it for a few moments before shrugging him off. "I'm fine. I'm just starving now."

"Make a sandwich," he said, pointing at the deli meat behind him. "Don't just snack on junk."

"Yes, Dad."

Laughing, Carter made a swipe at him, intent on putting him in a headlock for that tired joke, but Wren was too quick, hopping out of the way with a wild laugh and sprinting from the room. Carter shook his head and closed the fridge, knowing he'd be back to get his food in a few minutes.

"You didn't have to cook, Mama. We could have gone to the diner, or I could have made something." He didn't usually cook a whole meal just for himself, but he knew how.

She waved him off. "It's fine. Though we'll need to go to the store soon. You're woefully lacking in spices."

"Apologies," he murmured, grinning at the back of her head as he leaned against his island. He'd had the kitchen remodeled when he'd first moved in, making the space bigger and more open since it had always been the hub in his mom's house growing up. He'd always imagined the room being the same for him and his family, even if he hadn't had much luck on the family part.

Though, hopefully, that was changing, thanks to a sweet little witch.

She finished what she was doing and turned to him, running her eyes over him from top to bottom and then tilting her head to the side. "Something's different about you."

"I grew my hair out," he said dryly.

She rolled her eyes. "You were doing that when we saw you last year. Though it is getting quite long. Are you using a good conditioner?"

"Mama…"

She held up her hands. "Excuse me for wanting to make sure you're—" She froze, eyes narrowing on him. Taking a step closer, she inhaled deeply and gasped. "Carter, are you… Are you an Enforcer?"

He grinned sheepishly, even as he shrugged it off. "As of yesterday."

"What about your medical practice?" Onyx asked from behind him, his perpetually raspy voice always identifiable and giving him an almost hoarse sound.

Carter glanced back at him and let his grin widen at his brother's worried face. His pitch-black hair hung in waves to his chin, and his skin was nearly ghostly in comparison. "Rick isn't making me quit my practice. That isn't how things are done here. His Enforcers are more like advisors than anything else most of the time."

"Most of the time," Wren repeated, appearing over O's shoulder. "Except when you're about to go head-to-head with the fucking Council."

"Wren." Their mom's voice left no argument—she didn't abide by *coarse language* and never had.

"It's alright," Carter said to her, then fully turned toward his brothers, noticing Asher hanging back with his arms closed tightly over his chest. "Listen, I'm not going to lie. The Council and the O'Hare Coven are about to make their move against us, we think. War planning is already underway, and when the time comes, I'll be standing with my alpha to face off against them. I would have done that anyway though. Being asked to become an Enforcer… that's just Rick's way of showing the pack that he, you know, values my opinion."

He was a little embarrassed saying the last part, but his mom's hand on his shoulder lessened the feeling. "And we're very proud of you, aren't we, boys?"

"Yes, Mama," they all said together.

"And we'll be standing with you and Alpha Kincaid as well," she added, her grip tightening on his shoulder when he stiffened. "It's our choice, and we already talked about it. We could have waited to join until afterward, but that wouldn't have been honorable. We're here to support you and our new alpha."

He looked at her determined face and then at each of his brothers, a kernel of fear settling in the pit of his stomach. It wasn't that he hadn't had anything to lose before, but he'd been so focused on Damien and getting the Blood Oath removed that he hadn't thought about what might happen afterward.

Or that maybe not all of them would make it through the upcoming battle.

Swallowing, he said thickly, "There's someone I want you all to meet."

Getting Damien to his house to meet his family ended up being a lot easier than he'd anticipated. Apparently, once the beta guarding his apartment had realized he'd broken the cuffs the night before and gone the entire night and morning without them, she'd contacted the manor, and Rick had essentially thrown up his hands, ordering Damien to stay at *Wicca We Can* for the day where Tashmica could—theoretically—keep an eye on him.

When Carter and Tash called him again to ask if Damien could come to his house for dinner, Rick had growled at them to stop bothering him about it and handle it themselves as Enforcers. Which they'd taken as an agreement.

Carter's fingers were tingling as he pushed into the shop, ignoring the Closed sign on the door. He'd expected the front part of the store to be empty since the pack work was usually done in the small room in the back, away from prying eyes, but the place was *bustling*. There had to have been at least a dozen people moving around, pulling items off shelves, or reading out of one of the countless books strewn about on the makeshift tables that had been set up in the space.

With a jolt, he realized the entire coven was there. They'd all shown up to help prepare the spell for Damien, and that was… amazing.

Nearly overwhelmed with gratitude and feeling more hopeful than he had in days, he smiled in greeting as people waved or called hello to him. He didn't see Tashmica or Damien though, so he made his way through the room toward the back.

Just as he reached the colorful curtain of beads separating the room from the public space, he heard an angry female voice say, "You can't make me do this!"

He recognized it as Jess and hesitated just on the other side. He could scent her agitation, as well as Tashmica's worry tinged with annoyance, Keegan's impatience, and Damien's regret colored with grief. His mate's upset hit him like a physical blow, but he held his position, not wanting to interrupt just yet.

"Actually, I can," Tashmica said slowly. "As head of the coven, you answer to me. I can order you to perform any magic I see fit. If you don't want to do that or be part of this coven anymore, then you can leave."

He heard angry steps coming toward him, but Tashmica's next words stopped Jess cold.

"You can leave the *pack*. Just to be very clear: if you choose not to be a part of this coven, then you cannot be a part of this pack."

Jess sucked in a breath. "You can't just… kick me out of the pack. Kai would never—"

"Kai doesn't have a damn thing to do with it," Keegan said, voice clipped. "Pack law is clear. Magic users can't be a part of the pack if they aren't part of the coven and follow coven rules."

"If she doesn't want to help, we shouldn't make her," Damien said softly.

Jess talked over him like he hadn't said anything, her voice turning shrill and wavery. "This is ridiculous. My powers are too unpredictable! I could hurt someone. Please, Tash, don't make me do this."

He wished he could see what was happening in the silence that followed. While he felt for Jess—truly he did; she'd never been anything but sweet and warm to him in the years he'd known her—the fact that she wasn't willing to help her own brother, his mate, and was ignoring him was something Carter couldn't ignore.

"Fine," Tash finally said. "You don't have to take part in the Cleansing Ritual."

Jess's relief hit him clearly through the beaded curtain. Goddess, she really was scared of her abilities. "Thank you—"

"But if you don't stand with this pack against the Council and O'Hares, there will not be a place for you here anymore," Tashmica finished. "Nico's email went out earlier today, and Rick's feelings on the matter were the opposite of ambiguous —anyone unwilling to do their part to protect the pack is welcome to leave, but they won't be invited to come back when the fight's over. You're either with us or not, Jess. You can't hide in the shadows forever."

"If you stripped my powers like I asked—"

"That would kill you," Keegan said coldly. "Go ahead and ask me how my mother looked after the O'Hares did that to her. Not a fucking option."

"Jess," Damien said, but she cut him off.

"Don't. You think because we share the same mother, you

know anything about me? Just shut up!" she screamed and then was coming through the curtain fast, but Carter didn't move, jaw tense as she skidded to a stop in front of him and wiped at her tears. "Excuse me."

"Don't ever talk to him like that again. I don't care who your friends are," Carter said, voice low and even. "You can be as scared and angry as you want, but you do not get to take it out on him."

She stared up at him with wide, red-rimmed eyes, greasy hair pulled back in a ponytail, skin pallid, and cheeks hollow. She wasn't taking care of herself while she was locked away from everyone else—that was for sure—but he remained firm.

When she nodded shallowly and sniffed, he finally stepped aside, and she scurried past, heading straight for the door. He didn't watch her leave, needing to put eyes on his mate, the drive pushing him through the curtain and straight for his hunched form. As he gathered Damien in his arms, he heard the other two leave.

"Hey, baby boy. You ready to come eat dinner?" he asked softly, rubbing his hands over Damien's slender back, dying a little at the slight tremble he could feel as Damien clutched at his sides.

"I could eat," he murmured but didn't pull away from Carter's hold.

That was fine. He'd gladly hold him all night if he needed to.

Damien fit perfectly against him, his face burrowing between his pecs and arms wrapped tight around his waist. How someone of his small stature could be so damn powerful was a little amazing to him, even though Carter knew it was the same with shifters. Size didn't mean much, especially when the person was in a position of power, like Rick's tiny Enforcer, Vanessa.

He had zero doubt that even though he was an Enforcer too now—which came with untested new strength—she'd be able to put him on his ass without breaking a sweat.

When Damien sighed and tipped his head back to peer up at him, Carter smiled down at him. "She'll come around."

"Maybe." Damien shrugged and stepped back, running a hand over his dark hair and then tugging at the cuffs of his light blue button-up. He traced his fingers over his belt, checking to make sure the bottom of his shirt was still tucked in neatly.

Carter quirked an eyebrow at him. "Did you go change for dinner?"

Damien looked up at him with a small scowl. "Of course. Your family will be there."

"That's adorable." So was the tiny snarl he got at his words. His mate was hanging out with too many shifters. "My mom is going to love you, even if you wore a holey T-shirt, and my brothers don't matter."

Damien snorted and crossed his arms over his chest. "Yes, they do. They're your family. Their opinion of me—"

"Changes nothing." Carter tugged Damien's hands free and then used them to pull his mate back against him. "Just like nothing you did in the past will change things between us."

Damien sucked in a shaky breath. "You can't know that for sure."

"Yes, I can." Carter kept his voice steady, doing his best to exude confidence to try and ease his silly mate's worries. "We're destined for each other, beautiful. Built for each other. Made for one another. However you want to say it— you were put on this earth just for me, and I for you. Whatever you had to do to get here to me doesn't matter."

Tears welled in Damien's eyes, turning them into a liquid gold. "I want to believe that."

"Then believe it," Carter whispered as he lowered his head and pressed a soft, adoring kiss to the plush lips he hadn't been able to stop thinking about since he'd tasted them the night before. "You're mine, and I'm never giving you up."

CHAPTER SIXTEEN

D amien felt like he was floating the entire way to
Carter's house.

A tiny voice kept reminding him that Carter could still
change his mind after everything was out in the open, but it
was getting easier and easier to ignore it when Carter said
things like *You're mine.*

Damien shivered as he hopped down from Carter's huge
truck. Goddess, all he'd ever wanted was to belong to Carter
from the moment he'd met the big bear. To be so close to
actually having that was like slowly waking from a dream—
difficult to tell what was real and what were remnants of
sleep.

Honestly, if he was dreaming, he never wanted to
wake up.

When Carter took his hand like it was nothing, like they
held hands every day, and led him up to his large house,
Damien's heart started beating faster, his magic—truly
untethered for the first time in over a week—reaching for his
mate, wanting nothing more than to wrap around him and
never let go.

The door flew open as they climbed the steps to the wide, comfortable-looking front porch, a tall woman who looked remarkably like Carter standing in the doorway and smiling like he was the most important person she'd ever met.

Her brown hair—the same shade as Carter's—was half pulled back, leaving her beautiful face clearly visible. Her eyes were the same too, the small lines around them and the tiny streaks of gray the only signs of her age. He knew Carter was in his forties, putting her in her sixties probably, but he never would have guessed it.

Her smile softened as she wiped at the bright pink apron she was wearing over her voluptuous figure. "Oh, Carter, he's so handsome."

Damien's face flushed immediately. Chuckling, Carter put one of his big arms over his shoulders and drew him right up against his side. The heat from his body soothed his growing nerves so quickly it was like they'd never been there.

"He is. Damien, this is my mother, Claire Bell. Mama, this is Damien Alvarez. My mate."

She sucked in a breath as tears began to fall from her sapphire eyes, rushing forward to pull Damien out of Carter's hold and into her arms. "Thank the goddess. I knew that seer was right."

Her hold was strong, nearly crushing his ribs, but it felt amazing. He hadn't been hugged by his dad in ages, and it wasn't the same, but it was damn close. She was so motherly and welcoming, he found himself collapsing against her and hugging back nearly as hard as her.

"Oh, sweetie," she murmured, carding a hand over his head and rocking him lightly back and forth. "You smell so sad. Come inside and let me feed you."

Sniffling, he wiped at his nose and eyes as they separated,

a little embarrassed at how much he'd needed that. "Okay. Thank you, Mrs. Bell."

"Oh, please. Call me Mama, dear." She cupped his cheek tenderly, then ran her hand down his neck, scenting him. It was so casual, like she didn't even realize she was doing it, but her easy acceptance of him into her family nearly brought him to his knees.

"Give us a second, Mama," Carter said, placing a steadying hand on Damien's lower back. Once they were alone, the door mostly closed and the most heavenly scent wafting out to them, he turned Damien toward him. "You okay?"

"She's so nice," he said in explanation. "It just… caught me off guard, I think. And made me miss my dad."

Carter's jaw tightened as he nodded, cupping the back of Damien's head and pulling him forward so he could lean down and press another of those soul-stealingly gentle kisses on Damien's lips. "If he's alive, I'm bringing him back to you. I promise."

Damien shook his head. "Don't promise something like that. Just… just promise to help me."

Grunting, Carter kissed him a little harder, nipping at his bottom lip and making him gasp. "Have faith in me, mate."

Damien reached up and gripped the sides of Carter's neck, staring deep into his eyes. "You're the only one I have faith in, mi corazón."

The corners of Carter's lips tipped up as he puffed up with pride. "Yeah?"

"Absolutely."

"Good." He thumbed Damien's sensitive bottom lip and murmured, "What's mi corazón mean?"

Damien snorted at his terrible pronunciation, but a voice from the open doorway spoke up before he could answer, "My heart, you uneducated mammoth. Your boy speaks

Spanish, and you don't even know endearments? Tsk, tsk. Mama's gonna be so disappointed in you."

Growling, Carter tipped his head down until their foreheads rested against each other. "Go away, Ash. We're trying to have a moment out here."

"Yeah, well, the rest of us are starving, so hurry your ass up." The door slammed shut.

Clearing his throat, Damien said softly, "One of your brothers?"

"Yeah, but don't bother getting to know him because I'm going to smother him in his sleep."

"Hey!" a muffled voice yelled from inside the house.

Damien collapsed against Carter, laughing for the first time in what felt like decades. When he got himself under control again, he sighed happily and nuzzled against Carter's chest. "For the record, endearments are pretty much the only Spanish I know, despite my dad's best efforts."

"Is that his first language?" Carter asked curiously, seeming unwilling to break up their tender moment, even if his brothers were probably heckling him from inside the house.

"It's what my grandparents spoke at home, but he grew up in the States in a pretty white neighborhood, so he learned both from basically the time he started talking. His parents died when I was pretty young, so I never really learned myself. I think it reminded him of them too much for a long time. Though when people find out my dad's from Honduras, they always try and speak Spanish with me. So that's fun."

Carter laughed softly. "Maybe I'll learn so your dad will like me more than you."

Damien grinned, tipping his head back to look up at him. "He'd love that. I can just hear him saying something like, *'I'm glad one of my boys has bothered to learn.'*"

"Well, it's settled then. I'm downloading an app tonight."

Damien stared up at him, the realization that he was already well on his way to letting himself love this man hitting him like a truck. He swallowed the words down though, knowing it wasn't the time or the place and that it wasn't fair. Not until he could tell Carter everything. Hopefully, by the time the sun rose in the morning and he was free to share everything, Carter would still be looking at him like he saw forever in his eyes, and he'd have a chance to tell him how he felt.

"We should go in before your—"

"Damien."

He turned back toward the sidewalk, shock and wariness coursing through him when he saw Jess coming toward them, a determined set to her jaw. "Jessica. What are you doing here?"

She glanced at Carter before focusing on him as she reached the bottom of the porch steps. "I, um... I wanted to talk to you for a minute. If that's alright."

Carter's arms were tense around him, but Damien patted his chest reassuringly. "It's okay. I'll be right in."

Huffing, Carter leaned down and pecked a kiss to his cheek before slipping inside and closing the door behind him. As soon as he was gone, Damien wished he'd asked him to stay, remembering the pain he'd felt at the shop when Jess had lashed out at him.

He straightened his shoulders instead of calling him back though. He was the mate of a pack Enforcer—he needed to act like it. Stepping over to where a couple of wicker chairs with navy blue cushions sat in front of a large bay window, Damien settled into one and gestured at the other.

"Have a seat."

Her steps were slow, but she eventually lowered herself onto the edge of the other chair.

A long, awkward pause followed. When he couldn't take it a second longer, he cleared his throat and said, "If something goes wrong tomorrow, there's a letter for you in my apartment tucked inside a book titled *Becoming Your Own Familiar*. There's also one for my dad and another for Carter. Will you please make sure Carter gets his and try and get my dad's to him?"

Her head jerked up from where she'd been staring at her hands, picking at a cuticle. Eyes wide, she stared at him. "You wrote letters in case you die?"

Cocking his head, he studied her. "It isn't outside the realm of possibility. Tomorrow morning or another day in the near future... I wanted to make sure I'd have a chance to say certain things."

She licked her chapped lips. "Why can't you say it to my face?"

He raised a brow. "You haven't exactly been speaking to me lately."

Grimacing, she looked away. "That's fair. I actually came to say I was sorry. About earlier and I guess about... well, avoiding you since I found out everything."

"It's okay—"

"No, it isn't," she said wetly, then took a deep breath. Steadier, she said, "No, it's not. You're my brother, and I let myself assume the worst about you, even though I *know* how our mother can be." She looked up at him, tears trickling down her cheeks. "I knew before Keegan figured it out that she'd probably forced you to spy for her. I of all people know how cruel and manipulative she and the other members of the coven can be. But I was so scared and hurt and *angry*."

Tentatively, he reached over and laid a hand over one of her fisted ones, surprised when she didn't pull away. Instead, she turned her hand over and gripped at him so tightly he had to hold back a wince. "I forgive you. Can you forgive me? I've been a terrible big brother."

She sniffed and smiled, nodding. "I haven't been the best little sister either."

He shrugged. "Eh. Younger siblings are supposed to be terrors, I hear."

She laughed, the sound croaky and wavery, but still beautiful. "I'm scared to come tomorrow to help."

The change in subject should have startled him, but he'd been expecting it. He gave her hand another squeeze. "You don't have to do anything you don't want to. And I'll talk to Tashmica. You won't get kicked out of the pack."

"Thank you."

"But Jess?" He paused, trying to figure out exactly how to say what he wanted. "Can I give you a piece of advice?"

She nodded, pushing a few loose pieces of hair out of her eyes and looking young and vulnerable. A fierce protectiveness filled him, and he used his other hand to sandwich hers.

"From what I've learned since coming here, your entire life, people have told you you weren't good enough, that your magic was too unstable or unpredictable. That you'd never amount to much." He ducked down to catch her eyes when her gaze dropped. "Am I right?"

"Yes," she whispered.

"But they were wrong." He gripped her fingers tightly, pushing a small amount of his magic into the hold to draw out her own. Like recognized like—her powers surging forward, knowing him in a way they hadn't had a chance to get to know each other as siblings. Their magic, their blood, knew they were family. They were safety and home. "You're more powerful than our mother could ever hope to be. That isn't something to be afraid of—it's something to be proud of. You are *amazing*. And that terrifies her and every other weak-willed witch out there. Their jealousy can't douse your light though. Only you can do that. Don't let them win. Trust yourself. Trust your magic."

She stared at him, a tentative hope building in her eyes. "But what if I lose control?"

Smiling gently, he reached up and tucked the stray strands that had fallen back into her face behind her ear. "Then I will pull you back from the edge. Me and Tash and Keegan and all the others. We will keep you safe until you trust yourself enough to do it."

His grin widened when he felt her reach out to him with her magic, a small smile on her face.

"Okay." Some of the tenseness in her eased. "I... I'll trust you. And I'll be there tomorrow morning to keep you safe too."

He stood and pulled her up, grateful when she let him wrap her into a hug. "That's all I ask."

He was surprised when Jess agreed to stay for dinner, but Mama Bell took it in stride, hugging and doting on her just as much as she did him. Carter must have explained at least a little to his family about his and Jess's relationship and his inability to talk about certain things because the conversation stayed light throughout the meal. The Bell brothers were fascinating to watch, the four of them teasing and heckling each other until their mom gave them a look that would end things for a few minutes.

While Mama Bell roped Carter's brothers into helping with cleanup and Carter disappeared upstairs, he followed Jess out onto the porch, feeling more at peace than he had in years.

"This was nice," she said, looking out into the early

evening. Throwing him a teasing smile, she added, "You're good for Doc."

Damien pressed his lips together, trying not to look too pleased at that. "I'm sure he's better for me than I am for him."

She snorted inelegantly, looking and sounding more and more like her old self the more the night had gone on. "That's not really how mates work, and you know it, but okay. I just meant that you bring out a side of him I don't think he's let himself embrace before. He's usually so laid-back, but he's all growly and protective when it comes to you."

"I guess."

"It's hot."

He swatted at her arm as she skipped down the steps, laughing.

"Don't worry," she called back at him as she made her way down the sidewalk, "he's not my type, big bro."

Shaking his head, he watched until she reached her car, parked half a block away, and was safely inside it, engine started. He hoped that the evening was a precursor for the rest of his life, but he couldn't let himself truly believe it. It wasn't even that he thought he'd die in the morning—or when the O'Hares arrived in a couple of days—though it wasn't outside the realm of possibility.

No, it all just seemed… too perfect.

Like maybe the universe was giving it to him as a gift, a brief respite, before his life went back to fear and guilt and loneliness. It made his skin itch, his blood starting to heat from his magic. He had the urge to do *something*. Anything to make sure he'd get to keep… everything.

His sister.

Mama Bell and her boys.

Carter.

Goddess, he wanted to keep Carter. Wanted to bury

himself so far into his sweet bear that they'd never truly be able to separate. He wanted to carry his marks on his skin and feel their bond in his chest. To accept him inside his body and feel him dripping out afterward.

Shuddering, he pivoted and headed back inside, needing to find his mate.

His mom and brothers were still in the kitchen, but there was no sign of Carter on the first floor. He didn't hesitate to head up to the second, a thrumming drive urging him to put eyes on his mate. An urgent call from deep inside him, stirring up his blood and magic.

He found several bedrooms with half-emptied suitcases and bags before coming to the last door, and his magic heated inside him, recognizing his mate was on the other side.

Wiping his sweaty palms on his thighs, he took a deep breath and knocked. He wasn't sure why he was nervous after feeling so calm after their lovely family dinner. The hole left from his dad's absence had still ached, but being surrounded by his mate and sister and Carter's family had made it hurt a little less.

He wasn't prepared for the sight that met him when Carter pulled open the door. Wearing nothing but a towel around his hips, his wide, thick torso was still damp from a shower, rivulets of water tracing down the expansive hills and valleys from his dripping hair. A thick pelt of dark brown hair sprinkled with gray covered his plump, bitable pecs and soft belly, narrowing only a little before disappearing under the terrycloth.

Oh *goddess*. There was a smattering of cinnamon-colored freckles on his massive shoulders. Damien couldn't tear his eyes away, imagining tracing his tongue over each and every one.

"Is your sister gone?" Carter asked tightly, running his

fingers through his long hair. "I was just finishing up and then was going to come back down to get you. We need to talk."

A minute ago, Damien would have said he'd swallowed his tongue and perished on the spot, but the phrase *we need to talk* froze the arousal building in his veins.

Swallowing, he forced himself not to run away. "Are you okay?"

"No, Damien, I'm not." He stepped back, silently inviting Damien into his bedroom. As soon as he stepped inside, Carter shut the door with an ominous thud and then was standing in front of Damien at the end of his enormous bed, crossing his arms over his chest. Damien tried not to notice how it made his arms bulge. "We need to talk about what you told Jessica."

What he'd told Jess? "I... I don't know what you mean."

"The letters, Damien," Carter rumbled at him, uncrossing his arms and grabbing Damien's twisting hands. He tugged him closer and scowled down at him. "Why would you write those? Do you... Are you giving up?"

"What?" Damien gaped at him, digging his nails into Carter's flesh for a second in his surprise. "Of course not. I just... We don't know what's going to happen tomorrow. Or the day after that. Or the day after that..."

Carter shook his head hard, hair flying out around him and flinging water. "You can't think like that," he said fiercely. "I just got you. I'm not giving you up so easily, baby boy."

The words felt nice, but they were just words. Taking a deep breath to calm his heart rate back down, he focused on soothing his agitated mate. They could say all the nice words they wanted to each other, but they both knew that any number of things could happen over the next few days to take one of them away from the other.

Maybe they'd only have a single family dinner and night

together. And as horrible as that would be, Damien couldn't actually be upset about it. It had been one of the best nights of his life.

"I'm not giving up," he said clearly and calmly, slipping his hands free of Carter's tight grip and reaching all the way up to cup his stress-lined face. "I will *always* fight with everything I have to come back to you. I promise."

Carter made a sad, broken noise in the back of his throat as he turned his head and pressed a kiss to Damien's palm. "Me too, beautiful."

It was the best promise they could make to each other at that point, and Damien would take it. He pushed up onto his toes to lay a gentle touch of his lips to Carter's. "I should get back home. I'll meet you at—"

"*No.*" The snarled word shocked Damien, but not nearly as much as Carter dropping to his knees in front of him and pushing his face into Damien's stomach, rubbing back and forth. "You can't... I can't..."

His mumbled words were barely distinguishable, his arms like steel bands around Damien's back. Combing his fingers through the wet strands of Carter's shoulder-length hair, he said, "It's okay, mi corazón. Tell me what you need."

"*You.*"

CHAPTER SEVENTEEN

The guttural vehemence of Carter's answer was breathtaking.

"You have me. You've always had me. I've been yours since that first moment I laid eyes on you." Damien continued the steady pace of his fingers carding through Carter's hair, keeping his voice low and soothing. "Do you remember? I'd only been a part of the pack for a couple of weeks. Agnes had sent me to Momma's to pick up lunch, and you were there with the people from your clinic."

Carter's big shoulders rose and lowered as he sucked in a deep breath. "I remember. You stared at us like a little creeper."

Damien snorted and slapped at Carter's upper back. "I did not!"

Carter laughed, burying his face back into Damien's soft midsection and inhaling deeply. "You didn't, but I... felt you the moment you came in. It was so weird because I could barely scent you, but you caught my attention anyway."

Damien smiled at the lamp on the bedside table, oddly pleased to hear that. "I'd known my mate was here, somewhere. The second I saw you at that booth, laughing at something one of your employees said, I knew it was you. My magic was tamped down because of the tea I was taking to hide, but it still tried to reach out and touch you. Though nothing like it does now."

Carter made a questioning noise.

"Now that I'm not taking the tea or hampered by the cuffs," he said slowly, trying to think of the best way to explain something that was more of a feeling than anything else, "my magic vibrates when you're near. Like it's so excited to be close to you and always wanting to be even closer."

"My bear feels the same way."

They stayed like that for a long moment, quiet and holding on to one another, and then Damien whispered, "I'm sorry I didn't tell you. We could have had so much more—"

"Don't," he cut him off, but not harshly. Carter tipped his head back to look up at him, face solemn. "I understand why you did it. We found our way to each other when we were ready, and we'll have the rest of our lives together. I believe that with my whole being."

Damien wanted that. Wanted a thousand family dinners. A thousand evenings curled up on the couch watching movies. A thousand nights wrapped in each other's arms.

But neither one of them could *know* it.

"I can smell your fear and doubt," Carter rumbled, pushing to his feet.

Damien gripped at his arms, terrified he'd pull away. "I'm sorry. I don't mean—"

Carter shook his head, silencing Damien with a fierce kiss, big hands settling on either side of Damien's neck. His lips moved over Damien's like a man possessed, like he was just as worried they'd only ever have this little slice of time together.

Like everything would change come morning.

Tears pricking at the back of his eyes, Damien kissed back just as passionately, opening his mouth at the first touch of Carter's tongue and allowing him entrance. The brush of their tongues together set off a spark of electricity that jolted Damien's entire body, Carter growling as he moved one hand to Damien's lower back to hold him in place.

He couldn't hope to keep up with Carter's expertly delivered kisses. Instead, he let himself become lost to the moment, allowing the syrupy feeling of desire to build inside him and turn his limbs to Jell-O. Moaning as Carter sucked his bottom lip into his mouth, Damien planted his hands on his mate's furry belly.

Goddess above.

He couldn't stop himself from rubbing his palms over the soft hair, groaning under his breath as his fingers tingled. Too tempting to resist, Damien smoothed his hands to the sides and palmed the love handles just above Carter's hips, then pulled back to peek up at him to make sure it was okay. He hoped it was. He hoped Carter wasn't self-conscious of a single inch of his body because Damien thought he was beyond perfect, but he knew the world could be cruel.

When Carter didn't even seem to notice, simply grunting and trying to kiss him again as his gorgeous eyes glowed softly, Damien snickered and ducked out of reach. "Is your bear in control right now?"

That got Carter's attention, his eyebrows going up as his hold on Damien tightened a fraction. "No, beautiful. Though he's in agreement with me that I need to get my scent all over your naked skin."

Damien sucked in a breath and stared up at Carter, unable to form words as the images his mind created bombarded him.

A slow grin spread across Carter's face. "You like that idea too, don't you, baby boy?"

He could only nod, his mouth dry and palms damp.

"Full disclosure here," Carter said, turning a bit more serious. He pointed at the dresser behind Damien, right next to the door. There was a large flat-screen TV mounted on the wall above the dark walnut piece of furniture.

And a jar of Damien's bonding tea sitting innocently next to Carter's discarded wallet and phone.

Swallowing, Damien turned back to him. "Where did you get that?"

"The shop. Tashmica gave it to me earlier today." Carter studied him, thumb starting to gently caress the front of Damien's throat in a way that was thoroughly distracting as well as intoxicating. "You made that for us, didn't you?"

Stomach tightening and eyes wide, Damien nodded, worried Carter thought it was weird or that he shouldn't have shared it with anyone else or that he had no business trying to replicate something so primal to shifter couples or—

"Good. When you're ready, we'll use it," Carter said, giving a sharp nod like the conversation was over.

"Do you..." Damien paused, biting his lip.

"What?"

Shrugging, he looked away, unable to meet Carter's eyes. "I can't decide if it would be better or much worse for you if we were to use it tonight."

Carter cupped his chin and forced his face up, eyes narrowed just a little. "I'd bond with you in a second, don't doubt that, but I don't want you to just do it for me. Or because you're worried something will happen tomorrow and you want to give me something to remember you by."

Damien's stomach swirled uncomfortably. "That's only part of it. A more selfish part of me wants..." He grimaced and squeezed his eyes shut before forcing the words out. "There's a chance you won't want me after you learn... certain things about me. If tonight is all I get—"

Firm lips landed on his, moving slowly until Damien relaxed into his mate once more and then pulled back. "If that's the case, we're definitely waiting. I don't want either one of us to choose to bond because we're afraid or because we think the other person wants it."

"I do want it—"

Carter pressed one of his thumbs to Damien's lips. "Shh. I know. The fact that you spent so much time and energy creating the tea even when you never thought you'd really get to use it tells me everything, beautiful."

The scared part of him scratched at the back of his mind, whispering he'd never get another chance to bond with Carter again, but he shoved it back ruthlessly. Even if it took him two more years to win back Carter's trust after he learned everything, Damien would do it rather than trick him into bonding out of guilt or fear.

"But I still need to rub my come into your skin until you smell like mine."

The crass words were so surprising Damien choked on his own spit. "O-okay."

Damien half expected Carter and his bear to be so impatient and filled with animalistic instincts that he wouldn't be able to hold back. That he'd attack Damien with unbridled passion until they were both left sated and sweaty.

But it was the opposite.

Carter smiled at him softly, his eyes full of an emotion Damien did not have the courage to name, and then he leaned down, going so slowly he knew his mate was giving him a chance to pull away. To step back or change his mind.

He didn't want to. All he'd ever wanted was in front of him, and he was going to grab onto it with both hands, whether he deserved it or not.

He pushed up onto his toes and met his mate halfway, tilting his head to the side and locking their lips together. Damien breathed out a sigh at the spark of connection. He would never get over the way Carter tasted, the way he made Damien feel. It was like pure adrenaline and the softest of blankets wrapping around him all at the same time. He always wanted more, but he also felt so safe in Carter's arms.

Was it like that for everyone with their fated mate? Or were he and Carter just exceptionally lucky? Either way, he vowed to himself to never take their mating for granted.

Carter kissed him slowly, seeming to be in no hurry at all, taking his time to taste every corner of Damien's mouth. He nibbled on Damien's lips and then across his jaw.

Damien found himself becoming the aggressor, kissing back harder and gripping at Carter's hair as his patience deserted him, his arousal flaring. Every part of his body felt alive with anticipation, his skin tingling with need.

He nudged Carter backward—well, he tried to. His bear didn't move at all, but he did smile against the hinge of Damien's jaw and gave it a sharp nip that made his half-hard cock stiffen the rest of the way.

"Don't be impatient," Carter said without raising his head.

Damien shivered, the moist heat fluttering over his sensitive skin. *Goddess.* Everything with Carter felt so good.

"Please, I need more," he said shakily, sinking his fingers into the thick fur of Carter's chest. His bear grunted at the sharp tug but seemed to get with the program.

Damien sighed with relief as Carter stepped back toward the bed and pulled the covers down—then shrieked with surprise when big hands grabbed his hips and tossed him into the center. Carter was on him before he fully settled, moving so much faster than his size indicated.

"So needy," Carter murmured, trailing kisses down the

side of Damien's neck as his hands started tugging up at the bottom of Damien's button-up, pulling it out of his pants.

Tipping his head to the side to give his mate better access, Damien whimpered. "Is that bad?"

"Hell no." Carter's deep voice vibrated into Damien's body, lighting him up from the inside out. "I love that you need me. I love that you're impatient." He sucked at the thin skin of Damien's throat until he was arching and moaning beneath him. "I love that you hold nothing back. Your reactions are so honest."

Before Damien could say anything or question why anyone would want to hold back their reactions from their mate, Carter was gripping each side of his shirt and pulling, the sound of buttons popping off ricocheting around the room.

Damien gasped. "You just tore my shirt."

Carter didn't even reply, humming as he moved down to explore Damien's bare chest with his lips and tongue.

He forgot his annoyance as soon as Carter's mouth latched onto one of his nipples, shooting electricity straight to his balls. Who would have known the small brown peaks could be so sensitive? He fisted Carter's hair, his mate tugging at the stiff peak with his teeth until he was moaning and thrashing, his feet scrambling for purchase on the soft sheets.

Carter chuckled softly and reached down to grab each of his thighs, lifting and guiding Damien's legs around his hips before returning to his exploration.

Oh goddess, that was so much better.

It notched their hard cocks together and gave Damien something to hold on to and anchor himself with as sensations rolled through him. He ran his hands over Carter's back, sinking his nails in when his mate switched sides, giving his other nipple the same treatment as the first. He sank his teeth in just to the point of pain and then laved his tongue over it before sucking the bud into his mouth.

Damien rocked up against him over and over, frustrated at the layers between them. The towel Carter was still managing to hold on to somehow, as well as his pants and underwear. He wanted more of his skin. He wanted to feel everything, to see if he really was as big as he felt pressed up against Damien.

He carefully extracted his hands from where they'd somehow found their way back into Carter's soft hair, then shoved between their bodies to start undoing his belt, wanting to help in moving the process along. Unfortunately, that had the undesired effect of Carter lifting his head off his chest, but instead of reprimanding Damien or telling him again to be patient, he scooted backward.

With quick sure movements, he divested Damien of his belt and then his pants and socks. When he slipped his fingers beneath the waistband of Damien's briefs, he paused and looked up at him, eyes searching and wanting to make sure one last time that Damien was on board.

He nodded fast and loose, chest heaving from his panting breaths. He wanted more. He *needed* more.

Carter slowly lowered his underwear, and Damien gasped at the feeling of his rock-hard erection getting released and popping up to smack against his stomach, leaving a string of precome connecting his glossy head and belly. The snarling noise Carter made raised goose bumps down the back of his thighs. It would have been terrifying in any other context, but in that moment, it was thrilling. His mate was finally starting to lose control—because of *Damien*.

Intoxicated at the idea, he moaned and spread his legs, lifting his hips off the bed and presenting himself in a way that would have been embarrassing had he been thinking clearly. Staring at Carter through half-lidded eyes, he delicately rubbed at his sensitive pecs and down to his belly button, making his way toward his cock.

But his hands never made it.

Carter threw aside the underwear he was still holding with a growl, then snagged Damien's wrists before he could make contact with anything good. "Not so fast."

Damien whimpered as Carter gently forced his arms out to the sides, leaving him completely naked and exposed. No one had ever seen him like that. And while he didn't have rock-hard abs or bulging muscles in his arms and legs, the way Carter looked at him made him feel like he was the most attractive person on the planet.

He felt the same way about his mate. There wasn't a single inch of his body that Damien didn't adore and want to kiss and caress.

Before he could suggest that Carter remove the towel hanging precariously around his hips, his sweet bear with glowing eyes and sharpened fangs dove forward, running his tongue up the underside of his erection with a deep groan.

It felt *so* good.

Damien tried to push his hips upward, wanting more of that sensation, but Carter just moved his arms so his wrists were stacked on his sternum and he could hold both with one hand, then used his other to hold Damien's hips flat against the bed, easily controlling him and keeping him exactly where he wanted him.

He gave his arms an experimental tug, but there was zero give to Carter's hold. He moaned at the perfection of the moment, feeling so safe in his confinement. His mate tasted him exactly as slow as he wanted to, refusing to let Damien speed him up. All he could do was accept what Carter was giving him, and it somehow quieted the extra noise in his head, allowing him to sink fully into the moment.

Perfection.

As soon as he relaxed into the hold, Carter hummed and went back to exploring Damien's erection, dipping down to suck on each of his balls. Damien mewled, sliding his thighs as far apart as they would go, silently begging for more. Instead, Carter shifted over and sucked a bruise to the surface of the skin right where his groin and thigh met. Damien's leg spasmed as he moaned low in his chest.

"You taste good, baby boy," Carter murmured as he moved back to licking around Damien's aching cock. "Sweet like honey, even here."

"Oh goddess," he gasped, hips twitching as he tipped his head back and sucked air into his lungs. "*Carter.*"

Wet heat enveloped him as Carter sank down around him, sucking hard as he pulled back up. "Yeah, beautiful?"

All Damien could do was whimper and try not to orgasm too quickly. He didn't want the amazing things Carter was doing to his body to end.

Carter's tongue playing with his foreskin had Damien biting his lip to hold back his cries as white-hot ecstasy coursed through him though. He knew he was going to come way too fast, but considering it was his first time *and* it was with his mate?

He was going to give himself a pass.

Especially when Carter's lips encircled his ruddy, leaking glans and sucked like he was trying to pull Damien's soul out through his dick.

That was all he could take.

Calling out Carter's name, Damien's entire body stiffened as all of his muscles locked up at once, and pleasure like he'd never experienced by his own hand coursed through him, lighting up every single nerve ending in his body. His magic surged to the surface and then out through his fingertips, moving around the room like a tiny tornado.

Damien barely even noticed as he moaned and thrashed,

his cock releasing into the warm heat of Carter's mouth. He vaguely heard his mate make a sort of grunting sound of approval as he let go of Damien's wrists to wrap around his cock, working out every last drop of come Damien had in his entire body.

As his orgasm slowly faded, Damien flopped back against the mattress, a thin layer of sweat coating him and his dick feeling overly sensitive. He had to moan and push at Carter.

Raising his head, Carter smiled as he licked his lips, his damp hair wild around his flushed face. Holding Damien's eyes, he unknotted his towel and tossed it away. He never looked away, but Damien didn't have the discipline for that. His gaze moved down his mate's body, and he wished more than anything he had an ounce of strength left in his muscles.

His mate was so beautiful. Big and thick and strong. He couldn't wait for the opportunity to learn every inch of him. When he got to the junction of Carter's thighs, his eyes widened at the size of his mate's erection.

"You're…" He didn't know how to finish that sentence, his brains still scrambled from his hard release. When he glanced up at Carter's face, he swore his mate was blushing even as he fisted his long, thick cock in his giant paw of a hand, stroking himself.

"Yeah," Carter said, his voice little more than a deep rumble. "Bears are usually pretty big. It'll get a little bit more length after we bond."

Damien's eyes shot back down. He wasn't sure where Carter would put all of what he had already, and it was going to get *longer*?

"At least I don't have a bone in there," Carter added nonchalantly.

Damien looked back up at his face, shocked speechless.

Carter shrugged as he continued to stroke himself slowly, the muscles in his arm and chest moving in a tantalizing fashion and distracting Damien from their conversation until Carter said, "Real bears have bones. Keeps them erect for a long time."

The way he said it made it sound like they were having an ordinary conversation. Like they weren't in the middle of sex, talking about the anatomy of real bears versus shifters.

"How long will *you* stay... erect?" Damien asked, his face —which had finally been cooling after his mind-blowing orgasm—heated all over again.

Carter smirked at him. "Long enough."

Damien sank his teeth into his bottom lip, imagining Carter being able to fuck him over and over while never going soft in between. Was that really a thing they'd be able to do? Did it make him a slut to want to?

It didn't matter because he did. He wanted anything and everything with his mate.

Carter groaned as he fell forward, bracing himself on his free hand where it planted on the bed next to Damien's head. "Your scent just spiked. You like that idea, don't you?" Carter whispered. He leaned in to inhale right behind Damien's ear and then pressed a kiss against the oddly sensitive spot. "You're imagining me keeping you impaled on my cock for hours and hours, aren't you, baby boy?"

"Yes," he admitted breathlessly, though he wasn't quite sure if it was from his orgasm or from getting aroused all over. His dick was valiantly attempting to get hard again at Carter's crass words.

Carter hummed, the soft vibration of his lips sending a shiver down Damien's spine as he lowered himself so he was pressing Damien into the bed with his bulky body. He moved against him, rubbing his big, thick cock over Damien's spent and sensitive one, then over his hips and his belly.

Thrusts growing in strength and speed, Carter kept his face buried in Damien's neck, breathing heavily and groaning quietly. Damien wrapped his arms around his mate's wide shoulders, reveling in the feeling of his mate rutting against him. It was oddly erotic, the way Carter dragged the tip of his erection over as much of Damien's skin as he could. It was arousing but not enough for Damien to get fully hard again. Instead, it sort of soothed the ragged edges left behind from his intense release, and he sank into a soft headspace of safety and comfort.

And probably love—if he was letting himself think like that.

He sank his fingers into Carter's hair, petting him and urging him to take whatever he needed from Damien. He even found the strength to hitch his legs up around Carter's hips again, creating a better cradle for him to rock against.

It wasn't long before Carter's movements began to become erratic, each thrust dredging a soft groan from Damien as his deep grunts rang in his ears. He found one spot he seemed to particularly like at the junction of Damien's groin and thigh, right where he'd left a hickey earlier, and rubbed his hot, dripping cock over it repeatedly.

"Yes," Damien moaned, arching his hips to get more of the wonderful feeling. The smell of sex was so thick in the air even his paltry human nose was overwhelmed with it. "Leave your scent all over me."

A low snarl was Carter's only response as wet heat splashed against Damien's hip and belly, the muscles in Carter's back stiffening beneath his hands.

Then there was a sharp bite right where his neck and shoulder met. Right where a bonding bite would go. It wasn't hard enough to break skin, but the pain and meaning behind it were enough for pleasure to rocket through him. He gripped Carter with his hands and thighs as he whimpered and arched his neck, silently encouraging his mate to mark him. He grasped the back of Carter's head and pushed his hips up, rubbing his still-sensitive dick against his mate's furry belly.

Carter's movements began to slow, his teeth releasing. Damien shivered as he pressed the softest, most delicate kiss to the same spot.

It felt like... a promise. To himself and to Damien. The word never left his mouth, yet Damien felt it sink into his very soul.

Soon.

CHAPTER EIGHTEEN

Before the sun was up, Carter was blearily following Damien down the stairs, anxiety making him nauseous and his bear ready to rip apart anyone who even looked at Damien wrong. He doubted either of them had slept much, even after their spine-melting orgasms. Every time Carter had dozed off, he'd jerked awake minutes later, reaching for Damien, afraid he'd lost him. Damien never said anything, just ran his fingers through Carter's chest hair and hushed him softly.

He was surprised to see the lights under the cabinets in his kitchen turned on low, but then his tired brain kicked on, and he caught his mom's scent just before she appeared in the doorway, fluffy purple robe wrapped around her.

"Good morning, darlings," she said with forced cheer, her smile looking more like a grimace. "I was just about to turn the coffee maker on. Can I make either of you anything to eat?"

Goddess, he loved his mom.

"No, Mama," he said, walking over and giving her a kiss on the cheek. "We don't have time to eat."

"Thank you though," Damien added. "You didn't get up just for us, did you?"

She went right over to his mate and gave him a hug. Carter's eyes stung as he watched Damien grip her worn robe just like he had the day before, soaking up his mom's easy affection.

"I wanted to wish you good luck," she murmured, still holding on to Damien and rubbing her cheek against his messy bedhead. "I know you both are nervous, but have faith, my dears. The goddess has brought you together for a reason, and I don't believe it's simply for you to lose one another."

Carter's heart ached, thinking about the letters tucked away in Damien's apartment *just in case*. He couldn't even imagine what his life would be like if he lost Damien so soon after finding him. He'd let himself think he was so content, that he didn't need anything other than his work and his pack.

That was bullshit. He *needed* Damien.

He needed his sweet smiles and soft voice and gentle strength. He needed him in his bed and in his kitchen and curled up on his couch.

He just... he needed him.

They may have known each other for two years, but Carter felt like he'd just found him. Was only now seeing him fully, like his eyes hadn't been able to focus on him before. Even then though, he'd been drawn to him. If he'd gotten the balls to actually ask his witch out on a date, would he have said no?

Or would he have said yes and still kept their connection from him?

Stomach rolling, he shook off the thoughts. Wondering about what might have happened in the past would do nothing but drive him out of his mind. He couldn't know what would have happened between them if he'd gotten around to making a move before, but now that he knew? Now that he'd gotten a tiny taste of what it could be like between them?

He wasn't letting Damien go.

He didn't care how many damn witches tried to take him away—Carter would hunt him down and bring him back to his den.

It was still dark as they approached the small pond behind the manor, the beam of Damien's flashlight leading the way. Carter didn't need it, but he hadn't wanted his mate to stumble around in the dark, and he'd refused to let Carter carry him the whole way.

He heard the others before they came into view, the soft murmur of their voices and Tashmica directing the rest of the coven drifting to him on the chilly early morning air. Without thinking, he reached over and grabbed Damien's hand, needing the connection between them as things suddenly felt very real.

Damien looked over at him, face serious but calm, and nodded. "Have faith, mi corazón."

The soft reminder eased a little of the tension in his shoulders. His mom was right—why would the goddess or universe or whatever be so cruel as to finally reveal Damien as his mate just for him to lose him less than a week later?

Their story was just beginning, not coming to a tragic end.

He had to believe that.

As they came into the clearing, Damien clicked off the flashlight, the dozens and dozens of candles floating in the air combined with the waning moon enough to illuminate the area for him. It looked like the whole coven was there, some still setting things up while a few others were already kneeling at the water's edge, heads bowed and hands raised up above them. Carter wasn't sure if they were praying or meditating or what, but he hoped whatever it was helped.

"Right on time," Tash said, hurrying over to them, smile tight. She cupped Damien's cheeks, looking him over closely. "We can still try the other way…"

His grip on Carter's fingers tightened, and he took that as his cue. "No, he wants to try this way."

She glanced at him and then back at Damien, jaw set as she nodded. "I figured. Still thought I'd ask. You'll need to strip and get into the water."

Damien smirked at her and nodded.

Rolling her eyes, she stepped back. "Yes, I know that you know. Don't sass me, and just get in the water."

After she turned away, the tilt to Damien's lips dropped, all humor draining from him as he swallowed and faced Carter. "I—"

"Don't you dare say goodbye," Carter growled, gripping the back of Damien's head and tugging him none too gently against him. As soon as they collided, he bent and slanted his mouth over his mate's, reminding him of what he had to live for. Of why Carter wouldn't just let him give up. When Damien finally sagged against him, limp with submission, he gave one more swipe of his tongue inside his sweet-as-sin mouth, shuddering at the tiny whimper he got as he lifted his head. "Take off your clothes, baby boy."

Nodding loosely with adorably flushed cheeks, Damien started unbuttoning the shirt Carter had pilfered from one of his brothers. Carter knew he should turn away, that his mate wasn't used to nudity like a shifter would be, but he couldn't force his body to move, and Damien didn't ask him to. He shyly met Carter's eyes as he stripped off his shirt and then his pants, acting like Carter hadn't seen and touched and tasted most of him the night before.

Biting his lip, Damien kicked his clothes away before turning and padding barefoot to the edge of the pond. Carter bit back his groan at the sight of his perfect, tiny bubble butt jiggling as he moved.

Grateful he was the only shifter around to notice how turned on he was getting, even though it was completely inappropriate at the moment, he started to follow Damien, wanting to be as close as possible. Movement coming from the same direction he and Damien had drew his attention though, and he stiffened, scenting the air, only relaxing when the wind shifted and brought him the scents of his alpha and alpha-mate.

As they broke into the clearing, Carter was relieved to see the easy way they held on to each other, Rick's arm around Kai's shoulders and Kai's around Rick's waist, leaning on him a little. Kai looked like he'd rolled out of bed and thrown on the first clothes he'd found, hair adorably messy and eyes half-closed. Rick was as alert and awake-looking as ever as he took in the sight of his coven working.

They moved over to stand next to Carter, Kai smiling around Rick at him as the alpha said, "Morning, Doc. How is he?"

Carter followed his gaze to where Damien was wading into the water, already mid-thigh. "Scared but trying to hide it. He…" Carter cleared his throat and dropped his head, trying to compose himself. He was a damn Enforcer now; he needed to remember that and start acting like it. "He wrote goodbye letters. To me, his sister, his dad… just in case."

Rick's strong hand landed on the back of his neck, squeezing and offering comfort. "Tashmica assures me that her version of this ritual has a much higher probability of him surviving. Though it's possible it won't remove the Blood Oath completely."

Carter was glad to hear the chances of his mate dying were no longer *thirty percent*, but he turned to Rick. "What does that mean? I thought it either worked or it didn't."

Tashmica was already heading toward them, having spotted the couple standing next to Carter just outside the candlelight.

Before she could say anything, he asked, "Rick said the ritual might not completely remove the Oath. What does that mean?"

She glanced at her watch and then toward the east, but the sky was only *just* beginning to lighten. "Don't think of the Oath spell as a single complex spell. Think of it like an onion. It has layers to it. Most people—at least according to my research—aren't powerful enough to do more than one or two, but based on how complex Damien's is, I believe it has at least a dozen layers."

Carter shook his head. "Okay? What does that mean for him if the ritual doesn't work?"

"It'll work," she said confidently, "but my approach is a bit more subtle. I'm going to peel back the spell, layer by layer, whereas Damien's plan had been to basically pulverize it with a hammer. Sure, it would obliterate the spell completely, but it also might take him out too. This way, *my way*, the bottommost layer or two may still remain, but we can deal with that."

Eyes narrowed, Carter looked at where Damien was treading water, his olive skin glistening with droplets and looking darker than usual in the low lighting. "What would the bottom layers be though?"

She looked toward the pond, then her watch, sighing as she took a step away from them. "The first layer will probably be one that allows the caster to kill the wearer. From anywhere."

Carter's stomach dropped, and he was lurching after her without thinking, but Rick's strong grip on his shoulder stopped him. He whipped around and growled, "We can't leave that layer!"

"We'll see what happens and then deal with whatever remains afterward," Rick said calmly, though there was an edge to his voice that said he didn't appreciate Carter's tone.

Not that Carter really gave a shit at the moment.

He turned back around, teeth clenched so tight his jaw began to ache as he watched Tashmica gather the coven around her at the edge of the water. With a wave of her hand, she sent four candles out over the surface of the pond around Damien, one at each of the cardinal directions.

She held her hands out to the witches on either side of her—Keegan and Jessica—and quickly, all of them were connected. The scent of the herbs already in the water with Damien was beginning to tickle at Carter's nose as the coven began to chant in one voice just as the sun crested over the edge of the horizon and Damien dipped beneath the surface.

The surge of magic was immediate, whipping at the long grass and cattails near the pond's edge and disturbing the entire glass-like surface. The flames on the candles grew taller and taller as they continued to chant, repeating the words without pause or variation. A glow beneath the surface began to grow, drawing Carter's eyes. It was right where Damien had gone under, the bright orange color expanding with every harsh breath Carter took.

He realized the chanting was getting faster, the air around him crackling, as the bright spot in the water got to be too much, causing Carter's eyes to sting and look away. He focused on Tashmica instead, the glowing tattoos on her dark arms and fierce concentration on her face. Her loose curls were waving around her face, her long skirt around her calves, but her focus didn't waver even for a second.

Just as he was beginning to worry about Damien holding his breath for so long, the voices came to a crescendo, ringing in the early morning air, and then silence. The flames on the candles and light in the water extinguished from one breath to the next.

But Damien did not reappear.

Worry began to prickle at his skin, a ball of dread building in his gut as he took a few steps closer to the water, eyes searching for any sign of his mate. The water wasn't that deep, was it? The bright reflection of the rising sun was making it hard to see beneath the surface, but he should have appeared by now. The spell was over, wasn't it?

As he reached the edge, panic beginning to truly set in and rile his bear to the point his skin felt too tight, like he might burst through at any moment, he shot a look toward Tashmica and found her frantically searching the water as well.

"Where is he?" Carter growled, already shrugging out of his jacket.

"I… I don't know…" she whispered, voice breaking. She slipped off her sandals as Carter tugged off his boots. "He should… It should have worked."

"*Where is my mate?*"

His roar sent ripples across the surface of the pond—and then he was jumping in, praying for the first time since he was a cub to a goddess he barely believed in.

Please let him be okay. Please don't take him from me.

I need him.

CHAPTER NINETEEN

D amien didn't know where he was.

He was lying on grass—he was pretty sure anyway —but everything was dark and fuzzy, like a fog covered the ground and air around him. He wasn't in the water anymore, that was for sure.

One minute, he'd been surrounded by cool, soothing liquid, the tattoo on his chest growing hotter and hotter despite the water cocooning him. He'd felt the spell working, peeling back the tight grip the Oath had held him in for so long he'd stopped feeling it.

Just as the pain had grown to the point he worried he couldn't handle it, he must have blacked out. Had someone pulled him out?

Why couldn't he see Tash and the others? Where was Carter?

He pushed himself upright, afraid for reasons he couldn't explain, and squinted at the grayish landscape around him. "Hello?"

He ignored the tremble in his voice, hoping no one else heard it. As he climbed to his feet, he realized he was wearing his clothes and that they were dry. When he lifted a hand and ran it through his hair, he found that dry too.

What the hell?

"Damien?"

His breath froze in his lungs as his heart rate skyrocketed. He knew that voice. He'd know that voice *anywhere*.

"Taita?" His whole body was trembling as he turned, unable to believe he'd actually heard his dad's voice. It had been so long since he'd been allowed to talk to him. He'd feared the worst.

He blinked a few times, trying to clear his eyes and bring him more into focus, but it didn't help for some reason. But there was no mistaking his dad's short, stocky build, dark hair just like Damien's, and wide smile. The fog seemed to be swirling around his legs, concealing his bottom half from view, but Damien forced himself not to think about it, not to *let* himself think about what that meant.

"Hola, mi vida," his dad said. His voice sounded weird, like it was coming from far away, and even though he was still smiling, there were tears on his leather-brown cheeks. "It's so good to see you."

Swallowing thickly, Damien took a step forward.

Or... he tried to. It felt like he was moving, but the distance between him and his dad didn't change. He tried again and again—walking, running, stretching one leg out as far as he could go and then pulling the rest of him after it— but he didn't move. Or maybe his dad kept moving away?

Screaming out in frustration, Damien fell to his knees, breathing hard. "This isn't... I just want to hug you again."

"I know, mi vida. I want that too." His smile dimmed, turning sad. Now that Damien wasn't desperately trying to get to him, it seemed like the haze around him cleared a bit more, bringing him into sharper focus. "But you know that can't happen in this place."

Damien gripped the grass beneath him, trying to tear at it, but nothing happened. It was like the ground was there and not at the same time. His dad's softly spoken words were a sucker punch to his gut, forcing the air from his lungs and dazing him.

He focused on breathing for a minute, even though he knew he wasn't even really *there*, and then fell back to sit on his feet, not bothering to stand again. "She killed you."

"She did," his dad confirmed, voice even, yet the confirmation still felt like an icicle to his chest. "I'm so sorry, mi vida. I never wanted this life for you."

Damien absently wiped at his cheeks. "I know. It's not your fault, Taita. It's mine. I did this. I'm the one who—"

"No." His dad's sharp word cut Damien off, surprising him out of his downward spiral of guilt and pain. "You didn't know. I should have told you long ago who your mother was so you were prepared instead of curious. I failed you."

Damien shook his head hard, fingers digging into his thighs. He wondered why it hurt, why he could feel that, but he couldn't hug his damn dad. The spirit plane was a mess of contradictions, and he hated it. Hated everything—including himself. It didn't matter what his dad said, Damien was the one who'd used magic to try and find his birth mom, curious and frustrated with the rules and restrictions his dad put in place.

He'd had no idea that all those rules had been to protect Damien from *her*.

"You didn't fail me," he said brokenly. "You were the best dad. You loved me and protected me and taught me everything you knew about magic. I loved our life. I'm the one who blew it up, not you."

His dad clenched his jaw. "Mi vida, listen to me," he said fiercely. "I knew—from the moment I took you and ran—that she'd find us one day. I just hoped you'd be stronger than me, strong enough to beat her. I should have warned you. I meant to, but…"

"But what?"

"But I was worried you'd hate me for putting you in such a dangerous position. Or worse… that you wouldn't believe me and go looking for her anyway." He shook his head, looking away from Damien for the first time. "I was so foolish. I should have trusted you. I knew you were a good man, that you wouldn't let her draw you in with her manipulations, but I just wanted to keep you safe and unafraid for as long as I could."

Damien licked at his dry lips. "Why didn't you hide? You made a name for yourself, going out and helping so many packs and covens. If you knew she was looking…"

"I hid at first. I took you and ran back to Honduras and stayed with some family I still had there," his dad said slowly, eyes still averted. "I was so sure she wouldn't go that far. I knew that as her firstborn, you'd be important to her and her coven, but I thought she'd move on, have more children to fill in the ranks. It wasn't like she loved me or you, not really. I don't think she's capable of it, honestly."

"She did have more kids," Damien offered, not sure how much his dad knew about why he'd been sent to the Kincaid Pack. "Well, one more. A girl. She's here, a member of Rick Kincaid's pack too."

"I'm glad you have each other," his dad said softly, watching him thoughtfully. "Is she powerful like you?"

Damien chuckled wetly. "Probably even more powerful. But she's afraid. Scared of using her magic and losing control."

His dad hummed. "I see the family resemblance already."

"That… It's different," Damien muttered, glancing away.

His dad let the silence settle over them for a moment in that way he'd always done to force Damien to think about what he'd said. The ache of knowing it was the last time he'd ever experience it sharpened in his gut as his dad continued his story.

"I was wrong to assume she'd give up. When you were two, the village we lived in was attacked. Most of the people there weren't even aware a small coven lived among them, but the O'Hares didn't care. They... they killed everyone they could find as they hunted for us. I barely got us away."

Damien stared at his dad in horror. "What?"

He nodded and cleared his throat, voice raspy as he said, "My cousin and her husband were killed that night. Because of me. Because I'd been so naïve in thinking she'd just give up her chance at raising you to be the kind of witch she was and that she'd forget."

"Forget about me?"

"No, that she'd forget I outsmarted her. That *I* left her and took something of hers with me." His dad smiled gently. "After that night in Honduras, I knew it was only a matter of time before she caught up with me again. I moved around a lot after that, never staying anywhere longer than a month. I'd sell my skills to packs when I could, pick up a regular job when I couldn't. When you were around six, I met a young alpha who convinced me that running was no life for a kid. Especially one of your talent. He offered to let us stay with his pack, but I didn't want to put them at risk, so he suggested we form an alliance and that I form as many alliances with packs and covens as I could."

Damien nodded slowly, finally understanding. "Instead of making yourself invisible, you made yourself as visible as possible. So she'd think twice before coming after us again."

"I was skeptical at first, but after a few years, I began to relax. I wasn't sure if it was the allies I'd made or that maybe she really had moved on, but I convinced myself we were safe as long as we stayed away from her and her coven."

"And then I tried to contact her, ruining all of your hard work."

His dad crossed his arms over his chest and gave him a look he was *achingly* familiar with. "Mi vida, you must let go of your guilt. Don't let it consume you, or you may as well have died alongside me."

The reminder that he'd never see his dad in person again jolted Damien, his body rocking at the force of his sorrow. "How can I do that? It's my fault—"

"No, it isn't. You do not get to shoulder responsibility for her actions." The deep furrows on his forehead scowled at Damien in Disapproving Dad.

It made him want to smile and cry at the same time.

"She'll come for me," he whispered, letting his head drop forward, suddenly too tired to hold it up. Too tired to fight. Just... too tired. "I didn't do what she wanted, so she'll probably kill me too anyway."

"You're stronger than I was, and you have something I did not."

Flinching, Damien forced himself to lift his chin and meet his dad's eyes. "I can't use—"

"A pack, mi vida. You have a pack and a mate, yes?" He smiled at Damien when he didn't deny it—though Damien wasn't really sure he could count on the Kincaid Pack to defend him against his mom. And he wasn't sure he even had the right to ask. "Tell me about him, your mate."

"He's... brilliant," Damien croaked out, swiping at his wet eyes. "He's a brown bear shifter and a doctor. And I just met his mom and brothers, who moved here to help, apparently?" He laughed wetly, curling over on himself. "He's so beautiful and kind. He is... too good for me."

His dad made a disgruntled noise. "Nonsense. He sounds like he's maybe just good enough."

"No, Carter is—"

"Love him fiercely, mi vida," his dad interrupted, suddenly kneeling just in front of Damien. The ache to touch him was so sharp Damien wasn't sure how he'd survive. There was a gaping hole in his chest that would never heal, he was sure of it. "Love him and let him love you. Let go of your guilt and fear and live your life so full of joy and happiness I will feel it in the Beyond."

"Taita," he said, sobbing softly. "I can't say goodbye to you. I don't... I don't know how to do this without you."

Life. Magic. Family.

How could he do anything without his dad at his side, guiding him on the path?

"You'll never be without me, mi vida. I'll always be with you." He raised his hand as if he would cup Damien's cheek, like he'd done so often in Damien's life, but stopped short, his wavery hand mere inches away. "Go back to your mate. Go now, Damien."

"No, wait!"

His cry went unanswered, the hazy visage of the spirit plane darkening around him until he was surrounded by blackness.

And then he was gasping and shooting upright, strong hands holding him and sending a bolt of fear through him before he could focus his eyes. The sun was so bright above him, contrasting obscenely with where he'd just been, it was disorienting.

He twisted around, frantically trying to find his dad again. To ignore the numb certainty building inside him that told him that was the last time he'd ever speak to him.

Big, warm hands gripped the sides of his face, stilling his jerky movements. He knew those hands. He blinked rapidly, staring into the concerned face of his sweet mate, his blue eyes red-rimmed and glowing faintly. His comforting herbal scent engulfed Damien, slowing the panicky thoughts racing through his brain.

"Can you hear me?"

Damien swallowed, his throat feeling raw and parched like he'd been screaming. When he spoke, his voice came out hoarse and low. "Y-yes. I can hear you."

Relief relaxed the fine lines around Carter's eyes and the tenseness in his jaw. "Good, that's... that's good, beautiful. You scared the shit out of me."

He licked his lips and croaked, "She killed him."

Thick brown brows furrowed at him. "What?"

Grief was building inside him as he settled more fully inside his body, feeling the dewy grass beneath his bare legs and realizing he was wearing Carter's enormous T-shirt, his mate's torso naked. It felt like there was a vise around his chest, preventing him from taking a deep breath as tears burned in his eyes and spilled down his cheeks.

But beneath that overwhelming grief was something else.

Something white-hot and all-consuming.

Amelia O'Hare had taken something precious from him. A man who'd devoted two decades to helping others and keeping Damien safe. She'd *robbed* him of ever seeing his dad again.

As the heat spread out to his limbs, sparking and feeding his magic until it was pushing at his skin, wanting to get out, Damien vowed she'd feel the same pain he was. He'd destroy the one thing she cared about in the world—and then he'd destroy her.

Throwing his head back, he screamed, releasing his magic into the air around him. He heard a few people hit the ground and curse, but he couldn't even be bothered to look. His rage and anguish were all he cared about in that moment.

Safe arms wrapped around him as Carter tucked his face into Damien's neck and pressed a soft kiss to the thin skin there. He didn't try and stop Damien, didn't tell him to control himself or his magic.

He just held him.

And Damien...

He kept screaming.

CHAPTER TWENTY

Carter had never felt such utter terror like he had when he'd pulled Damien's limp body out of the pond. If he hadn't had his knowledge and training to rely on, he was fairly certain he would have lost his damn mind when he laid his mate on the ground and found him unresponsive and not breathing. He'd already started CPR by the time Tash hit the dirt next to him, holding a glowing hand over Damien's forehead.

Of course, when she'd ordered him to stop, he'd nearly taken her head off.

Luckily for them both, Damien had sucked in a breath at that moment and then coughed out half the pond. Carter had helped him onto his side, rubbing his back and telling him to try and take it easy. But when he'd stopped coughing and he still hadn't said anything or reacted at all, Carter had flipped him onto his back again and stared at his blank, unseeing eyes.

"What's wrong with him?" he'd asked even as his hands had run over Damien's head and chest, looking for an injury.

"Nothing," Tashmica had told him, placing a hand on his

shoulder. "He's... somewhere else right now. We just have to wait."

And they had. For twenty minutes, they'd knelt on the grass next to his unresponsive mate and waited for him to come back to himself. Carter had slipped off his shirt and then wrestled his limp body into it when he realized everyone was standing around them watching and his mate wouldn't appreciate being so exposed to them all.

When the whimpering started, Carter had nearly gone out of his mind, lifting Damien's body and cradling it against him as he rocked him, trying to offer him whatever comfort he could.

But the screaming... that had been the worst. Long, anguished cries that sent goose bumps down his spine. Something was very, very wrong.

He'd thought it was over when Damien finally seemed to wake up from whatever hell he'd been stuck in, the scent of relief nearly overwhelming him from so many people at once. But the hoarse cries of pain and rage continued not long afterward—as well as a wave of magic that had knocked everyone but Carter on their asses.

When his poor mate finally quieted, snuffling and clinging to Carter, he'd gathered him up and stood, looking to his alpha, who sat nearby with his mate resting against his shoulder.

Nodding, Rick stood and helped Kai up, then silently led the way back to the manor.

He heard Tashmica whisper a few orders to the coven, thanking them for their help, then followed them. Carter didn't bother looking back to confirm, his nose letting him know Keegan and Jess were trailing after as well. He hoped his mate's sister would be a comfort once he caught his breath and calmed a bit more.

As they traipsed into the manor through the back door

near the kitchen, Carter hesitated. Neither he nor Damien had eaten anything before the Cleansing Spell, and while he knew he was hungry, he wasn't sure about his little mate.

Seeing where he was looking, Kai peeled off and headed toward the sounds of the busy kitchen, sending Carter a soft smile.

When they reached the library, Carter stopped just inside. The rest of the pack's Enforcers and some of the betas were in there waiting, looking at him and Damien expectantly as soon as they spotted the two of them. The last thing Damien needed was to deal with so many people after what was obviously a very traumatic experience.

He started to back out of the room, thinking of nothing but protecting his mate, but Rick spoke up first. "No, you stay. The rest of you... we need the room. Gabriel and Bennett, stay."

No one questioned the alpha, simply standing and heading for the door. A few sent him and Damien sympathetic looks as they passed. Ericka was the only one who paused before leaving, asking softly, "Do either of you need anything?"

He started to shake his head, then thought better of it as he felt Damien tremble almost imperceptibly. "Could you grab us a blanket, please?"

She nodded and was off like a shot.

Walking into the room, he looked at Rick. "She was an excellent choice as Enforcer."

The alpha's lips tipped up in agreement as he dipped his head in acknowledgment from where he'd taken his usual seat. "Agreed. Few care as much about taking care of the pack as she does."

Carter chose a large chair near the middle of the seating area, knowing everyone would want to hear what Damien had to say and hoping his mate would be up to talking. He'd only just settled with Damien still tucked up against him, bare feet wedged between one of his thighs and the arm of the chair, when Ericka returned and helped him spread the thick, buffalo-plaid blanket over him.

"Thank you," Damien murmured hoarsely, sounding exhausted.

"You're welcome," she said, just barely touching Damien's still-damp hair before turning and heading out.

The door had barely closed behind her when Damien let out a breath and tried to sit up, but Carter held him in place. "Just relax a few minutes, baby boy. Kai's bringing up some water and food for you. You need to recover before doing anything else."

Damien peered up at him, dark smudges under his hazel eyes, but when Carter just stared back, he sighed and eased back down against Carter. "Okay," he croaked.

There was a tenseness in the room, but Carter was grateful no one tried to rush them or talk about what had happened. He felt like he was still trying to catch his own breath; he couldn't imagine how his mate was feeling. He smelled of sorrow and anger, but there was a hint of determination underneath that was troubling Carter.

Jess scooted a chair over so it was right next to Carter's and settled on the edge, worried eyes on Damien.

In less than ten minutes, Kai was bustling into the room with a tray of glasses, a water pitcher, and a coffee carafe, and one of the young women who helped in the kitchen was right behind him with one loaded with food. "I thought everyone could use some comfort food."

Large cinnamon rolls covered in thick icing were passed around, and the carafe and pitcher were set on the table. Kai came over with an already steaming mug and held it out, the scent of herbal tea strong.

"I put honey in it for your throat," he said gently, looking down at where Damien was nestled as close as he could get to Carter.

Slowly, like maybe his whole body hurt, Damien shifted around until he could accept the mug. "Thank you, alpha-mate."

Kai smiled sweetly, scented the side of Damien's neck, then walked over and climbed into Rick's lap. Carter wondered if anyone but him noticed he hadn't even looked at Jess—well, he knew she had. The pungent scent of hurt spiked for a moment, followed quickly by guilt.

Damien sipped his tea slowly but steadily. As soon as he finished, Carter took the empty mug and set it aside, then glanced at Jess. "Can you grab him a water and roll, please?"

She was nodding and jumping up before he even finished, Damien protesting the cinnamon roll weakly, but they both ignored him. Carter took the small plate, his own stomach growling at the heavenly scent, but he ignored his hunger, tearing off a piece and holding it to Damien's lips.

"Try and eat a little," he murmured, nuzzling into his mate's hair. He smelled a little like pond water, but his honey sweetness was still there, soothing Carter's agitated bear. "The sugar might help."

Damien grumbled, but the look on his face when he turned his head was full of adoration, stealing the breath from Carter's lungs. When he parted his full pink lips and accepted the gooey treat from Carter's fingers, his bear rumbled in happiness at providing for their mate, lust hitting him low in his gut.

Mesmerized, he tore off another piece and slowly fed his mate, who made no effort to take over, perfectly happy to let Carter care for him in this way. When he licked at a spot of icing and Carter growled lowly, someone chuckled, drawing his attention to the rest of the room.

Gabriel was shaking his head, grin on his face. "Damn,

you forget how single-minded a shifter can be when their unbonded mate is in the room."

Carter ignored the heat in his cheeks, refocusing on Damien. His mate was also blushing, but the small, pleased smile on his lips eased Carter's own embarrassment.

"Oh, please," Kai scoffed, waving a hand at the former hunter. "I seem to remember a certain blond *human* lurking in the hallways downstairs while his mates tried to do their jobs."

Gabriel grinned unashamedly. "Guilty."

"Yeah, I feel like I mooned over Nico way more than he did me," Keegan said with a snicker. "I had to actively stop myself from following him around when I moved here."

Carter rolled his eyes at the others, setting aside the rest of the cinnamon roll when Damien shook his head at another piece. He'd eaten half, so he wouldn't push for more. He picked up the remainder and ate it in a few quick bites, saying around his full mouth, "Pretty sure Nico did all his mooning before you got here."

A very faint *"Hey!"* made it to Carter's ears, he and the other shifters laughing at Nico's affronted tone. The other Enforcers must have only moved down the hallway—the soundproofing between the second and third floor was too good for them to have gone downstairs.

Rick was smiling softly, hand running up and down Kai's back and eyes at half-mast. He looked… content. Even with the upcoming battle they were facing, Carter could tell that his alpha was ready—maybe even a bit *eager*—to get the fighting over with. He knew Rick and some of the others had been meeting and talking about what would happen *after*.

After Rick succeeded in toppling the Council.

Alpha Okenapowet had even been brought into the discussions. She and her new second-in-command had apparently been wary of creating a power vacuum but were on board with helping to shepherd in a new governing body.

Once they got rid of the old one.

Carter wasn't surprised by that news though. She and her pack had been forced to seek refuge on Kincaid Pack land after they'd been attacked simply for agreeing to come to their aid in the event of an attack. They hadn't been the only pack either, but the others had withdrawn their support and begun rebuilding instead of coming to Rick for help.

He also knew—thanks to his new Enforcer status—that Drake was reaching out to the pack's closest allies. As the pack's former emissary, he had a lot of connections in other packs and knew who they could most likely trust with the truth about Garcia's and Voight's deaths, Rick's dad's plan and collusion with the O'Hares, and the ultimate goal of making sure not just the Kincaid Pack was safe but every pack, coven, and nomad was.

It was an insane plan, but Carter knew if anyone could pull together the forces they'd need and *actually* succeed, it was Rick Kincaid.

The mood sobered as Rick sighed and turned to Damien. "We noticed while you were... absent that the mark of your Blood Oath was still there, but it's very faint now."

Damien stiffened, then jerked the blanket out of the way, tearing at the collar of Carter's shirt to see his chest for himself. The ruin was just barely visible now; if you didn't know what to look for, you could maybe even miss it entirely.

"Dammit," Damien said, voice thick.

"I'd say all that's left is the base layer of the spell," Tashmica said carefully, uncrossing and recrossing her legs. "Do you know what that was?"

Teeth grinding together, Damien nodded. "I think it's the

same thing they always use for the base of the spell—the connection of life forces."

Keegan cursed, and Carter's heart rate picked up speed. "Is that the thing that…?"

Tashmica nodded as Damien looked up at him, eyes sad but resigned. "It means she can still kill me from anywhere at any time."

He'd been hoping Tash was wrong and felt so fucking foolish for having not even considered the possibility. He'd known—thanks to how Kai's dad and stepmom had died— that if the bearer of the Blood Oath *broke* the rules laid down in the spell, it could kill them. How had he not realized that Amelia O'Hare would *of course* have a failsafe built in so she could take out anyone she deemed a loose end?

Nearly panting, Carter held Damien even tighter. "What do we do? Can we do the Cleansing Ritual again?"

Damien reached up and ran his fingers gently over Carter's forehead, using his thumb to rub at the furrow between his brows, but it was Tash who answered. "No. The spell worked as well as it could. If we try and increase the power of it, we'd probably kill him."

Not the answer Carter wanted to hear. Staring into his mate's face, he whispered, "How have you lived for two years under the threat of her killing you at any moment? I think I would have gone insane…"

Damien took in a deep, shuddery breath. "I was really worried at the beginning, but the longer it went on without her doing it, the less I focused on it. There were too many other layers in the spell keeping me in line, I think, for her to ever worry about needing to silence me. And as long as I was potentially useful…" He shrugged, wincing. "She was motivated to keep me alive, exactly where I was."

"Spying on my pack," Rick said, voice hard.

Damien turned and faced the others, hands fisting in the blanket pooled in his lap. "Yes, sir."

"Tell us what happened," Rick instructed. "How did you end up here?"

When he hesitated, Carter covered one of his hands with one of his own, linking their fingers together. Nosing behind his ear, Carter murmured, "It's okay. Nothing will change. I promise."

Damien took one more deep breath and then said, "Two years ago, I cast a spell to find my birth mother. I... I didn't know my dad was hiding her identity to keep me safe. He was gone on a job, and we'd fought—" Damien's voice cracked, and he turned his face to the side. His scent soured with guilt and shame. "We fought right before he left."

"About your mom?" Rick clarified.

Damien nodded. "That and... about me leaving to find my mate. He kept telling me it wasn't safe to travel on my own, but I was twenty-three. I thought..." He laughed humorlessly. "I thought I was strong enough to handle anything that could happen on the way, and then once I found him... I'd be safe with him and his pack."

Carter's arms tightened.

"He told me we'd talk about it when he got home, but he always said that. So I waited until I was sure he was really gone, and then I cast a spell to find her. I figured I could stop and meet her on my way here," he said with disdain, shaking his head.

"You knew your mate was here?" Bennett asked curiously, speaking for the first time.

Damien nodded. "I'd been regularly scrying for him ever since I'd used a spell to find out I had a mate out there when I was sixteen. I knew he'd moved here, and I knew from my dad that this was Garrick Kincaid's territory. A strong alpha with a subpar coven." He shot Tashmica a small smile. "Obviously, that was because of your predecessor, not you."

Her own grin was wry. "It sure has helped to have you and Keegan join and to get Jess unshackled, but thanks."

"What happened when you cast the spell?" Jess asked softly, a touch of pink staining her cheeks at Tash's words.

Damien raised his eyebrows at her. "I'm sure you can guess. The map I was using started to lead me to her, but then it caught fire. Burned the entire thing and scorched the table underneath before I could get it to go out."

She nodded, looking unsurprised. "She and the others use magic to mask them from most locator spells."

"I thought it was weird—that I'd somehow messed up the spell." Damien audibly swallowed, eyes losing focus as he got lost in his memories. "It took her less than a day to show up with a half dozen coven members. I... I didn't know what was happening. One minute, I was packing my bags, trying to figure out what to write in the note I was going to leave my dad so he wouldn't be so mad at me, and the next..."

When he hesitated, scent spiking with remembered fear, Carter shifted him so he was perched on one thigh and his legs fully draped over the other, urging Damien to lean into him and take whatever comfort he needed. His mate's face burrowed into his neck for a moment, his breaths faster than they should have been and cheeks damp. No one spoke, even though the tension in the room was palpable.

After a few moments, Damien turned his head just enough that his voice wouldn't be muffled but kept himself plastered as closely to Carter as humanly possible. "They blasted through the warding we had around the house so forcefully it took out a chunk of the garage. It shook the whole place. There was so much smoke and heat, and I was terrified, but I tried... I tried to fight back. When they came into my bedroom, I was waiting and hit them with every-thing I had."

"You were so brave, baby boy," Carter murmured, rubbing his nose in Damien's drying hair.

Damien scoffed, his voice thick with recrimination as he said, "I really wasn't. I was stupid. I'd been so sheltered, even in my travels with my dad. I knew I was powerful, but I'd never... I'd never gone up against an opponent like that. Never had to fight for my life." His voice broke on the last word as he shuddered against Carter. "I stunned the first two, but the rest just kept coming, and they overwhelmed me easily. One of them could... He can stiffen your muscles to the point of excruciating pain, making it impossible to move or fight back. To barely breathe."

"Peter," Jess said softly, a world of pain and terror in that one word.

Damien jerked around to face her, reaching out like he could scent her distress as easily as a shifter. Hands clasped tightly together, they stared at each other in solidarity for a long moment before Damien relaxed back against Carter and continued without releasing his hold on his sister.

"I blacked out, and when I woke up, I was in a basement, chained to a wall."

Carter's bear roared inside him, but he managed to hold him back, only letting out a low, menacing growl. "She chained you to a *wall*?"

Damien shrugged, tipping his head back onto Carter's shoulder to see his face. "Apparently, I was deemed a threat. Though how they expected anyone to not react like I did when they came for me is anyone's guess. It was a while before she finally came down, leaving others to bring me food and water for several days. I don't know if she was honestly too busy doing other things to visit the prisoner in the basement or if it was—"

"A dominance display," Rick said, just as Jess offered with a fierce scowl, "A power play."

Damien nodded at them both. "My thoughts too. When she finally came down, I was weak from the spellwork in the chains and etched into the walls and just... so scared. No one would tell me what I was doing there or where I was. I still hadn't put it together that I... I was the one who'd caused all of it to happen."

"You had no way of knowing how awful she'd be," Carter insisted, slipping a hand beneath his shirt and rubbing his fingers against a soft spot low on Damien's belly.

"I should have realized there was a reason my dad hid her from me." Damien shook his head at himself, even as his body relaxed a fraction at the gentle caresses, responding to Carter's touch and his own instincts. "I was so foolish."

"Everyone is foolish at that age," Rick said unexpectedly, drawing his and Damien's attention across the sitting area to where he was holding a wet-eyed Kai. "Those who aren't... there's a reason for that. They had to learn lessons younger and harder than they should have."

Kai turned his face into Rick's shoulder, shuddering but making no move to leave the room. Hearing about an abusive-as-shit parent had to be hard for him. Carter glanced over and saw Keegan's bunched jaw and fisted hands. Jess's glassy eyes.

Goddess, so many of them had been robbed of a loving, supportive family, instead gifted with trauma and heartache.

Sucking in a deep breath, Damien let it out slowly. "She stared at me like I was a fascinating bug or something, not saying anything even as I-I begged to be let go so I could go home. That's when she finally said something: You are home, son."

CHAPTER TWENTY-ONE

It was so much harder to share what had brought him to that moment in Rick's library than he ever could have thought. He knew why though. He hadn't let himself—in the entire two years—consider the possibility of what he'd do if he couldn't save his dad. That he wouldn't even have the chance to try.

It made the sharp edge of guilt and despair he'd been fending off for years cut through him like a hot knife, leaving him bleeding and dying.

If he hadn't had Carter's strong arms around him, his solid torso pressed against his back in solidarity, he never would have been able to get through sharing his deepest secrets and shame.

Clearing his throat, he gripped Jess's hand tighter, taking strength from her unwavering presence as well. "I didn't want to believe her at first, but then she showed me a picture of her and my dad, a baby in her arms. She gave me a sob story about how my dad had stolen me from her and she'd been searching for me ever since. It was… compelling, even though it was unbelievable. She has this way of making you want to trust her, even when you know you shouldn't. But despite the fact that I'd gone behind my dad's back to try and find her, I knew he wasn't the monster she was trying to paint him as."

"Didn't help that she'd kept you chained in a fucking basement for days," Keegan snarled.

"It did not." Damien could remember those days like they'd happened a week ago and not over two years. How cold and damp the space had been. The sounds of *things* scurrying just out of sight. The creeping knowledge that he'd die in that terrible place. "Every day for weeks, she came down into that basement and tried to convince me that I should be thankful to her for saving me. That I owed her my loyalty."

"One of her active powers is projection," Jess interrupted, voice wavery. "It doesn't work well on other witches, but if they're weak enough or made weak by injury or other magic, she can sometimes use it on them."

"Projection?" Kai said, not bothering to un-burrow from Rick's chest.

"Sort of like mind control," Keegan explained with distaste. "You can *project* a thought or feeling into another and make them think it's their own. It's extremely rare, and a lot of covens have bans in place to prevent a member from joining with the ability."

"Nasty shit," Gabriel added. "I've known covens to put down witches with the ability to protect themselves, their packs, and the humans of their community."

Damien shuddered at his casual words. *Put down.* Like that was the only reasonable way to handle a witch with the ability. Or like a deadly, out-of-control witch would be as easy to kill as a rabies-infected dog.

"So that's why she kept you so long in the basement. She was trying to weaken your magic enough to implant the idea that you owed her your life and loyalty." Rick shook his head. "Damn, she's a real piece of work."

"One way of putting it," Jess muttered.

"When it didn't work, she took some of my blood and then left me alone again for a few days," Damien said carefully, trying to keep his words even. "Then one night, I woke up to the door crashing open and a body getting thrown down the stairs. It-it was my dad. He was bleeding and unconscious."

For the first time in weeks, Damien had finally felt something other than fear as he'd stared down at his dad's unmoving body for hours, watching and counting each labored breath. Right when he'd started to wake, his mom and a couple of others came down and tied his dad up, cruel hands pushing and pulling at his broken body until he was on his knees five feet from Damien.

So close and yet still out of reach.

He'd watched, horrified, as she'd gripped his dad's hair and forced his head up so Damien could see the damage. His pain-filled face and bitten-off groan were all Damien could see or hear for a long moment as his anger and frustration at his inability to stop them built inside him and whited out his vision.

Está bien, his dad had said, over and over, split lip bleeding and one eye swollen shut. *Está bien, mi vida.*

Except nothing would ever be okay again.

"Damien?"

He jolted, coming back to the library's warmth and safety at Carter's soft voice in his ear. "Sorry. I…" He cleared his throat and blinked the sting from his eyes. "Sorry. Um, where was I?"

"She brought your dad," Jess said, squeezing his numb fingers.

"Right." He tried to sit up a little, a restless energy hitting him and making him want to run away rather than talk any more about what had happened, but Carter's arms didn't relent. He rubbed his cheek against Damien's, soothing him. "Um. She told me that she'd tested my blood, and now that she knew what I was capable of, she had a job for me, and if I did it well, she'd let us go. I... I told her to go to hell."

Jess's grip on his hand became painful even as someone chuckled and said, "Good for you."

It had been the furthest thing from good for him.

"She hurt him," he whispered brokenly, letting his eyes fall shut so he couldn't see their faces. He focused as hard as he could on Carter's heat and strength behind him and Jess's hold on his hand, knowing they wouldn't last once he told them everything. "I wanted it to stop, pleaded for her to leave him alone, but I didn't want to agree. I was scared of what someone like her could need from me, afraid of what she'd make me do. But I... I couldn't stand it." He swallowed the bile trying to rise up the back of his throat as the echo of his dad's hoarse screams rang through him, the scent of his burnt flesh filling his nose. "I told her I'd do whatever she wanted."

"And she wanted you to come here."

Damien opened his eyes at the words, meeting Rick's unyielding gaze. "Yes, but not at first. First, she had me do a few other tasks for her. I-I think she wanted to test my abilities and see how far she could push me with my dad's life under threat."

"What did she have you do?" Carter asked, dread lacing the words.

Damien's whole body tensed, and he turned his face away from the others as he whispered, "Use my projection power on the alpha of the pack they reside with and... several witches who were considered enemies of the coven."

Carter stiffened behind him, freezing in place, as Jess

jerked her hand out of his and stood so fast she stumbled. "What the hell are you talking about?"

He flinched at her harsh tone, wrapping his arms around his middle and curling over. "I'm sorry. I never wanted to use it on anyone. I hated that I could mess with people's minds like that."

"Wait. You have the power of projection too?" Kai asked, peering over at him.

"Have you used it on anyone in this pack?" Rick spoke over his mate, his voice deadly calm.

Damien nodded as tears slid down his face. "A couple of times wh-when I had to. I'm so sorry."

Carter's arms loosened around him, and Damien thought he really would be sick. Taking the hint, he slid off his mate's lap and stumbled across the room, bracing his hands on a bookshelf. He'd known they wouldn't understand, couldn't forgive, such a violation. His knuckles turned white as he squeezed the edge of the shelf as tightly as he could and bit his lip until it bled, trying to stop himself from fleeing the room. The manor.

The pack.

Why should he stay? They'd never see him the same way again, never trust him, and it wasn't like his dad's safety hung in the balance anymore.

The reminder was like a knee to the gut, nearly dropping him to the floor before he caught himself. No, he'd stay and help them fight against his mom if they'd let him, and then, if he was still alive, he'd leave them in peace.

"Did you use it on me?" Carter's soft words right behind him startled him, and Damien spun around, staring up at his looming mate. His teeth were clenched together so tightly a muscle in his strong jaw twitched. He looked like he was barely holding himself together as he waited for Damien to answer.

"What? No! Of course not." Squinting up at Carter in confusion, he said, "Why would she have me project something on you? She doesn't even know about you or who you are to me."

It was Carter's turn to look confused for a second. "So you only used it when she told you to?"

The pain of his mate even asking him that had Damien jerking his head back like he'd been slapped. "Yes. I… My dad taught me how to control it, how it could be used for good, but I never felt comfortable with the power. I've only *ever* used it when I couldn't do what she wanted or get the information she asked for another way. I'd… I'd never use it on you."

"You used it on Agnes when you joined the pack, didn't you?" Tashmica spoke up from where she still sat on the couch, sounding unsurprised at the revelation.

Damien swiped under his eyes as he nodded, looking around Carter at her. "I needed to make sure she let me into the coven. I didn't want to leave even a chance she could turn me away since pack law doesn't allow for witches to be members if they don't belong to the coven."

She nodded like that made perfect sense to her. "Who else?"

He swallowed. "Rick."

A nasty snarl filled the room as the big alpha pushed to his feet, depositing his wide-eyed mate on the chair and then stepping in front of him, putting himself between Kai and Damien. Protecting him. "When?"

"When you started the War Council," Damien whispered, shame coursing through him as he did his best to hold his alpha's eyes. "Y-you told Tashmica to only bring Jess because you didn't need three coven representatives there. I… changed your mind so I could sit in on them."

Rick seethed at him, the tips of his fangs poking out. "And how much of those meetings have you shared with her?"

Before he could answer, Carter was turning and facing Rick, wide body blocking Damien's view and vibrating with tension. "Rick... your aggression is really agitating my bear."

Damien poked his head around Carter's arm, terrified the two would come to blows because Carter's bear hadn't gotten the memo that Carter didn't like him anymore. Rick's eyes glowed brightly for a second, but then he squeezed them shut, taking several deep breaths. Damien was impressed, having figured things would escalate and they'd have to be separated, but then he saw Kai's fingers curled around Rick's wrist.

The sight wasn't even overtly sweet or romantic, but the reminder of how much influence mates could have on each other was just another blow to Damien's already severely damaged heart. He'd foolishly let himself get his hopes up, let himself believe that his and Carter's connection really would be strong enough to withstand the truth of what Damien was. What he was capable of and the acts he'd committed against the pack.

He should have known better.

Carefully, he stepped around Carter and looked at Rick, ignoring the disgruntled look Carter gave him at moving. "I swear to you, I only ever shared with her what I absolutely had to. I know you have no reason to believe me, but that's the truth. Mostly, her interest was in Jess, not you or the rest of the pack since I don't think she actually saw you as a threat. For the first year or so, she barely checked in with me, but after Agnes was killed, she started asking me for more. Wanting to know if anyone had figured out who Jess was, how powerful she was getting. Things like that."

"You told her about me?" Jess asked from the other side of

the room, looking two seconds away from fleeing. Or attacking.

"Only what I had to," Damien said, pleading with his eyes for her to understand. "If she asked a direct question, I had to answer, but I'd be as vague as I could, I swear. I'd never…"

He trailed off when she looked away, mulish expression on her face and hands fisted at her sides. He looked around the room, seeing most people looked vaguely uncomfortable, if not angry like Rick and Bennett. Tashmica was the only one who still seemed unperturbed.

"You said your dad taught you how to use the ability for good," Keegan spoke up, still eyeing Damien warily. "What the hell does that mean?"

Damien shrugged, not sure it really mattered. "He thinks —" He stopped, sucking in a sharp breath and slamming his eyes shut as fresh grief hit him. *Goddess.* Clearing his throat, he said thickly, "He *thought* that I could use it to help people. Ease pain from injuries. Lessen g-grief. Things like that." He looked away from them all, tucking his chin against his chest. It hurt so much to even think about his dad. He wrapped his arms around himself, suddenly very, very tired. "My dad always thought I was a stronger witch and better person than I am though."

There was a heavy silence following his words. One that made the skin on the back of his neck crawl.

"Can you really do those things?" Kai asked curiously.

"Probably." Damien resisted the urge to shrug again, instead tightening his grip on himself. "It's been a long time since he and I trained, and people and emotions are… complex. But yes, I… Yes. I can do those things."

"As well as trick your way into my pack and onto my inner council."

Damien flinched at Rick's words. "That too. Suggesting things people are already open to is easy."

"Your gift could be a game changer," Tashmica said, standing and smoothing her dress over her hips.

"*Gift*," Damien scoffed derisively, tears pricking at his eyes. "It's not a gift, Tash. It's always only been a curse, and now it's..." He shook his head, barely able to get the words out. "Now it's killed my d-dad and cost me—"

He couldn't finish his sentence, but he also couldn't stop himself from casting devastated eyes at his—at Carter. He was frowning, arms crossed over his chest as he looked over at Tash, but like he could feel Damien's eyes, he glanced over and scrunched his brows at him.

Right. He probably didn't want Damien airing their business in front of everyone.

Clearing his throat, Damien forced himself to look away, meeting Rick's hard gaze and refusing to even imagine that the alpha's face had softened. "They'll be here at sundown tomorrow. We need to be ready. I don't know if she's bringing the entire coven, but that's what I'd guess if she promised your dad this pack."

His words hung in the air around them, suffocating them all with the reminder that no matter how they felt about *him*, he wasn't the biggest problem the pack had to deal with.

Sighing, Rick shook out his shoulders, nodding. "We'll talk more about this... ability of yours later. For now, we need to adjust our plans now that we know the O'Hares will be coming for us so soon. How have you been communicating with her? Can you get more information?"

Damien pressed his lips together, then looked at Tash. "Do you think she felt us messing with the Blood Oath?"

She tilted her head and thought about it for a long moment. "Maybe? Though since we weren't able to break the lifeforce bond between you, it's very possible she isn't aware that you aren't still her unwilling puppet."

He looked at Keegan, who nodded his agreement.

Turning back to Rick, Damien said, "If that's true, then I may be able to get more details out of her. There's a journal in my freezer at my apartment that we've used to—"

"Wait."

Damien's teeth clacked together at Carter's sharp voice, jerking toward him to stare at him with wide eyes. Surely he didn't think Damien couldn't be trusted to help fight the woman who murdered his dad?

"What's wrong, Doc?" Kai asked, grabbing one of Rick's hands and threading their fingers together.

Carter didn't look away from Damien, ignoring the alpha-mate's question. His brows were furrowed, creating that groove between them that Damien always wanted to smooth out, but he knew his touch wasn't welcome anymore.

When Carter didn't say anything else for nearly a full minute, Damien glanced around the room before taking half a step closer, relieved when Carter didn't move away. Softly, even though half the room could still easily hear them, he said, "I know you're upset right now, but we need to focus on protecting the pack."

"You said…" Carter closed the distance between them so fast that Damien nearly jumped back at the unexpected move. Then his big, warm hand was gripping the side of Damien's neck, tipping his head up, up, up to meet his softly glowing eyes and exposing his neck. "You started to say it cost you something. Your dad and something else. What else did she take from you?"

"Carter—" someone said, but his low growl shut them up. Damien couldn't tear his eyes away from his bear's to bother to see who it was, and his brain was buzzing with a weird sort of anticipation, making it too hard for him to think to identify them. Maybe Keegan?

It didn't matter. His mate deserved the truth.

"Something just as precious," Damien said, not bothering

to wipe away his tears anymore. Goddess, he'd never cried so much in his entire life as he had the last few days. Hell, the last couple of weeks.

"What?"

"You. Your trust. I tried to warn you that I—"

His words were cut off with a violent kiss, a kiss meant to silence him and possess him all at once. To take everything Damien had to offer and then hold those jagged pieces fiercely, protecting him from the world.

Whimpering, Damien sagged against Carter as soon as he got over the shock of having his lips on him again, unwrapping his arms to grip at Carter's furry chest as tightly as he could, unwilling to let him go even if the whole pack tried to drag him away. He wasn't sure why he was getting another chance at tasting and holding his mate, but he wouldn't question it.

He was too selfish. He'd take what Carter was offering and hope he never realized how much better he could have done than a traitorous witch with a terrifying power.

Carter growled against his lips, prodding at the seam of his mouth. Damien opened to him with a sigh, willing to give his mate anything, everything. When his tongue swiped inside, Damien hummed and pushed up onto his toes, wanting to get closer, wanting more.

The hand on his neck shifted forward until his rough palm pressed against the front of Damien's throat, fingers on one side and thumb on the other.

The possessive, controlling hold sent goose bumps cascading down his limbs as he fell back onto his heels, easily submitting to that guiding hand instead of pushing for more.

"Jesus." The soft curse somehow cut through the drugging effect of Carter's mouth and hands, jolting Damien back into his body and the awkwardly quiet library.

He tried to pull back, heat suffusing his cheeks, but

Carter's hand tightened just a fraction, just enough to let Damien know he didn't want him to go anywhere. His other hand smoothed down Damien's back, chasing the shivers racing down his spine, then palmed Damien's ass in a blatant display of possession.

As if the way they'd just been kissing and the hold on Damien's throat weren't clear enough.

Carter's lips slid over his several more times, making Damien's toes curl, and then he finally pulled back just enough to say, "You can never lose me, mate. My love will never come with conditions. I'm sorry I asked if you used your magic on me; I was so shocked that I wasn't thinking straight. I know you'd never do that."

He brushed his mouth against Damien's slack one. Had he just said...? "You love me?"

"Mhm." Carter nibbled on Damien's bottom lip, completely unconcerned with the fact that he'd just declared his love in front of everyone or that Damien was so surprised it felt like his heart was going to pound out of his chest. "How could I not love someone so sweet and perfect?"

Damien flinched, trying to turn his face away, but Carter adjusted his grip up to his jaw and held him in place. "Carter... I'm the furthest thing from perfect. Haven't you been listening?"

"Haven't you?" Carter growled back at him. "You aren't responsible for the things Amelia O'Hare made you do, baby boy."

"Maybe. But I—"

"And doing what you had to do to protect yourself and your dad doesn't make you a bad person."

"Okay, but—"

"And wanting to meet a biological parent is so fucking normal. You had no way of knowing what kind of person she'd turn out to be."

Eyes stinging, Damien swallowed. "But no one here will be able to trust me again."

"Then we'll go somewhere else." He said it like it was obvious. Like it was no big deal.

Like he wasn't willing to give up his whole life for Damien.

"The hell you will," Rick snarled, standing a foot away from them and glaring at Carter in a way that had Damien's magic surging to the surface despite the fact that he knew Rick would never actually hurt him. "Everyone will get over it once Damien here *earns* their trust back, right?"

"He can't be held responsible for things he did under duress and threat of violence," Carter snarled.

Damien's eyes widened. Goddess, maybe the two would come to blows after all.

"No, Rick's right. I came here under false pretenses and lied for years. The reason why doesn't make it magically better," Damien said quickly, placing a calming hand between Carter's thick pecs. "If the pack is willing to give me another chance, I'll use it to show they weren't wrong to place their trust in me before."

"Excellent." Tashmica clapped lightly and sat back down. "Why don't we come up with a plan to beat these assholes and remake the parahuman world then, hm?"

CHAPTER TWENTY-TWO

Carter had never been so amped up and exhausted at the same time.

He'd never been a big fighter, more interested in using his brains to heal than his bulk to maim, but there wasn't a question in his mind that if he got the chance to gut Damien's mom, he'd do it. And not feel a single ounce of regret.

He had a feeling there would be a line of people behind him wanting the honor too.

Despite how his delusional little mate seemed to see himself, Carter knew that once the rest of the pack knew the truth of what happened to Damien—and his dad, *fuck*—and had a chance to catch their breath after everything was over, they'd remember why they'd opened their arms and hearts to him in the first place.

And if they didn't... well, Carter hadn't been bluffing when he'd said they'd leave.

As he pulled his truck into an empty spot in front of *Wicca We Can*, he frowned at the number of Closed signs on businesses up and down Main Street. As disconcerting as the sight was, he hoped that meant Chief Baskin and the mayor were following through on their promise to evacuate as many humans from the town as possible.

Even though Kincaid Pack territory expanded far beyond the city limits, the town of Meyerville was the hub of the pack. Which made it—and the innocent people living in and around it—easy targets. Carter had heard the police chief and mayor were going to tell people there was a massive gas leak or something to get folks out of town for a week or so, but there was no guarantee everyone would leave.

Carter and the rest of the Enforcers had spent all afternoon going through the list of pack members who could potentially fight and those that would need to be protected. Cubs and those too old had automatically been added to the second list, obviously, but others who weren't as physically strong or weren't interested in fighting had been too. Nico had started reaching out to them—along with the help of several betas—to let them know where to hunker down during the fighting in the coming days.

Robson Medina had been evaluating pack members ever since he'd joined and had started the two lists based on his combat experience. He—along with Gabriel when the hunter had become an official member—had been working with the eligible fighters, those who already knew how or were willing and able to learn. Many of those Robson had deemed potential fighters had been studying under Gabriel and the other retired hunters at their training facility for months, and Carter had finally gotten out to see it that afternoon. The building was utilitarian but still impressive, creating a massive space for the hunters to keep up with their own training, as well as teach the stronger but less skilled shifters.

Carter had even gotten the chance to go a few rounds with Drake, his friend goading him into it by claiming that even with Carter's increased strength—which he hadn't had time to really test out, but holy *shit* was the power boost unreal—he'd still beat his ass with one arm.

Which he had, but Carter had held his own pretty damn well, he thought. In his family's pack growing up, he'd been trained in fighting before he'd left for med school, choosing a life of science instead of violence.

Pushing open the door to the shop, he was surprised that the front was empty. He'd expected it to be full of coven members preparing for the upcoming fight like they had for Damien's cleansing spell. Maybe they were done? He glanced around, noticing the empty spots on some of the tables and shelves, like items had been taken that were usually there.

He was halfway across the room, intent on collecting his mate and going home to slowly take him apart and taste every inch of his silken olive skin, when the voices in the back penetrated his crowded head.

"—like getting hit with a wall of emotions," Tash was saying, sounding pensive. "I should have realized right at that moment what you were capable of."

"I'm sorry. I know it can be... uncomfortable." Damien's voice was soft and tired and full of regret. "Not that I've ever lost control like that, but my d-dad used to say it felt like I was poking at his brain with a stick when I first started learning to control it."

"It must not feel that way now if you can do it to people like Rick without them noticing."

"No. Once I learned control, it became more like... using a tiny needle. So thin you can't feel it and much more accurate results."

Carter knew it was ridiculous, considering how he'd initially reacted to the revelation of Damien's ability, but he couldn't help the little surge of pride at his mate's words. Considering it sounded like he rarely ever used the power, it was impressive that he still had such control.

And it was… oddly sexy.

Carter may have been physically bigger and stronger, but he would have put money on his tiny mate kicking his ass if need be. He was incredibly powerful, and Carter sometimes got the feeling that Damien was always holding back.

What would it be like for him to really let go?

Shivering, he paused at the beads when Tashmica said, "I'm sorry Jess took off again. She'll come around."

"I broke her trust. Again. She has every right to be upset."

"No offense to either of you, but if she hadn't considered the fact that you having been sent here to keep an eye on her might mean you'd have to actually report back to your mom about what she's doing, then she isn't as smart as I thought she was."

Carter snorted as he pushed through the beaded curtain, drawing both witches' attention. "That wasn't very nice, but I was thinking the same thing."

Damien was frowning and fussing with a hex bag in his hands, not seeming willing to let himself off the hook. He and Tash were standing by the round table in the middle of the room, a large paper map laid out on it and two bloody streaks leading from the middle of Michigan's lower peninsula down to just past the state's southern border.

Carter nodded toward the map. "Alistair and Amelia are in the same place then?"

Tashmica had been confident that with the spell still binding Damien and his mom that they'd be able to track her without the whole shop going up in flames. Wanting to keep track of Rick's dad, he knew the witches had brought back some of the alpha's blood to use to find him too.

Tash and Damien glanced at the map before Damien nodded, and Tash said, "Yes. There's no telling how many are with them, but he must plan on joining the fight. Maybe to make sure the O'Hares keep their promise of delivering the pack to him."

Sounded about right. Alistair was the kind of person who never kept his word, so he no doubt couldn't imagine anyone else doing it either. Considering what he'd already done in the name of becoming alpha of a pack again, there was no telling what else he was capable of to get what he wanted.

"How'd prepping go?" Carter jerked his thumb toward the front of the shop. "I was surprised the others were already gone."

She smiled at him like he wasn't very bright. "We got a lot done, but everyone was drained from the cleansing this morning and needed rest. At this point, we have no reason to believe the O'Hares won't give Damien the whole five days, so we have tomorrow to get ready too." She glanced at where Damien was still fiddling with the cloth bag in his hands, not looking at either of them, and her smile gentled. "In fact, why don't you two head home. I'm going to clean up a few things and then go get some sleep. We can meet back here tomorrow morning, okay?"

She aimed the last part at Damien, who nodded and finally set the hex bag on the table before immediately picking it up again and walking over to an overflowing crate of them by the back door. "Sounds good. You sure you don't want help cleaning up?"

Was his mate avoiding being alone with him?

"Let's go home, beautiful," Carter said, keeping his voice low and rumbly like he knew Damien liked and was satisfied when he saw him shiver.

"I'm good, but thank you, sweetie," Tash added, shooting Carter a wink.

He was going to bring that woman the largest cup of coffee *Magic Beans* made in the morn—oh *shit*. The coffee shop was owned by a non-pack human. People were going to be so mad when they couldn't get their caffeine fixes, assuming the owner had followed orders to leave town.

When Damien grabbed a leather-bound notebook from a side table before heading toward him, Carter did his best not to curl his lip. He knew his mate needed to keep the journal with him in case his mom contacted him or gave him more instructions, but he hated that thing. During the meeting at the manor, Damien had shared a bit about how it worked— and what had happened to him when he'd tried to write a lie once.

They quietly left the shop, Carter going around to the passenger side to open the door for his mate. He smiled to himself as he watched him awkwardly climb into the tall truck, making a mental note to add a step bar for Damien as he closed the door and circled around the front to his side. He couldn't help but get excited at the idea. He knew the next few days would be stressful as hell, and there was every possibility that not everyone in the pack would survive the encounter with the O'Hares.

But in his gut, he knew that he and Damien would be okay. That they'd have the rest of their lives to add steps to his truck. He had to believe that. And that meant after everything was said and done, he and his mate would have all the time in the world to love each other and to be happy.

And to put up with his brothers' ridiculousness.

As he backed out of his parking spot, he tried not to frown at the fact that Damien hadn't actually said the words back to him when Carter had confessed his love back in the library. He knew his mate felt the same way. He could feel it in his bones, see it in the way he looked at Carter, taste it when he sighed into their kisses, and scent it in his honey sweetness as it intensified anytime Carter was less than three feet away from him.

He glanced over at Damien and felt his heart ache for

him, knowing he would wait as long as it took to hear the words back.

His poor mate had been through the wringer, not just from the cleansing ritual but finding out about his dad and sharing about his projection power and then spending hours and hours helping Rick and the rest of the War Council come up with a plan before heading to the shop to prepare with the rest of the coven. Damien had to be exhausted and grief-stricken, as well as still scared of what could happen during the confrontation with his mom.

It would be a lot for anyone.

As he pulled into his driveway, he put the truck in park and turned it off but reached over and grabbed Damien's hand before he could open his door to jump down. Damien looked at him, brows furrowed in question but his eyes bleak and exhausted.

"Tell me how you're feeling," he said, threading their fingers together and using his other hand to cup Damien's cheek. His skin was so soft it was distracting, but Carter forced himself to focus.

Damien sucked in a shaky breath as tears welled in his eyes, but he blinked them away. "I want to say I'm okay, but we both know that would be a lie. I don't even know if I'll ever be okay again. It's still really hard for me—" He stopped and swallowed thickly, giving his head a small shake. "It's still really hard for me to accept that he's gone and there won't be some... heroic save to get him out of her clutches. I hate her for that, Carter. I *hate* her."

Carter hummed, leaning in to rub his nose against his mate's small pert one. "I know, baby boy. I hate her too. For the way she treated you, for the things she made you do, for what she took from you."

"I'm going to kill her," Damien rasped. It came out as a confession in the dark, enclosed space. He licked his lips and looked up at Carter, nervousness spiking in his scent. "Please don't try and talk me out of this."

Carter tightened his hold on Damien's hand and face, imagining pushing strength into his mate through their connections. "I would never try to talk you out of that, but I am going to ask that you make me a promise."

Damien watched him warily.

"I need you to promise me that you won't sacrifice yourself to take her out. If you can promise me that, then I will stand right by your side as you do it. I will hold you afterward if you need to fall apart." He rubbed his thumb back and forth across Damien's gorgeous, high cheekbone. "If you want, I will even slice her throat if that is what you need from me, but I need to make sure that you plan on coming back to me."

Damien stared at him for a long moment, and Carter could see it, could see that at least a part of Damien didn't want to agree. That his grief over losing his dad—as well as everything else that woman had taken from him—was so strong in that moment he wasn't sure how he would keep going after she was gone.

Carter would need to show his mate there was a lot left to live for.

"Okay," Damien finally whispered. "Alright, mi corazón. I promise to come back to you."

Carter leaned in and rubbed their cheeks together, inhaling his sweet scent and letting it settle his nerves. "Let's go inside, baby."

They walked up to his front door, hand in hand, in silence tinged with sadness and exhaustion. The lights were on inside his house, and he could hear his brothers bickering as they played some video game. He hoped it wouldn't be overwhelming for his mate. Carter almost stopped and offered to take him back to his apartment, but his instincts told him there were too many bad memories in that place for Damien to ever truly relax.

And his bear—and him—*really* wanted Damien in his home, layering his scent over Carter's.

Besides, what his mate needed was to be surrounded by family.

Opening the door, he ushered Damien inside and steered him toward the kitchen when he started toward the stairs. "You need to eat something first. Have you had anything since that half of a cinnamon roll this morning?"

Damien shot him a cute, disgruntled look but didn't deny it. He could hear his brothers in the living room cursing at each other, but he wasn't surprised to find his mom sitting at his breakfast nook in the kitchen, reading on her tablet and already in her pajamas.

As soon as they walked in, she gave them a soft smile and pushed to her feet. He'd shot his family a text earlier, letting them know a little about what had happened to give them a heads-up about Damien's dad and how hard of a day it had been.

His mom didn't say anything, just walked right over to his mate and wrapped him in a strong hug. He half expected Damien to let go of the tight grip he had on himself, collapsing against her and crying in her safe embrace, but if anything, it made him stiffen. He returned the hug, but it was obvious he was holding himself together with great effort, his body looking taut as a guitar string.

His mom seemed to sense it, pulling back and cupping Damien's face gently with both hands and dropping a kiss to his forehead. "I saved some salmon for you two. Let me just reheat everything."

Carter nodded as he nudged his quiet mate toward the table with bench seats his mom had been sitting at. Once he had him seated and he didn't look like he'd bolt as soon as

Carter turned his back, he went and helped his mom to get the food prepared.

He brought a tall glass of water over to Damien with his meal and then gave his mom a look. She smiled back at him, but she still collected her tablet, scented Damien one last time, and then headed for the door. "I'm going to bed, my loves. I'll see you in the morning."

She called a good night to his brothers, who chorused it back, and then it was just the two of them again. Carter didn't try and make conversation. He focused on eating and making sure that his mate did as well. Once they were finished, he rinsed their dishes, stacked them in the dishwasher, and then went and collected his half-asleep mate.

Towing him toward the stairs, he said his own good night to his brothers but didn't wait for their responses. As soon as he had Damien in his room, he didn't waste a moment. He closed the door and efficiently stripped them both. Not with any sort of sexual intent. That wasn't what his mate needed. He needed to be cared for at the most basic level. Shown that no matter what, Carter would always be there to hold him and put him back together.

Damien didn't say anything, just watched him with half-lidded eyes framed by dark circles and a downturn to his lips. Carter pressed a chaste kiss to the corner of his mouth, grateful when it eased the slight frown, and guided him into the connected bathroom. He turned on his shower, relieved he had such a large glass-enclosed stall. He'd had the space redone after he moved in because he always felt too big for regular-sized showers, and that meant that there was plenty of room for him and his mate.

It didn't take long for the water to heat up, and then he was urging Damien into the stall and under the spray, following closely behind. The long, ragged sigh Damien let out as Carter eased up behind him and the water rained down on them let him know he was definitely on the right track.

The quiet intimacy in the enclosed space settled something deeper inside Carter as he gently washed his mate's hair and body, using easy but firm strokes to make sure Damien stayed present in the moment even as he relaxed. They didn't talk, but they didn't have to. The moment felt more profound than that, making words unnecessary. Taking care of Damien, showing him that he still had someone who loved him and wanted to care for him, was more important than trying to find empty words in an attempt to make him feel better. He knew nothing but time would do that.

Damien was practically boneless by the time Carter was finished, so he propped his mate against himself and quickly shampooed and conditioned his own hair, then focused on just washing the important bits of his own body, wanting to get his poor mate horizontal as quickly as possible.

As soon as they were out of the shower and Carter was drying him off, Damien seemed to wake up a bit more, and he watched Carter with a serious look on his face. Like he was thinking hard about something.

After Carter haphazardly dried himself and hung both the towels, he turned back to Damien and nearly slipped on the floor when his mate clearly said, "I love you too."

Tears burned Carter's eyes. Oh good, his mate had gotten the message.

Swallowing, Carter nodded and wrapped his arms around him, giving him a tight hug and wishing he could take some of his sorrow away. Damien's grip on him was almost painful as he felt a few tears hit his chest. *Finally.*

Carter didn't know how long they stood like that before Damien's fingers loosened so his nails weren't digging into

Carter's back anymore and his shoulders stopped shaking with his silent sobs.

"Let's go to bed," he said softly, brushing his lips against Damien's ear.

He nodded and peeled himself off Carter's body, wiping surreptitiously at his cheeks as he headed into the bedroom and straight for the king-sized bed. Carter stopped to turn off the lights and grab their phones before crawling in next to him.

He didn't hesitate to wrap his big body around his mate's smaller one, doing his best to shield him from the outside world. Damien scooted back so they were plastered as close together as humanly possible and wrapped his arms around the one Carter had tucked over his chest.

"I know you need to go to the shop tomorrow," Carter said into the darkness, "but will you do something with me first?"

Damien didn't hesitate. "Anything."

Carter pressed his face into Damien's hair and smiled. He'd only have a couple of hours, but he was going to show his mate a glimpse of what their future could look like once all of the danger and bullshit was said and done.

That way, his mate would be more likely to not break his promise.

CHAPTER TWENTY-THREE

R ick was eavesdropping on his mate, and he wasn't even sorry.

In fact, he was glad that he had seen Jess come into the manor because he had a feeling Kai wouldn't have told him otherwise. So while his mate and the woman who was supposed to be his best friend spoke a few rooms away, Rick lay on the floor on his back with his pups jumping and tumbling on and around him, giggling madly and occasionally chasing after their dog, Loki, who kept trying to get in on the playing, and listened in.

To be fair to Jess, she was saying all of the right things.

"I just freaked out so bad," she was saying, having already apologized profusely—while crying—for ghosting Kai the last couple of weeks. Rick had a feeling his mate had hugged her after that or, at the very least, was offering her comfort, even though he was the one who'd nearly lost his mate when Rick went off to play the big damn hero.

"I get that," Kai said. "It was just really difficult. I was freaking out about Henry, and the one person besides Rick who I felt like I could really depend on suddenly wasn't there. And then when he disappeared…" Kai stopped, his voice thick with emotion. Even from three rooms away, Rick could hear the rise in his heart rate, and he had to squeeze his hands into fists to stop himself from getting up and storming in there to comfort his mate. But Kai had wanted to talk to Jess alone, so he had to respect that. Finally, Kai said softly, "I didn't know if he was coming back, and you were nowhere to be found."

"I know. I'm so sorry," she said again. The long pause after that definitely made him think they were hugging again. Especially when her voice dropped to barely more than a whisper. "I promise I'll never do that again. You're my best friend, and you guys have been so good to me. All I could focus on were my own fears. I couldn't see anything else. I couldn't see the pain you were in. I couldn't see what it must have meant for Damien to have been sent here. All I could focus on was the idea that I would destroy the world with my magic. Like, literally destroy it."

"That's so ridiculous," Kai said fiercely. "You would never do something like that. I don't care who you're the reincarnated spirit of. You're *you*. You're Jessica freaking Macey. Strong and nice and the best friend that I have ever had."

"I know that it sounds dumb," she said, "but in a way… it made sense."

"What do you mean?"

Rick groaned as he nearly took a tiny foot to his groin and missed the first part of what Jess said. He playfully snapped his teeth at Callie as she screeched and ran away. "No, Papa! Don't eat me!"

"—always felt… I don't know. Like, unstable? I guess that's the best way to describe it." Rick frowned, focusing more closely on what she was saying. "I've talked to Tashmica and Keegan about it a little, and the way they describe their magic and how it feels inside them is so different than mine, you know? Like theirs is this… steady, warm presence that sort of moves around as needed, but it's a part of them. It's completely under their control."

"But it's not like that for you?"

"No, and it never has been. I thought it would get better," she said slowly. "Growing up, no one wanted to train me because of who my dad was. I didn't really get any kind of formal teaching the way I should have, and then when I came here, Agnes just… ignored me for the most part."

"Well, and gave you that stupid amulet that messed with your powers," Kai interjected, still sounding mad about it a year later. His sweet, protective mate.

"Right," Jess said. "I thought after I finally started getting the proper training and got rid of the amulet, my magic would settle. That I would feel more… in control. But it hasn't. If anything… it feels bigger every day."

"Bigger?"

"Yeah. Like, now that I'm actually trying to hone my skills and my abilities, it's freed up whatever was holding me back, and it just keeps getting stronger and stronger. So when I heard about that dumb legend…"

"It felt true," Kai finished for her. "Like the magic inside you will keep growing until you lose control."

"*Yes*," she said vehemently. "I'm terrified it'll keep growing until it consumes me and then… goes looking for more."

Rick moved Henry off his chest and pushed to his feet. He'd be the first to admit that he wasn't an expert on magic, but what Jess was describing did sound dangerous. How much had she actually told Tash about what she was experiencing? Did they maybe need to take steps to lock down her abilities? Maybe with another amulet or some kind of spell. He wasn't sure if it was feasible, but he did not like what Jess was sharing. It put his wolf on edge, his instincts screaming at him to get Kai away from her.

He still refused to believe that Jess would—or *could*—ever destroy anything, let alone the entire magical world, but was he really willing to put his family and his pack on the line? Could he really be one hundred percent sure?

Before he could go and find the two of them, Samantha eased through the cracked door of the den, halting him in his steps. She looked at where her siblings had finally sacked out with exhaustion on the floor, cuddling each other with Loki pressed against Callie's side. The TV was playing some kids' movie, but the volume was turned down low so the songs wouldn't drive Rick crazy.

Smiling at them, Samantha shut the door and leaned back against it. When she turned her attention to him, she crossed her arms over her midsection and nibbled on her bottom lip, her long hair falling forward to hide part of her face.

He took in the fragile way she was holding herself and took a step closer. "What's wrong?"

She studied him for a long moment, and even though she'd cut her hair a couple of months ago, it still passed her shoulders and was her favorite way to hide when she was feeling nervous or vulnerable. He could feel the intensity of her gaze through the thick brown curtain.

Slowly, he closed some of the distance between them, his wolf growling in agitation. "Samantha, what is it? You can tell me."

She sucked in a ragged breath and then blurted out, "I didn't know if you were coming back."

The vulnerable ache in her voice hit him in the chest like a sledgehammer. Fucking hell, how could he have been so thoughtless? In the moment, all he'd been able to think about was saving Henry from that damn prophesy and his mate from driving himself crazy.

But thanks to his shortsightedness, he'd hurt so many people he cared about. While things were going better between him and Kai, he obviously still had a long way to go to repair the damage he'd inflicted on the rest of his family.

"Come here," he said gently, holding his arms open.

Thankfully, she didn't hesitate, letting him know he hadn't completely broken her trust. She dove into him, hitting his chest nearly at a run, and wrapped her arms around him so tightly it hurt and nearly cut off his breath. But it was a good kind of ache, deep in his bones. The kind that reminded him he was alive and his family needed him.

"I'm sorry," he murmured into her soft hair. "I was so thoughtless, but I'll never do anything like that again. I want you to know though—what kept me alive when that poison was doing its best to kill me was knowing my family needed me."

She sucked in a sharp breath and pressed her face harder into his neck. "We do need you," she said, her voice muffled. "I thought Kai was going to lose his mind, and I didn't know what to do to make it better."

"It's not your job to worry about that." He rubbed a hand up and down her slender but strong back, giving her one more squeeze before separating them. Keeping his hands on her shoulders, he studied her wet, tired face. "I love you, kiddo, and it's your brother's and my job to worry about things like that."

Her eyes darted away, landing on the pups on the other side of the room. "I love you too. I know our relationship is different than what you have with Henry and Callie... but no one except Kai had ever been there for me before you. I don't... I can't lose that. Not on top of everything else."

"You'll never lose me." He cupped the side of her neck and scented her, trying to ease her agitation. "What else is on your mind? The prophecy about Henry?"

She shrugged. "Yes, but also..."

"But also what?"

283

She looked toward the door and then back at him, lowering her voice. "It's just that... I got something really wrong somehow."

He wasn't sure what that meant, but he sure as shit didn't like how heartbroken she looked and sounded. Her usual soft, floral scent was souring with it. "What's that?"

"I thought someone was my mate," she said slowly, not meeting his eyes. "But then they did something I'm not sure I could ever forgive, so that must mean they aren't, right?"

Understanding dawned on him, but he tried to keep his face neutral, even as his ears perked up to try and catch anything Jess and Kai were saying. "Being—and having—a mate doesn't make either one of you perfect. You can make mistakes just like any other person in a relationship."

She didn't look like she believed him, but Rick reminded himself that she and Jess were still quite young. Hopefully, one day, Samantha would be able to understand and forgive Jess for the mistakes that she'd made. He knew that family was the most important thing to Samantha, so the fact that Jess had abandoned Kai in his hour of need was no doubt something she truly felt like she couldn't ever forgive.

He gently tucked her hair behind her ears and then chucked her beneath her chin. "Besides, you're way too young for a mate."

Just as he'd hoped, she rolled her eyes at him, some of the tension leaving her. "Okay, *Dad*."

He knew she was only saying it teasingly, but it still warmed his heart. They hugged one more time, and then she collected her younger siblings to take upstairs. Despite their protests, she loudly declared they were both rank and in need of a bath. As she carried Henry past, Callie trailing slowly behind, he promised that he and Kai would be up soon to help put them to bed.

It wasn't long after she and the pups disappeared that he

heard Jess and Kai heading toward him. The soft smile on his mate's face and his scent full of contentment were enough for him to forgive her pretty much any transgression.

Before he could ask if she felt ready to face her mother and old coven, he pulled his focus from Kai and truly looked at her. Even though his mate seemed calm and happy, Jess still had an air of unease about her. He raised his arm to allow Kai to settle in next to him on the love seat and frowned at her.

"Is something wrong, or are you just worried about what happens when your mom gets here?"

She twisted a piece of hair around her finger, face scrunched up. "Both. I... had a vision."

A feeling of foreboding crept over him at her words. He exchanged a look with his mate, wrapping his arm securely around Kai's shoulders. "What did you see?"

"It was while you were gone," she started, speaking slowly and softly. "I woke up in a cold sweat and tried to convince myself that it had just been a bad dream."

"But it wasn't."

Kai didn't say it like a question, but Jess still shook her head before saying, "No, I can tell the difference, and it was definitely a vision." She hesitated, and he thought he would have to coax the words out of her, but then she met his eyes and said clearly, "I think it was a vision of me destroying the pack."

Rick tensed at the words, his wolf on high alert after what she'd confessed to Kai in the other room. "What *exactly* did you see?"

She sat on the couch across from them, wrapping her arms around herself as she rocked back and forth. "I-I was walking down Main Street in town, and all the stores were destroyed. Everything was either on fire or looked like it had been blown up. And th-th-there were bodies in the road and on the sidewalks. None of them were moving. Most looked... too broken to be anything other than dead."

Kai sucked in a breath, the scent of his fear filling the space between them and riling his wolf further. His hand landed on Rick's thigh, fingers digging in. "What else?"

She swallowed thickly. "Then... I was here at the manor, but part of it was m-missing. A whole section had just been... blown away. I walked through the place, but I didn't find anyone. Just... blood and scorch marks."

Rick stared at her for a long moment and then asked, "Is that everything?"

She nodded, spilling the tears that had been swimming in her eyes. Wiping furiously at her face, she asked hoarsely, "Isn't that enough?"

"You didn't actually see yourself doing any of those things? Destroying anything or killing anyone?"

"Well... no."

"So it could be someone else. Probably the O'Hares," Kai interjected, turning to Rick. "That's what you're thinking, right? That maybe our plan is going to fail and Jess saw what would happen to our home and town."

He nodded slowly, mind racing. The plan they'd come up with depended heavily on drawing the O'Hares into a trap and then getting them to surrender and leave by showing their superior strength and numbers. But if what Jess had seen was what the O'Hares intended... "Yeah, maybe. But we've stopped her visions from coming true before. I think... I think we should consider it a warning and adapt our strategy."

"How was it a warning? We already know they're coming for us." Jess's voice was higher than normal, her panic obvious even without Rick's heightened senses.

"I think this tells us just how serious things can become. That if it looks like they aren't going to get what they want, they won't just give up and leave like we'd hoped. They're fanatics, after all. They'll go down fighting."

"Okay," Kai said, brows furrowed. "So what you're saying is—"

"We have to kill them all first," a deep voice said from the doorway.

Rick looked over his shoulder at his second-in-command. "Yes. We have to kill them first."

Bennett nodded, crossing his arms over his wide chest, and then gave them a tired, crooked smile. "Here I just thought I would stop in for the Rick Kincaid Apology Tour. I didn't realize I'd get to help plan death and mayhem, but let's get to work."

CHAPTER TWENTY-FOUR

D amien was already awake the next morning when someone knocked on Carter's bedroom door. He wasn't quite sure how long he'd been awake since he hadn't bothered to look at the time and had simply been staring at his sweet mate's face for a creepily long time.

The way Carter had taken care of him the night before had shifted something inside him, easing the fractured pain of grief. Not completely, but enough that he no longer felt overwhelmed by it. Maybe if he hadn't spent the last two years terrified of what his mother might do to his dad, he would have been more surprised and devastated.

And he *was* devastated, but he wasn't surprised. He had just hoped that she would have found it useful to keep him alive a little longer.

Carter snorted adorably at the knock, blinking his eyes open and then squinting down at where Damien was half sprawled on his chest. He smirked when he found him awake and staring.

"Good morning," he rumbled, palming the back of

Damien's head to drag him up as he leaned down, pressing their lips together chastely.

"Good morning," Damien murmured back, happiness bubbling up inside him at the idea of getting to have moments like that every day for the rest of his life.

"Yes, yes, it's a good morning for everyone," Mama called through the door. "And I wouldn't be bothering you, except there is a very large man at the door who says he would like to speak to you two. He smells like a tiger."

Damien stiffened. Why would Bennett be at Carter's house looking to talk to them? He'd barely said two words to him since Rick had woken up, and based on the scowl on his mate's face, he was guessing that Carter hadn't forgiven the man for insisting on putting Damien back in his cuffs.

Not that Damien truly blamed him, but that didn't mean he'd appreciated the way he'd been treated. He'd never really known B to say a mean word to anyone, and yet he hadn't seemed to have any patience or empathy for Damien or for his and Carter's... situation.

"Dear hearts..." Mama said from the hallway when they didn't respond.

"Yeah," Carter said gruffly, rubbing at his face. "Yeah, we'll be right there." He looked at Damien and pressed a kiss to his forehead before climbing out of bed. "I suppose we should see what he wants."

"I suppose."

Though in all honesty, Damien wasn't really in the mood for anything but spending time with his mate before having to return to the shop to finish prepping for sundown. He wanted to make sure they had as many exploding and freezing hex bags as possible, not to mention vials of certain potions that could do as much damage as possible. His mom's coven may have been stronger and bigger than Damien's, but with the pack, they had way more fighters.

He prayed she'd be smart enough to surrender and give up her crusade after being confronted with their strength.

They each took a turn in the bathroom, and then just as Damien was about to pull on his clothes from the day before, Carter opened his closet and sighed heavily. "I knew I shouldn't have told that woman where you lived."

Not understanding, Damien stepped closer to take a look inside the closet and then slapped a hand over his mouth to stifle his chuckles. All of his clothes appeared to be stuffed in next to Carter's, his shoes lining the floor. He took a step back and looked around the room, noticing several boxes stacked in the corner for the first time.

The night before, he'd been too out of sorts with grief and exhaustion, not noticing anything but his mate and the bed. That woman... she'd made her feelings about Damien's apartment quite clear, and he couldn't help but love her pushy, caring nature.

He went over and opened the top box, and sure enough, it looked like she'd collected all of his books from his place and brought them over too. Damien didn't have much else in regards to personal effects, but he'd have to go through the boxes and make sure to get the picture of him and his dad if she hadn't found it. They'd taken it while on vacation when he was eighteen. Standing on the beach of the Gulf of Mexico, they had their arms wrapped around each other's backs and were smiling widely. The water behind them had been so blue, and their cheeks and shoulders were a little red from the sun. He'd been so happy, and it was one of his favorite pictures—the only one he'd bothered to print from his phone after arriving in Michigan.

Remembering the trip made him ache at the idea of never seeing his dad again while also easing some of his grief. He had a lot of happy memories to look back on when he was missing him.

After he quickly threw on clean clothes, he followed Carter down the stairs and into the kitchen, where they found the pack's very large second-in-command seated in the breakfast nook. A cup of coffee and a bagel were in front of him.

Carter rolled his eyes, sending his mom an exasperated look as she bustled out of the room, smiling at the both of them.

"You don't have to eat that if you don't want to," he said to Bennett as they approached the table. "She just really likes feeding people."

"My mom was the same way," Bennett said almost to himself, staring down at the plate. He cleared his throat and said louder, "It was sweet of her to offer."

He picked up one of the cream-cheese-smeared halves and took a large bite. As he chewed, he studied Carter and Damien, his eyes dropping down to their clasped hands and then lingering on their scar-free necks.

Damien stiffened, not appreciating feeling like he was being examined or found wanting in some way. He kept his mouth shut though. After everything, the last thing he needed was to piss off the pack's second even more than he already had.

"I talked to Rick last night," Bennett finally said after nearly finishing his entire bagel. "Well, to him, Kai, and Jess."

That got Damien's attention. He would have thought that she would have been holed up in her apartment again based on how upset she'd seemed the day before.

"There's going to be a change of plan," Bennett continued. "You'll get more details later this morning, but suffice it to say, based on a vision Jess has had, Rick wants to adjust the strategy."

"Adjust in what way?" Carter asked.

Bennett took the last bite of his bagel and then wiped at

the corners of his mouth and took a deep sip of his coffee. His dark umber skin seemed to absorb the early morning light in the kitchen, turning it richer and even more beautiful. "The new plan will be similar to the old one, except our main objective is no longer to drive away the coven."

Damien's brows furrowed as he glanced up at his mate and then back at Bennett. "Okay, what's the new objective?"

"Kill them," Bennett said dispassionately and then swallowed the last of his coffee and pushed to his feet, rising to an intimidating height. "Kill all of them."

Damien's blood hummed in his veins, and he was a little surprised at his eagerness. Sure, he'd already planned on not letting his mother leave Kincaid Pack territory alive. He couldn't. He couldn't just let her get away with what she had done to him, to his father, to Jess, and to who knew how many more. She and the rest of her coven had terrorized anyone they'd deemed a threat, and he'd planned on at least taking her out.

But if Rick's new plan was to eliminate the coven altogether...

"That won't be easy," he said carefully, Carter's hand twitching in his.

"We know," Bennett agreed, coming to stand in front of him and Carter. "Based on what Jess saw though, we believe it's the only way to keep the pack safe, long-term. People like her and her coven have been allowed to do whatever they want. They've preyed on smaller, weaker packs and covens. They've paid hunters to eliminate challengers. This shit ends, and it ends now."

"I'm not disagreeing," Carter said slowly, "but if all of this is going to be relayed later today, why are you here first thing in the morning to tell us personally?"

Bennett sighed and then looked straight at Damien. "Because I owe you an apology." He met Carter's hard gaze.

"You too, Doc. I wasn't in a good place when Rick was injured. That man is more than just my alpha; he's my best friend and has been my entire life. I would follow him into the fires of hell. And the fact that he left me here and took a human hunter as backup instead..." He paused, glancing away from them. His face tightened with a grimace. "It felt like I'd failed somehow. Like he couldn't trust me to have his back, and then for him to come back on the edge of death and have to rely on a witch we didn't know if we could trust—"

Carter's low growl interrupted, and Bennett held up his hands, smiling.

"I know. But at the time, we didn't. We did not know if we could trust him," he said, enunciating clearly. "But we had to put Rick's life in his hands anyway. And I took out my fear for him and my anger toward him on you. I'm truly sorry."

Damien swallowed and nodded. "Thank you. It didn't feel great, but I understand, and I'm glad he's okay now."

When Carter didn't say anything, he gently elbowed his mate in the side, causing him to huff and then mumble, "I understand too."

Bennett grinned at them. "You're well matched. I look forward to getting to know you better, Damien, and earning back your friendship, Carter."

Carter rolled his eyes and stepped forward, surprising Damien. Based on how Bennett's eyes widened when Carter enveloped him in a hug, he was a bit shocked too.

"You don't have to earn back anything. I *may* have been a little touchy after figuring out who Damien was to me. Especially with everyone's emotions so heightened while we waited for Rick to stop being so dramatic."

Bennett laughed and clapped him on the back. "He sure did take his time, didn't he? And to be fair, I wasn't much better when I was fighting my tiger's instincts about Kieran. I get it, and I'm sorry if I caused either of you more pain."

Damien smiled softly at the both of them. "Thank you."

After another moment of embracing and reaffirming their bond, Bennett stepped back from Carter. He reached up and quickly scented his neck before absently doing the same to Damien, already moving toward the door before Damien realized what was happening.

"I need to get back to the manor. You're gonna get an email soon from Nico, asking you to come later." He paused in the kitchen doorway, turning back to them. "Take the next few hours for yourselves. No one knows what's going to happen, and you deserve to spend time just the two of you."

And then he was gone.

Carter grasped Damien's hand once more, holding on almost too tightly. "Now that the pack has sanctioned our alone time, are you still okay with coming with me somewhere instead of heading right to the shop?"

Damien grinned up at his mate, ignoring the trepidation growing in his belly. "Mi corazón, I'd go with you anywhere."

He may have spoken too soon.

"Where are we going?" Damien finally asked after traipsing through the woods for nearly ten minutes.

He hadn't said anything when Carter had made him sit out on the porch while he'd gotten things ready. He hadn't said anything when Carter had come out of the house carrying a cooler and a large cloth bag over his shoulder, looking like a mom ready to take her kids to the beach. And he hadn't said anything when Carter had driven out of town for several miles before pulling over in the middle of nowhere and telling Damien they had to walk the rest of the way.

But now that he was scratched from random branches, had a blister forming on his left heel, and more than a few mosquito bites on his arms, he was beginning to question his mate's judgment. And his own for following the man without asking any questions.

"We're almost there," Carter said, laughter clear in his voice from where he marched ahead of Damien.

Sighing, he tried to speed up to close the distance. "You know, I think when Bennett suggested we spend the morning together, he might have meant in more of a *bedroom* capacity. Not a nature hike."

The heated look his mate threw him over a shoulder nearly made Damien trip and fall over a fallen branch. "Patience."

Before he could point out that he *had* been patient, Carter broke through a cluster of trees and then halted. Damien did the same, and his breath caught in the back of his throat. There was an honest-to-goodness babbling brook ten to fifteen feet from where they stood at the edge of a large meadow filled with bright, colorful wildflowers.

"It's beautiful," he said softly, completely forgetting his complaints and ailments.

Carter smiled over at him, looking pleased. "I found this place during a pack run a few years ago. Most people either gather at the manor or at the southern edge of the territory, but after seeing this, I've tried to come back as often as I could, especially while the flowers are blooming."

Damien took a few more steps forward, taking a deep, cleansing breath. It was still early, but the sun was already beginning to heat the day. Fluffy white clouds dotted the brilliant blue sky. There was a soft hum of insects all around them, and he caught sight of a fat bumblebee meandering from one flower to the next.

It was... perfect.

Turning back to his mate, he said, "I love it. Thank you for bringing me here."

Carter cupped his chin and pressed a soft kiss to his lips before moving closer to the brook and setting down his cooler and bag. He opened the canvas tote and pulled out a large gray-and-blue blanket that he spread on the ground, several plastic cups, and a wireless speaker, which he connected his phone to and started playing soft music. Not enough to disrupt the peace of the clearing, just enough to enhance the moment.

He waved Damien over. "Take a seat, beautiful."

Completely enchanted with his mate, Damien lowered himself onto the blanket, rubbing his hand over the fuzzy material and staring as Carter opened the cooler and pulled out bottles of orange juice and champagne. He doctored up a mimosa for each of them, and they clinked their plastic glasses together while grinning at each other.

He took a drink as Carter pulled out a large bowl of freshly cut mixed fruit, then a covered plastic container that he couldn't see inside of. Damien leaned forward a little, eager to see what else was tucked in there.

"I didn't have a lot of time to put this together," Carter said, sounding almost embarrassed. "For our next picnic, I'll be better prepared and be sure to have more options."

Damien shook his head and downed the rest of his drink. He pushed up to his knees and clambered over next to his mate. "No one has ever done anything like this for me. It's perfect."

A hint of color filled Carter's cheeks as he wrapped his strong arms around Damien, lowering his head to capture his lips in a soft, sensual kiss. Damien had half a mind to forget about their breakfast, but even as his fingers began to trail down his mate's yummy chest, Carter grinned against his mouth and pulled away.

"Not so fast. You're not distracting me from our date."

Date.

Damien had never been on one of those. For some reason, it hadn't occurred to him that that was what they were doing until Carter pointed it out. Nearly overwhelmed with feelings of gratitude and love, he scooted back to his side of the blanket and sat on his heels, more than happy to let his mate pamper him.

And pamper him he did.

The covered container had freshly made biscuits—courtesy of Mama Bell. Carter pulled out a jar of fresh honey and one of softened butter. Damien had to bite his lip not to make a comment about bears and their honey. After he slathered one of the biscuits with butter and then drizzled the honey on it, Carter offered it to Damien on a small paper plate. He couldn't help but be impressed. They were so delicious, light and fluffy and perfect.

He scarfed it down faster than was probably dignified, and as soon as he finished, Carter was right there, holding a slice of strawberry to Damien's lips. He stared into his mate's eyes as he opened his mouth, accepting the sweet, juicy berry onto his tongue and biting into it.

He moaned at the sweetness, and Carter's eyes began to glow. He picked up a red grape and offered that to Damien next, licking his lips as he watched him chew with an intensity Damien could feel all over his body.

Slowly, without exchanging any words, Carter nourished him. He wasn't just feeding his body. In a very primal way, he was nourishing Damien's soul, binding them in a way he'd gotten a glimpse of the day before. First, when Carter had carefully fed him the cinnamon roll, and then when he'd gently washed Damien's body and held him afterward.

Despite knowing each other for two years, Damien was getting the chance to learn about Carter in a new and wonderful way. Damien might have known where Carter had gone to med school and that he enjoyed research just as much as working with patients and that he visited his family as often as he could and loved his brothers, even when he pretended to be annoyed by them, but in that perfect, warm morning, he fell in love with the sensual, caring side of his mate.

Carter dragged a piece of melon across Damien's bottom lip before popping it into his mouth, then diving forward to chase the juice with his own tongue.

Damien knew, without a doubt, no one had ever loved him the way Carter did, and no one else ever would. As he stared up into his sweet mate's face, caressing his bristly, unshaven cheek, he knew deep down in his soul that he would never let anyone take this man from him.

CHAPTER TWENTY-FIVE

C arter's bear was humming with happiness in his chest, hardly able to take his eyes off his smiling mate as he drove them back into town. His plan to show Damien how much he had to fight for—how much he had to *live* for—seemed to have gone even better than he had hoped. And while he wanted nothing more than to drive them straight back to his house, carry his mate up to his room, strip them both naked, and bond completely with him in a frenzy of pleasure and adoration, the real world was already beckoning them.

Damien frowned at his phone. "The email from Nico came through. Rick wants to do another strategy meeting at one and discuss 'a change in tactics.'"

The way he said the last part made Carter think that was a direct quote. Nodding, he slowed for a Stop sign and then paused at the intersection, despite there being no one else around. "One should be okay. While you're at the shop, I need to go into the office and go through messages. Make sure I haven't missed anything urgent."

When Damien didn't say anything to that, Carter turned

to him, studying his mate's concerned face. "I'm sorry your schedule got so—"

"Hey." Carter waited until he stopped talking, then reached over and laid his hand on Damien's surprisingly strong thigh, giving it a squeeze. "You don't have anything to be sorry for. I've seen the few patients I couldn't reschedule between all the chaos, but things won't be like this for much longer, and then we'll be able to find our everyday rhythm."

Damien swallowed, looking hopeful and scared all at once. "That sounds… oddly nice."

Snorting, Carter leaned over the console for a kiss, something warm and *boundless* unfurling in his chest when Damien met him halfway without hesitation. He meant for it to be quick but found himself lingering, reveling in the sweet sigh his mate breathed against his damp limps when he finally leaned back.

"I was thinking," he said gruffly, "if you want to try out using that power of yours for good, there's a young cub who's terrified of needles that has a vaccine appointment coming up. Maybe you could come and help him relax?"

He tried not to hold his breath as he waited for Damien to answer, worried he'd overstepped. Or worse, that he'd hurt his mate just by suggesting it. He knew how sensitive a subject it was, but he had a feeling his dad had been right—Damien hadn't been given such an amazing gift for nothing.

"I don't know," Damien said, dropping his eyes for a second before raising them to meet Carter's again. "I doubt his parents would be okay with it."

"I'll talk to them ahead of time, and if they aren't, then it's no big deal." Carter let himself smile gently. "But they're pretty exasperated themselves, so they may be willing to try a little magic on their tiny terror."

One side of Damien's perfect, pink mouth tipped up. "*If* they agree, then we can talk a—" His phone started ringing in his hand, the sound loud and annoying in the enclosed space. Damien frowned down at the device. "It's Jess."

Carter was surprised but settled back into his seat. "We'll talk about this later, beautiful."

The smile he got back felt a bit indulgent, but he'd take it. He was just pulling into the still-deserted intersection when Damien answered with a tentative "Hello?" and Jess's loud, panicked voice blasted through the phone's small speaker.

"Where are you right now?"

Damien looked around them in confusion, and Carter let his foot off the gas, a bad feeling beginning to grow in his gut. He rattled off the name of the roads they were currently in the middle of bisecting.

"She's there! Go! Get out of ther—"

The blaring horn of a semi cut her off, and Carter jerked his head around even as he tried to stomp on the pedal to get them out of the damn intersection, but nothing happened. His truck stayed frozen in place, and the semi didn't slow at all, barreling down on them.

He didn't think. His hand was on his seat belt, unbuckling himself before Damien even realized what was happening, his confused face morphing into terror as he turned toward his window and saw the large red-and-black big rig coming straight toward them.

There wasn't time to jump free. All Carter could do was shield Damien's fragile, human body with his own as best he could, wedging himself between his mate and the door and wrapping his arms around him to tuck his head into Carter's chest.

And then it hit them.

The sound of shrieking metal combined with fiery pain.

Damien screaming his name.

He felt the truck crumbling around them even as it rolled, his body slamming against the roof. Grunting, he tried to ignore the pain and stay focused, not get sucked into the black spots covering his eyesight and fuzzy edges of his consciousness. Sweet honey mixed with the acidic burn of fear.

Despite his best efforts, he must have blacked out because he lost time. One moment, he was holding on to Damien as hard as he dared, gritting his teeth, and then the next thing he was aware of was getting dragged across the bumpy ground, the sound of Damien screaming his name pushing his bear to the surface.

He must have made a noise because whoever had a hold of him stopped, dropping Carter's head and shoulders onto the hard ground.

"Oh no you don't, beast," a low, feminine voice sneered at him. "Get control of him, Peter. We can't let him shift."

His thoughts weren't firing quite fast enough, but he followed enough of that to bare his teeth and swat at the man hovering behind him. He blinked the fuzz from his eyes and brain, focusing on the towering figure standing down near his feet. The first thing he noted for some reason was that she looked nothing like either of her children, yet there was no doubt in his head that the woman curling her lip at him was Amelia O'Hare.

He snarled, his fangs dropping, and he started to push to his feet, searching for Damien while trying not to look away from her. When he finally found his mate, he lunged forward, intent on ripping the arms off the big witch holding Damien by his throat.

Before he could make it farther than his knees, all his muscles seized up, and he groaned at the excruciating pain. Oh *fuck*. He remembered Damien telling them about Peter's ability now. He couldn't move so much as his pinky fingers as every muscle group in his body locked him in place. It was all he could do to keep breathing, the pressure on his chest agonizing.

Grinning, Amelia swept toward him, using her green-painted fingers to pick at his long hair.

"Honestly, Damien, *this* is who you've chosen to betray us for? Your father will be so ashamed." She turned away from Carter so he couldn't see her face anymore, but he saw his mate's as she said with faux sympathy, "Oh, how rude of me. I mean, he *would* have been ashamed. If I hadn't already had Peter snap his neck."

Damien's face crumpled at her words, devastation and sorrow clear from a dozen feet away, and Carter fought the magical hold on him, desperate to reach him, but it was no use. His head was clearing though, and he took stock of their grim situation. Somehow, Amelia and three other witches had snuck into the territory, and based on the slumped form he could just make out in the cab of the semi, she'd used her own projection power to compel the driver to hit them.

They were only maybe a mile from the hunters' training facility, but even if he could distract Amelia and the other two witches long enough for Damien to get away—and communicate to his mate where to go—Carter was pretty sure no one would be there to help provide backup. Not this late in the morning.

Damien had been on the phone with Jess when they were hit, and she knew where they were, but how long before she could gather reinforcements? He had a feeling Amelia wasn't going to wait around for a pack of shifters to realize she had snuck into their territory.

Jaw tight, Damien tore at the hand on his throat as he stared daggers at his mom. "Fuck you."

Carter had never heard Damien curse like that, and based on how Amelia's step froze and her spine stiffened, she hadn't either. He was more than a little proud.

"So crass. Is that what you've been reduced to after two years of living among these animals?"

Carter was going to rip her throat out. Hippocratic Oath be damned.

"What do you want? I told you I'd bring Jess to you at sundown," Damien gritted out, and Carter was impressed with how convincing he was. They'd had him use the journal to tell his mom that he'd bring Jess outside the warding but that he'd been unsuccessful in offing Rick while he was injured.

They'd never intended for things to get that far; the plan —at least before whatever had changed the night before to cause Bennett to show up on his doorstep and Nico to send out the email about the meeting—had always been to lure the O'Hares into a trap.

The trap, it seemed, had been sprung on him and Damien instead.

Amelia tsked as she turned back to Carter and smiled down at him in a way that would have made him shudder if he could. She was beautiful in a classical way, skin an alluring peaches and cream and hair a wavy strawberry blonde. Her long legs were encased in skintight dark-wash jeans, and her black tank top showed off her... considerable assets, even under her thigh-length light-knit cardigan.

Next to the ripped jeans and U of M T-shirt he'd thrown on, she looked like a model.

"Let's not pretend anymore, darling," she said to Damien as she gently tucked Carter's hair behind his ear. The bizarre gesture was so disconcerting it threw him a bit off-balance, and he nearly missed her next words. "We both know you compromised the Blood Oath and never had any intention of bringing me the abomination."

Abomination. Mother of the fucking Year she was not.

Damien stared at him, not answering her for a long

moment, then seemed to decide something and gave the tiniest nod. "You're right. I never planned on letting you so much as get within a hundred yards of her. I do, however, have every intention of killing you."

He said it calmly but with such conviction Carter knew it stunned Amelia, her face turning to stone, but she kept her focus on him, not her son. "Matricide, really? We both know you don't have it in you. You've always been too... soft."

The idea that his mate's sweet, gentle nature was a flaw riled Carter up even more, and he could tell when his eyes began to glow, his vision sharpening. Amelia cocked her head at him, like he was a curious bug she was about to stomp on.

"Maybe I used to be," Damien said quietly, "but not anymore."

The spot on Carter's neck where he hoped to have a bonding bite one day soon began to heat and pulse. He stared at his mate in confusion, not sure what was happening, but Damien was calm as he held Carter's eyes, head tipped back just slightly from the grip on his throat.

Amelia said something else, her tone cutting, but Carter couldn't hear it over the buzzing in his ears. A sad smile curled Damien's lips, there and gone so fast Carter wondered if he'd really seen it, and then he heard Damien's voice in his head. A firm command that rocked him to his core.

Shift.

Without thought or hesitation, Carter released his bear, his form growing in just a few moments, thanks to his new position in the pack. Shifting, for whatever reason, seemed to break through the hold the witch behind him had locked him down with. He heard a few people shouting—confused and afraid, which his bear *loved*—and he didn't wait even a second after his four paws hit the dirt to turn and swipe at the man scurrying away from him.

Not fast enough.

Carter's claws caught his soft midsection, the scent of blood mixing with the witch's fear and pain, his brown eyes widening in shock. Roaring, Carter was on top of him from one breath to the next, his teeth sinking into the vulnerable flesh of his throat.

Pausing to think about the fact he'd just killed a man wasn't an option. His mate was still in danger. Wheeling around, Carter huffed and growled as he took a few steps forward, looking for an opening to help. Damien had gotten away from the man who'd been holding on to him, but he was alternating between holding a protective barrier against his mom's fireballs and shooting his own magic at the male witch. It looked like he was tossing tiny lightning bolts at him as the guy dodged and ducked, doing his best to get behind Damien so as to divide his attention.

Carter ambled as fast as his bulk could toward Amelia's defenseless back, intent on coating his claws and teeth in her blood, but he only made it halfway. She spun around, narrowed her eyes at him, then raised her arms over her head and clapped. The air rippled out from her hands, and Carter felt the magic coasting over him. He roared, expecting some sort of injury to hit him, but the sensation just kept going right over him.

He paused, confused. Just as he started toward her again, ears flat and head lowered, he caught the faint sound of a metallic clang followed by low growls. He tilted his head, trying to hear better without taking his attention off the witches in front of him. Damien had used his mother's inattention to focus completely on the other one, backing him against Carter's wrecked truck and then hitting him in the chest with his lightning over and over until the man was on the ground, unmoving.

Amelia clenched her jaw as she turned and saw what

Damien had done, but her tone remained haughty as she called out, "Impressive, but let's see how your bear fairs against *my* beasts."

Understanding dawned on him as he whirled around and caught movement along the low branches of the trees five hundred yards away. Even as the first one stepped into the sun, Carter was remembering the horrible wounds Marcus's friend Wendy had suffered from one of the heinous things.

Carter counted at least five more lingering in the shadows behind the first.

It made its way toward him, loping like a wolf, but it was far from it. The best Tashmica and the others could figure, the O'Hares had used some fucked-up magic to create mindless, killing beasts. They were bigger than regular wolf shifters but disfigured too—like they'd been caught partway through a shift and forced to stay that way.

He edged over to put himself between the thing and his mate, unable to stop himself from turning to glance back at Damien, needing to see him... one more time. He was staring at the approaching creature with a horror-stricken face, and Carter hoped he couldn't make out the rest yet. He wasn't sure why they weren't attacking all at once, but he knew they wouldn't hang back for long.

His mate was so beautiful. There was a streak of blood on his forehead, and his shirt was torn at the neck, but Carter still thought he was nothing less than breathtaking. His olive skin and dark hair practically glowed under the morning sun.

His only regret was not bonding with Damien when he had the chance. He knew from when Keegan had bonded with Nico that it had amped up the man's magic like getting plugged directly into a powerplant. Would his mate have had a better chance fighting his way out of there if he'd had access to that kind of juice?

Carter clacked his teeth in agitation at the thought, forcing himself to face the oncoming threat. The thing was moving steadily toward him but didn't seem to be in any kind of hurry, the rest still holding back, though he could see two more clearly as they stepped out from beneath the trees.

"Carter," Damien whispered, his voice cracking. "*Run.*"

He felt the urge in the muscles of his legs, but he snorted and shook it off, bracing himself for the attack. Damien made a muffled noise behind him, his scent terrified and stinging Carter's sensitive nose.

"*Run!*"

It was easier to brush off the instinct to follow the command that time, and Carter realized what his mate was doing, what he'd done to break the hold Peter had had on him. His sweet little mate was using the power that scared him more than anything to try and save Carter's life, to get him to run away and save himself.

That would never fucking happen.

Amelia tutted behind him. "Oh dear, it seems you're out of practice."

Damien let out a frustrated yell, running toward Carter, but he couldn't turn to look at him, the beast nearly on them. He felt a burst of heat though, and nearly spun around when Damien cried out in pain, but the thing was there, snarling and lunging at him. Carter couldn't lose focus, had to trust that Damien was only hurt, not... something worse.

Roaring, he reared up and swatted at the beast, knocking it back with a yelp, but he didn't pause to see if it would run away or how injured it was. Narrowing his attention to the threat in front of him, he trusted his mate to deal with the one behind. To stay alive and protect his back.

Then he attacked.

CHAPTER TWENTY-SIX

D amien felt like his heart had jumped out of his chest and was currently fighting to the death with the ugliest thing he'd ever seen. He didn't know why his projection had failed to make Carter run, but he could barely breathe, unable to completely tear his eyes from the brawling fight to focus on his advancing mother.

His head was thumping painfully from where he'd hit it during the crash, but that was nothing compared to the burn on his right forearm where his mom's fire had hit him. She hadn't even been trying to kill him—just get his attention off his mate and back on her. Toying with him.

The metallic taste of adrenaline was thick in his mouth, and it was possible he'd throw up from the dizzying pain before everything was said and done, but he'd die fighting to protect his mate before giving up.

He just wished backup would hurry up and arrive.

Jess had been on the phone with them when they'd been hit, trying to warn him that their mom had somehow gotten past the warding without them realizing it. Why hadn't she brought help yet?

"How'd you get through the wards?" he asked, hoping he could stall her while Carter fought off the beast.

She rolled her eyes like he'd asked the dumbest question she'd ever heard. "You let me in."

He sucked in a breath. "No, I didn't."

"You might as well have," she said, shrugging and flicking her fingers at him. A dart of fire flew at him so fast he almost didn't get his shield back up in time.

Stupid, don't let her distract you.

"I knew you'd overcompensate after those two idiot hunters used my device to trick your warding," she said, examining her nails like they were discussing the weather over tea and not standing less than ten feet from Carter and one of her mutated beasts fighting and snarling at each other. "Greedy, simple-minded Lars Morde was so easy to manipulate—I didn't even have to use my powers on him."

Damien swallowed. Gabriel's brother and another hunter had used a powerful—and very clever—device to hide their breach through the warding when they came to kidnap Gabriel to bring him back home. Afterward, Damien had obsessed over the thing, trying to figure out how it worked and where it had come from without much success. Instead, he'd increased the power in the wardings as high as was safe, which also meant they had more false alarms.

Like the one the day before.

"The tree yesterday," he said, stomach dropping as the pieces started to fall into place. As well as the realization that he'd been played.

"The tree yesterday," she agreed, smiling at him like a proud parent, but her pale eyes were ice-cold. "Your little coven's response time was impressive, I'll give you that, but we were still well hidden by the time you arrived."

He'd been so annoyed, using his telekinesis to lift and throw the tree out of the line of the border ward and resealing it. Anything bigger than a small dog set it off after he'd upped the power, whether it was a parahuman or not. Where it crossed roads in and out of the territory, the warding was less powerful but more complex, protecting against violent intentions as well as magic.

His gaze darted toward the road leading into town, and he swore he could just make out a car in the distance, but his mom laughed and said, "No one's coming. The rest of the coven and my beasties are keeping them well occupied far away."

Dread weighed down his limbs even as the car grew closer.

She smiled, turning to look. "Well, no one but your sister is coming." She pulled a familiar device out of her pocket, and Damien stared at his phone, patting uselessly at his pockets. "'We're okay. I fought her off, but the truck is totaled. Can you come pick us up?'"

Bile rose at the back of his throat. "You sent that to her?"

Tossing the device away carelessly, she sighed and shook her head. "Silly little half-breed still has no control over her visions. You're both such... disappointments."

There was a loud yelp and then a thud behind him, but he didn't look away from her until he heard an annoyed snort. Unable to help himself, he glanced back, pulse hammering in his ears. There was a dead beast at his bear's feet, but two more were circling him, drool falling from their gaping snouts.

Farther away, three more were lingering near the tree line, their glowing eyes locked on him and Carter.

Goddess.

The loud squeal of tires decelerating too hard had his head whipping around to find Jess staring at their mom in horror from behind the wheel of her crappy car. Concentrating, he *pushed* at her, urging her to drive away, but just like Carter, she shook it off, turning narrowed eyes on him.

Slowly, she climbed from her car, refocusing on their mom, who was sneering at Jess with distaste. "Hello, Mother."

"Jessica, lovely of you to join us." She turned her cold, dead eyes back on Damien. "Kill her, right now, and I'll let you and your *mate* live."

Jess's steps faltered, causing her to slip the rest of the way down the small slope at the edge of the road and land on her backside in the muddy trench. "Fucking awesome."

"Are you okay?" He moved over to use his shield to protect her as well, even though it killed him to leave Carter more vulnerable.

"Fantastic," she snarled, pushing to her feet and then shaking the mud from her hands. "I take it you didn't send me that text?"

He shook his head, eyes on their waiting mom. "Get back in your car and get out of here."

"Shut up, Damien. I'm not *abandoning* you and Carter to die."

He flinched at her fierce words, darting a look at his mate. He was still fighting, but Damien knew it would only be a matter of time before he was overwhelmed by the sheer number of beasts. Carter was doing well, but he wasn't a trained fighter like the other Enforcers.

"Damien." Amelia's voice snapped through his worries, her hands clenched at her sides. "Do it. You know she's too dangerous to be allowed to live. She'll destroy—"

"*Shut up!*" Jess screamed, throwing her hands up and sending their mom flying backward.

Damien used the distraction to lower his shield and call up his magic, shooting sizzling lightning at the closest beast. The high-pitched noise it made hurt his ears, but he hit it again. And again. Moving forward slowly, he gathered his magic in his chest, feeling it heat and grow and then forcing it down his arm and out his fingertips.

The smell of burnt flesh made him gag, but he refused to feel bad for the twitching thing on the ground, whirling to help Carter with the other one. But his mate had it in hand, sinking his teeth into the thing's side and *tearing*.

"D-D-Damien!"

He whipped around and found Jess floating ten feet in the air, convulsing. He didn't stop to think, forgetting that his projection power hadn't worked the last two times he tried to use it, and punched his way into his mom's mind.

Stop.

Jess fell to the ground with a grunt, not moving but breathing heavily. Damien kept his eyes on their mom, grateful whatever blip had caused the power not to work seemed to be gone.

Amelia shook her head, brows furrowed, then locked in on Jess's panting body.

You don't care about Jessica.

A blankness came over Amelia's face for a moment, and then she turned to him and raised her hands, flames licking at her fingers. A horrible, terrible idea popped into his head, steadying his runaway heart. He heard his dad telling him he was powerful, Carter whispering to him that he was brave, Jess promising to have his back as long as he had hers.

Straightening his shoulders, he stared at the woman who had tortured him, forced him to betray those he loved, and killed his father. The man who raised and loved him, protected him from her. Taught him how to use his magic to help others.

The fiery rage he'd felt the day before still licked at him, but it was tempered by a conviction that he *was* stronger than her. And he didn't have to be afraid anymore.

"Goodbye, Mom," he whispered, then *pushed* his projection into her mind, not stopping until she turned her hand toward her own throat. Her eyes widened a second before her fingers closed into a fist.

Her knees hit the ground as her mouth moved wordlessly, but there was nothing to be done. She'd crushed her own windpipe using the telekinesis both he and Jess had inherited.

He watched, dispassionately, as she crumpled to the dirt, face contorting horribly and skin flushing purple. The moment felt... surreal. He'd expected relief or even vindication at her death, but he just felt empty.

He'd just used the power she'd so admired in him to kill her, and he felt... nothing.

Slender arms wrapped around one of his, jarring him out of his thoughts. He turned his head to find Jess staring at their mom, a bruise already beginning to rise on her jaw from her fall and dirt sprinkled like freckles over her cheeks and nose.

"Are you okay?" he croaked again, hit with a weird sense of déjà vu.

"I... I think so. I feel like I can breathe for the first time in my life. That's weird, right?"

He shook his head, opening his mouth to tell her he understood exactly how she felt, but snapped it shut once more when his naked mate skidded to a stop in front of them, worried eyes running over both of them. There was a deep gash over one of his pecs and a bite mark on one of his meaty thighs, but otherwise, he looked okay.

"Holy fuck," Carter breathed out, gripping both of them on the sides of their neck and looking back and forth between them. "Are you hurt?"

Damien looked over his shoulder and rubbed at a dull throbbing on his chest, feeling like he was in a daze, but didn't see any sign of the other three beasts, only the three he and Carter had killed.

They'd killed... a lot of people.

"We killed people," he blurted out, interrupting Jess from telling Carter she was fine, just a few bruises.

Both of Carter's warm hands clasped his jaw, bringing his focus back to him. "We did. We protected ourselves and each other and our pack. I need to call the manor and get some more people out here to track down those things and whoever let them out."

"No one's there," Jess said. "Except for anyone who needed to hunker down there for safety. All the Enforcers and betas are out fighting."

"Where?" Carter asked her, voice clipped but fingers so gentle as they moved over Damien's face, paying special attention to the bump and cut from the accident.

"All over," she said with a sigh, scrubbing at her face and then wincing when she hit her jaw. "There should be someone at the shop, though, to help coordinate efforts, but I didn't stick around to find out who. I... I needed to put eyes on Damien after the vision I had of our mom k-killing him."

Her trembling voice and wet eyes finally seemed to break through the wall of ice he was stuck in. Turning, he wrapped her in a tight hug, murmuring into her hair, "Thank you for coming for me."

Her grip on him was too tight and perfect at the same time. "Always."

"Yeah, it's Doc," Carter was saying into a phone. "Tell me what's happening."

It took all day to track down every beast and O'Hare coven member who'd breached the territory. Damien had grabbed some blood from one of the dead beasts and used it to help scry for the others, but it had still taken a lot of coordinated effort to put down each one.

He and the betas—along with some of the less skilled pack members—handled that while the Enforcers, the rest of the coven—led by Tashmica in black fatigues that looked weirdly good on her—and any remaining pack fighters took on finding and eliminating the O'Hares.

And then there was Alistair Kincaid.

They didn't realize Alistair was inside the territory too until he tried to surrender just after nightfall. Damien was at *Wicca We Can*, a bandage over his burned forearm and a hovering mate feeding him snacks every half hour, using three different phones to communicate with the teams in the field as he triple-checked his scrying bowl to make sure they'd found all of the beasts and a map of the territory to pinpoint the last few O'Hares. A fist landing on the front door startled him, but the protective warding had already thrown Alistair back so hard he was sprawled on the sidewalk.

He looked like he'd been running through the woods all day. Dried mud caked his loafers and the bottom of his black slacks, and one of the buttons was missing on his red button-up, a sleeve nearly completely torn off just above his left elbow.

And there may have been twigs in his disheveled hair.

Damien and Carter didn't open the door, his mate pulling out his phone and calling Rick. "Yeah, your dad just showed up at the shop... Mhm... Okay, see you soon."

Damien glanced up at him. "He's on his way?"

"Yup. He said not to risk going outside, but how do you feel about using your projection power one more time today?"

Damien smirked up at him, flicking the lock open with a twitch of his finger.

By the time Rick and the others arrived, Damien and Carter had Alistair trussed up like a turkey in the middle of Main Street. They'd had to gag him too, since he started to yammer at them every time the projection forcing him to shut up wore off.

Rick raised his eyebrows at his dad, then glanced over at Damien and Carter. Carter was pressed against his back, face buried in his hair and arms around him, one hand dangerously close to slipping down the front of his jeans.

"I thought I was clear," Rick said, though he didn't sound upset.

"We didn't want to risk him trying to run again," Carter said, his rumbly chest sending shivers down Damien's spine.

Rick crouched in front of Alistair and pried the sock out of his mouth, tossing it over his shoulder. As soon as he finished coughing, Alistair started talking. "Council law dictates you return me—"

"*Stop talking*," Damien said, a headache forming in his temples. He wasn't sure if it was from using his power so much after barely ever using it before or from the semitruck to the head he'd taken.

Probably the second.

Alistair opened his mouth, but nothing came out, his eyes glowing with hatred as he stared at Damien. Rick swiveled, looking at Damien over his shoulder, eyebrows raised. "Handy. How long does it last?"

"Only about ten minutes," he admitted. "That's why we gagged him."

More Enforcers and witches began arriving, some on foot but most in SUVs. Robson was limping, his mate supporting his weight and watching him with concern. Most of the others looked okay, if not dirty and tired. He noted Tashmica was grinning in a way he found disturbing as she bounced on the balls of her feet, looking like she was eager to go another ten rounds with O'Hare witches.

When she sidled up next to him, he said out of the corner of his mouth, "You enjoyed today too much."

Keegan and Nico exited a car and walked up to them, the normally happy Enforcer scowling fiercely at Alistair as Damien tried to decide if he had blood or mud on his T-shirt.

She shrugged, lacing her fingers together and stretching her arms out in front of her, magic crackling around her hands. "Disagree. I enjoyed it just the right amount. Been a long time since I got to really let my magic loose."

"Agreed," Keegan said, stopping next to Tash. "This was the first time I really got to test the new limits on my powers since bonding."

"And?" Damien asked, more than a little curious. He didn't hide it well, based on Carter's deep chuckle into his hair.

"Didn't find one," Keegan said, grinning just as manically as Tashmica. "I'm pretty sure I'm tapped right into the pack bonds, which means I have to be careful not to funnel too much magic through me and fucking fry myself from the inside out."

"Lovely, sweetheart," Nico muttered.

Rick pushed to his feet, eyes back on his dad, who twitched and jerked in his bindings but wasn't going anywhere. The alpha planted his hands on his hips and took a deep breath. As he let it out, the tension in his shoulders slowly released.

"You know," Rick said idly, looking around at the dark storefronts, "I thought it would be harder."

"Wasn't exactly easy," Robson said petulantly, blood still seeping from the gash in his thigh.

"I don't just mean what we did here." Rick dug in his

pocket and pulled out his phone. Everyone was quiet, waiting. Crouching back down in front of his dad, he turned the device so they could both see, then hit Play on the video that had come through two hours before.

Gabriel Morde's Southern drawl came over the speaker clearly. "As you can see, the last of the buildings are nearly finished burning. Admin personnel was evacuated, and the Council's coven was nowhere to be found. I'm guessing they got our message about what Daddy Kincaid and his merry band of witches were up to."

Alistair's eyes were bugging out of his head, his perfectly tanned face draining of color.

The video continued, Gabriel sounding pleased as punch. "Any Council members who fought back were neutralized. The couple who surrendered were collared and will be returning with us."

The magical collars would prevent the shifters from being able to use their abilities at all, rendering them as weak as humans. One of his and Tash's more impressive inventions, if he did say so himself.

Rick slipped his phone back into his pocket and thumbed at Nico over his shoulder. "My Enforcer there, he sent out notices on all of the online forums, informing everyone about what you and Amelia were doing, everyone you killed or tried to kill to accomplish your goals, and letting them know the time of the Council is over."

Alistair fought so hard against his bindings he fell onto his back, getting stuck like a turtle. Damien must have been more tired than he'd realized since he had to slap a hand over his mouth to muffle the laughter that bubbled up inside him at the thought.

Rick shook his head at his dad. "Don't bother getting upset. You can't fight it. I did warn you about what would happen if you came after me and mine though, didn't I? But don't worry—you won't be here to see what comes next."

Faster than Damien could track, Rick swiped his extended claws across his dad's throat. Damien turned and pressed his face into Carter's chest and his hands to his ears, tired of seeing and *hearing* people die in front of him. Carter ran his hands up and down his back, soothing him.

When Carter tapped on his butt, Damien flushed but uncovered his ears and peeked over his shoulder. Alistair's body was already gone, the taillights of an SUV halfway down the street. He turned around and looked at the tired but victorious group around him.

"I can't believe it's actually over," he said softly, shaking his head. He rubbed the spot on his chest where the Blood Oath mark had been, the last of it having burned away with his mom's death.

"Are you kidding?" Nico asked, already on his phone and typing. "The hard part is just starting."

The wide, satisfied smile on Rick's face eased the worry Nico's words had planted in his belly. "We just changed the world, yes. But that means we get to remake it into a better version."

Damien couldn't even really imagine how much work was facing them over the next weeks, months, maybe even years, but for the first time in a long time, he felt *hopeful*.

"What do we do now?" someone asked, sounding as exhausted as Damien felt.

"Rest," Rick said, walking over to where Robson and Marcus were and scenting them. He started moving his way around the disjointed circle they'd formed around him and Alistair. When he got to Carter and Damien, he paused to study Damien.

There was a deep understanding in his alpha's eyes and a hint of pain. Just like in Damien. They may have hated their parents, but they'd still been forced by selfish choices and fate to be the ones to end their lives. Neither would forget that.

Rick palmed the side of his neck, scenting him, then reached up and did the same to Carter. After he finished making his way around the circle, he took a deep breath and looked at his witches and Enforcers. Those who had fought and killed for him. Who would stand behind him as he remade the parahuman world.

"Tonight, we rest. Tomorrow… we get to work."

CHAPTER TWENTY-SEVEN

"We're supposed to be *resting*," his mate singsonged at him as he darted out of Carter's hands and up the stairs to their bedroom.

Carter gave a playful growl and thundered up after him, delighted at Damien's small squeal.

While it was true Rick had told everyone to go home and rest, that had been over two hours ago. Everyone—hell, nearly the entire *pack*—had gathered at the manor for an impromptu celebration. There were way too many members —even with the ones who had jumped ship when Rick had told anyone not willing to support him and the pack against the fight with the O'Hares to get the fuck out—to fit inside the manor for a feast, so Beth and her helpers, along with Cole and the others from Momma's, had pulled grills from somewhere and started cooking for everyone. He'd seen his own mom jump in after she and his brothers arrived shortly after him and Damien.

Carter had forced himself to only hug his brothers and not check them each for injuries, nodding as they told him about battling a pair of beasts alongside a couple of betas.

Carter was pretty sure he'd grown a few gray hairs during their retelling.

Other folks arrived, bringing tables and chairs from their homes, as well as dishes to pass. Nico somehow rigged up speakers to play music, then went back to typing away on his phone, only putting it down when Keegan and their daughter dragged him onto the makeshift dance floor.

A few of the Enforcers helped carry the large dining room table outside, and Rick sat at the head most of the evening, holding court as pack member after pack member streamed over to thank him for protecting them and vowing their fealty to the Kincaid Pack once more. In turn, he'd scented each one, thanking them for their loyalty. It had been oddly somber for the celebratory mood, yet completely natural. Even Carter and Damien had made their way over and gotten scented again.

Kai alternated between sitting next to his mate and running after their pups until tiny, blonde-haired Callie climbed onto the table, a half of a peanut butter and jelly sandwich in either hand, and screamed, "Sammiches!"

At that point, Rick and Kai had excused themselves, Rick throwing the madly giggling young girl over his shoulder, and gone inside to put her and Henry to bed.

Carter had seen Alpha Okenapowet making her rounds, thanking Rick and all of the Enforcers for their hospitality and protection. Most of her pack members who were able to fight had gone with Gabriel, his mates, and the rest of the hunters to Mehko to take out the Council and its headquarters. Once they returned the next day, she and her pack would return home and begin rebuilding.

Carter had eaten until his bear was finally satisfied and then pulled his mate into his lap and hand-fed him the rest of his own plate. Damien had blushed prettily, embarrassed to have Carter taking care of him like that in front of the entire pack, but when Kieran and Bennett—who'd been sitting across from them at the small square table while they discussed the backlog of patients needing to be rescheduled at the clinic—didn't so much as blink, his mate had finally relaxed against him.

A lot of people had come over and congratulated him for becoming an Enforcer and then him and Damien on their mating. Only a handful seemed uncomfortable with his mate, and Carter knew they'd come around in time. There was no way someone could get to know his sweet mate and not love him.

After Rick and Kai headed inside, the gathering slowly began to break up, those with young cubs being the first to leave. Carter had been anxious to get his mate back home as well but hadn't wanted to seem rude by disappearing too early.

When B stood and clapped him on the shoulder with a chuckle, he took that as permission and excused him and Damien.

The drive home had been quiet but full of delicious tension.

Stalking down the hallway to their bedroom, he said, "Do you honestly think Rick and Kai are sleeping right now and not—"

"La la la la." Damien shoved his fingers in his ears and squeezed his eyes shut. "I can't hear you."

Snorting, Carter closed the door behind him but didn't stop until he collided with his mate. Hazel eyes popped open in surprise, then crinkled with a smile as Damien rested his arms on Carter's shoulders, combing his fingers through the loose strands of his hair.

"Hey," Damien said softly, eyes traveling over Carter's face.

"Hey." He kissed the inside of Damien's elbow, taking

note of the way he giggled and flinched. "How's your arm? Do you need something for pain?"

His sweet, innocent mate dropped his eyes to Carter's crotch and said, "I can think of one thing that might help."

Laughing, he grabbed the back of Damien's thighs and lifted him effortlessly. "Are you saying my dick will make you feel better, baby boy?"

"I mean... I didn't *say* that..." Damien wrapped his legs around Carter's waist and arms around his neck, clinging to him like an octopus. "But if you think we should try, you know, for science, then I'm willing."

"For science," Carter repeated, leaning in to run his nose up the slender throat in front of him.

"Yeah," Damien said breathlessly, tilting his head back. "Where's your scientific curiosity, Dr. Bell?"

He laughed against his mate's sweet skin, pressing a few kisses to each of the places that made him squirm. "How about this instead: you make that special tea of yours, then we use our *scientific curiosity* to figure out how powerful you are once we're bonded. How's that sound?"

Damien sucked in a breath, tipping his chin back down to meet Carter's eyes. "Are you sure?"

"I've never been more sure about anything in my whole life," Carter said, holding his gaze so he could see just how serious he truly was. "If you aren't ready though—"

Damien shook his head quickly. "I'm ready. I-I... Yes, I want that, Carter. I want to be bonded with you. I want to be *yours.*"

"That's good. I want that too, baby boy." He didn't release his hold though. Instead, he sealed their mouths together in a light, lingering kiss, refusing to deepen it no matter how many times Damien pushed for more. When Damien grunted in annoyance and pulled away, Carter grinned. "No distracting me. Go make your tea."

He let Damien slide down his body, biting back a groan at the delicious pressure on his hardening cock. Damien smirked up at him before dancing away when Carter tried to snag him again.

"Now, now. No getting distracted. I'll be right back," Damien said, smiling at him over his shoulder as he grabbed the jar of herbs off the dresser and slipped out of the room.

That man was perfect.

Sighing at his own luckiness, Carter stripped out of his clothes, then pulled back the covers on the bed, tossing the lube onto one of the pillows. He ducked into his closet to pull out the dozen candles he'd stashed in there the other day. Spreading them around the room, he lit each one before hitting the lights and turning on his Bluetooth speaker, picking a playlist on his phone that was made up of violin covers of popular songs.

He was just setting the speaker and his phone on the bedside table closest to the door—his side now that he couldn't just starfish in the middle—when it opened behind him, cool air hitting his back and ass.

"Carter," Damien gasped, and he turned to find his mate looking around the room with wide, wet eyes, his steaming mug of tea cradled against his chest. "This is..."

"The least I could do." He walked over and rescued the mug before it could be dropped, setting it next to the speaker, then taking Damien into his arms once more. "My sweet mate, you've been waiting for me for so long, the least I could do was make the moment special."

The tears spilled over as Damien pushed up to lay a breath-stealing kiss on Carter. His bear hummed with happiness, more than ready to tie them together, and Carter had to agree. Their breakfast picnic seemed like weeks ago, not earlier that day. So much had changed and yet was the same.

It didn't matter to him what the future held for the pack

—or anyone else, for that matter. All he cared about was loving his mate, taking care of his patients, and keeping his brothers from getting into too much trouble.

Oh, and eating plenty of his mom's cooking.

Slotting their mouths together over and over, Carter trailed his hands down Damien's slender torso until he reached the hem of his shirt, then slipped underneath and made the same journey in reverse. He stopped to rub the spot low on Damien's belly that made him gasp, as well as lay both of his hands over his ribs to give a squeeze. The size of his hands compared to his tiny mate's rib cage made him groan. He was so damn delicate and yet full of immense power. The contradiction was intoxicating.

He shifted his grip so he could use his thumbs to circle Damien's nipples, tracing the flat discs until the peaks were stiff and Damien was whimpering against his lips and sagging against him.

"You're so sexy," Carter rumbled, dragging his lips across his sharp jaw all the way to his ear, then sucking the lobe into his mouth just to hear him make the same gasping whimper again.

"Me?" Damien asked, sinking his hands into the mat of hair on Carter's chest and then trailing them down to his belly. "You're the sexy one. You're so big and strong."

Carter grunted as he ripped Damien's shirt over his head and tossed it aside. "You like that I'm bigger than you, baby boy?"

Damien sucked in a breath and nodded, dropping his chin to watch Carter unbutton his jeans and draw the zipper down. "So much. Makes me feel safe."

Carter had just stuck his hands into the back of Damien's pants and into his underwear to palm his perfect little ass, but he stilled at his words. Pulling one hand out, he cupped his chin and brought his face up so Carter could look him in the eyes as he said, "You are safe with me. You always will be. Forever."

Tears welled in his mate's eyes once more, but he held them back, sniffling and nodding. "I know. I trust you."

"I trust you too," he said clearly. "With my heart. With my life."

Damien sucked his lower lip into his mouth. "Carter..." He swiped beneath his eyes and cleared his throat. "Is there usually so much crying during a bonding?"

Carter snorted. "I wouldn't know, beautiful. This is my first one."

"Only one," Damien corrected, laying a hand over Carter's heart. "This is your *only* one, mi corazón."

"That's right." He didn't hate how possessive his little witch was.

He dropped to one knee, taking Damien's jeans and boxer briefs with him, and helped him step out of them before tugging off his socks. Once his mate was naked, Carter leaned forward and nuzzled into the fragrant space where his thigh and groin met. They'd both showered earlier, Carter carefully bandaging Damien's arm and the small cut on his forehead. But after so many hours, the scent of soap on his mate's skin was almost completely overtaken by his natural honey and musk.

"Carter," Damien moaned, sinking his fingers into his hair as he rocked his hips forward. His hardness brushed against Carter's cheek, but he ignored it, burrowing into his mate's dark pubic hair and just breathing him in.

"How long does the tea need?" he asked, lips brushing against the base of Damien's cock in the cruelest of teases.

Fingers tightening in Carter's hair, Damien tried to nudge him over where he wanted him so desperately. "Umm. Few more minutes probably."

Carter peered up at him. "Really? Or are you just hoping I'll suck you while I'm down here?"

They'd all heard the stories about how Marcus and Robson had let their tea steep too long, and Robson had practically been stoned when they bonded—not that either had minded. But unlike them, it was his and Damien's first time together. Hell, it was Damien's first time *ever*. He wanted his mate's full wits about him.

Damien smiled down at him. "I took the relaxing additive out since I won't have to stay... well, *relaxed* to take a knot."

Carter grinned back up at him. "In that case..."

He ran his tongue down the side of his mate's cock, then pushed to his feet.

Damien huffed in annoyance but then gasped when Carter picked him up and carried him over to the bed, gently laying him in the middle. He was about to climb up when Damien popped onto his knees.

"Um. Actually, can I taste you?"

Carter's dick twitched at the very idea, and Damien—eyes glued to his considerable *attributes*—licked his damn lips. Like he could already taste Carter's precome on his tongue.

"If that's what you want," he said, trying to play it cool and failing spectacularly, but Damien was too busy staring to notice. He hauled himself up onto the mattress and lay down on his back, Damien kneeling next to his hip. "Don't feel like you have to do anyth—ah, *fuck*."

It took everything in him not to flex his hips and push his cock up into the warm heat encircling his head. His mate had scrambled over his thigh, zeroed in on his target, and just *gone* for it. His tongue was tentative as he ran it along the ridges of Carter's glans, but when he groaned and rasped, "So good, baby boy," he seemed to gain confidence, hitting that same spot again and again.

Damien moaned when Carter rested a hand on the back

of his head, the vibration traveling down his shaft and into his balls. He didn't push him down farther or try and guide Damien's movements, simply touched him softly, letting his fingers drift from the top of his head down to the base of his neck and back.

"Show me what to do," Damien said, pulling off with a wet sound that hit Carter in the belly. "I want you to like it as much as I did."

"I do," he assured him, cupping his face and thumbing at his slightly swollen lips. "I'll like anything you do to me because you're the one doing it. And just like you belong to me, I belong to you. You can explore all you want. Learn what you like as well as what makes me lose control."

Damien's eyes lit up with interest at his words, like he hadn't considered that every part of Carter now belonged to him. Peeking up at him, Damien rested his hands on Carter's thighs, then slid them down to the inside and put the slightest pressure there.

Grinning, Carter slid his legs apart easily. Damien sucked in a breath and caressed his legs from knee to hip. "I like how much hair you have."

He whispered it like it was a confession, but to Carter, it was just one more way they were made for one another since he liked how silky smooth Damien's skin was. "I'm glad. Maybe you should drink your tea first so I don't get caught up in how good you're about to make me feel."

The cutest pout appeared on Damien's face, even as he clambered back up so he was straddling Carter's belly and could lean over to reach the mug. From up on his perch, he grinned down at Carter, then downed the tea as fast as humanly possible, shuddering as he returned the cup to the nightstand.

"Ugh. So gross."

Carter chuckled, smoothing his hands up Damien's legs

to his hips and then easing him backward just enough for his cock to nudge between his cheeks. Eyes widening, Damien met his gaze and rocked himself, riding the hard shaft.

"Oh." Damien moved back and forth a few times, cheeks and chest flushing with arousal.

Groaning, Carter held him steady with one hand on a hip as he reached up with his other to tweak a tantalizing nipple.

Damien gasped and ground down. Hard. "*Carter.*"

"Feels good?" His adorable little mate was driving him out of his mind, chasing his pleasure as he rode Carter's cock, rubbing it on the sensitive skin of his channel and hole.

"So good."

"Then you're going to love when I sink inside you."

Moaning, Damien ground down again, precome seeping from his ruddy head and down his more petite shaft. It was perfectly proportioned to his petite mate. "Not yet. I wanted... I wanted to taste you, remember?"

His mate's eyes were barely open, his body's instincts driving him to chase down his orgasm and find his own pleasure, and yet he was still worrying about getting his mouth on Carter's cock.

So fucking precious.

"I remember. You want to climb down and do some exploring?" he asked with a grin.

It seemed like it took a lot of effort, but Damien halted his rocking, breaths unsteady. "Y-yeah. Then you'll get me... ready, right?"

He gripped the back of Damien's neck and dragged him down for a long, drugging kiss. "That's right. Then I'll make sure you're ready to take my cock."

Shivering, Damien nodded loosely and scooted back down between Carter's legs. He took a few steadying breaths as Carter snagged the other pillow to prop his head up, wanting the best view possible. His mate's olive skin glowed beautifully in the flickering candlelight, his hungry eyes riveted between Carter's legs.

He wasn't sure what he'd been expecting, but tiny kitten licks on his balls wasn't it. But, fuck, did it feel good. Groaning, he tipped his head back and spread his legs as wide as he could, giving Damien as much access as he could. He hissed as wet heat enveloped one, then the other testicle, his mate sucking lightly on each before releasing them.

"You smell good," Damien murmured, nuzzling farther down and running his tongue over Carter's taint.

His whole body twitched, and he arched his hips, silently encouraging Damien. He could only really see the top of his mate's head when he felt a shy lick over his hole, fiery pleasure ricocheting through him.

He gasped, and Damien jerked back, peering up at him with pupils so wide with arousal he looked like the tea *had* gotten him stoned. "Was that not okay?"

"It was more than okay," he quickly assured him. "It felt good."

"Do you think… one day…" Damien bit his lip. "Would you ever want to… bottom?"

Carter grinned and sat up, giving his mate's weeping cock a firm stroke. "I'd bottom for you any day, baby boy. There is no right or wrong between us. If we both enjoy it, then we can do it."

Nodding eagerly, Damien ran his teeth over his bottom lip. "But not today."

"Well, not this first time if we want to complete the bonding." Carter played with his mate's foreskin a little, loving how he nearly toppled over, mouth hanging open. "But if you want a turn afterward, I'm game."

Damien was wrapped around him, kissing him furiously a second later. Carter did his best to keep up, running his hands over his smooth back all the way down to his ass, gripping each cheek. When he ghosted his fingers through the cleft between, Damien ripped his mouth away and moaned, thrusting his wet dick against Carter's stomach.

Chuckling, Carter carefully peeled his eager mate off him and laid him out on the bed next to him, following so he was pressing him into the mattress as he nibbled along his jaw. Without looking, he patted around where he'd thought he'd left the lube but came up empty. Grunting in annoyance, he lifted his head and looked around.

"Did you see where the—" He spotted the bottle down by their legs—what the hell?—just as it rose and shot toward his outstretched hand. He turned and smiled at his mate. "Thank you."

He gave him another lingering kiss, licking deep inside and then pulling back to settle between Damien's thighs. As he wet his fingers, he ran his eyes over his debauched-looking mate, knowing his eyes were glowing and his fangs were starting to descend.

"Have you ever played with yourself back here?" he asked as he slid one slick finger between Damien's cheeks and tapped against his hole.

Blushing hotly, Damien stared right back at him as he nodded. "Sometimes."

"That's good," he praised, rubbing at the tight opening to get him to relax. "You know what to expect then."

"You're a lot bigger than my fingers," Damien protested, even as he bent his legs and tipped his pelvis up to give Carter more room to work.

"True, but you'll learn to appreciate that." Carter gave him a cocky grin as he pushed, sinking his middle finger inside his mate for the first time. He paused halfway, using his other hand to glide up Damien's chest and flick one of his nipples. "Just remember to relax."

"How can I relax when it feels so good?" Damien gasped, rolling his hips and taking in more of Carter's finger.

Far slower than his mate seemed to want, Carter worked that one digit in and out, loosening him while playing with his nipples and leaking cock. When he pushed in a second finger, he played with Damien's frenulum, distracting him from any discomfort and causing him to arch beautifully as he tugged at the bedding.

He leaned over him, needing his mouth on him, as he thrust his fingers inside a little faster. As he curved his fingers and found that special spot that made Damien yell his name, he growled with satisfaction, sinking his free hand into his mate's hair to hold him still, and devoured his mouth.

"I'm going to come," Damien gasped as soon as he tore his mouth free, his body undulating beneath Carter's in a sensual wave. "Please, need you. I'm ready."

He shook his head. "Not yet. One more. I don't want to hurt you."

Damien groaned, pulling at Carter's shoulders, but he held firm, working a third finger into his tight hole. The soft hiss he got in response slowed him down and let him know he was right to have been cautious.

It didn't take long, though, before Damien was humping back against his hand, taking all three without issue and begging him for more. Carter was so aroused he wasn't sure how he hadn't already come, spraying his load all over his mate's sexy body.

Sweat ran down his spine as he positioned himself, palming the back of Damien's thighs and guiding his legs up, resting one in the crook of Carter's arm and the other over his shoulder.

Damien stared up at him with wide eyes, swollen lips damp from Carter's rough kisses. Holding his gaze, Carter slicked himself with more lube and positioned his wide head at his mate's loosened opening.

"Ready?"

Damien nodded.

As he started to push inside, he said gruffly, "I love you so fucking much."

Face lighting up, Damien caressed Carter's cheek. "I love you too, mi corazón. Now, bind us together forever."

"Forever," Carter grunted as he popped past the first ring of muscle.

It took quite a while for him to work his whole length inside Damien, though he was probably being overly cautious based on how his mate kept squirming on his dick and pleading for more. But he'd never forgive himself if he hurt him. So he took his time, rocking in and out, adding more lube than strictly necessary, and making his way deep inside Damien until he couldn't go any farther.

He could feel his mate's racing pulse all around his cock and was about thirty seconds from exploding. Lowering himself to his forearms, he peppered Damien's damp face with kisses. "Okay, baby boy?"

"No."

He froze. "No?"

"No," Damien said, grinning. "I need you to actually *move*."

Shaking his head, Carter smiled down at his mate as he drew his hips back and then drove forward. Damien's head shot back as a guttural moan ripped from deep in his chest.

"More, Carter. Faster."

In that moment, he knew he'd do absolutely anything for the man panting beneath him. Including fucking him into the mattress.

After their lengthy buildup, he knew he wouldn't last long, but he made sure to make it as good as possible for Damien, adjusting his thrusts until he found his prostate.

The throaty whimpers Damien released each time were driving Carter insane, his orgasm building at the base of his spine.

Grunting, Carter sped up as he buried his face in Damien's neck and licked up the salty column. "Touch yourself. Make yourself come."

He felt Damien wiggle a hand between them, grasping his cock and stroking it feverishly. Just as Carter was sure he couldn't hold on another moment, Damien squeezed around him so hard he groaned.

"*Carter!*" Damien bowed beneath him, his back arching off the bed as far as Carter's body above him would allow. Wet heat spilled between them, the scent of his mate's come filling his nose and sending him straight over the edge.

Teeth clenched, he shuttled his hips back and forth a few more times, then pressed as deep as he could and released, filling his mate with his scent. Instincts took over, his fangs lengthening fully, and he was biting into the crook of Damien's neck before he realized what he was doing, needing to claim his mate more than anything in that moment.

Damien moaned again as Carter *felt* his magic surging, tasted it in his honey-sweet blood, and then Damien's own teeth were sinking into him.

Claiming him right back.

He felt his cock lengthening where it was still buried inside Damien, causing his mate to moan against his skin. They released their bites at the same time, Damien's hands smacking down onto the mattress as he stiffened and moaned again.

Carter watched, entranced, as his mate's whole body seemed to vibrate and glow a faint teal, feeling it when his magic swirled around and through Carter, like it was checking him over. Mouth hanging open, Damien silently screamed as the glow left his skin and concentrated in his hands before shooting out and whipping around them and the room.

Then Damien sagged into the bed, a soft smile on his lips. "Whoa."

Shaking his head, Carter slowly eased down and kissed that happy mouth. "Whoa?"

"Keegan was not kidding about the power boost." Damien blinked his sleepy eyes open and met Carter's semi-concerned gaze. "I'm okay. It was just… a lot. And now I can *feel* you. My magic is connected to you in a way I can't even explain."

He could feel Damien too, a warm glow in his chest letting him know how pleased and satisfied his mate was. When Damien shifted, his eyes widened, and he stared down between them.

"You're still…"

"Yeah. Part of the bonding. Until I learn to control it, I'll stay erect… probably at least a couple of hours." Carter knew it varied between bonded pairs, and he could get it to go down faster if he orgasmed a few more times, but there was no way his mate could handle going again so soon.

He started to pull out, biting back a moan as his warm, slick channel rippled around him, but Damien wrapped his legs around him, stopping him. "Wait. Do you have to…?"

"I don't want you to be uncomfortable."

He shook his head and urged Carter more onto his side so he could relax without crushing Damien and still keep them connected. "I'll tell you if I do, but I… I like it."

Groaning, Carter buried his face into Damien's neck as his cock flexed involuntarily inside him. "You can't say things like that."

His mate's soft laugh and gentle hands smoothing over

his heated skin settled him back down, but he still wasn't sure he'd be able to sleep.

But that was okay. He'd gladly watch over his mate for as long as necessary.

"Good night, my mate."

"Good night, mi corazón."

CHAPTER TWENTY-EIGHT

Six Months Later

"Kieran!" Carter bellowed, slamming his keyboard down onto his desk.

"Good lord, what?"

He jerked his head up, not expecting him to be standing in the doorway of his office. Kieran's smirk let him know he was damn proud of himself for sneaking up on Carter.

Huffing, he gestured at his computer. "It's frozen. *Again.*"

Rolling his eyes, Kieran crossed the room and leaned over the desk, blocking Carter's view of the screen. Thirty seconds later, he stood up. "There. You should be all set, but aren't you already supposed to be gone?"

Carter grunted, navigated to the patient file he'd been trying to update, and started typing his orders. "Yes, but what else is new."

Despite things settling back into normal—or as close as possible—Carter had been busier than ever, making it more and more difficult for him to get out at a reasonable time, let alone early on days he had Enforcer meetings at the manor.

But since it was Rick's fault he was swamped, the alpha could just fucking deal.

Kieran clucked his tongue. "Did you have a chance to look over those resumes I gave you... last week?"

He sighed, checked one other patient's chart, then started shutting down his computer. "Not yet."

"We need at least one more doctor, but a mid-level or two would also help. You're taking on too much."

It wasn't a new argument, so Carter ignored him and kept working on getting his ass out the door. He was right though. Meyerville was *booming*, and the influx of families meant more patients for Carter. Another private practice had already popped up on the other side of town, but it still wasn't enough. He needed to bring on another doctor to share the workload, but he was finding it hard to trust another person with his business and patients.

But after the dust had settled—or ash, since the hunters had literally burned Mehko to the ground—some packs had been furious, accusing Rick of being a power-hungry alpha looking to become some sort of parahuman dictator. Thankfully, Gabriel and his team had known what they were doing and had pulled boxes and boxes of materials out before torching the place, and a lot of what he'd brought back was incredibly incriminating.

Not to mention Alpha Okenapowet publicly stating what had happened to her and her pack and how Rick had allowed them to stay in his territory for more than half a year.

And of course, there were the pictures and firsthand accounts of the beast things Alistair and the O'Hares had cooked up.

Nico had been busy as hell processing and sharing documents, pictures, and videos on the online forums used by most packs. And anyone who wasn't convinced—some even accusing Rick and the pack of fabricating the evidence—had been invited to come and see everything for themselves. There had also been dozens and dozens of video conference calls where Rick and a few other alphas and coven leaders who'd experienced the violent side of the Council's "leadership" or been targeted as a "threat" by the O'Hares Coven painstakingly shared the details of what had happened to the Kincaid Pack and the others over and over again.

Mostly Rick kept his cool. But there were definitely days where Carter and the other Enforcers got a heads-up from Jamie or Kai to avoid the manor to stay out of the line of fire until Kai could calm him back down.

None of that would have made the town explode or brought an influx of patients to Carter's practice. The fact that Rick had insisted that the new governing headquarters be built just outside his territory?

That had caused Carter's issues.

It hadn't taken much more than the evidence or phone calls to get the majority of packs in the country on board with the new plan of democratic representation. A lot had wanted the new House of Guardians and Prime Alpha lodgings to be rebuilt on top of the Council's old ones, but Rick had put his foot down. And since it was obvious to most that he'd be the first elected Prime Alpha, he'd gotten his way.

As the closest town to where the Guardians would meet —the representatives from the packs and covens around the country who would pass laws and hear complaints—they'd expected an increase in tourism and such while the House was in session. And some pack's representatives had already moved to the area, interested in helping to get things going, even though the first session wouldn't happen probably for another six months.

What they had not anticipated were the *hundreds* of requests to join the Kincaid Pack.

Rick was still being somewhat picky about who he

accepted, but he'd loosened up some. As he'd told the Enforcers and betas, it'd probably be a long time before anyone tried to attack them again, considering what they'd done to the Council and O'Hares.

"Doc, are you—"

"Yes, I'm listening," he said absently as he pushed away from his desk, then paused, eyes locking on his open door when the scent of honey hit his nose.

A few seconds later, his smiling mate filled the doorway. Carter grinned back, surprised but pleased with the visit.

Kieran laughed as he headed out. "Never mind. I'll pester you about this tomorrow. Bye, you two."

Damien flushed as he scooted out of the way, murmuring a goodbye and then shutting the office door and leaning back against it. "Hello."

Carter tilted his desk chair back, unabashedly running his eyes over his mate's slender form. "Hello, beautiful. What's the occasion?"

"I saw your truck was still next door when I got back, so I thought I'd come and see why you weren't at your meeting."

Carter glanced at the clock on the wall and grimaced. "Yeah, I'm running really late. I had someone who got squeezed in today because of a 'weird asthma attack,' but it turned out he was having a heart attack, so we had to call the ambulance and get him to the hospital. Threw off the whole rest of my day."

"Is he okay?" Damien asked, brows furrowed with concern.

Carter nodded. "He will be. We got him there in time." He spotted the edge of the hickey he'd left on Damien's bonding scar popping up over the collar of his polo and lost his train of thought. "Come here, baby boy."

Damien sucked in a quick breath. "Carter..."

He beckoned him with a finger. The flush in his mate's

cheeks deepened as he crossed the room, nibbling nervously on his lower lip. His face said he was embarrassed, but his scent and the tent growing in his slacks told another story.

His bear surged to the surface, wanting nothing more than to get his hands all over his perfect little mate.

As soon as Damien rounded his desk, coming up next to him, Carter rolled his chair back. "Drop your pants and bend over the desk."

A soft, hungry sound fell from his parted lips, chest moving faster with his panting breaths. He turned to look back at the door though. "I didn't lock it."

Carter studied him, waiting for his mate to meet his eyes once more before saying, "Do you want to lock it? Because if not, I want you over my desk so I can have a snack before my meeting."

"*Gracious.*" Damien glanced back at the door one more time, then moved his hands to his belt, making quick work of it and his pants. As soon as he lowered his zipper, he let his pants drop and pushed his underwear down to his thighs.

His cock was already hard, foreskin beginning to pull back and expose his damp head.

Delicious.

But not what he was in the mood for.

Bottom lip caught between his teeth, Damien slowly turned and lowered himself until his forearms were braced on top of the desk, right over the random loose papers always covering it, his perfect little peach of an ass right in front of Carter's face.

Humming, he ran his palms up the back of Damien's thighs, knowing how sensitive the skin was there. He grabbed a cheek in each hand and pulled them apart, revealing the light dusting of hair around his hole.

"You're already late. Rick's going to be upset," Damien whispered, pretending like he wasn't craving Carter's mouth even as he stretched his arms out in front of him and arched his back like a contented kitten, chest flat on the desk.

He grunted as he lowered his head and said right over the furled opening, "You're right. I should probably get going."

He watched gooseflesh erupt on Damien's cheeks and thighs at the teasing of his breath.

"Probably..." Damien agreed, wiggling his ass in Carter's face until he tightened his hold on him.

His soft moan made Carter grin. "Then again... I'm already late."

"It's a *representative* body of *elected* members," Rick said very clearly toward the cell phone sitting on the table in front of him, a hand shoved into his hair and the other pinching the bridge of his nose. "You cannot appoint yourself, Alpha Zimmerman."

Carter paused just inside the library, waiting for him to finish his call. He stuck his hands into the pockets of his chinos, chagrined at the fact that he and Damien had gotten a little... carried away and he'd missed the entire Enforcer meeting.

Rick really was going to be pissed.

He heard the person on the other end of the line—Alpha Zimmerman, apparently—huff and say in a creaky voice that pegged the man at eighty. At least. "Rick, there's no need to explain it to me like I'm a child."

"My apologies, sir," Rick said as he shook his head and straightened, waving Carter farther into the room. "That wasn't my intention. I just wanted to make sure you and your pack understood an election would have to be held to select a representative. It's not just up to you."

"Hmph. It's a good thing I like you a lot better than I did your father."

"Yes, sir." Rick smiled and rolled his eyes. "I've got another meeting, Alpha Zimmerman—I'm going to need to let you go. I look forward to your visit."

"Sure you do. Goodbye, son."

"Goodbye, sir."

Rick ended the call and then stared at the device like he was contemplating throwing it against the wall. Or maybe out the third-story window. "I swear, between these cantankerous old alphas and the shit that mobster in Chicago is getting up to, I'm starting to regret burning down the Council."

"No, you're not," Carter said, snorting.

Rick sighed. "No, I'm not."

Lowering himself into a chair across from Rick, Carter cleared his throat, trying to decide how to explain his absence. "Uh, Rick. I'm sorry I missed today's meeting. I... Well, you see..."

He wasn't sure what to say. He didn't want to lie, but he also didn't want to admit what he'd been doing instead.

Sighing, Rick leaned back in his chair and balanced an ankle on his opposite knee. "You know your office manager is mated to my second-in-command, right? I already know what you were doing."

To his horror, he felt heat rise in his face. He had ten years on Rick probably, and yet he felt like he was getting scolded by a parent. "Right. Well."

Rick stared at him for a long moment, and then a grin broke across his face. "I'm fucking with you, Doc."

Carter just barely kept from sagging in his seat. "Seriously?"

"Yeah." Rick waved a hand. "I get it. You two are newly mated. Plus, you've got your family staying with you and a busy practice. Not to mention your Enforcer duties. It's understandable that you occasionally… lose track of time."

He scrubbed at his face. "It can be difficult to find time for each other."

"Of course. But I'm glad you came by because I wanted to check in." Rick's smile fell away as he studied Carter. "Kieran says you're putting off hiring more help. Are you concerned about something I should be aware of?"

He shook his head. "No. I'm just finding myself… protective of the clinic. But I'll prioritize getting someone in there."

"Good. Also, I wanted to see if you'd changed your mind and would like to step down as Enforcer."

Carter sucked in a breath, feeling like all the wind had gotten knocked out of his sails. "Are you asking me to—"

"No," Rick said clearly, dropping his leg and propping his arms on his thighs to lean forward. "I still firmly believe you are a valuable adviser and friend who more than earned his place, *but* I know you're burning the candle at both ends, and your patients have to come first, agreed?"

Carter nodded reluctantly. "Yes, but… if you're sure you still want me, I'd prefer to stay as an Enforcer. It is a lot of work—especially right now—but it's *important*. I'm sorry if you felt like I didn't appreciate that or wasn't prioritizing those duties."

"That's not how I feel at all," Rick said calmly. "Like I said, I wanted to check in. I already talked with Tashmica and Gabriel, and they are both also choosing to stay on. I just wanted to be sure that now that things are less chaotic—or at least less dangerous—you didn't regret letting me harangue you into taking the position."

"It's an honor," Carter said, and it was. He loved being a doctor, but there was something about serving his pack as an Enforcer that was fulfilling in a way he'd been missing. He hoped his brother Asher felt the same way. He'd been tapped to become a beta recently after Harry—the asshole who'd bruised Damien—had been demoted. "And not one I take lightly, even if I miss the occasional meeting."

"Excellent." Rick clapped his hands on his knees, smiling. "And don't worry about that. Jamie and I are discussing a new system. Getting everyone together for a weekly meeting is getting impossible, so we'll probably switch to either a bi-monthly or even monthly in-person meeting and then do a conference call the other weeks." He shrugged his well-muscled shoulders as he pushed to his feet. "We'll get it figured out. How's Damien doing?"

The change in topic nearly gave Carter whiplash as he also stood and followed Rick over to the overflowing table he used as a desk. There were maps and blueprints and proposed regulations for the House of Guardians' duties and powers, as well as the Prime Alpha's. There also appeared to be several crude drawings of Rick and his family done with pink and lime-green crayons.

"He's doing really well," Carter said honestly, grinning proudly as he thought about his blossoming mate. "It took a little while for some of the coven members to get on board after they learned about his projection power, but they've all since come around. Fortunately, I think it helps that his ability doesn't work very well on pack mates." They'd done some testing after Carter and Jess had both been able to throw off his commands and found that if the pack member didn't want to accept the projected thought or emotion, they could ignore it. "He also seems to really enjoy working at *Wicca We Can* while Jess is... away."

His mate's sister was the one dark spot in their otherwise happy life. After their mom's death, she'd talked to Damien at length about everything: him passing information to Amelia, his projection power, her own fear of her ever-growing powers. Damien had tried to reassure her, talking to her about stepping in to help train her and help her gain control, and she'd seemed interested…

And then one morning a few weeks later, they'd found a letter taped to their front door, and Jess was gone. Her phone had been left in the small house she'd been living in ever since Kai and his siblings had moved in with Rick, her few possessions packed into boxes with a note taped to them requesting they be stored for her.

Kai had gotten a letter too, but Carter didn't think he and Damien had ever compared what she'd said. He knew that she'd told her brother she needed to figure out who she was and how to be comfortable with her powers and how to stop them from growing. And she'd promised to come back.

Considering how Damien had sobbed on his lap for two days, Carter wasn't overly comforted by her promise to return.

"That's good," Rick said, gaze distant like he was thinking about the wayward witch too, or maybe about one of the thousand other worries stacked on his shoulders. Not to mention, Carter knew that he and Kai were still concerned about what could happen when Henry grew up and the possibility of him unleashing some sort of monster Armageddon.

Rick was silent for another moment, and Carter wished he could do more to ease the weight of the man's burdens. But then Rick seemed to shake off his thoughts and reached under the table, setting a small white box in front of Carter. "There's one more thing."

Carter furrowed his brow as he stepped forward to read the label on the box, his stomach tightening when he caught the words *Funeral Home and Crematorium*. "Is that…"

"Yes." Rick rested a hand on top. "It took longer than it should have because Amelia had moved him, probably as a precaution against Damien breaking the Blood Oath and coming to rescue him. We had to track down where he'd been held and then where he'd gone after she killed him. Since we didn't know when exactly it had happened..." Rick sighed, a wealth of emotion in the soft sound. "Anyway, he'd already been cremated as a John Doe."

"You're sure it's him?"

Nodding, Rick gently patted the box. "I'm sure. The owner of the funeral home recognized the picture Damien gave us of Pedro right away. It was a small town in a small county, and his place handles all John Does for the county's morgues."

Carter shuddered at the thought of such a job. "At least Damien can finally put him to rest."

"I hope it brings him some peace."

He hoped so too. Taking a slow, shuddery breath, he tore his eyes off the box and met Rick's sad eyes. "Thank you, Alpha. My mate and I owe you."

"You owe me nothing." Rick stepped closer, clasping a hand to the back of Carter's neck and tugging him forward to press their foreheads together for a brief touch. The love and respect Carter felt for the man made his chest tight even before Rick said, "I would do anything to ease your mate's pain, brother."

Eyes burning, Carter was three seconds from shedding actual tears when the door to the library burst open and two little tornadoes crashed into the room.

"Papa!" Callie screeched, running right up to Rick without sparing Carter a glance as he and Rick separated. "Henry took my princess doll!"

Carter glanced down at the youngest King sibling. His hair, which had been dark like Kai's, was starting to lighten— though it wasn't nearly as blond as Callie's—and was getting long with a bit of curl to it. His bright green eyes were full of unrepentance as he held the doll nearly as big as him up to Carter.

Laughing, he accepted it and handed it over to Rick, scented the boy, and then extracted himself before Callie's volume reached ear-splitting mode. His hands were careful as he carried the box of his mate's father out of the manor, sorrow weighing him down.

"Are you sure? We could take him back to your house in South Carolina or even Honduras," Carter double-checked as he parked his truck, the new car smell still lingering in his sensitive nose.

Damien nodded without looking away from the box in his lap. "I'm sure."

Nodding, Carter got out and came around to help his mate down, putting an arm around his shoulders while they waited for the others to disembark. Damien wiped at his wet cheeks as car after car parked behind Carter's truck on the side of the road.

"I didn't think they'd all come," he said softly.

"That's because you don't realize how much you are loved," Carter murmured, leaning down to press a kiss into Damien's hair. "They want to support you."

Every single member of the pack's coven was present, as well as most of the Enforcers and their mates and Carter's mom and brothers. There were a few others, like the therapist, Helena, that Damien had been seeing after killing his mom, and the owner of *Magic Beans*, who hadn't left town when he'd been advised to and caught an eyeful of what some of the town's residents got up to behind his back.

Once the crowd of friends was gathered around them, Carter pointed in the direction they were going. "It's a little bit of a trek, sorry. But thank you so much for coming. It means the world to us."

"It really does," Damien added quietly, not bothering to wipe his tears anymore.

Tashmica came forward and pressed a quick kiss to his cheek. "Let's offer him and you some peace, hm?"

Their group traipsed through the woods, and Carter was reminded of the first time he'd made the trip with Damien, how he'd fussed about the distance. He smiled softly at the nice memory as he tightened his hold on his silent mate.

Before too long, they were emerging into their meadow. Unlike that first time, there was a thin layer of snow covering the grass, not wildflowers, and the brook was still and low, close to freezing.

"Sorry it's not quite as beautiful right now," he offered Damien, who shook his head and peered up at him with wide, luminous eyes.

"It's not just the flowers that gave it beauty. It is almost spiritual in its tranquility." A shadow of a smile graced his lips. "And it's *ours*. This is a very good place for Taita to rest."

Tash had already gotten everyone organized into a circle, and Keegan was handing around thin white candles. Kai stepped forward with the large paper bag Rick had carried and offered it to Tashmica.

She smiled as she reached in and started pulling out a wide variety of flowers, spreading them around the open space inside the circle. Damien sucked in a breath and mouthed *Thank you* to their alpha and alpha-mate. A lighter was produced to light the candles, and even though it was cold, the wind held off, seeming to know better than to disturb the tiny flames.

"Whenever you're ready, Damien," Tash said, stepping to one side as soon as she was done.

Taking another moment, Damien looked around the

circle at each person, smiling and nodding. "Thank you again for being here today while we usher Pedro Alvarez to the Beyond." He paused, swallowing. "We are taught as witches not to fear death. That it is a changing of seasons, not the end. That through death, we find new life. Today, we honor that change and Pedro's life and h-h-his death. We remember him with fondness and love and look forward to joining him in the Beyond one day."

Tears were streaming down Damien's cheeks, his grief fresh once more, but his brave mate kept going, carefully removing the cremains from the box and slowly releasing them onto the ground as he walked around the perimeter of the circle.

"What was will be again," he said thickly.

"What was will be again," Tashmica and the other witches repeated. As Damien passed, they blew out their candles and bowed their heads.

"What was will be again," Damien said again as he rounded near Carter.

He caught his mate's eyes and said clearly, "What was will be again," and blew out the candle he was holding.

A soft breeze caught Carter's hair, raising goose bumps on the back of his neck. He closed his eyes, imagining it was Pedro. That he really was watching from the Beyond as his son honored him.

Don't worry. I'll keep him safe. I promise.

He felt the touch again, an acknowledgment, and opened his eyes, feeling at peace.

Damien wrapped up the short ceremony with a prayer to the goddess asking for guidance and strength, and then Tashmica burned some herbs, wafting the smoke at everyone. She hugged Damien afterward and led the others back through the woods, Keegan cursing where he walked between her and Nico as he nearly rolled his ankle somehow. Carter's mom stopped and hugged them both, his brothers clapping Damien on the shoulder and scenting him.

Rick and Kai each offered their condolences, their sensitive alpha-mate grabbing Damien in a fierce hug with tears in his eyes.

Soon though, it was just the two of them in their quiet, peaceful meadow. Damien stood among the flowers, eyes squeezed shut.

"He really would be proud of you, you know," Carter said gently as he closed the distance between them, taking the empty box and bag and setting them on the ground at his feet. "You are a good man, Damien Alvarez, and a powerful witch."

"I'd give up every ounce of power I have to have him back," Damien said without opening his eyes.

"I know, beautiful." He wrapped his arms around his mate and held him as he cried. Big, heartbreaking sobs racked his body, but Carter held him tightly, offering as much comfort and support as he could.

It passed quickly, his mate having already done most of his grieving months ago. Still, Carter didn't release his hold, and Damien seemed content to stay leaning against him as his breathing slowed and he was reduced to just the occasional sniffle.

Carter managed to maneuver a hand into his coat pocket and pulled out a travel-sized pack of tissues, silently offering it to his mate.

Laughing wetly, Damien accepted them and blew his nose and cleaned up his face. As soon as he finished, he wrapped his arms around Carter's torso again and gave him a squeeze. He nuzzled into his favorite space between Carter's pecs and said quietly, "I love you, mi corazón."

"I love you too, mate."

No matter how much the world changed around them or

how many responsibilities they had with the pack, they made sure to never lose sight of what was most important. Their family, their friends. Their devotion to one another.

Carter's life had never been so full, and he knew exactly who to thank for that. The hardships they'd faced to get where they were just made him that much more grateful. For every quiet moment. For all the soft touches and heated kisses.

For every single time Damien sighed and relaxed against him, like he knew down into his very bones that Carter would hold him up and keep him safe.

His heart was full to bursting, and he wouldn't have it any other way.

Letting out a quiet breath, Damien tipped his head back to peer up at him, a soft smile on his beautiful face. His hazel eyes were shining from his tears and practically glowing with love. "Let's go home and snuggle on the couch."

Carter framed his face with his hands. "Whatever you want, baby boy."

Always and forever.

Want more in the Kincaid Pack Universe? Don't worry, you don't have to wait long. The Mobster's Mate *is coming later this year and will feature the mysterious Quinten Amato, human mobster in the parahuman world.*

On your Kindle? Scan the QR code with the camera on your phone to jump to my website to sign up!

A NOTE FROM KIKI

THANK YOU. THANK YOU. THANK YOU.

Thank you for reading *The Witch and His Doctor*. If you enjoyed Carter and Damien's story, please consider leaving a review to help other readers find this series!

Wanna never miss a release or sale?
Follow me on BookBub or on Amazon!

To always make sure you know what I'm working on, have the opportunity to read early copies of my books, and get freebies, subscribe to my newsletter!

Free to download at www.kikiclark.com/newsletter!

Injured and terrified, Victor runs for his life and right into the arms of the last person he expected to find: his true mate.

Living in a pack who viewed imperfections as weaknesses that needed to be eliminated, Victor is lucky to escape alive. He's heard of the Kincaid Pack's strong but fair alpha, but he has trouble truly believing he won't be targeted once more if his shameful secret is discovered.

When Cole meets a young man with fear in his eyes and pain in his scent, he recognizes him as his mate on sight. His excitement is short-lived, however, when they find out Victor's life is still in danger from what his old pack did to him.

After a lifetime of being abandoned by others, Victor has an important decision to make: Will he choose to trust the mate fate gave him?

Or will he run again?

A New Pack for New Year *features an eighteen-year-old wolf in need of some TLC, a thirty-something lion dying to give it to him, sexy times in an inappropriate place, found family feels, and hurt/comfort that will warm all the corners of your heart.*

EXPAND YOUR TBR!

Once you're finished bingeing the Kincaid Pack series, you might like to try one of my contemporary romances!

LAYING PIPE features an age gap, dad's best friend, bisexual awakening, and adorable rescue pets. All the books in my Blue Collar Hearts series can be read on their own and have characters who work blue collar jobs.

Available in eBook, Paperback, Audiobook, & Kindle Unlimited.

RECKLESS is the first in my Leather & Chrome series which focuses on the Devil's Hands Motorcycle Club and the exploration of kinks. Tank and CJ's story features a prison pen pal program, an age gap, exhibitionism, and a tough biker only soft for his kinky virgin.

Available in eBook, Paperback, Audiobook, & Kindle Unlimited.

ALSO BY KIKI CLARK

Forever Family Trilogy
Favor (Declan & Jeremy)
Easy (Simon)

Scythe Series (written with EM Lindsey)
Until His Last Goodbye

Many of my books are also available in audio! Check them out on Audible or on my website, www.kikiclark.com.

ABOUT THE AUTHOR

A small-town Michigan girl, Kiki has enjoyed reading since she first picked up a YA fantasy novel as a child. After that, she devoured everything she could get her hands on and dreamed of one time writing her own books that touched people's hearts.

In her early twenties, she discovered LGBTQ romances and had a realization: these were her people and this was where she belonged.

Nearly ten years later, she proudly joined the ranks of authors releasing character-driven, emotionally satisfying books showcasing that everyone deserves to find love.

To keep up-to-date with Kiki, sign up for her newsletter: www.kikiclark.com/newsletter.

Keep in touch by following her on any of these platforms:

facebook.com/kikiclarkauthor
instagram.com/kikiclark2017
amazon.com/author/kikiclark
bookbub.com/authors/kiki-clark
goodreads.com/kikiclark